THE BOXCAR OF FUN

THE BOXCAR OF FUN

The memoirs of
Arthur Dandoe, 1910-1913

Chris England

Published in Great Britain in 2016 by
Old Street Publishing Ltd
Sulivan Road, London SW6

www.oldstreetpublishing.co.uk

ISBN 978-1-910400-27-2

10 9 8 7 6 5 4 3 2 1

A CIP catalogue record for this title is available from the British Library.

Typeset by JaM

Printed and bound in Great Britain.

For my mother.

EXPLANATORY NOTE

AS I explained at the start of the first volume of these memoirs, entitled *The Fun Factory*, they came into my hands quite by chance.

When my wife and I moved into the house in Streatham where we have lived for the best part of twenty years now, we became friendly with the elderly lady who lived in the ground floor flat next door, a Mrs Lander. One day we happened to be talking about my interest in comedy and comedians, and she said:

"Of course, my grandfather knew Charlie Chaplin."

"Really?" I said.

"Oh yes," Mrs Lander said. "They were really quite thick, apparently."

Eventually Mrs Lander moved to a residential care home, and then a few months later her daughter dropped round to tell us that sadly she had passed away.

"She wanted me to thank you for your kindness," the daughter said, "and asked me to make sure you had this."

The battered old trunk she left me - which was brown, reinforced by wooden ribs, and secured by what looked like an army belt – had been used as a repository for the memorabilia of a career treading the boards. There were wooden swords and shields, in the Roman style, and a lion skin (somewhat past its best). There was some old-fashioned football kit, a red shirt with a lace-up collar, long white pantaloons, and big boots that laced above the ankle. There was also a big black cape, of the sort you might see a magician wearing, and a top hat, and a mechanical contraption with a couple of off-white feathers clinging to it.

Underneath all this, lying flat at the bottom of the trunk, were papers, including posters from old music hall and vaudeville bills, mostly featuring the sketches of the great Fred Karno. Tucked in amongst these charming relics were old black-and-white photographs of groups of young men and women posing together, sometimes in theatrical costume and make up, sometimes formally dressed, often posing in front of a railway carriage.

Who were they, I wondered, and what had they been doing?

———

I inspected the old photographs more closely. Surely that dapper young fellow with the toothy smile was Charlie Chaplin? And who was *that* one, standing over to one side, captured in an instant glaring at young Chaplin as though he would cheerfully throttle him till his eyes popped out?

Well, the answers were to be found in a brown leather satchel right at the bottom of the trunk, in the memoirs of the owner, one Arthur Dandoe, comedian.

The first volume of these, *The Fun Factory*, covered the period in which Dandoe worked for Fred Karno in the Edwardian music halls of Great Britain.

Karno – who called himself 'the Guv'nor' – was the entrepreneur king of the British music hall. He operated out of a base in Camberwell he called the Fun Factory, where he created hugely popular and spectacular sketches with brilliant effects and enormous casts of 'supers', or extras. These spectacles would sit squarely in the middle of a music hall bill between the singers and the banjo-playing clog dancers, and up to a dozen Karno companies would be touring the length and breadth of the country at any one time, playing something from his massive repertoire. Each of these companies would operate on a strictly hierarchical basis, with a number one comic, the star, at the apex, but it was always Karno's name that put bums on seats, as the saying goes.

Arthur Dandoe joined Karno's organisation at the same time as another young hopeful called Charlie Chaplin, and both developed the same burning ambition – to rise to become the number one comic of a Karno company.

Chaplin, however, was not content to let the matter be resolved in a fair fight. He used underhand methods and downright dirty tricks to undermine not only Arthur's chances of advancement with Karno but also his blossoming romance with a beautiful young actress called Tilly Beckett. Arthur eventually discovered what Charlie had been up to and threatened to expose him to the Guv'nor unless he dropped out of an upcoming tour of America.

At the last minute it turned out that leaving Charlie behind would not only be the ruin of Arthur's bitter rival, but also of his good friend Alf Reeves, the company manager, and so Arthur relented. He found Charlie, unshaven, drunk, and wallowing in despair, and hurried him to Southampton to join the rest of the American Karno company on board ship. The two rivals were then all set to cross the Atlantic together, in a state of uneasy truce.

This is where the second volume – the one you are holding in your hands – begins. It covers the period from autumn 1910 to the end of 1913, when Arthur Dandoe, Charlie Chaplin, Tilly Beckett and their friend Stanley Jefferson were touring the United States in Fred Karno's comedy company, during what was the golden era of American vaudeville.

I have no reason to doubt that the memoirs represent a truthful account, and where Dandoe touches upon verifiable historical fact he is invariably accurate – considerably more so than his contemporary managed in his 1964 autobiography, at any rate. Indeed, this memoir covers a period very swiftly – one might almost say, dismissively – dealt with in that other volume.

Readers can judge whether or not Dandoe is to be believed regarding more personal matters. In editing the papers, I have confined myself, more or less, to the addition of a few historical notes.

C. W. England
Streatham, December 2015

PART 1

1
OFF TO AMERICA

WE were all gathered on the foredeck for our first proper sighting of the New World, a faint grey strip on the distant horizon, when our number one comic suddenly astonished us all by leaping up onto the railing, throwing his arms wide and declaiming:

"America, I am coming to conquer you! Every man, woman and child shall have my name on their lips – Charles Spencer Chaplin!"

The company hooted good-naturedly at this almighty hubris, and the little fellow turned to give us a mocking bow and a flourish, his dark mop of hair whipping wildly in the wind.

"You do know that's Canada, don't you?" I called out, raising a pretty decent laugh at his expense, I thought. I glanced over to see if Tilly was laughing, or at least smiling, and she was, she was, she was smiling the smile that only she could smile, the smile that had haunted my dreams since we first met at Fred Karno's Fun Factory, the smile that warmed my heart and my loins, and could make me feel like everything was going to be all right.

But was she smiling that smile for me, or was she smiling it for him...?

"Pfft! Canada, America, what's the difference?" Charlie scoffed with a dismissive wave. Albert Austin, his ever-faithful beanpole lapdog, was preparing to capture the moment with his trusty box camera, but he wasn't quick enough with the tripod legs. Charlie had already leapt back down onto the deck and grabbed a life-belt, which he slung around his neck.

"Look at me!" he cried. "I'm Monsieur Mal-de-mer!" He tousled his hair and slumped against the railing in an extravagant pantomime of sea-sickness, while his acolyte scrambled to capture this fresh comedy gem from the master for posterity.

He was trying, I had to give him that.

It was the October of 1910, and the famous Fred Karno comedy company, of which I was a member, were travelling to New York to begin a tour of the United States.

We were supposed to have made the crossing in the lap of luxury on board the RMS *Lusitania*, no less, the pride of the Cunard line and holder of the Blue Riband, and would indeed have done so if only Mr Chaplin had turned up on time. We had all boarded, and had enjoyed a tantalising glimpse of our obscenely luxurious cabins – First Class, thanks to a deal done by our company manager Mr Alf Reeves, whereby we would provide entertainment for the swells – before it was all whisked away and we were unceremoniously disembarked with our trunks onto the quay at Liverpool dreaming wistfully of gold taps.

The whole company had then been obliged to traipse down to Southampton to catch this ailing rust-bucket instead, once the tardy Chaplin had been located (by me, as it happens). Located, and delivered, but not forgiven by his colleagues, not by any means. Because you see the SS *Cairnrona* was not exactly the absolute apex where trans-Atlantic travel was concerned. In point of fact it was a converted cattle boat, and they hadn't converted it quite as much as they might have.

The company's resentment was compounded by the fact that the cattle boat's propeller shaft sheared in two halfway across the pond, and the replacement took interminable days to fit, while we bobbed around under unfriendly grey skies, tossed this way and that by the waves like a cork in a bathtub full of over-excited toddlers.

With our meagre rehearsal days being swallowed up by the delay, we had been frantically trying to practise our show, *The Wow Wows*, in the ship's dining room, but a combination of the rolling and yawing of the vessel and the smell of the recycled grease coming from the kitchen would quickly drive us all up onto the deck where we'd grimly compare the greenness or otherwise of our gills and try our level best to hold onto our breakfasts.

As if that wasn't enough, the damn'd tub wasn't even heading to New York, it was chugging with aching slowness towards the St Lawrence River and Montreal, where we would have to embark upon a gruelling overnight railway journey which would only just get us to our destination in time to step straight onto the stage for our first performance, under-rested, under-washed and under-prepared.

None of us was particularly happy about any of this, and Charlie was squarely taking the blame, which was why he was desperately clowning about the place with the charm turned up to full blast, trying to get us all back onside.

"Come on everyone!" he cried. "How about a team photograph, eh? Something to remember this whole..."

"Ordeal..." Mike Asher muttered.

"Nightmare..." Emily Seaman chipped in.

"Experience, I was going to say. This... adventure! Come on Arthur, help me whip this miserable bunch into order!"

3

Some memento this was going to make, I thought, with all the scarves and hats and upturned collars hiding our wind-slapped faces, but I watched as Charlie ushered the company into two lines, one standing and one sitting or kneeling, like a football team.

Chaplin himself sat in the middle of the front row, the team captain, with the lifebelt still around his shoulders, framing him, picking him out, setting him apart, while the rest of the company huddled around him in their winter coats, trying to force a smile into the teeth of an Atlantic gale.

There was our sturdy foursquare company manager Alf Reeves and his wife, lovely Amy Minister. I had been a guest at their wedding just a few months earlier, a slap-up affair which anyone who was anyone in British music hall had attended. Fred Karno himself had been the best man, mainly because Alf hadn't dared ask anyone else to do it. Amy was a lovely girl, but her marriage to the boss had brought out the latent school ma'am in her, and while she might still join in giggling mischief with the rest of us she was just as likely to tut her disapproval.

There were two more married couples on the strength, namely George and Emily Seaman, and Fred and Muriel Palmer. The Seamans were hardened Karno lifers, and had quickly taken the younger Palmers under their wings on this benighted crossing.

Frank Melroyd and Bert Williams I didn't know particularly before this trip, but they seemed to be stand up fellows. Frank was a paunchy, comfortable fellow, who would happily sit on the sidelines, rarely contributing much to conversations, he would just be... there. He was balding, a project only a couple of years away from success, I'd say, and he nearly always wore a dark blue knitted cardigan instead of a waistcoat, which made him seem a generation older than he really was, somehow. Bert was also quiet, and had a very distinctive laugh that whistled through his

4

teeth – "Sss, sss, ssss!" – which may have been a ventriloquist thing: he once had a solo act with a dummy that he unfortunately lost in a card game to a rival, and which sadly went on to have a more successful career without him.

Then there were the young bloods, my friends Stan Jefferson, Mike Asher and Freddie Karno Junior, the Guv'nor's son, who was to be performing with us for the first time.

Stan was great company, a terrific giggler, with a laugh that transformed his whole long thin face. His bright red hair grew vertically upwards out of the top of his head and wouldn't sit down flat whatever he did to it.

Mike Asher was a dapper little fellow, slightly round-shoul-dered, but always immaculately turned out, his hair oiled and slicked down just so, with a centre parting you could use to navigate by. "America is the land of opportunity," he was saying often around that time, "and you never know when that opportunity may come, be it business or romance, so it's imperative to be ready to advance at all times."

Freddie Junior, by contrast, always looked as though he'd been dragged through a hedge backwards. It was strange, we all agreed, since his father, the Guv'nor, was famed for his trademark shiny shoes, that you would often find Freddie in a disgracefully scuffed and flapping pair of old boots, on occasion not even laced up.

He would jam his unruly hair under a herringbone newsboy cap that would drive Mike to despair. "You know, Fred," he'd say. "I don't know if I should even be seen out with you – who knows what chances may go begging." Mike's habit was to sport a rather fancy felt fedora, unless he had been so careless as to leave it lying around, in which case it would likely be jauntily perched on Tilly's head, that being the fashion for independent-minded ladies at that time.

There was Albert Austin, a tall, thin, pale, lugubrious chap of a type that my mother would have characterised as "a yard of pump water". Albert believed that the Sun shone out of the Chaplin backside, and since that pretty much chimed in with the little man's own view of the grand scheme of things, he and Charlie were fairly matey. He finished showing a *Cairnrona* crewman which lever on the camera to press and when, and then skipped into the front row to crouch beside his hero.

On Chaplin's other side, I couldn't help noticing with a sour feeling in my stomach which had nothing to do with the movements of the boat, was Tilly Beckett, her arm linked ever-so chummily with his.

And lastly, stuck on the end of the row, the glowering narrow-eyed expression on his face captured in black and white forever – I have the photograph still – was me, your 'umble narrator, Arthur Dandoe (yes, it's my real name).

Now when I called us 'the famous Fred Karno comedy company' I mean, of course, that we were just one of the many comedy companies belonging to the famous Fred Karno organisation. At that very moment there were probably at least a dozen similar aggregations of music hall journeymen (and journeywomen) travelling up and down the British Isles trawling for laughs. This particular company was just the one that happened to be heading for America, and vaudeville.

But before I start telling you about what happened when we got there, perhaps I should tell you a bit about how we got this far.

Chaplin and I had joined Fred Karno at about the same time, some three years before, arriving at the Guv'nor's Fun Factory by very different routes. Charlie was born into show-business, with parents who were both singers on the halls. He was a performer as a child, appearing in all kinds of stage plays, and comedy routines, and as a clog dancer for a time believe it or not, before his half-brother Syd, who was already working as one of Karno's most trusted number one comics, managed to pester the Guv'nor into giving his kid brother a go.

My family, on the other hand, were no help at all. They were all servants at a Cambridge college, and I was a junior porter there when I somehow got myself involved in a Footlights production which required me to be eaten by a large and frankly dangerous mechanical dinosaur. Karno came to see the beast, which didn't impress, but he ended up giving me a job.

We learnt the ropes together, Charlie and I, touring the country picking up the Karno repertoire as we went, making our way up the company's hierarchy, and naturally enough a rivalry developed between us. Finally there came a time when the Guv'nor was looking to promote someone to number one status, and couldn't decide between the two of us.

He set up a contest, which captured the imagination of the whole music hall community. We would both play the lead role in Karno's hit sketch *The Football Match* on the same day, Charlie playing the matinée and myself the evening show, and then he would make his decision.

The situation was complicated somewhat when Fred Karno took me aside and promised to swing the thing in my favour if only I would help him out with another little problem of his. He wanted to divorce his wife but she was having none of it, so he asked me to 'compromise' her, and testify to her infidelity in court. Well, Edith Karno was a friend of mine, and the mother of my chum Freddie Junior to boot, and so (in the end) I told the Guv'nor in no uncertain terms that I would not oblige him.

Nonetheless, on the big day the contest was going pretty well for me until a malicious heckler disrupted my rhythm, and one of the ex-professional footballers in the cast contrived to break my knee, and Charlie became the new number one while I retired to Cambridge and contemplated leaving the business altogether.

I did return to Karno's Fun Factory, but without enjoying the favour that had been mine previously. Then I discovered that Charlie and his brother Syd had been deliberately sabotaging my chances all along. They'd hired that heckler to undermine me, and had paid the footballer to put me in the hospital.

Now by this time Charlie was looking forward to making this trip to America as a number one. He had recruited my friends, Stan and Mike, and had lined up Tilly too, hoping to drive a wedge, a considerable geographical wedge the size of the Atlantic, between us. I, naturally, had been labelled 'Not Required on Voyage'.

However, I was able to use what I had found out to... well, to blackmail him, not to put too fine a point on it. I forced him to add me to the strength, and then the understanding was that he would fail to turn up for the crossing or else I would go straight to Karno, spill the beans about his dirty tricks, and that would be the end of his career.

It didn't quite work out that way, as you will have gathered. At the last minute Alf refused to travel without his number one, so I had to get Charlie to come along or the whole trip would have been off. I went back to London to find him, and when I did he was in a sorry state indeed. Hadn't eaten, hadn't shaved, hadn't been taking care of himself at all. I thought for a horrible moment that he might even have done himself in.

When he realised that we really were heading for the boat train and that his career had been given a stay of execution he perked right up. He grasped my hand and thanked me profusely, then he shot me his most dazzling toothy smile and said: "Friends?"

"Friends," I had agreed.

Ever since he had been as nice as pie to me. Nicer even. It was gratitude, of course, for me letting him off the hook, but it wasn't just that. He knew that I still had all the evidence that I had collected during my stint as an amateur detective, and I could still pass it on to Fred Karno at any time. That card was lodged firmly up my sleeve, and that is where he wanted it to stay.

Charlie Chaplin trying so hard to be my friend wasn't easy to take, let alone reciprocate. The memory of the many underhand ways he had tried to do me down was still raw.

However, I suppose I had more in common with Charlie than I did with most people walking the planet. Civilians, in other words. People who would never get to wield what I called The Power, that feeling that I got onstage when everything was going my way, time seemed to slow down, and the audience was in the palm of my hand.

We both had our sights set on making it to the very top of the comedy business.

We had each tried to come to America without the other, but had been obliged to travel together.

And there was one other significant thing we had in common. I'll come to that.

2
CITY LIGHTS

WE finally arrived in New York on a Monday at the crack of dawn, and as we straggled out into Grand Central station, grey, aching, travel-soiled and sleep-deprived, lugging our trunks and the costume cases behind us, none of us was feeling remotely funny. Which – considering we were due onstage later that same afternoon, and again twice more that evening – was not ideal.

The station was still being built, or extended, or finished off at that time, and consequently a cacophony of head-ringing hammer blows greeted our arrival, and we spilled out onto the street wearing a fine film of granite dust. Outside we slumped on our bags on the pavement while Alf set about finding some transportation for us.

It had been a brutal journey. The *Cairnrona* had meandered slowly up the St Lawrence to Montreal in Quebec several days behind schedule. Once there we'd all hustled to the railway station to embark on a seven-hour train journey around the northern shoreline of Lake Ontario to Toronto.

With barely a moment to catch our breath we then bundled ourselves and our baggage straight onto an overnight train down to New

York, crossing into the United States at Niagara Falls in the early evening (but without so much as a moment to stop off for sightseeing).

Alf had been unable to secure sleeping compartments so we were all condemned to sit bolt upright as we rattled through the night. Every now and then a clanging bell and a cloud of hissing steam would signal a station stop, often a place with a name that was familiar yet somehow disorientating – Rochester, Rome, Amsterdam – or else an increasingly alien collection of syllables – Utica, Schenectady, Poughkeepsie…

Now we just wanted to sleep for about a week.

Even though it was early in the morning the city was coming to life. Throngs of people were streaming out of the station and heading to whatever work they had to do, and we watched them go by with the thespian's traditional pity for the early bird.

On the opposite side of the broad thoroughfare, we could see some fellows sitting out on the pavement reading the *New York Times*. Their seats were raised unusually high, so that they would have to clamber up a couple of steps to get on board, and they were smart-looking chaps, too, with top hats and smart topcoats. Then the crowd of pedestrians passing in front of them thinned momentarily, and we realised that there were other fellows crouching in front of them shining their shoes.

Stan wrinkled his nose at this. "Not a particularly dignified way to start the day, is it?" he sniffed. "I don't think I'd like to have the horse muck scraped off my shoes in front of the world and his wife."

Charlie, though, was at that moment inspecting his own shoe, one leg thrust out straight, turning his ankle from side to side. He was just about to cross the road to see about getting a shine when Alf Reeves returned, leaping down from the front of the first of two horse-drawn carts he'd managed to hire.

11

"All aboard!" he shouted, clapping his hands. "Let's get these bags on the back, shall we?"

"I'll thank you not to refer to my wife that way!" said George Seaman, beating the other married man to the punch by a split second. Fred Palmer grinned amiably at this defeat, and reached for his luggage. Charlie swung his own trunk up onto the second cart, then turned round and grabbed the handles of mine.

"Here Arthur, let me get that for you," he said with a cheerful grin.

"That's all right," I said, but he was already hefting it up onto the back board.

"No trouble, old pal!" Charlie cried, and then skipped up to take a seat. Stan gave me a quizzical look, but I just shrugged and climbed up too.

The carts swung out across the road then, and we got our first look at the great metropolis, its wide roads, its improbably tall buildings, and its people scuttling every which way. The middle of the main roads was given over to trolleys. These were slow-moving, and pedestrians stepped out right in front of them almost as if they were not there. They oozed along, only twenty or thirty yards apart, and they were enclosed, not like the open omnibuses of London. The impression they gave was that the humans were sharing their city with a race of giant molluscs.

We reached Broadway and swung North through the theatre district. Of course we weren't seeing it at its best, lights off, doors shuttered, the much-vaunted playhouses looking like closed shops. I saw the Victoria go by, the famed vaudeville house in Times Square, and the Gaiety, where someone called Hale Hamilton was appearing as 'Get-Rich-Quick Wallingford', who I presumed would be a character in the Mike Asher vein. My friends were all looking around, eyes wide, and I could tell they were thinking the same as I was. Broadway! Is this... it...?!

We clopped slowly on and on. The theatres were fewer and farther between now, Broadway became a great wide boulevard lined with comfortable-looking residences, and just when we were sure that we were out of the theatre district altogether, we came upon the Colonial Theatre, our home for the next week.

We had wondered on the way over how different the American vaudeville theatres would be from the music halls we were used to back in England. As it turned out, the Colonial was built by a crazed enthusiast of British music hall, so once we filed in through the stage door it could hardly have felt more familiar. The effect was just anti-climactic enough to suck the last bit of life from our weary bodies, and we slumped into the seats in the tiny green room – which smelt, as green rooms everywhere smelt, vaguely of feet – without even bothering to take our coats off.

"Hmmph. Long way to come for this..." Asher muttered, folding his arms and closing his eyes for a kip.

Tilly sat beside me, and gave me a weak smile. "So, this is the start of our American adventure, eh?"

I shrugged, tried to think of something breezy to say, but I was just too tired. In any case Tilly wouldn't have been awake to hear it, and the whole company seemed to be winding down, like a set of clockwork automata that had lost its keys.

Suddenly there was a tramping of boots on the stairs outside, and we were joined by a snorting presence akin to a bull that was minded to lay waste to a china shop.

"What ho! Hail fellows, well met at long last! What news of old Blighty!"

Ruddy of face and jovial of demeanour, and distressingly well-rested, it was our missing colleague Charles Griffiths. We hadn't seen him since he had gone to his cabin on the *Lusitania* for a bit of a nap. He'd woken up to find he was making the crossing solo, and he'd been in New York for a week and a half.

His arrival was greeted with groans, and the odd moan of "Leave me alone...!" coupled with a mumbled "Keep it down, can't you...?!"

"Well, aren't you a sorry-looking bunch of sad sacks!" Griffiths bellowed. He might have been talking normally, but to our tired ears he did seem to be bellowing. "I must say I was most surprised to wake up on the *Lusitania* and discover that the rest of you had made alternative arrangements. You missed a rare treat, you know – ah, what luxury! I have never seen the like of it! The food! The comfort, the service! It was without a doubt the very best week of my entire life...!"

This monologue brought on some jeering, and a boot thrown by an unseen hand clipped Griffiths' trilby from his head, at which he laughed heartily.

"Alf! There you are!" he cried, spotting our company manager in the corridor. "Got your wire, and I've organised the accommodation just as you asked. Here..." He fumbled in his jacket pockets for a piece of paper. "We can all move in tomorrow."

Alf gaped at him. "Tomorrow? Where will we sleep tonight?"

Griffiths was amiably perplexed. "Aren't we going to be going out on the town? Celebrating?"

Everyone was following this conversation, and this was greeted with a chorus of jeers.

"We'll need to sleep somewhere, you lummox!"

Alf's shoulders sagged. Like the rest of us he had hardly slept at all on the train journey down from Canada, so this felt like the final straw.

"I'll go and book us all into the hotel next door," he said.

"Now don't you all fall asleep, you lot, we've got the band call, and then we've got a show to do. *Two* shows. Mr Griffiths? You are responsible."

"Aye aye, captain," Charlie Griffiths said.

Alf headed out towards the stage door, and Griffiths clapped his hands together. "Come on, everyone, wakey-wakey!"

There was a loud moan from the assembled company, and no one made a move to get to their feet. Indeed, one or two people began rolling their coats into pillows for their heads, and stretching out on the chairs and sofas.

"All right," Griffiths said. "Five more minutes." He sat down, stretched his legs out across the rug, and placed his hands together across his ample belly.

I could barely keep my eyes open, but I did stay awake long enough to see Chaplin sidle over to where Tilly was lying with her head resting on the dozing Amy's legs, and he placed a coat solicitously over her shoulders. Her eyes half-opened and she smiled her thanks.

I gritted my teeth.

Because Tilly Beckett was the other thing Charlie and I had in common.

The important thing to remember is – I saw her first. At the time Charlie was mooning around after a young dancer – a very young dancer – called Hetty Kelly, and he was wafting into work every morning waxing lyrical about the divine smell of her soap and such like. No wonder she gave him the bum's rush.

Tilly and I first met down at the Fun Factory, Karno's head-quarters in Camberwell, and I was captivated at once. She was bright, and funny, and so attractive, with her cascade of blonde ringlets and twinkling green eyes – I just couldn't stop thinking about her.

Soon Tilly and I both found ourselves supers in a Karno show called *Wontdetainia*, in which we were required simply to cling to the railings of a vast ocean liner as it bucked and tossed in a fake storm. To alleviate the tedium of being merely human scenery we concocted a storyline for ourselves in which we were secretly married and eloping to America together, just a bit of harmless flirty fun to pass the time.

However, Tilly then blurted out one evening that we were *actually* married in order to deflect the amorous attentions of young Freddie Karno Junior, who was then working on the admin side of things for his old man. Freddie, meaning well, added her to the strength of the company that I was touring with at the time, and saw to it that we were assigned married accommodations. Well, I suppose we could have straightened out that misunderstanding there and then, but we didn't, and we passed several happy weeks living as man and wife before the roof fell in.

So you see, our romance was all the wrong way round, beginning with married bliss before we'd had a proper courtship.

Anyway, Charlie got wind of our little charade and either out of jealousy or a desire to see me, his nearest rival, knocked back, he went to his brother, Syd, who was the number one of the company, and shopped us.

Tilly was booted out, and I was offered the choice of leaving with her or staying without her. My girl, or my career. I should have gone with her, I see that now, but at the time the idea of giving the Chaplins the satisfaction of getting shot of me just stuck in my craw, and before I really knew what had happened she was gone.

I didn't see Tilly again for more than a year. I did everything I could think of to track her down, even going to Southend to search for her parents to see if they had word of her whereabouts, but to no avail.

Then I was in Paris, with Charlie, appearing at the Folies Bergère in *Mumming Birds* (about which, more in due course). While we were there he struck up a clandestine romance with a chorus girl from the headline act, which was the celebrated French singer and comedienne Mistinguett. I stumbled across Charlie having supper with his new paramour one evening, and lo and behold, it was Tilly Beckett.

A furious fist fight ensued, during which Charlie and I attempted to knock seven bells out of one another – I'm pretty sure I knocked at least five out of him, maybe even six. And then I declared myself to Tilly, told her how miserable I had been and how I felt about her, but la belle Mistinguett had plans to marry her off to some ghastly German aristocrat from the Hohenzollerns, and I left Paris convinced that I would never see her again.

I was wrong about that, though, because Tilly suddenly wrote that she was returning to England and auditioning for Karno. I was thrilled, but then Freddie Junior told me exactly what an audition with his father consisted of. When I saw Tilly I could not shake the mental image of her and the Guv'nor together, and I rejected her, drove her away. Stupid, stupid boy.

Shortly after that I left Karno to nurse the broken knee which Charlie had kindly arranged for me, as I mentioned earlier, and when I returned Charlie had resumed his courtship of Tilly, and I was forced to watch him pressing his oleaginous attentions on her.

His scheme, quite clearly, was to whisk her away with him to the States leaving me, his rival, behind. I'd had a similar plan, of course, but as it turned out there all three of us were in New York, our fortunes bound inextricably together for the foreseeable.

But where did we stand, really...?

Suddenly I was hauled abruptly back from the Land of Nod by an anguished cry.

I looked up, rubbing my eyes, and saw that the whole company, all fifteen members, was snoozing. Right in the middle Charlie Griffiths lay with his feet up, snoring away like a champion.

"Griffiths, you big lump!" Alf was shouting. "Didn't I say you were responsible?"

"Oof! Aha! Alf!" Griffiths spluttered, struggling to his feet.

"You've missed the bloody band call, and the matinée has already started. We are on in twenty minutes. Twenty minutes! Up! Everyone! Up! Costume! Make up! Come on!"

Grumbling and mumbling, the company stirred into a faint simulacrum of life, and we traipsed up the stairs, with Alf Reeves goading us all the way.

Once on the stage a modicum of professionalism kicked in. We launched into the sketch without intro music and only a rough idea of where our props might be. We were able to work out how to get on and off without breaking a leg (not as lucky as theatre people make it sound, by the way), because the English-style Colonial Theatre was so very like so many we had played before that we could almost do this in our sleep. Which was a bit of luck.

We didn't exactly set the place on fire that day, either in the matinée or the evening. *The Wow Wows* wasn't Karno's finest offering, not by any means, but his very best work on its best day would have struggled to maintain a proper comedy momentum if four - yes, *four* - members of its cast had actually nodded off onstage at various points during the performance.

I put my arm around Alf's shoulders as we walked into the hotel next door at the end of the night. "Never mind," I said. "Be better tomorrow."

"It'll need to be," he muttered. "Or not even Karno's name will save us."

3
THE WOW WOWS

THE next morning I woke early, realised that I was hungry, and was reminded of one of the hard and fast rules of the travelling life – never, *ever*, miss a hotel breakfast. My roommate, Freddie K Junior, was dead to the world so I dressed and went down without him.

On the way I tapped on the door of Tilly's room. It took a minute or so to get a response, and then she opened the door a crack and blearily peered out.

"Come on, sleepyhead," I said. "Hotel breakfast?"

Tilly groaned. "I think I'll give it a miss..." she started.

"No, no, get dressed, come on," I insisted. "We don't have to be at the theatre until twelve, so let's go for a walk, explore a bit. We're in America! I don't feel like we've actually arrived yet."

"I feel like we spent the last fortnight arriving," Tilly muttered, but she finally relented and agreed to join me shortly down in the dining room.

My spirits were even higher after an excellent breakfast of strong coffee and scrambled eggs on toast. There was a wide variety of ways in which they were prepared to cook eggs, evidently, but scrambled was the only one I was absolutely certain I recognised so I had that, and then set off to make my first foray into the big city with Tilly yawning by my side.

At the end of West 63rd Street we came to a park entrance, and strolled through onto a tree-lined path. The noise of the streets, the horses' hooves, the trolleys and the automobile engines faded behind us.

"This reminds me of Hyde Park," Tilly said with a smile. "Our first walk out together, do you remember?"

"Of course."

"Yes, and then tea at the Trocadero, I was most impressed."

"I'm glad to hear it," I said, remembering the echoing void that particular afternoon had created in my wallet.

"In fact," Tilly went on, "it's not so very different from London altogether, is it? The traffic, everyone speaking English. And that theatre could have been shipped here from any English town brick by brick."

"The weather's better," I said, and indeed New York was enjoying an Indian summer. Like they have in India, I mean, not the kind enjoyed by the lads in the feathered headdresses.

"Mmm."

"Come on," I said. "Aren't you even a little bit excited? We are in America! One big city is much like another, I suppose, but just wait till we start crossing the country, see the wide open spaces, the prairies, the Rocky Mountains!"

"Yes, well, we're going to be here in New York for a couple of months, aren't we? And unless someone books us onto one of the circuits we could be home by Christmas."

"We're going to be a hit, don't you worry. They love the Karnos over here."

"They haven't seen the wretched *Wow Wows* yet," Tilly muttered.

We strolled on through the trees in silence for a while.

"Tilly?" I said eventually. "There's something I want to... I mean, there wasn't ever a chance on the crossing to talk about..."

"To talk about...?"

"Well... us."

Tilly kept her eyes on the path straight ahead, nodded slightly, said nothing.

"You know how I feel about you," I ventured after a moment.

"I thought I did," she said. "We have been special friends, you and I, Arthur, and you know that you mean a lot to me. But I have twice been in a position where I looked for your support, and you didn't give it."

"I know," I winced.

"Once when I was sacked that time we were caught pretending to be married, and you chose to stay with Karno rather than leave with me..."

"I know, and if I had it to do again..."

"You preferred your obsessive little competition with Charlie."

"I did, I know."

"And again when I came back from Paris, precisely because you had been so lovely to me there, and so sad, and lost, and then you turned your back on me."

"I did, and I'm sorry. I didn't understand. Please let me apologise again."

"Your apology is accepted, Mr Dandoe," she said, with exaggerated formality.

The path took us past a sports field of some kind, a nice round open space that would have been perfect for a cricket pitch, except that it looked like it was marked out for some other game, which some players were practising. One of them suddenly shouted out: "Strike two!" which was a little on the nose, I thought.

"But even so, it was hurtful, Arthur, you hurt me," she went on. "We can be friends, of course we can, we can be good friends, we *are* good friends, but if you want... more than that, I need to know that I can trust you to put me first. To put your feelings for me above this stupid rivalry with Charlie, for example."

"You know it was Charlie who got you the sack back then, don't you?" I muttered.

"So you say, but I don't see how you could possibly know that for certain."

I did know it, just as surely as I knew anything, but it was never easy to speak to Tilly about the ways Charlie had done me down. She never seemed prepared to believe the worst of him – it was infuriating, but I let it go.

"Are you and Charlie courting?"

Tilly laughed. "Courting? Good Heavens, no. No, no, we are friends, that's all. Sometimes he likes to play at being romantic, but it's just one of his characters. You know that about him, surely? He's always playing a part of some kind, and sometimes he likes to play at courting, that's all it is. Just a bit of fun. And it is fun, sometimes, to have a man make a fuss of you."

We strolled on a little further. I wondered whether Charlie knew he was just playing a part, or whether he himself had a quite different impression.

"You should get to know him better, you know, "Tilly said. "He's a nice chap, deep down, and he doesn't make friends easily."

"He told you that himself, did he?"

"Yes, he's really quite shy, you know."

"Shy?"

"Yes. Why do you think he keeps himself to himself so much of the time?"

I had always put that down to arrogance, myself, a contemptuous disdain for the rest of us, who simply couldn't understand how hard it was to be a *genius*...

"So you are friends, then?" I said.

"Why shouldn't a woman have male friends?"

"You'll be wanting the vote next," I said. Tilly gave me a hard punch on the arm for that one.

"It is not easy for me, sometimes, you know. I am the only unattached girl in this company, so I really have to be one of the lads. You surely don't think I should only socialise with Amy and Emily and Muriel?"

"Of course not."

"Well then. So I am going to be chums with all you boys, aren't I? Not just you and Charlie. Stan and Mike I know, Albert and Bert seem perfectly agreeable, I haven't really spoken to them much yet. That Frank Melroyd has a way of looking at me that... oh well, never mind."

"What?"

"Nothing, it doesn't matter."

"I'll have a word with him."

"You will do no such thing."

"Well," I said as a clock somewhere outside the park began to chime the three-quarter hour. "We'd best get back to the theatre, hadn't we?"

Tilly took my arm, and we set off back the way we had just walked, this time in companionable silence. At least I had broached the subject, but I wasn't altogether sure that things were any clearer than they had been. Still, it seemed that if I was going to make sure of Tilly, I was going to have to curb my desire to compete with Charlie.

I glanced over, and she gave me one of those smiles. She was worth it, she was most definitely worth it. And I'd still need to keep a close eye on him, I thought.

━━━━━

The company convened in the green room at the Colonial Theatre at noon, and my colleagues seemed to be all the better for a good night's sleep. There was a gale of laughter as Tilly and I arrived, and at the centre of it was Stan Jefferson.

Everyone liked Stan. His laugh was incredibly infectious, and transformed his whole visage, making it seem like his eyebrows were trying to fly off the top of his red head.

"Whatever is it?" Tilly asked, and a couple of helpless gigglers simply pointed at Stan's feet.

He was wearing maroon-coloured carpet slippers, with a nice little embroidered bedtime candle on each toe, very much the sort of thing Wee Willie Winkie might have worn to gad about the town.

"You forget to put your shoes on today, Stan?" I said.

"Mmm!" he said, winding himself up to tell the story again. "It's the darn'dest thing. I put my shoes out last night to be cleaned, you know, as you do, and this morning they were gone. I asked the porter, and he said they don't actually clean shoes in hotels in this country, so someone must have just walked off with them. My only pair, too!"

By now Tilly and I were laughing along with the rest.

"Some ordinary fellow, probably, just walking along the corridor minding his own business, then 'Hey, what do you know, free shoes!' Ha ha ha!"

A blob of tan coloured sauce plopped at Stan's feet, dripping from the strong-smelling fried sausage he was clutching.

"Breakfast? Or lunch?" I pointed.

"Fellow in the street selling them from a stand," he said taking a bite. "It's called a Frankfurter. Three cents, or two for five. Marvellous!"

Alf Reeves was amongst us then, arriving unnoticed in all the merriment, and he cleared his throat to get our attention.

"Morning everybody – or afternoon, is it? Just. Ha! I hope you all had a good night's rest, and are refreshed and ready to give of your best today at four and eight?

"Yes, Alf," we chorused.

"Wide awake this time?"

"Yes, Alf!"

"Keep the noise down, will you?" Charlie Griffiths muttered, pretending to be having a nap. Alf acknowledged this witticism with a long suffering sigh.

"Now, before we talk about the arrangements for your accommodation here in New York I need to have a word about behaviour." Here he waved a letter on Fun Factory paper above his head. "The Guv'nor has made it clear that he expects you all to maintain the very highest standards of propriety while you are representing the Fred Karno company..."

"Oooh!" came the jocular response from the room.

"Some of the towns we may end up playing over here are quite... prudish. There is a very strong... what would you say... *churchy* element, maybe not here in New York City, but certainly once we hit the road. Some of the vaudeville theatres we could be visiting have been fighting a running battle against elements in their communities that would like nothing better than to close them down completely as dens of iniquity."

"Shame!"

"So if you must..." Alf stopped, searching for the right phrase, and alternatives were immediately supplied from all sides.

25

"Sow your wild oats?"

"Practise the blanket hornpipe...?"

"Play a little rumpscuttle...?"

"Sss, sss, ssss!" Bert Williams sniggered.

"Seek a companion with whom to make the beast with two backs...?"

"Oh Charles, you are awful!"

"My dear lady, that was Shakespeare..."

"All right, all right, that's enough!" Alf cried above the smutty chuckling. "If you must indulge in... any of those extraordinary things, then please try to do so with the utmost discretion."

"Oh! Courting! You're talking about courting!" Frank Melroyd was just catching up.

"Simmer down, you lot, please. We shall be in New York for the next few weeks, and Mr Griffiths here has secured rooms. We shan't all be staying together, I'm afraid – or perhaps you are relieved to hear that, eh? So the single lads, Charlie, Stan, Arthur, Albert, Frank, Bert, Mike and Freddie, you're in four rooms on Forty Third Street, two in a room, got that?"

We nodded, and Alf went on.

"The married couples and the single girls – well, that's just you, Tilly, isn't it? – are to be accommodated in a nice house over on Forty Eighth Street."

Tilly and Amy started giggling about something, but I was a little disappointed. Tilly was to be five whole blocks away?

"Now, both of these buildings have very, shall we say, *attentive* landladies. The Guv'nor has made it abundantly clear that any suggestion of 'moral turpitude' will result in the immediate termination of your employment by the company."

"Moral turpitude? What's that?" Fred Palmer asked.

"It's the stuff they were just talking about, the rumpscuttling and the blanket hornpipe," his wife said, nudging him quiet.

Alf had said his piece, though, and wrapped up the meeting. "Well, there it is. Here's the addresses, back here at three everyone!"

Freddie came over, pretending to bite his nails with fake anxiety. "Moral turpitude, eh?" he said, giving me a nudge in the ribs. "Oh yes, one of the great ironies, my old man taking a moral stand of any kind, given his own outstanding turpitudinousness."

We single lads found our allotted rooms in a brownstone house just off Forty Third Street, pretty much where the Times Building now stands. It was a depressing little dive, with a busy laundry in the basement, and the damp odour of drying clothes permeating every room and landing. Like all Karno men we were acutely aware of the company hierarchy, and so we naturally deferred to Charlie.

"Well," he said, stroking his chin. "Clearly the farther from the steamery the better. What do you think, Arthur? Shall you and I take the top floor room?"

I blinked. Charlie wanted to share with me now? We could be living here for weeks, months even. Could I trust myself not to throttle him in his sleep?

"Oh," I said. "I thought I'd be sharing with Freddie as usual."

Charlie beamed, completely unperturbed. "Fine. You two take the top floor, Stan and I will be one below, and you chaps" – he waved breezily at Albert, Frank, Bert and Mike – "can take the two rooms on the first floor."

As we dumped our luggage Freddie grabbed my arm. "What just happened? Did we just get the best room? What's the catch?"

"No catch," I said. Just Charlie trying to stay on the right side of me.

27

Inside the building, because of the sweaty humidity caused by the laundry constantly on the go, there were fingers of damp grey mould everywhere, reaching down from the ceilings and up from the stairs, so the title 'best room' was a slightly hollow one in any case. We were only going to be there for a few weeks so it wasn't like it was our job to fix it, but I did wonder how mouldy it was in the place where Charlie Griffiths himself was staying.

We rode the trolleybus back up Broadway, and as the matinée approached, the Karno dressing room was abuzz with excitement, the lads bouncing jokes off one another, throwing props and costumes around. The day before we had sleep-walked through the whole performance, both the matinée and the evening go, barely even noticing how we had been received. Now, though, with a good night's rest and a couple of square meals under our belts, we were raring to go, and our professional pride was kicking in. This felt like the real first night, the start of our American adventure proper, and we were determined to put on a good show.

Fred Karno's reputation ensured that we were the headline attraction, and the other acts on the bill were wary of us and more than a little resentful. There were fifteen of us, and so we had commandeered a substantial chunk of backstage real estate. The previous day our new colleagues had been preoccupied, but now, on this second night that felt like the first, they all gathered in the wings to watch us, coolly assessing whether we were worthy of holding top billing over them.

So as the moment drew near for *The Wow Wows* to begin, and the jaunty chords of our signature music rang out, we were on pins, nervous. Confident, certainly, but nervous nonetheless.

The Wow Wows was billed as a 'farcical sketch in three scenes', the first of which was set at a campsite by a river. A group of young gents – played by yours truly, Mike Asher and Frank Melroyd – are getting up to face the day. My character, 'Blazer', is trying to shave, but keeps getting his elbow bumped by passing boatmen swinging oars around. Melroyd as 'Bottles' moans about always having to pay for the fourth member of our party, one 'Archibald Binks', who never opens his wallet for fear that his collection of moths might escape.

Early on we were not expecting too much response from the audience. The real laughs were due to arrive with the entrance of Binks, who was Charlie Chaplin of course. On he came, in his too-white make-up, looking like death warmed up, with one end of his moustache pointing up and the other down. When we performed the sketch in England his very appearance would start the crowd a-sniggering, but here in New York City you could almost hear the audience thinking: "Come on then, you dumb limeys, make us laugh."

Charlie's first gag was to hold out a tea cup to Frank Melroyd, saying:

"I say, Bottles, do you mind giving me a little water?"

'Bottles' replies: "Certainly, what do you want it for?"

And then Charlie's topper: "I want to take a bath."

In England this used to go down big, setting Binks up as the sort of upper class twit that the music hall would reliably milk for laughs. Here, though – nothing. Nothing at all.

Charlie blinked hard, knowing, as we all did, that the next few minutes were all in this vein. On came Amy Minister as Lydia, Archie's girlfriend, to ask about his morning dip.

"Did the water come up to your expectations?"

"No, only up to my knees."

We'd have taken a groan, frankly. Anything to indicate that the audience were still actually alive. But no, there was just the same cavernous indifference to our efforts.

Once Archibald Binks departs, my character Blazer would take the lead as we make a plan to revenge ourselves on the skinflint by faking an initiation into a secret society, inflicting various indignities upon our number one. The audience actually perked up at this a little bit, quite keen to see Chaplin hurt.

We ploughed grimly on through the second scene where Binks was prepared for the ordeal ahead, and then the climactic third scene of the initiation itself. For this we all wore long black robes and conical headpieces that concealed our faces, which felt like a blessing at that time I can tell you. The get-up was Karno's idea, and he based it on some ecclesiastical picture he'd seen of monks in Spain. We genuinely had no notion that our costumes had any other resonance than that, not until *The Birth of a Nation* came out.[1]

Anyway, there was no end of silly business, paddling poor Binks back and forth as he howled, and electrocuting him on a so-called magic carpet, before we reveal ourselves and let him know why he has been taught such a salutary lesson.

The slapstick of the finale went down a little better than the opening, but not much, and the feeling lingered that the audience had only enjoyed the humiliation of the main character because they really didn't like him.

At the end we slunk offstage into the wings, stunned and humbled, and just stared at one another wide-eyed. Most of our American colleagues seemed to have drifted away during the course of the performance, but at my side, all of a sudden, was Edgar Pendulo, hypnotist and mind-reader. He gave me a sorrowful look, and whispered:

"Never mind, old bean. Perhaps tomorrow I could go on and hypnotise the whole audience into thinking they are British, what-what?"

He smirked unpleasantly then and sidled off to tell someone else his brilliant witticism. I think that may have been the very start of my hatred for Americans trying to do a British accent.

We told ourselves that the matinée was a fluke, just one of those crowds you sometimes get, but the second house was no better, and it was a dispirited bunch that gathered to drown their sorrows in the bar around the corner at the end of the night.

"I told him," Charlie said, shaking his head over his glass of port. "I told the Guv'nor we shouldn't do *The Wow Wows*, but he was convinced that it was just the thing for America. He's got it into his head somehow that the place is just crawling with secret societies."

"Secret societies of silly Englishmen, though?" I said, doubtfully.

"Exactly my point, Arthur, exactly. It's too English, isn't it, with its lame puns and its endless haw-hawing. The pantomime parts, the business with the oars at the beginning, and the initiation, they're universal enough to play, but the rest of it is just too..."

"English," said Stan.

"Right. It's too parochial."

The fact is *The Wow Wows* was simply a dud, not fit to lace the boots of *The Football Match*, let alone toss a derisory orange at *Mumming Birds*. We all knew it, we all hated it, and we all knew we were stuck with it.

"It'll be all right," Tilly said. "No Karno company has ever failed in America."

"There's a first time for everything," Charlie muttered darkly.

4
BLITHERING, BLATHERING ENGLISHMEN

TWICE a day for the rest of that week we attempted to breathe life into our much-hated show, but without success. The audiences remained determinedly unimpressed, and our American colleagues began to avoid us backstage as though we had the plague. One night we stood in the wings waiting to go on, and Charlie was next to me in his pale drunk's make-up, and he whispered:

"It feels like we are lining up to get shot."

He got no argument from me. And then on the Friday *Variety* came out.

This weekly rag was a forty-page trawl through everything connected with vaudeville, principally the New York scene, but gathering titbits from all around the world to pack its pages. That autumn I remember reading the salacious developments in the Doctor Crippen case, which qualified as a *Variety* story because his missing wife, Bella Elmore, had been a British music hall artiste.

There was a particular slang used in *Variety* that you had to pick up. You would read, for instance, that: "Irwin and Herang are at the Fulton, Brooklyn this week for their New York opening on the Morris time." This meant that the act in question were going to be working on the Morris circuit of vaudeville houses, beginning in New York. 'Time' was the word used to describe the various circuits an act could be hired to play, so if, for example, you were working the Pantages circuit you would say you were "on Pantages time". In those days there were any number of circuits, of all sizes. The 'big time', such as the Keith and Orpheum circuit, was where you would find the top acts such as Mr Al Jolson or Houdini, and they would be playing large theatres in big cities across the country. Less prominent acts you might find plugging away at a more modest list of venues limited to a particular city or state, working 'small time'.

It was trivial stuff, maybe, but there was no getting away from the fact that vaudeville was very big business indeed. The must-read pages contained the reviews of vaudeville acts, with nothing escaping their gaze, nor their withering scorn.

A *Variety* review could make or break a vaudeville act in less time than it took to read the thing. We were new to the New York scene, of course, and so were not expecting it, but one of the other acts had helpfully left a copy on the dressing table in our room lying open at the offending page.

The reviewer began by describing Charlie as 'typically English', and he didn't give the impression that this was a good thing. Despite this, he grudgingly reckoned that 'Chaplin will do for America'. However, he went on to dismiss the rest of us as "the most remarkable collection of blithering, blathering Englishmen New York has seen in many a day."

Most of us were pretty cast down by this, but those who were most dismissive of *The Wow Wows* were feeling vindicated. Tilly brandished the paper with what looked like triumph.

"See? What have I been saying? Listen: 'The three women in the act are not needed. One has a scene with the comedian' – that's Amy, of course – 'the others simply walk on and off a couple of times'. I hate *The Wow Wows*, hate it!"

Fired up by this, an impromptu council of war assembled in the bar after the Friday night show. Poor Alf Reeves was in the hot seat, fingering his bow-tie nervously, surrounded by a surly and unhappy mob. Charlie, as the number one, should really have been taking the lead, but he sat still, detached, legs crossed, inspecting his nails, so I stepped up, banged the table and began: "Listen everyone. It's not been a good week, we all know that, and now there's this piece in *Variety* that is going to hang around our necks wherever we go. What can we do?"

Everyone had an opinion, it seemed, and they were all versions of the same one.

"Dump *The Wow Wows*!"

"Bring out *Jimmy the Fearless*! Or *London Suburbia*!"

"Or *Mumming Birds*!"

"How about it, Alf?" I said. "We could drop *The Wow Wows*, and we all know *Mumming Birds*, I'm sure, we've all played it before back in England."

"Hear hear!" came the cry from all parts, along with a nodding hum of confirmation that this was a feasible plan of action.

Alf raised his hands for silence, and the urgent murmuring died down. "I know that's what you all want," he said, "but there's simply no chance."

"Why not?" Charlie asked languidly.

"The last three Karno companies who have come over here have played *Mumming Birds*, that's why. It's run its course. The Guv'nor wants to break this new thing in, and he's convinced it will play. You want to tell the Guv'nor he's wrong?"

Charlie blinked, and the rest of us looked at our beers.

"No, I thought not. You want me to do it for you, that's it, isn't it? Well, no, thank you very much. We're going to give it a fair go, and that's all we can do. Understood?"

━━━━

The next week we moved to the Alhambra, where *The Wow Wows* was no better received. Charlie was pulling out all the stops, throwing in new bits of business, introducing fresh pratfalls and extravagant mugging, but all to no avail. It was clearly beginning to get him down, and he stopped coming to the bar for a drink afterwards, gloomily disappearing into the night.

I wanted to talk to Tilly about this, and about how things were going generally, but it wasn't proving easy to grab a moment with her. After the performances we would all - apart from Charlie, of course - tip into the bar next door and commandeer a large table. If I could, I would take the seat next to Tilly, but more often than not I would find that Frank Melroyd had taken the opportunity to shuffle in beside her, sometimes even trapping her in a booth. He was a funny fish, Frank. He would sit next to her all evening, not saying much, just enjoying his proximity to a pretty girl. It was infuriating, not least because he was so intent on holding onto this prime spot that he very rarely made a trip to the bar.

And then whenever we decided to head for our accommodations he would be steering Tilly to the trolley bus, or sometimes calling a cab for the two of them – which he could afford with all the cash he was saving not buying anyone a drink, by the way – and making sure that he was the one who saw her safely to her door. On one occasion he was so anxious not to miss out on this chivalrous little treat that he stood squarely on my foot and clumsily shoved me face first into a hat stand.

So one morning I strode the five blocks over to the brownstone building where Tilly was staying and knocked on the front door. It was opened by a sturdy woman whose features seemed set in a permanent frown.

"Good morning, madam," I said, in my most polite English manner. "Is Miss Beckett at home?"

"No gentlemen callers allowed in the rooms," the landlady said firmly.

"Of course," I said. "I wouldn't dream of suggesting otherwise. But I am a colleague of hers, and if you would be so kind as to let Miss Beckett know that I am here, then perhaps she would like to take the air?"

The woman grunted, shoved the door almost to, and disappeared into the darkness leaving me standing on the step.

After a minute or two Tilly appeared in a rush, still fastening a hat to her hair, and we set off along the street, with the landlady watching us all the way. I could feel her dark little eyes boring into the back of my skull.

"Thank goodness you came over, Arthur," Tilly said, taking my arm. "I was going stir crazy in there. Emily means well, but... you know?"

I did. Emily Seaman was one of those people who think of themselves as bouncy and irrepressible, and consequently was quite tiring company. The first time she greeted you with the phrase "Hello, wonderful to see me, isn't it?!" or responded to an offer to put the kettle on with a chirpy "It won't fit you!" was all well and good, but over and again every single day was enough to make a saint start grinding his or her teeth.

"Let's head for the park, shall we?"

We took the trolley up to Central Park, and strolled in down a wide avenue that was already pretty heavily populated with walkers, many of them ladies with spud-faced children in bassinets swaddled to within an inch of their lives.

"Aaahh," Tilly sighed, her spirits visibly lifted by the trees and the open air. "You know, if you want to avoid that battle axe there are two mornings a week where she attends a temperance gathering to conquer her weakness for the demon drink."

"Oh really?" I said.

"Yes, apparently they are hosted by a rather striking gentleman from the 'hell fire and brimstone' school of performing, and she has a considerable weakness for him as well."

"She's under his spell, eh?"

"I have heard you speaking about the... what do you call it? When things are going well?"

"The Power, do you mean?"

"Yes, that's it. The Power, it sounds tremendous."

The Power was the name I had given to that feeling of control that I had onstage when the audience was completely under my spell. I first felt it back in Cambridge when doing an impersonation of my head porter father at a college smoking concert, and had felt it periodically since. It was an intoxicating feeling, and one that I had not enjoyed at all while performing *The Wow Wows*, let me assure you of that. I had forgotten that I had even mentioned it to Tilly. I'm not sure it was a subject I would have broached with any of the lads, for fear that they would rib me about it mercilessly.

"I should like to feel something like that," she went on. "I have approached it, I think, on occasion. Sometimes, you know, even when I am just one of a dozen girls onstage I can feel that the whole audience is watching me."

"I can imagine," I said, gallantly. "I know I would not be watching anyone else."

"Ha!" she said. "You know, with Charlie I think it is different. He is always pursuing the perfect performance, one where he ticks absolutely every box. He wants to get every single laugh that is in there, and touch people at the same time, but he never talks about controlling the audience in the way that you do. He feels, I think, that if he gets everything just right, then he will naturally get the reaction he deserves as his due."

"It doesn't seem to be happening at the moment," I said.

"I know, and I think it's hitting him quite hard." Tilly frowned.

"It's not exactly a picnic for the rest of us, is it?"

"I know, I know, but I do feel sorry for him. He feels it's all on his shoulders, you know?"

We strolled on a little further.

"One day," Tilly said suddenly. "One day I should like to be centre stage."

"Well, I'm afraid the Guv'nor's repertoire isn't exactly stocked with roles for leading ladies."

"No, I know, perhaps not with Karno, but at least a woman can think of making herself a career on the halls, can she not? After all, who is a bigger star than Marie Lloyd?"

"Well, no one. Maybe Robey..."

"And he is your hero, isn't he?"

"He is," I agreed.

"And so if you dream of becoming George Robey, why should I not dream of becoming the next Marie Lloyd? Or Vesta Tilley?

Or Florrie Forde? Or Fanny Brice?"

"No reason, no reason at all," I said.

"I just wish I could show what I can do. There is just no chance in the stupid *Wow Wows*, for I am required to do nothing, nothing at all, in the comedy line. I walk on, I walk off. I might as well be a shop mannequin on castors."

I had to admit she had a point. And I was surprised, actually, because Tilly had never really spoken about her own ambitions before. Maybe she had, and I'd been too busy talking about mine to listen.

"So you want to be the next Marie Lloyd, then?"

"What's wrong with that?" she said sharply.

"Nothing, nothing at all," I said, quickly.

Time was getting on, and so I looked around to try and spot which path would lead to an exit from the park. As I did so I thought I saw a familiar figure a little way off.

"Isn't that...?" I said, my hand half-raising to wave a greeting, but the figure had turned and gone behind a fountain, and then was lost in a crowd of perambulators.

"Who?"

"I thought I saw... Frank Melroyd."

"No, really?"

"Just out for a bit of a walk, I expect."

"Yes..." Tilly murmured, turning thoughtful.

━━━━

Speaking of ambitions, I realised I was less preoccupied with the idea of becoming the company number one just then. In fact I had hardly thought of it at all since we landed on foreign shores. Had I come to terms with Charlie's superiority now? Was I prepared to concede him his ultimate triumph? Not likely.

For the time being I was content to be a mere foot soldier and let Captain Chaplin carry the can for the *Wow Wows* debacle. In fact we all were going through the motions, rather. That evening, though, the performance was livened up somewhat by an unexpected incident.

During the opening scene, my character, Blazer, tries to shave at the campsite while a passing boatman, played by Stan Jefferson, swings a great oar around the place, nearly knocking me over. Stan and I had worked out some careful near misses, and it was usually a serviceable enough piece of slapstick. On this night, though, Stan swished his oar past my head a couple of times – and it was a hefty wooden item, by the way, pretty solid – and then headed for the wings as per, when suddenly Frank Melroyd, as my supposed chum Bottles, leapt to his feet, grabbed the oar, and back-swung it straight at my face.

Well, it was a surprise and no mistake. Fortunately my reflexes were at their best onstage and I was able to fling myself backwards to avoid the swipe, and also managed to duck the return, which swished past my ear.

I gasped. "Steady on Fra... I mean, Bottles, old chap!"

I landed on my backside, and in my confusion I thought I heard a strange sound, a sound we hadn't heard for a while. It was the sound of an audience laughing.

In the dressing room afterwards I gave Melroyd a shove in the chest.

"Blimey, Frank, what were you thinking? You damn nearly knocked my block off!"

Frank shrugged: "It was just a bit of business, I thought of it on the spur of the moment, thought it might perk things up a bit."

"It certainly got a laugh," Stan said, somewhat dubiously.

Just then Charlie came in, and said the first words he had spoken to any of us for days: "Yes. Well done, Mr Melroyd. If only the rest of you were trying as hard maybe we wouldn't be in the pickle we find ourselves in."

———

In our third week we played the Bronx Theatre. This was a brand new venue, opened just a fortnight before with a great fanfare, and it was the most prestigious booking we had. They ran shows from one o'clock in the afternoon to 11.30 at night, so it was a slog of a week, especially the long slow cab drive back from 145th Street over the Third Avenue Bridge and through Harlem, counting off the streets all the way down to 43rd.

The Bronx was a rough sort of area, but the crowd was generally upwards of two thousand, which greatly increased the odds of some patrons being tickled by *The Wow Wows* and carrying the thing along. Humiliatingly, however, the bill was changed around on the Thursday, and we went from top of the bill to closing the first half, an unheard-of demotion for a Karno troupe in America, or anywhere else.

Alf took it on the chin. "I just hope to God the Guv'nor never gets to hear about it," he muttered bleakly.

For Charlie, however, this indignity was the final straw, and he plunged even further into the depths of his depression. On the Saturday night he was so low that Stan cornered Freddie and me in the corridor behind the wings, and confided that he was beginning to worry about our number one. As his roommate and his understudy, Stan was closer to Chaplin than any of us, and was privy to the full range of his moods.

"Listen, lads," he said, keeping his voice down. "After the show tonight come straight back to 43rd Street with me and Charlie. We need to cheer him up, and I've an idea that a bit of home

41

cooking might do the trick. Save us all a bob or two, as well, eh?"

Freddie and I agreed. We'd already noticed our pay wasn't going very far in this brave new world. Perhaps we were spending too much of it drinking away our sorrows at the end of the night, but belts needed tightening. Home cooking, though? It sounded intriguing.

So once the curtain came down on another dispiriting rendering of the cursed *Wow Wows*, the four of us – Stan, Charlie, Freddie and me – hustled straight for the trolley bus back downtown. Charlie was brooding, as usual, and communicating only in grunts, but Stan was effervescent, and clutching a parcel of bacon and a couple of loaves of bread that he had bought with our joint contributions between the (bleak) matinée and the (grim) evening show.

We made our way up to Stan and Charlie's room on the second floor of our brownstone building with a certain amount of forced jollity, trying to warm Charlie up, and we were fascinated to know how Stan proposed to cook up the meal without access to a kitchen.

"Are you going to take it down to the laundry and wait for it to steam slowly?" Freddie asked. "Because if you are, I'd like my money back."

"No, no, we've got it all worked out, haven't we, Charlie?"

Charlie sighed, as if to say "Are we really going to do this?", but Stan's eager grin must have broken through the gloom, because suddenly something clicked on, he winked, and the two of them went into action. It was like watching a finely-rehearsed little routine – in fact one or other of them will certainly have used it at some point since.

Charlie whisked the lampshade off the gas jet, while seemingly out of thin air Stan produced a skillet, which Freddie and I recognised merrily as filched from the campsite scene of *The Wow Wows*. In went the bacon, and Stan climbed up onto a chair, placed with perfect timing by Charlie, so as to reach the flame.

In a minute or two the bacon was sizzling away nicely, and beginning to smoke. Now cooking in the rooms was completely forbidden, of course, however nicely choreographed, but the possibility of detection by the landlady had been considered. Charlie briskly threw open the windows, then handed Freddie and me two towels, indicating by pantomime (as was his way when in this playful mood) that we were to waft the smoky smells out and away. Then he grabbed his violin and began to play, striding around the room ever more manically, getting into a character. This covered the tell-tale noise of the bacon sizzling, but also deterred any nosey parker from knocking on the door and disturbing the crazed maestro in full flow.

So Stan reached up to tend to the pan, like the greatest gas-jet chef in the world, Charlie whirled around, a musical dervish, and young Fred and I wafted for all we were worth. I don't know when a meal was ever more fun, and when I ever worked up such an appetite.

Mind you, bacon always has that effect on me, don't know about you.

And for a short while at least, the aroma of a good old English fry-up blotted out the stench of our embarrassing American failure.

5
THE GENTLEMAN'S GENTLEMEN

THE next two weeks saw the company running over to Brooklyn to play the Greenpoint Theatre and the Orpheum – just filling in rather than actually starting to work the Orpheum time, more's the pity. Then we found ourselves travelling back up to the Bronx to play the Loew's National, another brand spanking new palace of fun, where we fared no better.

One late night Charlie and I found ourselves tramping up the stairs of our mould-ridden brownstone lodgings together, while Stan and Freddie were acquiring the fixings for another gas-jet fry-up.

"Well," he said with a shrug. "It looks like this will be our last week. Alf has been trying to book us onto every circuit going, you know, but no one will give him a look-in. We're too big for small time, and not big enough for the big time. It's pretty hopeless."

"I didn't know that."

"No, that's right. We didn't want company morale to drop any further."

I flinched at this unsubtle reminder that Charlie and Alf were officer class while I was a mere private. We reached Stan and Charlie's room, and he let us in, before going on:

"I suppose I'm resigned to it now, but you know we will be the first Karno company to slink back from America with its tail between its legs, don't you? And the Guv'nor's to blame for insisting on that dreadful piece, it's no wonder no one likes it. But d'you think he will see it that way? No, neither do I."

I could see that Charlie was bitterly disappointed with how the American venture had gone, and fearing the awful stigma of returning a failure. When Stan and Freddie turned up with the ingredients of our late dinner, Charlie threw himself into his violin playing even more manically than usual, as if trying to obliterate his troubles with noise and movement.

———

Our final week headlining the bill with *The Wow Wows* at Loew's National was not a hit. It was the sort of huge auditorium that swallowed up an act like ours. Everything had to be bellowed at top volume, and gestures had to be wide and sweeping, so all subtlety was lost. Not that subtlety was the speciality of *The Wow Wows*, of course. Did I tell you this one?

> Archibald (Charlie): I say, what's for breakfast?
> Blazer (Me): There's two eggs for you, but they're both rotten.
> Archibald (Charlie): What, that one bad and that one bad?
> Blazer (Me): Yes.
> Archibald (Charlie): Oh that's too bad.

One for the Comedy Hall of Fame, *that*, I'm sure you will agree.

Anyway, after the show one night in that last week at Loew's, I was sitting alone at the bar, a gloomy place, furnished and finished in dark wood, with dark tiles on the floor, and stained glass in every window. In the wide-arched mirror ahead of me, surrounded by fancy green and turquoise tile work, I could see that Charlie was holding court, having come out of his slump somewhat now that hope was pretty much gone. I had decided to take a stool in the hope that Tilly might slide over and join me, which however she showed no sign of doing, and I found myself pondering an uncertain future in the bottom of my glass, both romantically and professionally.

The prospect of returning to England after only a couple of months in America was very disheartening. If only we had made a go of it, I might have seen some of the country that had sparked my imagination ever since I was a lad, reading about cowboys and Indians, and wagon trains and prospectors in my penny bloods, but the Rocky Mountains and the sweeping prairies seemed as far out of reach as they'd ever been.

Even more unsettling, though, was the certainty that after a notable failure such as ours Karno would split the company up and we would be at his mercy. Charlie would be all right, he'd be heading up a new company sooner or later, but the rest of us would be scattered to the four winds. Would I end up touring with Stan again, or Mike, or Freddie? Unlikely. And Tilly, what about her? I watched her and Charlie chattering together amongst the crowd on the far side of the room and felt sure that Charlie would engineer for her to accompany him wherever he was sent, just as he would be sure to fix it so that I did not.

Perhaps I would have to play the card that I still held up my sleeve, the knowledge that would finish Charlie with Karno, just to stay close to Tilly. Not a move that was likely to create a particularly friendly atmosphere, I thought, but still it might have to be done.

I raised my hand and called the barman over. "Another one, please, my friend," I said, and as the fellow reached for another bottle for me I became aware of a figure standing beside me, looking down at me with a slight frown on his face.

"Help you?" I asked.

The man became flustered. "Excuse me, sir, I didn't mean to offend, it's just... you are from England, aren't you?"

"Eh?" I said.

"The accent is unmistakeable," he said.

"Yours too."

He smiled, and then the barman returned with my drink. Blow me if this English fellow didn't insist on paying for it, too. I decided to let him, even though I realised I was letting myself in for more conversation.

"Your very good health," I said, clinking my glass against his, which was a small one with what looked like sherry in it. "My name is Dandoe."

"Jobson," my new acquaintance said, and we shook hands.

"Well," I said, happy to let him do the talking. "What line are you in, Mr Jobson?"

"I am currently employed as a butler," Jobson said, taking a small sip.

"A butler, really? An English butler in New York, eh? How about that?"

"There are more of us than you perhaps imagine," he replied. "English serving staff are quite the prize. We are a status symbol, I believe the term is."

"Well, well. Good for you."

"Yes, it seems the Americans are extremely jealous of the British class system," he went on. "They like the idea that we come from a long and distinguished history of servitude."

His deadpan delivery masked a dry sense of humour, and I found myself laughing. "Maybe I should look into that line myself," I said, taking a long swig of beer.

"You could certainly do worse," Jobson said.

"Oh, I'm pretty sure I am doing," I said. "I'm a comedian, appearing at the brand new theatre next door, Loew's National. I am with the Fred Karno company. You've heard of us?"

"Oh, indeed. A most reputable marque."

"You are familiar with the vaudeville scene, are you?"

Jobson allowed an enigmatic smile to reach his lips. "You could say so. And I should very much like to see your performance."

"Well, you'd better be quick. We're off next week, back to dear old Blighty to face the music," I said, bitterly.

"Oh I see. Well, then I shall certainly do what I can to attend."

And with that he gave a little bow, and moved off. "Yeah, I'll bet you shall," I muttered to myself, and to be honest I didn't think any more about him.

Then, a couple of nights later, we all stood in the wings waiting our turn, like condemned men lining up for the gallows as usual, just waiting for the executioner to finish with the preceding "Stunt Cycling and Ball Punching" team. I never got to see their act, by the way, as I was always behind the curtain when they were on, but from their bill matter I winced to imagine it.

"Oh well," I muttered to Mike Asher next to me. "Only a couple more and then we're done with all this." Mike nodded grimly, steeling himself.

A spattering of applause marked the end of the preceding turn, the curtains whisked open, and *The Wow Wows* were off again.

Frank Melroyd and I began our feeble crosstalk, and... hang on, what was this? Laughter? They never laughed at this bit, but... here it was! Gales of laughter rolling in from the stalls, the sound of people really *really* enjoying themselves. We'd almost forgotten what that was like. I glanced over at Frank, and he flicked his eyebrows at me, and we began to enjoy ourselves too.

Then Charlie came on as Archibald Binks, and they adored him. Everything he said, right from the start, just absolutely hit the spot, thumped them right on the funny bone, and that was what it was like for the whole turn that evening. Every half-arsed bit of business raised the roof, every stinking pun brought the house down.

We rode this roller-coaster of mirth for all it was worth, and when the curtain came down the cheers almost blew it back up again. Six curtain calls we were obliged to give, having got used to slinking down the stairs to the green room to hide our sorry faces, and the whole audience seemed to be on their feet, red-faced, beaming, tears streaming down their cheeks.

You never saw anything like it.

Afterwards we spilled down the stairs, laughing, clapping one another on the back, and I grabbed Charlie by the shoulders.

"That's more like it, eh?" I said, and he shrugged, bewildered. I could see from his face that he was as delighted and surprised as anyone, and we surrendered ourselves to the sheer joy of the night. Everyone hugged everyone else, and at least if we were going down it was with all guns blazing.

In the midst of our celebrations, a well-built gent – square-faced, middle-aged, with his greying hair scraped and oiled into a severe centre parting – poked his head round the door of the green room, and waved his pale broad-brimmed hat from side to side to attract our attention. "Hey fellas?" he shouted above the din. "That was a swell show, a swell show, yes sir!"

We had never before heard the word 'swell' used as an adjective, but we were all in a great mood, so we smiled benevolently. Our visitor beamed back. "Who's your manager, guys? Who makes the bookings?"

Freddie K stepped forward. "Mister Reeves is his name, sir, Alfred Reeves."

"Reeves," the burly gent repeated, committing it to memory.

"Excuse me, I hope you don't mind my asking," Freddie said. "But what would you call the style of that hat?"

"This? Why it's the Boss o' the Plains, the finest hat in these United States. Perfect for sunshine, perfect for rain, and stylish as all hell. D'you like it, son?"

"I do, sir," Freddie said.

"Then it's yours and welcome," the stranger said, winging it across the room. "I've a dozen more at home. Now where will I find this Reeves of yours?"

"Oh! Thank you, that's very kind!" Freddie cried. "Alf'll be backstage securing the set just now, but if you'd like to leave your card I'd be happy to... sir?"

The newcomer was already heading for the staircase, clearly intent on searching for Alf right that very minute. Freddie tried to hold him back, but just missed his sleeve.

"Sir?" Freddie hissed. "I'm afraid you can't go up there, members of the public are not allowed..."

The gent flashed him a big toothy grin. "Oh, I don't reckon anyone will mind little old me," he said, then winked and disappeared into the shadows.

"Little?" I said. "That fellow's built like a brick outhouse."

We got changed in record time, and decamped to the bar next door in high spirits, particularly Freddie, who was highly delighted with his new hat.

"I suppose it's an improvement on that ragamuffin old news-boy cap," Mike muttered. "But it does make you look like a cowboy."

The whole company was there, around one big dark wood table, and Charlie stood everyone a drink, so he must have been in an exceptionally good mood.

"Well," Stan said, raising his glass to us all. "Perhaps *The Wow Wows* isn't as bad as all that."

"Oh, I'm pretty sure it is, you know," Tilly said, and everyone started laughing all over again.

All of a sudden I became aware of a presence beside me, which seemed to have ghosted there without my noticing, and which announced itself with a polite cough. "I wonder if I might disturb you for just a moment, sir?"

I turned, and there was Mr Jobson, the English butler.

"Hallo!" I cried, full of the joys of a long-overdue success. "Of course! Join us!"

"No, thank you. I would not presume. I just wanted to thank you for your excellent suggestion."

I was puzzled for a moment. "My... what? Hmm?"

"When we met the other evening you suggested I should pay a visit to the new Loew's National to see the Karno comedians – a very good evening to you all, by the way..." he nodded courteously at the group now earwigging instead of minding their own business.

"Oh, so you came? Excellent! You picked a good one. Did you enjoy the show?"

"Very much, very much indeed. And so did all my esteemed colleagues." Jobson's answer seemed to be imbued with a weight of hidden meaning which eluded me.

"I see," I said, not really seeing. "Well, we are very pleased. Aren't we lads?"

"And lasses," Tilly put in, as everyone raised their glasses to my friend and gave him a hearty "Cheers!"

Jobson gave a small smile at this, and then leaned in to continue as a hum of conversation began again around the table. "Allow me to explain. You see, yesterday I took advantage of a free afternoon to pay a visit to the New York Society of British Butlers, Valets, Nannies, Maids and Gentleman's Gentlemen, of which I am a founder member, only to find that their annual social event was on the point of falling through. Miss Alma Wray had double-booked herself and she elected to fulfil the other engagement rather than theirs."

"Right," I said, sympathetically. "Oh dear, that's bad luck."

"Indeed. Well, I used to be the chair of the entertainments committee, and they all still look to me for guidance because the gentleman I work for is 'in the business', as they say, so when I suggested a trip to see the Karnos the motion was carried *nem con.*"

I laughed. "Hey! Everyone! Are you getting this? There was a whole party of butlers from the old country in!"

"Not just butlers. Butlers, valets, nannies, maids, and gentleman's gentlemen, to be precise."

"Good Heavens! How many of you were there?"

"Oh, upwards of two hundred, I should say."

Stan's mouth dropped open in astonishment. "Two hundred?" he said.

"And all of them laughing their heads off, too!" I cried.

"Well, I think all of us know what it is like to deal with a Mr Archibald Binks, eh?"

Charlie grinned and bowed his head modestly – most unlike him.

"So who is this gent you work for now?" I asked. "Is he English?"

Jobson shook his head. "No, in point of fact he is from Seattle. His name is Mr John W. Considine. And here he is now, sir."

At that moment, right on cue as it were, the street door opened to admit Alf Reeves, accompanied by the square-and-bare-headed gentleman who had been so eager to congratulate us just a short while ago.

Mr Jobson glided around to Freddie and murmured softly in his ear: "If I might offer a tip, sir, a toothbrush dipped in warm soapy water will freshen up the sweatband." Then he swished away and ghosted over to attend to his employer, while Alf came over to our table, as thrilled as I had ever seen him.

"Listen everyone" he hissed, "don't get too excited, but I have just been speaking with Mr Considine there, who owns the Sullivan and Considine circuit, and he would like to book us for a six month stint headlining in his theatres, if you can believe such an extraordinary thing."

"We can," said Stan. "His butler is a friend of Arthur's."

"Is that so?" Alf said, as Charlie suddenly enveloped me in an emotional hug. No one was more surprised than me, but I gathered my wits well enough to catch Tilly's eye over Charlie's shoulder, as much as to say "See? I'm not competing. We can get along just fine."

"Well," Alf went on, "the important news is this – we're staying in America!"

6
MUMMING BIRDS

OUR elation at not having to return home as failures was tempered by the realisation that we had been booked on the basis of a pretty freakish night's work, and the prospect of playing *The Wow Wows* for another six months to audiences not entirely composed of sympathetic servants from old Blighty did chill the blood rather.

Then I mentioned to one Georgie Lockerbie who was sharing the bill at Loew's with us ("Feats of Strength") that we had been booked to play the Sullivan and Considine circuit. He nodded ominously and said: "Ah. Siberia time."

It appeared that Considine was based in Seattle, on the far side of the continent, while Sullivan, his partner, was a New York man – a former New York Congressman, no less. Their vaudeville chain stretched the entire width of the country, and included some houses in Canada. The rise of the railways made it feasible to have a national circuit, but the distances and travelling involved were brutal, apparently.

We picked up some titbits about our new bosses as well. John Considine had begun by becoming known as Seattle's 'Baron of the Box House' – box houses being a disreputable combination of brothel, saloon, gambling den and low-class theatre – and had made his fortune by entertaining prospectors on their way to and from the Klondike. He had moved up-market in recent years – but not before shooting a police chief to death in a feud – becoming one of the first pioneers of the vaudeville boom.

There was another impresario called Alexander Pantages who had a rival circuit, with theatres in many of the same cities as Considine. Their rivalry had developed into a vicious feud, with each side poaching the other's headline turns and committing various acts of sabotage.

Sullivan, the partner, was a character known everywhere as 'Big Tim' Sullivan. He'd been a big cheese in a political organisation called Tammany Hall, before settling in the Lower East Side to count his kickbacks and take care of the many pies he had his fingers in. Not a man to mess with, by all accounts, unless you fancied taking a walk on the bottom of the East River in chain-link boots.

Considine loved *The Wow Wows*, and was the only man we ever met who fitted Karno's notion that Americans were obsessed with secret societies. He himself had started an organisation called, if you can believe this, The Independent Order of Good Things, so maybe our stupid brotherhood of Wow Wows had genuinely struck a chord with him.

Our misgivings were forgotten, however, on the last night at Loew's National when the set and costumes for *The Wow Wows* were not just packed away, they were labelled 'For Storage'.

"What's this, Alf?" Mike Asher said, slapping a packing crate. "There's some mistake here, surely?"

"Oh, didn't I say?" Alf grinned smugly. "I have spoken to Mr Considine, and he would very much like us to play *Mumming Birds* from now on."

We were all stunned by this development. "But... what about the Guv'nor?" someone said.

Alf's grin got even wider. "Well, what he doesn't hear about won't hurt him, now will it, and...?"

Whatever else he was going to say was drowned out with whooping and cheering. The hated Wow Wows were dead, and there was a whole damn'd continent to see.

Things were looking up.

———

Mumming Birds, the sketch we were now going to rehearse up and play, was a legendary Fred Karno piece. We were able to inherit (and air out thoroughly) costumes and a set that a previous company had left in storage, and all of us had played it back in England at one time or another. It was like a rite of passage for a Karno performer, the most important single item in the repertoire.

It was a simple idea. *Mumming Birds* was essentially a music hall bill-within-a-bill, featuring a series of acts of deliberately excruciating awfulness, with the comedy coming from the raucous reactions of a fake audience, housed in two pairs of fake boxes constructed on either side of the stage.

The principal comic part was "The Inebriated Swell", a disruptive audience member who would stagger in late and drunk, disturbing the first act, and thereafter would clamber or fall out of one of the lower boxes, getting involved in arguments and even fights with the various turns. Charlie could hardly wait to ditch the pale persona of Archibald Binks for the more reliable physical comedy of the Swell.

In one of the opposite boxes you would find "The Naughty Boy", dressed in a child's Eton suit and armed with buns and a peashooter, and his exasperated guardian, a dotty old uncle.

The acts themselves, all introduced by a number man, would vary according to personnel, but usually there was a hapless vocalist reciting *The Trail of the Yukon*, a female singer – the Swiss Nightingale – who would massacre a ditty entitled *Come Birdie and Live With Me*, and a singing group known as the "Rustic Glee Club". A moustachioed magician, who insisted on the description 'Prestidigitateur', would present a conjuring act of spectacular incompetence, and then the climax saw the introduction of the Terrible Turkey, a self-styled champion wrestler, who would challenge all comers for a small cash prize. Naturally the Swell would take him on, and a free-for-all would ensue.

Charlie was going to play the Swell, of course, it was the number one part. Stan would understudy him, and also play the Naughty Boy. I would take the Magician, the principal number two part, and Tilly would play my assistant and also join in with one of the singing numbers. She was delighted to have something to do that was more than just walking on and looking attractive – although she did that too, of course.

So that was *Mumming Birds*. In the States it was billed as *A Night in an English Music Hall*, as Fred Karno was always very anxious to play up the "Englishness" of his comedy company.

———

That evening we all gathered to celebrate. We abandoned the gloomy bar in the Bronx and journeyed down to a brighter and more cheerful saloon called Brady's, on Seventh Avenue between 41st and 42nd Street, near to our accommodation. As it was in the theatre district, they were accustomed to actors and actresses, so our ladies could come and go without being challenged by saloon girls jealously protecting their territory. We liked it there – it was a welcoming oasis of warm, thick, fermented odours of hops, malt and barley.

We were in high spirits because of the change of sketch, not to mention that the spectre of failure had been banished from the tour, at least for the time being, and the to-and-fro around the three tables we had pushed together was getting pretty noisy. Even Charlie, who usually contented himself with a small port, had taken a stein or three on board, and he was bullishly predicting that we would sweep all before us once we headed out West.

A stranger appeared at his shoulder, a serious-looking stocky individual with tight curly hair and a suit that seemed to be about a size and a half too small, judging by the way his muscles bulged. He bowed politely, and said in a soft and faintly Eastern European accent: "Pardon me, but you are Charlie Chaplin, are you not?"

Charlie turned in his chair to squint up at the newcomer. "Who wants to know?" he said.

"I am sorry to disturb, but I believe we have a mutual friend."

"We do?"

"Yes indeed."

"And who would that be, might I ask?"

"He is from Scotland. His name is Dr Walford Bodie."

"Ha!" Charlie barked. "Bodie? Really?"

The stranger had piqued our interest now, that was for sure. We had all heard of Dr Walford Bodie[2], as he was reputed to have been the highest-paid entertainer back in our home country for years. His shows featured hypnotism, ventriloquism and demonstrations of electricity, the most startling of which involved an electric chair such as they used to dispatch murderers in America. Bodie would invite members of his audience onstage and electrocute them, stopping short of killing them outright, obviously, but making blue sparks fly from their hair.

The real show-stopping routine, though, was the hypnotism. Not only would Bodie have members of the public scrabbling around like farmyard animals or hopping on one leg, he would also claim to be able to cure ailments that had baffled the medical profession by means of hypnotism or electricity or both. Bodie had come a bit of a cropper a couple of years earlier, owing to a court case brought by the Medical Defence Union, during the course of which a former assistant had revealed many of his trade secrets, and he was now widely believed to be a quack.

"He offered me a role in his *Bodie Show*, you know?" Charlie confided to the table at large. "Before I joined Karno."

"Really? That would have been a good move, wouldn't it?" Alf Reeves said. "Harry Lauder started with him, you know, and George Formby."

"One could not wish for a better mentor," the curly-haired stranger said softly, nodding.

Charlie snorted derisively. "Well, first of all, I already had a job, working for Casey's Circus. And Syd was pretty certain of getting me into Karno's, so I wasn't looking just then. Most of all, though, I didn't want to end up as a stooge to a pompous fraud."

"A fraud, you say?"

"Oh yes. It happened that his stage manager did a remarkable impersonation of a rooster. The so-called Doctor would pretend to haul him up from the stalls and put him into a trance, and then the fellow would simply do his party piece. After I knocked him back I started doing a lampoon of him for Casey's, and d'you know what? I hadn't even seen Bodie's show. Didn't need to. I just put on that absurd upside-down moustache of his and strutted up and down like the big I-am. I called myself Doctor Awful Bogie."

He quickly jumped to his feet and gave us a quick sample of his self-important quack pastiche. The assembled company laughed heartily at this, as they were all in a good mood, but I noticed that the stranger remained stony-faced, and after a moment or two he simply turned on his heel and walked away.

A little while later I found myself at the bar, standing alongside the stranger who had approached Charlie.

"I'm afraid my friend was somewhat harsh earlier," I said.

The stranger looked up, and said: "Yes, it was... disappointing. I was interested to meet Chaplin because I have heard people speak well of him, but I was not prepared for this arrogant sneering puppy."

He paused to take a drink, and I stayed perfectly still, not wanting to throw him off his stride. Sure enough, after a sip or two the man continued his complaint.

"Yes, Dr Bodie is a braggart, but this is part of being a showman, and I know him to be a generous man, a philanthropist. I even think he might be a kind of genius."

"Oh, well there you are," I said.

"What do you mean?"

"There's only room for one genius in Charlie's world view, I'm afraid."

The stranger's face hardened, and he turned to fix Chaplin with a glare that could have melted a glacier.

"So," I ventured. "What line of work might you be in, sir?"

"I am appearing at the Orpheum," he said, still not switching that hostile glare off. "My name is Harry Houdini."

———

The Sullivan and Considine dates would not begin until January, and Alf managed to book us in for a five-week residency at the American Music Hall to keep us ticking over until Christmas.

Now that we were performing a different piece there was another opportunity for the ubiquitous *Variety* to have its say. On the Friday Alf and I arrived to find Chaplin staring into the dressing room mirror with a face like thunder, and a copy of the paper crumpled angrily in the waste bin.

Alf groaned and fingered his bowtie as though it was a tightening noose. "Oh, don't tell me it's another stinker!" he muttered, discreetly retrieving the offending item from the trash and flattening it out on the table at the far end of the room from Charlie. "We really cannot afford to put the wind up Considine just now, you know...?" He found the review of *A Night in an English Music Hall*, scanned through it and then frowned.

"What's up, Alf?" I said.

"Nothing. Nothing at all. It looks perfectly fine to me, won't do us any harm at all, thank goodness."

He went to fetch his scissors to clip it for his collection, and a few of us mustered around to see what was what. And this is what we read: 'The current crop of Karno comedians features one or two very likely lads and lasses. We are going to be seeing and hearing a lot more of Mr Arthur Dandoe, you mark my words. Stanley Jefferson's comic timing sparkles, with able support from Muriel Palmer and Charles Griffiths.'

No mention of Chaplin C. at all. Not a peep. No wonder it ended up in the bin.

———

The American Music Hall was on West 42nd Street, and we were still living over on 43rd Street, in the distinctly humid brownstone building above the laundry, just a short step away, which meant we had a little more free time on our hands.

Often in those weeks I would call on Tilly and we would step out together. We liked to ride the trolley down to Battery Park and watch the boats on the Hudson, with the Goddess of Liberty silhouetted on the skyline beyond. If the weather was too inhospitable we would sometimes go into the Aquarium, where there were crabs the size of side-tables and a distinctly malevolent octopus.

One fine day, we agreed, we'd ride the ferry out to Liberty Island and take a closer look at the statue, but the wind whipping in from the Atlantic kept putting us off.

Then there came an occasion when I called round to see her and she was not there. It was a day when I knew her landlady would be out battling the bottle, and so I knocked particularly loudly on the door so as to be heard in the rooms upstairs. After a minute it was Amy Reeves who answered:

"Oh, Arthur, hullo. What can we do for you?"

"Good morning Amy. I have come to call on Tilly."

"Tilly? She went out a little while ago."

"Oh."

"Yes, she and Charlie, all wrapped up warm. They're going to see that Statue of Liberty, you know the one. On the island, in the river?"

"Yes," I said, my guts falling down into my boots. "I know the one."

At a loose end, and preoccupied by unwanted speculations, I found myself a saloon and got on the outside of an unprofessional amount of beer for a three-show day, one foot up on a rail and my elbows resting in pools of overspill. I lurched over to the theatre in time for the matinée, arriving just in time to see Tilly and Charlie getting out of a cab, giggling, their faces still flushed from the autumn wind.

I followed them inside, telling myself that I'd wait for her to tell me about her excursion, and she did. Once Amy had told her that I'd been round to call, I surmised, sourly.

"It was great fun," she said. "You really must go."

"I was planning to," I said, adding "with *you*" under my breath.

Another morning, I remember, I called at the 48th street building, and the landlady told me Tilly was already out with another gentleman, giving me to understand with her shrivelled prune look of disapproval that this confirmed everything she had always suspected about the girl.

I traipsed back the five blocks to my own room, intending to lie on my back and stare at the ceiling while I imagined Tilly and Charlie out together. On the stairs, however, I met the little man himself, clearly just woken up and heading out in search of coffee and breakfast.

"Morning," I said, surprised, and his reply was distorted by a yawn so wide I had a sudden mental flash of shoving a whole doughnut in there. He shuffled on down, and I frowned to myself. Here was a puzzler...

So later at the theatre I cornered Tilly and asked her about it.

"I called round this morning," I said.

"Oh, did you?" she said, looking a little shifty, I thought.

"And you were out."

"Yes."

"With?"

Tilly bit her lip. "If you must know I went for a very pleasant stroll in Central Park with Frank."

"Frank? Frank Melroyd, you mean?"

"Yes, of course, how many Franks do you think I know?"

"But...?" I said, feeling that a little more explanation was required.

"The landlady came to my door, said there was someone to see me, in that way she has of implying that I will go straight to Hell, and I thought it was most likely you, or maybe Charlie, so I grabbed my hat and coat, came downstairs, and there was Frank on the doorstep. I couldn't very well turn him away, could I? And anyway, he's quite sweet, and a perfect gentleman, so we spent a lovely morning together."

"I see."

"We just walked and talked. I did most of the talking, of course, chattering away. He's a really good listener."

"Well, that's because he hasn't an original thought in his head or anything interesting to say."

"Now, Arthur, you behave yourself. He's a friend, that's all. I'm friends with all you boys."

I forced myself to smile, and she patted my arm.

"I see I shall have to get myself a system," she said. "Like the dance cards you can get at a ball."

I watched Frank Melroyd closely that evening. He struck me as a dull fellow altogether, and I noted his receding hairline and the paunch pushing at his cardigan. Perhaps he wasn't much of a threat. And at least she wasn't out with Charlie.

———

A week or so before Christmas I was just leaving my room to set off for the theatre, a little early. Alf Reeves was on a fortnight's trip out west to make some preparations for the upcoming tour, and so we'd been left to our own devices, which had made us if anything slightly more conscientious than usual. The cat was away, and the mice were on their best behaviour, kind of style.

Young Freddie was still sleeping one off, the beginner, but I was confident that he would make it in time for the show and I fancied some air. Or possibly some liquid...

Anyway, I heard a furtive whistle, looked round, and there was Stan leaning halfway out of his doorway, beckoning me, with a finger pressed to his lips for quiet. I followed him into his room, and he was on pins, tremendously excited for some reason.

"What's up?" I said. "Why the sneaking around?"

"Arthur," he began, and then stopped, a big grin on his silly chops.

"What? Whatever is it?"

"I'm not supposed to tell anybody, but I can't see how to do it without your help."

"How to do what? What is it, you fool? Stop giggling!"

"All right, all right!" Stan calmed himself. "The thing is: I need you to tell everyone in the company that I am unwell, and they will have to cover for me. It will be easy enough to do, tell Freddie to do the Naughty Boy, and we can manage without anyone in the top box."

"Unwell?" I said, puzzled. "What's the matter with you? You look as fit as a flea..."

"Yes, yes, I'm fine, and I will be there, but..." He bit his lip.

I threw my hands up. "You've lost me, I'm afraid."

"Oh, look, Arthur, here it is, but you cannot tell a soul, understand?"

I nodded, puzzled.

"Charlie and I have a wager, you see? I say a wager, it's more of a challenge."

"A challenge...?"

"The thing is, I have more or less perfected an impersonation of Charlie, and in the last few weeks I have been doing it in front of him, when we are back here in the room at night, just trying to get him to cheer up, really, trying to make him laugh at himself. Anyway, last night he challenged me to pass myself off as him, because that would be the clinching proof of my impression of him. And the more we talked about it the more cocky I became, and the more, I don't know, *arrogant* he became about his own... uniqueness."

"Yes, I can certainly imagine that," I said.

"Until I ended up saying I could take his place in the show and no one would be any the wiser."

"I bet that went down well," I said.

"And he said, Charlie said... 'Go on then!' And so that's what I'm going to do."

"No!"

"Yes!"

"When?"

"Today, this afternoon, this evening!"

"You're kidding!"

"I'm not!"

"Alf'll have your guts for garters, man!"

"Alf's not here is he?"

I found myself grinning almost as widely as Stan himself. "So... wait a minute. You need me to tell people that you are ill?"

"Yes, that's it. I shall be there, you see, as Charlie, but Charlie isn't going to take my place."

"As if he could," I said.

"Well, exactly," Stan grinned. "So *I* will be the one who is missing, you see?"

I nodded, appreciating the scheme.

"Also," Stan went on. "Since you know about it now, you can help me get into the theatre without anyone noticing. Once I'm made up no one will give me a second glance, they'll just assume I'm Charlie, won't they? All I really have to do then is look bloody miserable and not talk to anyone."

In a fizz of excitement the two of us headed off to the theatre, without (for once) stopping off at a saloon for a stiffener. We slipped in at the stage door and climbed the stairs, with Stan lingering one landing behind me until we were sure the coast was clear. The only member of the Karno company already in situ was Amy Reeves, on hand to take care of any problems arising in her husband's absence.

"What ho, Amy!" I cried, sweeping her into the ladies' dressing room. "Any word from Alf? How's the wild Wild West treating him? Has he shot any Indians?"

Amy tutted and wriggled free. "You idiot...!" she said. "He's in Chicago, you know, not Desperado Gulch."

I trusted that Stan had quietly nipped into our dressing room while I was distracting our manager's wife.

"Oh, by the way," I said. "I don't think Stan is going to make it today."

"What?"

"Yes, he was looking distinctly under the weather. He had the look of a man who would not dare to stray too far from the pan, if you get my drift...?"

"Hmmph!" Amy said, folding her arms in her best disapproving school ma'am style. "I suppose you lads pushed the boat out again last night, did you?"

"Who, *us*?" I said.

"Oh well, I'd better tell Charlie," Amy said, making for the door. I stepped into her path, and she frowned.

"He knows," I said.

"Aha. Leaving it to me to sort out, is he? Typical."

Happily Amy decided to leave 'Charlie' alone just then, and she made a brief announcement once the company was assembled later. The news that he was stepping up from super to the featured part of Naughty Boy took care of Freddie's hangover pretty quickly, and nobody gave more than a fleeting glance towards the Swell in his finery, adding a perfectionist's finishing touches to his make-up rather than engaging in dressing room banter. Already Stan had Charlie off to a tee, I thought.

Even though I had been sworn to secrecy I was absolutely bursting to tell Tilly about the challenge, wanting to share the excitement, so I lurked outside the ladies' dressing room hoping to grab a moment with her before we went up to the wings. As the company bustled up the stairs I saw Emily come out, and Muriel, and Amy, but no sign of my Magician's assistant.

"Hsst! Amy?" I hissed. "Where's Tilly?"

"Oh, she is unwell, I'm afraid. You can manage without an assistant today, can't you? After all, it's not as though any of the tricks have to actually work, is it? Ha ha!"

"Unwell?" I said, with a sinking feeling.

"Yes, both Tilly and Stan missing at once. I hope there's not something going round, don't you? Come on, we'd better get up there, chop chop, eh?!"

She skipped away, leaving me standing alone in the corridor, a chill sense of dread sweeping over me. Because I knew it wasn't Tilly and Stan who were missing.

It was Tilly and Charlie.

7
A NIGHT IN THE SHOW

I had to doff my cap to a supreme comic talent. I could have done the Inebriated Swell, I think, and I certainly believed I could – *should* – be the company number one, but I would be playing *my* Swell. Stan played Charlie's Swell, and played it to perfection, but it was also, somehow, his as well. They were close, Stan and Charlie, and each had unwittingly picked up a mannerism or two from the other. I could see, knowing it was Stan, that the performance was subtly refined, but no one else picked up on it at all. They just thought Charlie was having a really good night.

As it happened, that was precisely what I was afraid of. My enjoyment of Stan's triumph was overshadowed by the dark cloud of my imaginings, my wonderings where Charlie and Tilly had gone off to, and what they were getting up to together.

So once Stan had come off stage, thrilled and flushed with his brilliant coup, and had revealed himself to our astonished colleagues, all of whom fell about laughing or fell over themselves to pat the lad on the back, I pulled him to one side to ask him the question that had been tormenting me since before the matinée:

"Where is Charlie, then?"

"I have no idea, why?"

"Well, did you not notice that Tilly is off sick today as well? As well as '*you*', I mean?"

"No, I... oh my dear chap, I had no idea." Stan's face fell as he caught up. I felt guilty then for raining on his parade, so I summoned up a big smile from somewhere and said:

"Never mind, we'll find out soon enough. Congratulations! You were every bit as good as Charlie. Better even!"

Stan beamed. "Do you really think so? Thanks Arthur!"

The company was abuzz with excitement, and we all repaired, as per, to Brady's saloon on 7th and 43rd, where we commandeered a large table at the back. The chatter was all about Stan's terrific impression of Charlie, of course.

"Do you know," Charlie Griffiths was saying, "I think the exchanges with the Uncle were better than ever, they certainly got more laughs than usual."

He might have been right, as well. Stan was a more generous person to be onstage with, and if you had a laugh coming he was happy to help you get it, while Charlie was always more concerned about drawing attention to himself.

That drip Albert Austin, Charlie's most ardent admirer in the company, tried to claim that he had suspected all along, and he was roundly shouted down. Amy, who was jammed into the corner next to him, slapped him with her hat. After that, though, everyone started conjuring up moments when they'd allegedly come close to catching Stan out.

"I tried to talk to you on the stairs, remember?" Muriel Palmer said to Stan, "and you just turned and hustled away. I thought it was just typical Charlie, no time for the supporting cast, but now I get it. If I'd seen you right up close I'd have spotted it then."

Austin spoke up again. "It's actually rather good of Charlie, isn't it, to take such great care to think of the good of the company, ensuring that the understudy is up to scratch?"

This notion brought him another slap from Amy's hat, as everyone knew that Charlie had just wanted a sly night off while Alf was out of town.

"What do you think he got up to?" Mike Asher wondered.

"Cathouse, probably," George Seaman muttered with a wolfish grin.

"And what do you know about it?" his wife cut in, indignantly. "Charlie's not that sort. He's a nice boy."

After a while the conversation started to get me down. My mind was already churning with speculations where Chaplin was concerned, so I took myself over to the bar. I ordered myself a big jar of beer, drank it straight down, and ordered another, looking forward to the numbing stupor that a couple more would bring. As well as the Tilly-related imaginings, I was beginning to be nagged by the feeling that Stan had somehow stolen a march on me, and my status as number two in the company might not be as secure as it had been.

To take my mind off it all I glanced at my nearest neighbours. Alongside me at the bar was a trio of individuals whom I supposed had been amongst the audience that evening. There was a big straw-haired fellow chomping on a cigar, leaning forward on his elbows, and holding forth pretty much non-stop about something or other. Listening to him was a lugubrious-looking chap with a long thin face, and, most eye-catching of the three, a small girl, barely more than a child by the look of her, in a bright green dress. I gave her more than a couple of passing squints as I drank – she was a stunner.

The barman came over to the little group beside me, however, and said to the big guy: "Perhaps a bar isn't the place for your daughter, this time o'night."

The blonde chap chomping the cigar drew himself up to his full height, and threw his shoulders back, and all of a sudden he looked a formidable fellow to have a row with.

"My daughter?" the big lad said, indignantly. "Don't you know this is the Gibson Girl?"

"Huh?"

"You have seen her promoting hats, cold cream, umbrellas and shoes, and she is now, I am pleased to say, a leading actress for the Biograph moving picture company!"

Snowed under by this avalanche of references, the barman moved away. The big fellow bit the wet end off his cigar and turned to spit it out onto the floor, catching me watching the three of them. "Help ya?" he said, with more than a hint of left-over belligerence.

"I beg your pardon," I said. "But did you mention the Biograph company?"

I directed the question at the young lady, who smiled me a smile that I felt judder in my central nervous system, but it was the straw-haired giant who answered.

"That's right, buddy." He turned around and leaned his back on the bar. "You know, I used to come in this saloon all the time, when I lived not far from here. Coupl'a blocks over, in Hell's Kitchen. Had to move, though. Got into a thing with a hooker called Lucille, and her pimp went for me with a razor. I figured a move'd be good for my health."

His companions laughed indulgently at this colourful titbit, and he waved a meaty paw in their general direction. "This here's Griffith, and Miss Mabel Normand, and my name's Sennett," he said, then squinted at me. 'Hey! You were the magician, weren'tcha? The magician from the show!' he added, to his companions.

72

"Dandoe, Arthur Dandoe," I replied, shaking his hand, nodding to the others.

"Yes, we work for Biograph, studios down on East 14th. You seen any of ours? *Sunshine Sue? Two Little Waifs?*"

"I... er..."

"They're your standard melodrama. Griffith likes that kind of stuff, don'tcha D.W.? Eh?"

The lugubrious fellow's face got even longer. It didn't look like he even knew how to smile.

Sennett went on: "D.W. there, he wants to make a real long feature, five, six thousand feet, tell a real meaty story, but Biograph think a long film is gonna hurt people's eyes, they're worried about getting sued. For my money, I think trying to put across serious drama in a moving picture just looks silly. You're in the business, aren't you, kinda? What do you reckon?"

"I think you're probably right," I said.

"Exactly. People just wanna laugh when they go out, like tonight. This was our last night out on the town, and we went looking for a laugh. We leave tomorrow for California, we're going to spend the winter there. We need the sunshine, you see, to make pictures, and the Sun's not due to come out again in Manhattan till around Easter-time."

Sennett called the barman over and bought a round of drinks, including me in, which was most affable of him. I was starting to feel pretty drunk now, but luckily he was planning to do the bulk of the talking.

"We should be making comedies, that's what I think. Biograph now is concentrating on 'feature fiction products', that's what they call 'em, an' I keep saying. Make 'em *comedies*, that's what people want."

"You keep telling 'em, Mack," said Mabel, clinking her glass against his.

"One day," Sennett went on. "One day, I'm going to set up a studio all of my own, just for comedies, what do you think of that?"

"I think... good luck to you, my friend," I said.

"It's a million dollar idea, I'm telling you," he said, shoving his cigar into his big mouth. Mabel shot me a long-suffering grin, while Griffith looked like he wanted to go home.

I thought that Sennett was right about people wanting to laugh, but that anyone genuinely searching for comedy would take themselves to one of the city's magnificent vaudeville houses, where the comedians were in colour, and in three dimensions, and could speak and shout and sing, rather than the sort of low dive where films were shown on a sheet for a nickel. As this trio themselves had done.

"Say," Sennett suddenly said, jabbing his cigar at me. "Your show tonight... That little drunk feller was aces, we thought, didn't we doll?"

"Sure Mack," said Mabel. "He was a scream."

Griffith suddenly leaned over. "He was remarkably limber," he said, seriously.

"Exactly," said Sennett. "Now, *he's* just exactly the sort of feller who should be in pictures, in comedy pictures, and when I set up my studio that's the sort of guy I'm gonna be talking to."

"Yeah, one day," said Mabel.

"What's his name? The little drunk?" Sennett said.

I looked over at the far end of the room, where Stan was laughing, revelling in his great success. I wished I was in the mood to join them, but I was still brooding on Charlie and Tilly.

"His name? It's Jeff..." I began, distracted.

And suddenly through the alcoholic haze a lightning flash seared across my brain. What if this chap, this straw-headed

74

Sennett, actually managed to talk Biograph into letting him make comedy pictures, why, it might be just the opportunity I was looking for. Not for myself, I was not remotely interested, but Charlie might have an itch to scratch where the flickers were concerned, so it could be, couldn't it, that if somebody offered him a chance he might take it, he might leave us, leave Karno? My imagination began to soar...

And so even though I was happy for my friend, and proud of his success that evening, I suddenly felt it was important, *vital* even, to deny him the credit for it, so as to grab the chance, however remote, of ridding myself of my rival once and for all.

Which is why my drunk mouth, lagging ever-so slightly behind my drunk brain, said this:

"Jeff... er... plin."

"What?"

"Jeffplin..."

"Eh?"

"Jafflin..."

"Jafflin?"

"No, Ch, Cha... Chaff... Chaff... in."

"Chaffin?"

To be frank, Sennett, Griffith and the lovely Mabel were all looking at me a bit strangely now, and I thought better of trying to correct myself any further.

Chaffin. Near enough.

8
AND THE NEW YEAR IN

On New Year's Eve our last performance finished just after eleven, and we all hustled quickly out of our costumes and into our going-out clothes, eager to dash the short distance to Times Square. Hats were jammed on heads, scarves slung around necks, gloves fumbled out of pockets, and all would be needed because it was fearsomely cold outside.

We all thought we would be able to stick together and celebrate the turn of the year, but there was such a swarm of people on the streets that it was impossible, and I quickly found myself walking alone. I say walking, it was the sort of shuffling half-step that all around me were doing to avoid stepping on the heels of the half-stepping shuffler in front.

Mind you, if I thought the side streets were busy, then that was nothing compared to the square itself. It was packed. Thousands upon thousands were milling about, trying to find a little elbow room – gentlemen, ladies, workmen, tramps, children up way beyond their bedtime, and here and there the sort of ladies that those children didn't need to know about yet. The square was lined with wagons selling food and drink, many with signs suggesting that they had been hauled up from Coney Island for the occasion, and the thick aromas of frankfurters and cotton candy swirled around in the lightly falling snow.

I found myself a vantage point, out of the glacial flow of humanity, and took in the scene properly. At the far end of the square the tall slender Times building was brightly lit from sidewalk to flagpole, as if a giant had stabbed an illuminated pencil straight into the ground. The show we had all gathered to see was on top of this, where the Times Square ball was poised to drop at the transitional moment. This was a seven hundred pound wood and ironwork sphere, five feet across, illuminated by two hundred-odd electric light bulbs (according to the papers), and I could just make out half a dozen silhouetted men taking the strain with the ropes that held it, partly masked by coloured streamers.

I looked around at the crowd, gauging the impossibility of recognising anyone in all the hubbub, but then all of a sudden the masses parted like the Red Sea before Moses. An enormous man strolled across the square like royalty on a ceremonial progress, with a couple of equally massive bruisers flanking him and elbowing the populace aside. I saw caps doffed, I saw forelocks tugged, it was quite a thing, and then the waves of flesh could stand the pressure no longer and crashed together once more in their wake.

I turned to a fellow who had shinned halfway up a lamp post to see better. "Who is that?" I asked.

"You don't know? That, friend, is Big Tim Sullivan."

"Good heavens, is it really?"

I was still trying to keep our celebrated co-promoter in sight when I felt a fumbling movement to my side, and turned sharply thinking some sneak was making for my wallet. To my astonishment it was Tilly, shyly hooking her arm in mine and pulling herself close.

"Hello stranger," I said, and she gave me a little smile. Well now, what was this, I wondered. We had barely spoken two words to each other since the night she missed a show "sick" and spent the evening with Charlie. I confess I had been pretty fed up for the last fortnight, not only imagining the two of them together, but also missing her. She had definitely been avoiding me, and in a two-shows-a-day company like ours I was not likely to have been mistaken about that.

Even on Christmas Day, when Alf Reeves, bless him, had organised a great lunchtime dinner for us in a local restaurant, with two geese and all the trimmings (you've got to have trimmings, and all of them too), Tilly had contrived to seat herself at the far end of the table from me, with the unctuous Melroyd in close attendance. And yet here she was, hugging my arm almost as if nothing had occurred. I looked down at her blonde ringlets, spilling out from under her hat and sprinkled with twinkling snowflakes, and I racked my brains trying to come up with a smooth way to start a conversation that might tell me what I wanted to know.

"And?" I said. "Yes?"

Tilly sighed. "Oh, Arthur," she said. "I couldn't bear for this... awkwardness... to go on any longer."

"Ah. Right-o," I said, awkwardly.

"I never told you about the day Charlie and I missed the show."

"Yes," I said. "I mean, no. Stan was brilliant, you know, by the way."

"I know," she said. "I saw."

"You saw?" I said, baffled. "You mean... you were watching?"

Tilly nodded. "It sounded like a bit of fun, you know, a bit of a laugh. Charlie told me how he and Stan had a bet that Stan could take over and nobody would notice."

"Nobody did, neither, not till after."

"I'm not surprised. And so Charlie persuaded me to play sick the same day, and you know, have a day off, and, well, we've been doing two-a-day, seven days a week, ever since we got here, and so I was just about ready to see a bit of New York, have a bit of fun."

"So?" I said. "What fun did you get up to?"

She looked sharply at me then, but continued. "Well, you'll never guess what Charlie's idea of fun was?"

"What?" I breathed, bracing myself.

"Going to see the matinée of our own show! The show I thought we were taking a sneaky day away from! So yes, we were there, and we saw Stan doing Charlie, and very fine he was too. And the Prestidigitateur seemed to manage very well without his assistant, by the way."

"He'd rather not, though," I said, and she smiled again.

"Yes, Stan was funny, really funny, and that... well, that was the problem."

"What do you mean?"

"Well Charlie, do you see, he watched the whole thing, stone-faced, like he was in a trance. I was laughing away with everyone else to begin with, but after a while I started to get worried about him, and by the end he was trembling and murmuring to himself. I had to help him outside, because God knows I didn't want to sit through that dancing dog act, and we went out onto the street. He came to himself a little then, and said in a very courtly fashion: 'So, what shall we do with our night off, Miss Beckett?' And I suggested we might go dancing – I haven't danced in so long! Or maybe we could go and take a walk by the river, or go and have a swanky meal in a fancy hotel, or even a little bit of all three, you know?"

I nodded, digesting the thought of Charlie and Tilly enjoying these activities together.

"But do you know what he wanted to do? We had dinner, an early and rather quick dinner, which was nice enough. I tried to talk about Stan, because he'd been a marvel and I wondered what Charlie had thought, but he just went quiet, like he was in a world of his own. Then we went to the Metropolitan Opera House, if you can believe it, and saw something called *Tannhäuser*."

"Funny?"

"Not much. And long, oh my goodness me!"

"Good story?"

"Well, it was in German, so I couldn't really tell you. It seemed to be mostly about two rival singers competing for the love of a beautiful Queen. I was bored very nearly to death, but Charlie was really affected somehow. I was about to suggest we might leave before the end, but I saw that he was weeping, actually weeping, really big hacking sobs. And when I asked him whatever was the matter he said that the opera seemed to him to... wait, what was it now? 'Sum up all the travail of my life'. What do you think he meant by that?"

"I can't imagine," I said.

"Anyway, he was so wrung out by the end I had to help him back to his building, and he just disappeared inside, still crying. I mean, it was the strangest evening of my life, I think. And ever since I have been dying to tell you about it, but I have just been... well, a bit embarrassed, really, I suppose. Do you understand?"

"Of course I do," I said, and the relief was so overwhelming that I felt like crying myself, although that would have been a peculiar thing to do after the story she had just told me.

"So... are we all right, do you think?" she said, looking up at me rather timidly, it seemed, rather apprehensively. And after a moment I smiled, and nodded.

Down came the globe to a massive roar, and as it reached the bottom of its pole there was a blinding flash, and the figure '1911' was illuminated in great letters of fire that seemed to conjure all the colours of the rainbow. At least, that's what it said in the newspaper, I didn't see any of it. I had my eyes shut, and Tilly's soft lips pressed mine, and I'd pretty much lost interest in everything around me. I'll see it another time, I thought.

—————

A month later, I found myself in the freight yard of the Philadelphia railway depot with the rest of my colleagues, all fifteen of us yawning, shivering and clutching our bags. It was five-thirty in the morning, just six hours after we stepped off the stage at the Nixon Theatre – where we had played four fill-in weeks awaiting the start of our Sullivan and Considine engagement – for the last time.

A little way off we could see cattle being herded slowly up a slippery ramp into a wagon – with rather more consideration than we felt was being shown to us – and further on still some pig iron was being noisily manhandled onto a flatbed truck.

Why were we there? Alf Reeves, our estimable company manager, had something to show us all, apparently.

We'd had a good little run in Philly. Another brand new theatre, a nice hotel overlooking Wanamaker's department store, which had a pair of Marconi masts on it, like two Eiffel Towers, for wireless telephony (whatever that was), and everyone was much happier playing *Mumming Birds*.

I'd been seeing quite a bit of Tilly, after we had made up on

New Year's Eve, and she had enlisted my help in sidestepping the clumsy advances of the stodgy Frank Melroyd.

I didn't tell Tilly this, for fear she would think I was still obsessing over my rivalry with Chaplin, but I spent a fair amount of time mulling over what she had told me about him. It was clear to me that his strange behaviour was in response to seeing Stan being every bit as good as him. He had been shocked to the core, because he lacked the temperament or the grace to be happy for his friend, he only saw another rival to put in his place.

As for his overwrought reaction to the opera, well, plainly he could only have identified with the hero, the central character, as he was not psychologically equipped to think of himself in a supporting role. So what were the 'travails of his life' that all the Teutonic bombastery brought so vividly to mind? His romantic rivalry with me, I thought, considering that he was sitting there watching it with Tilly. But there was also the rivalry of the two performers, the two singers, Tannhäuser and Wolfram (I had to look that up, I'll admit it). I wondered whether he might not have been thinking of me as he wept, but of good old Stan.

I glanced over to where Charlie and Stan were shivering together, jacket collars turned up, hugging their slender frames, two peas in a pod. Where was Alf?

The company manager had, you will remember, disappeared for a couple of weeks while we were at the American Music Hall in New York, to do a recce of our first Sullivan and Considine dates and make some preparations. Finally he appeared, striding over from the station offices.

"Ahem," he began, drawing us to him. "Now, as you know, America is a big place. It's not just a country, it's a continent. I have had to work out how to transport the whole company, all our set, and props, and costumes, and baggage to all the places we will be playing over the next six months, and this is by far the most practical and economical way to do it."

"We're travelling with the cattle?" someone piped up, appalled.

"No, no, no. Look. Over there." Alf turned us round to face the other way, pointing at his prize acquisition. "Da-daaah!" he said.

It was a train carriage, sitting all by itself in a siding. Green in colour, like most of the stock you would see on the main lines at that time, it looked like the illegitimate offspring of a passenger carriage and a goods wagon. One half had windows, rounded rather stylishly at the top, with canvas blinds halfway drawn and visible behind the glass, while the other half was enclosed, with two big sliding panel doors held together with a heavy duty padlock. On the side there was the painted legend 'Private Car', and along the top was the typical raised section which housed the skylights for letting in a bit of sunshine. And at each end there was an observation platform, enclosed by a railing, so that passengers could stand out in the open air.

"Am I missing something?" Charlie Griffith yawned, "apart from another six hours kip?"

"This is ours," Alf said, pleased as Punch. "It's the Karno Company boxcar. At least it started out as a boxcar, it's been converted so that half of it is fitted out for passengers. We travel in that end, and the other end has all our set and props and costumes in it. Already loaded by the hands from the Nixon."

"And how do we get it to Chicago? Are there holes for us to put our feet through?"

"Sss sss ssss!" That tickled Bert Williams, despite the cold.

"Don't be daft. The Pennsylvania Special will be along any minute to hook onto us. Now get on board, everyone."

Suddenly our tiredness was forgotten as we swarmed all over

the boxcar like kids on Christmas Day, with Alf beaming like a benevolent Santa. We bundled up the steps – *our* steps – and whisked up the blinds, and shoved our heads and shoulders four at a time out of the windows – *our* windows – while Albert Austin set up his box camera on the tracks outside to capture the moment for posterity. Of course, if we'd realised how much time we were destined to spend in the thing we'd have been a little less anxious for a memento.

It was exciting, though, to feel the whole thing jolt as the Chicago train reversed up the siding into us, and to hear the heavy clunk of the coupling engaging. And then off we went, feeling like royalty, a whole carriage all to ourselves.

Not that there was anything particularly luxurious about the inside of the boxcar. It was not a plush Pullman-style carriage, not by any means. The fittings were what was known as 'tourist' standard – hard woven straw seats and basic tables. We had to ransack some of our stage furniture for cushions to make them bearable, because after two hours on those 'tourist' seats you felt like you'd slipped a disc.

Alf made a little speech as we rolled out of Philly. "I want you to think of this boxcar as the Fun Factory away from home," he said. "A Fun Factory on wheels. Any problem you might have, that you want to talk about, then the boxcar is the perfect place to catch me. Because I can't go anywhere, can I?"

"At the end of every week, as the boxcar takes us to our next exciting engagement, that's when you'll get your pay. It'll be just like the way the Guv'nor does it at the Enterprise. I'll set up a little office at the end there, over by the prop compartment door, and you can come and see me, we can have a bit of a chit chat, and I'll let you have your cash. All right?"

"Yes, Alf," came the murmured reply from fifteen mouths.

And that's how we began our love-hate relationship with the Karno boxcar, our home away from home. Every week we would pile into the thing, often very early in the morning, to be taken hundreds of miles to the next engagement. We would eat, sleep, read, drink, chat, fall out, smoke, write letters, look out of the windows at the scenery, rehearse and play cards. For hours on end.

George Seaman took charge of the card game, and it always seemed to be on the go. Players would get drawn in, stay for an hour or two, drop out tired or broke, but George always seemed to be dealing. There would be a fug of smoke hanging over the table, and the constant flick of the cards and the tinkle of coins being won and lost.

It was problematical for some of the boys to get paid their week's wages right there in the boxcar, actually, because old George was lurking just a few feet away to relieve them of it, and hours of boredom would eventually drive them into his arms. There was nothing more dispiriting, believe me, than arriving in a strange new city after a ten-hour trip on the boxcar knowing that you had no money for food because you'd lost all your wages at poker as soon as you'd got them.

There were a couple of camp beds that hinged down out of the wall and were suspended overhead on diagonal chains. On the very long haul journeys these were in considerable demand. Alf had to institute a ballot system to ensure that everyone felt they were having a fair crack, but even so not everybody got to use them because the tickets were accepted as currency in the poker game.

Another favourite boxcar activity was hair styling. The girls would do their hair, and redo it, endlessly. If Emily wasn't fiddling with Muriel's curls, it was Muriel fiddling with Amy's, or Amy tinkering with Tilly's. I could never spot much difference afterwards, but that didn't stop them badgering me to see what I thought.

I would get drawn into the card game from time to time, but I liked to sit and watch America sliding by the windows, especially if I could contrive for Tilly to sit beside me, as it would never take too long for the motion of the car to send her to sleep on my shoulder. Not exactly moral turpitude, but nice, all the same.

Early on that first tour someone painted an extra line alongside the 'C' on the side so that the sign there read 'PRIVATE KAR'. No one from the railroad ever mentioned it – I doubt if anyone ever noticed – but it helped to make it ours.

And even though it was hot as a blast furnace in the summer, cold as an icebox in winter, and uncomfortable as all hell, it did come to feel a little bit like home.

But if I'd known some of the things that would go on in there, I might never have set foot in it.

9
CLAMBER CLOSER
CLARA

THAT first long run from Philadelphia to Chicago was the start of our Sullivan and Considine time, which was eventually to take us all the way to the other side of the continent and back. The whole journey was in the region of 760 miles, taking around twenty hours, which we passed in games of dice and cards, and trying to make the boxcar tolerably habitable, but by the time we arrived at Chicago's Union Station the novelty had most definitely worn off.

I actually have very fond memories of the hotel we stayed in on uptown Wabash Avenue, though. Alf's injunction that the male and female performers were to be quartered in separate establishments still held, but Karno's hopes that this would put a stop to any 'moral turpitude' were soon made a mockery of. Alf had booked us lads into this particular hotel during his advance trip, but by the time we took up residence the nature of the clientele had, shall we say, subtly altered.

I awoke from a deep slumber the first morning we were there, still bone-tired and pore-clogged from the marathon train journey, to find Mike Asher standing over me, a towel slung jauntily around his neck.

"Hey, Arthur?" he said, shaking me by the shoulder.

"What? What is it?"

"Just a word of friendly advice," Mike said. "This hotel is absolutely packed to the blooming rafters, and there's been quite an ugly queue for the bathroom. But if you nip down one floor there's a bit of a lull just now, so if I were you I'd get in while the getting is good. Go on, old man, chop chop!"

"Oh, right, um, thanks," I muttered, blundering into my bath robe and grabbing a towel of my own. "Appreciate it."

It was a rule of the travelling life always to take advantage of a free bathroom first thing, so I stumbled, half-awake and yawning, down the stairs to the floor below ours, and sure enough there was no queue outside the communal facility. "Good old Mike!" I thought to myself, and pushed the door ajar.

The mirror on the wall was steamed up, so I wiped it with my towel and gave a cursory inspection to my sallow features, before turning my attention to the claw-foot bath tub.

"Hiya sugar!"

Sitting there in the tub, slippery, pink and naked as the day they were born, were two gorgeous young women, right in the middle of the act of soaping each other down with the bubbles that were spilling luxuriously over the edge.

"Where have *you* popped up from, honey?" one of these visions said with a twinkling smile.

I took half a step back in amazement, clutching absently at my suddenly thumping heart. The two young women gazed at me curiously, their hands still pushing bubbles around each other's curves, and I felt I had to say something, so I blurted out; "Good morning, ladies. I do beg your pardon, I had no notion the room was occupied."

One of the girls cocked her head on one side, without even thinking of covering herself up, and she said: "Oh, I do so *lurve* an English accent, don't you, Belle?"

Belle, the other one, gave a little sigh and said: "I surely do, sister, it makes me go weak inside..."

Covered with confusion I excused myself and stumbled back out into the corridor. The girls gave me cheery little finger waves as I went, and smiled. I think they did, anyway, it was all I could do to look at their faces.

Every door to every room on the floor seemed to be open as I scurried back to the stairs, and every room seemed to have a girl inside either getting dressed or undressed. None of them was in the least bit embarrassed, they just sang out a 'Coo-eee!' or a 'Howdy, sweetheart!' as I passed, as though I were an old friend.

Back in the sanctuary of the room I was sharing, as usual, with Freddie Junior, I collapsed onto the bedstead, panting. Mike and Freddie were there, laughing their heads off, and I realised I'd just been suckered.

"Boys!" Mike exclaimed. "This hotel... may just be my favourite hotel in the whole world!"

"What's happening?" I gasped.

"There's a burlesque house on the next block, right? Well, the girls are all staying here! Twenty-three of 'em! I just found out exactly the same way you did. They don't care! They hadn't even bothered to bolt the door!"

"Holy...!" I muttered, as Freddie and Mike hugged themselves with glee, rocking back and forth on the other bed, making the springs squeak noisily.

"We are going to have such a time!" Mike said, rubbing his hands together gleefully.

And they did.

Tilly was highly amused by the lads' exploits when I explained it all to her a few days later. We were in Jackson Park looking out over Lake Michigan, which stretched millpond-flat to the far horizon and beyond.

"Mike and Freddie are like kids in a sweetshop," I said, "playing up the English accents for all they're worth, with their 'What-whats!' and their 'Don'tcha knows!'"

"And the girls love that, do they?"

"They positively swoon. Stan is utterly in love, mooning around after a lass called Sally, and she hasn't had to pay for anything this whole week."

"That sounds about right. A fool and his money, eh? What about the other single boys?"

"Well, I don't know if I should say…"

"Oh, don't be such a tease!"

"Well, Charlie Griffiths is very popular, I'll tell you that for nothing. He's the odd man out, the one with a room to himself, so everyone is pestering him to swap."

Tilly's mouth dropped open. "You're joking!"

"No, I'm not. I've had the big lump sharing with me a couple of times already, because Freddie has come to some arrangement or other with him."

"Good Heavens!"

"Bert Williams is in clover what with his ventriloquist tricks. He's not only got the English accent going for him, he can make it appear to come from wherever or *what*ever he wants."

"You don't mean…? Oh, never mind. Well, what *do* you mean?"

"You know what I mean."

"What? He can make it… *talk?*"

"See, you're interested now."

"I am not!" she protested. "And what about Albert Austin? Surely no one's chasing after that oddball, are they?"

"Do you know, I think Austin's having the best time of all? The girls are positively queuing up to pose for his camera, all wanting to be captured in their prime, and he's so prim and polite with them that they all trust him implicitly. It's a good ploy, and he's made a bob or two from illicit copies of those photos, as well."

"The little scamp. Who else?"

"I've seen Frank Melroyd bouncing a girl on each knee, looking red-faced and sweaty while they play with his hair."

"Aha." A little pause. "And Charlie?"

"No," I said. "He doesn't seem interested in indulging. I think the burlesque girls are a little vulgar for his taste."

"I see. And you, what about you, Arthur Dandoe? Has one of these buxom beauties caught your eye?"

"Well, no, not really," I said.

"Come on, you can tell me."

"Really, no."

"And why is that, pray?"

"None of them could hold a candle to you."

She went quiet then, gazing out over the water.

"Well, you asked," I said after a minute.

"Poor Arthur," she said. "So you're missing out on all the fun!"

"Are you saying it's not fun listening to Charlie Griffiths snoring away like a hog?"

"Ha ha! Not what I'd call fun. Come on, let's walk."

She took my arm and pulled in close to me, and we strolled back towards the city.

The next day I called on Tilly again but she was already out and about so I set off for a stroll through the neighbouring blocks by myself. So far I had not seen anything that much resembled the Wild West of my penny bloods, as first Philadelphia and now Chicago were both big cities that were not so very different from New York, with their tall buildings crammed together thrusting into the sky and trolley buses crawling up the middle of their wide thoroughfares.

After I'd walked away from the city for a little while with no particular aim in mind, though, I suddenly began to feel that this was a bit more like it. I found myself on a street that was not metaled, just hard-packed mud flecked with patches of grey-brown ice. Motorised traffic had thinned out to almost nothing, and here and there rough-looking fellows were tying their horses up outside saloon bars with swinging doors.

I strolled along the wooden boardwalk in front of a row of basic establishments, drugstores, and butchers and barbers and bars, and could almost imagine the crackle of gunplay erupting all around me, except it was mid-morning, and a weekday, and everyone was disappointingly civilised.

There was a constant gently amiable rattling noise, though, and I noticed that pretty much every store, every drugstore and bar, had a dice table set out in front of it, and hardy old-timers in tatty fingerless gloves were encouraging passers-by to try their luck – perhaps they'd be able to afford that little treat they were denying themselves after all.

I was just thinking to myself that I wouldn't have fancied sitting out in the freezing cold all day long when my eye was taken by an item hanging in the window of one of these drugstores – a long, black coat, much warmer-looking than my thin jacket, that would be just the thing for a mid-Western winter. I took a closer look, steaming the window with my breath, and the storekeeper came bustling out to stand shivering beside me in his shirt sleeves and apron.

"Handsome, ain't it?" he ventured. "Just one previous owner, and it'd fit you nicely, I'd say."

"How much?" I said, just making conversation, really, because I feared it would be out of my price range, and when he mentioned the figure he had in mind I realised I was right.

"Why not try a roll or two, sir?" the storekeeper said, thinking that if he couldn't clean me out for the coat, at least he'd winkle a couple of bucks out of me.

As it happened, I was well-versed in the ways of the dice table, having picked up the intricacies of High-Low and Chuck-a-Luck while shooting dice backstage with one of the troupes we'd shared a bill with in New York, and I had won a pocketful of cigarette coupons that were no use to me unless I happened upon a similarly attractive overcoat in a United Cigar Store.

Long story short, I got on a bit of a roll – literally – and shortly afterwards set off back to the hotel with a jaunty spring in my step, wearing the coat and smiling at the memory of the storekeeper's rueful expression as he'd reached it down from its high hook with a long pole.

———

After the evening show I headed to O'Flanagan's, the Irish bar round the corner (there always seemed to be an Irish bar around the corner), with everyone else for a drink. Stan, Freddie and Mike nursed their beers, all watching the door and waiting for their burlesque girls to arrive, their tongues practically hanging out. When he wasn't in the company of his particular favourite, a buxom Latin lovely by the name of Lucia, Mike liked to spend the time talking about her.

"She calls me 'Maieek!'" he explained for the umpteenth time, "as though she has just seen a mouse halfway through saying my name. Which is adorable, by the way."

"What have you been up to, then?" Freddie asked me, with something close to pity in his voice.

"Actually," I said, "I bought myself a coat. It's good and warm, apart from at the back, where it is split up to the waist for wearing on horseback so it gets a bit draughty. Second hand."

"Second hand, eh?" Stan murmured absently, glancing at the door and fingering his watch.

"Yes. Obviously I'd have preferred to have salvaged it from the frozen body of a dead prospector and found a map of a gold strike crumpled in the pocket, but, you know, this is not quite the Wild West, is it?"

I was talking to myself by then, though, as Lucia and Sally had come in, with assorted other lovelies in their wake, and my friends were lost to me. Charlie was sitting in the corner, pointedly reading a slim volume of poetry in Latin, if you please. Or maybe he wasn't actually reading it, but it was open in front of him. There was no sign of Tilly, and I presumed she had gone back to her hotel with Amy and the other married ladies, so I decided to call it a night.

Back in the room I lay on my back in the dark alone. Freddie, I imagined, was busy coming of age elsewhere in the building, and mercifully hadn't needed to turf Charlie Griffiths out of his single accommodation to do it.

I watched the lights of the elevated trains playing on the wall like a kind of private bioscope, and my thoughts turned, as they so often did, to Mr Charles Chaplin and Miss Matilda Beckett.

The longer the tour went on, and the further we got from the Fun Factory, the less concerned Charlie seemed about keeping on the right side of me. Maybe he thought that Karno would not be especially agitated about all his previous misdemeanours. He didn't know the Guv'nor as well as he thought he did, if that was what he was thinking.

Now Tilly and I were seeing a fair bit of one another, and I was trying to at least give the impression that my rivalry with Charlie was not so important to me. He, I was itching to point out, had tried to make a move on her back in New York, and that had backfired on him precisely because of *his* obsessive rivalry with *me*. And with Stan, too.

Then my reverie was cut short by a light tap on the door.

"Who's there?" I called, but there was no reply. Instead the handle turned slowly, and the door began to open, revealing a very comely figure silhouetted in the corridor outside, dark hair piled on top of her head and tumbling down onto her bare shoulders.

"Hello?" I said. "Are you looking for Freddie, because I'm not quite sure where he... um... is..."

"No, sugar, I ain't a-lookin' fer Freddie. I am lookin' fer you, an' I reckon as how I've found you. Now why don't you invite me in, in that gorgeous accent of yours, an' we two can get ourselves better acquainted?" Her voice was as rich and sweet as honey, and carried the distinctive twang of the South. Which, coincidentally, was where I was beginning to feel definite stirrings of interest.

I knew I should be sending this alluring creature away, but I couldn't quite summon up the words. Instead I heard myself saying, in as plummy an English accent as I have ever heard myself using: "Forgive me, where are my manners? Let me just get the light..."

"Never you mind about the light, honey," she said, whoever she was. "We can manage just *fine* in the dark. Much more... cosy."

She stepped inside then, and closed the door behind her. In the darkness I heard the high heels of a pair of spring-sided boots clicking on the floor as the temptress walked slowly towards me, and I could just make out her shapely legs, sheathed in black silk stockings that swished lightly together as she moved, and a red and black basque that seemed to be offering up a creamy white bosom for my inspection.

"I... erm... well..." I ventured, impressively. "I should perhaps introduce myself properly before we... erm... go any further."

"As you wish, sugar," my visitor drawled. "But I'm happy just to go further."

"Dandoe, Arthur Dandoe," I burbled, as she sat next to me on the bed, her thigh pressing urgently against mine, her intoxicating perfume filling my head. "And you are...?"

"Call me Clara," she breathed, and began nibbling on my ear.

"I supp-o-o-ose one of my friends has arr-a-a-anged this, have they?" I managed to say.

"You could say that, honey pie," Clara murmured, moving down to my neck.

"Which...one, I wonder...?" I said.

"Well, let me see," said Clara, placing a finger to her lips thoughtfully. "Would you have a friend by the name of...?"

"Of...?"

"Matilda Beckett?"

"Matil...? What, *Tilly* arranged for you to...?!"

Clara sat up straight beside me then, reached up, and pulled a sumptuous black wig from atop her head, allowing her own distinctive blonde curls to tumble free. Just then an elevated train

96

rattled past outside, and there was just enough light to see the triumphant beam on her lovely face.

"Ha! Arthur Dandoe! Your face!"

"Tilly! What the...?!"

She stood up then, to give me the full effect of her disguise before the train passed by entirely. "I borrowed this clobber from Lucia, Mike's special friend. Such a lovely girl, by the way. Do you like it?"

"You look... incredible," I said, still recovering myself.

"I just didn't like the thought of you missing out on all the fun," Tilly said.

"It's... not been easy," I said.

"So...?" she said, tilting her head to one side, hands on hips. "I'm more or less finished with this disguise, wouldn't you say? Perhaps I should... take it off?"

"Oh, please," I said. "Allow me..."

10
OUT WHERE THE
BLUE BEGINS

THE next morning I awoke to the rustlings and swishings of Tilly relocating her various items of borrowed exotic clothing. When she saw me stir she rolled back onto the bed beside me and kissed me on the cheek.

"I need to go," she whispered. "I don't want to be missed at breakfast, now do I?"

"You're going back to your hotel?" I said, blearily. "You can't."

"Yes, dear, I must," she said, pulling herself away from my embrace and retrieving the dark wig from where she had thrown it..

"Not like that, though," I said. "You can't walk the streets dressed like that – or rather you certainly could, but you probably shouldn't."

"Hmmm..." Tilly glanced down with a frown at the revealing costume she had borrowed from Lucia.

"Take my coat," I said, fetching it from the wardrobe.

Outside the door, she stretched up on tiptoes and kissed me goodbye, and then skipped quickly along the corridor to the stairs and away. The saddle-cut of my new coat afforded me a pleasant view of her silk-clad legs and her high-heeled boots, and I drank it in till she was out of sight.

I heard a little cough, looked round, and there, also watching, was Frank Melroyd, on his way back from the bathroom in his dressing gown and slippers, a towel slung round his neck.

"One of the burlesque women, eh?" he mumbled.

"Yep," I said, and winked.

━━━━━

At the end of our second week in Chicago the burlesque girls moved on, but Mike, Freddie and Stan were not too downcast. The hotel manager had let slip that the replacement company at the burlesque house had booked the whole of the second floor for the next fortnight.

"Fresh meat!" Mike said gleefully, and he was not wrong. Mike, Stan, Freddie and Albert tiptoed down the stairs on the day of their arrival, having heard saucy feminine giggling, but they quickly came scurrying back, sweating and trembling.

The new troupe were known as Billy Watson and His Beef Trust. Watson, the host, star comedian and producer of the show was an odd-looking fellow, bald, but with a spike of hair on top of his gleaming pate, much like the Marconi aerial on top of Wanamaker's department store. 'His Beef Trust' was the unflattering name of his revue, which featured 'nearly a ton of feminine flesh' – according to his own publicity posters – in the form of twenty enormously fat middle-aged women parading around in corsets and tights. They were no less openly lascivious than their predecessors. They were, however, vast, and you did have the impression that any one of them could have eaten poor Freddie alive.

"I'm going to have to put this back," Mike shuddered, something metallic clinking in his pocket. It was the lock from the second floor bathroom door.

———

The one we were all mustard keen to take a squint at was the International Aviation Meet, which was taking place at – or strictly speaking above – Grant Park. So one late morning the whole gang of us headed over there and joined the thousands of spectators thronging the park, all craning their necks to peer upwards into the bright spring sky.

The park itself formed a natural arena for the event, sandwiched between a towering row of impressively grand beach-view hotels, all their balconies packed with lucky enthusiasts, and the great flat expanse of Lake Michigan. Boats of all sizes were lurking offshore, yachts and small steamers, with still more watchers leaning over their railings and pointing to the crisp blue heavens.

There were already more than a dozen aircraft swooping and swirling in the sky when we arrived, with more on the far lawns either just landed or waiting to take off. It was coming up to Good Friday, and I couldn't quite shake the impression that the sky was full of flying crucifixes. There were monoplanes darting like swallows, biplanes too, some with straight pairs of wings, some with wings bowed in at the tips giving them an oval aspect, and one triplane that looked like nothing so much as a flying slice of quivering cream cake. The noise of their engines was faint and distant, like a far-off wasps' nest, or a children's party dissolving into raspberry-blowing anarchy.

Tossed this way and that by the breeze coming in off the lake, like children's kites only without the strings, it seemed that there must be a collision any minute, but somehow the aviators were able to control their crafts sufficiently to twitch and weave out of each other's way. After I'd watched them for a while it seemed more and more to me that they were deliberately flying close to one another, to give the spectators an extra thrill, perhaps, or to put the wind up a particular competitor up there.

They looked impossibly flimsy and dangerous, especially when you saw them stationary and ungainly on the grass, with the wind rippling the light canvas of their wings and the skinny struts holding them up flexing under their weight. Sometimes the pilots would stand up in their cockpits to take the acclaim of the cheering crowds, and their little machines would wobble from side to side with every wave of their leather caps and goggles.

As we weaved through the strolling throngs, I was desperate to get Tilly on her own. All I'd been able to think about since that night she came a-calling as Clara the hot little burlesque piece was – what did it *mean*?

Had Tilly finally put aside all her misgivings about me, about resuming a relationship with me? Was I finally forgiven for my previous misdemeanours? For choosing my career over our pretend marriage back in England, and for rejecting her when I thought she'd succumbed to Karno's casting couch? Had I finally convinced her that I would put her first, ahead of my rivalry with Chaplin?

I went over to a stall selling something called Fairy Floss. I'd never seen anything like it before, it was like a cloud on a stick, made, as it turned out, from sugar heated and spun in a special machine shaped like a little bathtub. I bought a couple and took them over to Tilly, and, as I hoped, the sickly-sweet novelty lured her away from the others, particularly the ubiquitous lingering Melroyd, and soon we were walking along together towards the shore of the great lake.

A man with a megaphone announced that a certain Lincoln Beachey had just created a new altitude record of something over eleven and a half thousand feet.

"How do they know that?" I said. "That's one hell of a long ruler he must have taken up there with him."

"Or eleven and a half thousand small ones," Tilly said. "It's funny this stuff, isn't it? You take a great big bite of it, and suddenly it's like there's nothing in your mouth at all."

"I was hoping I might see our friend Clara again before we leave Chicago," I ventured.

"Oh, were you?"

"Very much so."

"Well, I'm afraid Clara was a one-night-only performance."

"Oh? Why is that?"

"It was just meant to be a bit of fun, you know, a joke."

"A joke?"

"Yes, you know. You were telling me all about what Freddie and Mike were getting up to, and I thought why should we miss out, eh?"

"I see."

"Anyway, your hotel is full of those enormous beef women, now, and I could hardly pass myself off as one of them, now could I?"

"I don't suppose so," I said.

"Oh, Arthur, don't tell me you've been taking it all too seriously. Thinking it was a new start, and now we are engaged or something. I knew you would, I knew I shouldn't have done it, but it was such a good ruse, and such... I mean, your face! You had no idea, did you?"

"No," I admitted, my head spinning. "You were... brilliant."

"Why, thank you," she said, with a little curtsey. "Mind you, I nearly got caught by Alf when I got back to my hotel, you know."

"Did you?"

"Oh yes, it was a very close thing, I passed him on the stairs going down for his breakfast. Luckily I had that black wig on, and your big coat."

"Ha ha!" I managed a laugh.

"Yes, that would have been a real nuisance. Quite apart from all that 'moral turpitude' nonsense he is perpetually banging on about, I do have my reputation to consider."

"Huh, your reputation," I snorted, without thinking.

"What?" she turned sharply. "Why did you say it like that? 'Your reputation'?"

"Like what?"

"So... scathing!"

"I didn't mean anything."

"Didn't you? It sounded like you thought that I didn't have much of a reputation to consider."

"No, no, not at all. I mean, as long as people don't find out..."

"About what?"

"About... well, you know..."

I was in agonies. How on earth had I ended up seemingly criticising her for the very thing I most wanted her to do again? Meanwhile Tilly's indignation was picking up momentum.

"I suppose you are saying to Mike and Stan and Freddie and the others that they shouldn't have a good time while they can, eh? That they should think of *their* reputations?"

"No, of course not, I..."

"So why should it be any different for me?"

"I... I don't know..."

"And you, you were quite happy to be seduced by a complete stranger, for all you knew."

"Yes, yes I was..."

"Well then!"

I held my breath, and the little storm seemed to blow itself out. We walked along, nibbling at the last of the cotton candy, which was making my teeth itch. A biplane buzzed slowly along the same line as our footpath, and when we looked up we could see the aviator's feet, and the bottom of his canvas seat.

"When I was in Paris last year, at the Folies Bergère," Tilly began again, "the girls there would quite cheerfully go out with several gentlemen friends at once. 'Why not?' they'd say. 'No one owns us, we do what we want'. It didn't mean they were looking for someone to settle down with, necessarily."

"I see," I said.

"Like the Neame sisters, d'you know them? Both singers on the halls, both now the mistresses of wealthy men who saw them there. One's calling herself 'Lady Fortescue' now."

"Ha!"

"Some were after a ring, of course, especially if it came with a castle and an obscure European title."

"Like that Hohenzollern fellow I found you with," I said.

"Mmmm," she said. "But it is an invigorating attitude to have, quite liberating really. Why should I worry about breaking the rules in a society that won't even let me vote? Why should I not pursue what I want? Why can't I make the most of myself, as a performer, for instance?"

"No earthly reason," I said, spotting my cue. "But that's not all you want, surely? What about...?"

"What about what?"

"Well... love."

"Oh, love, love is all very well, but why does it mean I have to be tied down? Why shouldn't I have the freedom to fly, soar around the sky like these chaps?"

104

It must have felt like a pretty straightforward connection to make, but unfortunately just at that very moment one of the biplanes was going into a crowd-thrilling dive, plummeting down towards the watching public, who scattered in all directions like a group of pigeons being chased by a small boy. The plan must have been to level off just above our heads, buzzing away like a giant insect, but this particular fellow was coming in too fast and about a hundred feet up the wings just tore off his plane all at once and spiralled away to either side, while the pilot nosed straight down into the turf with a sickening thump.

Tilly gasped in horror and covered her face with her hands. I looked away, but not before seeing one of the crumpled pairs of wings collapsing slowly on top of a knot of spectators, squashing them helplessly to the ground, and temporarily at least they were crushed.

I knew how they felt.

11
'E TAKES A MEAN ADVANTAGE

AFTER Chicago we played a week at the Empress in Milwaukee, further up the finger of Lake Michigan, then boarded the Karno boxcar for a long haul across the wild wintry wastes of Wisconsin to play the Unique in Minneapolis.

There was a good deal of snow on the ground, and every little lake we chugged by was frozen over. My colleagues were absorbed in the card game, in which George Seaman was once again relieving Stan of his wages, but I was only interested in the view. We rattled into a deep forest, the branches laden with snow and icicles, and I became frustrated peering out of the steamed-up window. I decided to take a ride on the boxcar's observation platform, so I slipped into the props compartment and made my way through to the back door. For this trip there was no guard's van attached behind us, as we had been added behind it, so I could stand there watching the rail track snake away through the trees through miles of beautiful desolation.

It was enthralling, but bitterly cold, so I was glad of my new winter coat, despite the draught in the rear. I pulled it closer round myself, remembering Tilly in her burlesque outfit slipping out of the hotel wearing it, and smiled wistfully as I recalled her returning it to me that evening at the theatre.

"Your coat, I think, Mr Dandoe," she'd said, and I had given her a courteous bow in return.

"Why thank you kindly, Miss Beckett."

Then our exaggerated discretion had made us both snigger, which would have been a dead giveaway to anyone paying us any mind...

Suddenly, from out of nowhere, I felt an almighty thump in the middle of my back, and in an instant I was toppling over the railing. For a long moment I was suspended in mid-air, staring down at the wooden sleepers flickering below my face at what seemed like fantastic destructive speed, and then I flung out a desperate arm and grabbed hold of the length of chain that secured the back gate of the boxcar. My lower half flipped over the railings then, and I was dragged along behind the train, my toecaps scraping and bouncing on the sleepers, before I was able to scramble up and straddle one of the buffers.

I sat there for a minute or two, trying to get my breath back, and waiting for my life to stop flashing before my eyes. I glanced at the frozen forest rushing by on either side. If I'd gone off the train there I'd have been miles from human habitation, miles from help, never mind thinking about what injuries I might have had from the fall. As it was I had a big bruise on my shin beginning to make itself known, and my bad knee was complaining too.

I turned to look back up at the observation platform and there was Frank Melroyd looking down at me.

"Was that...? You?" I gasped.

"Sorry," he said. "Must have slipped. Bit of ice here. Just clumsiness."

"Clumsiness?"

"Yes."

Only then did he reach out a hand to help me. Something struck me as not altogether right, but in my bewilderment I couldn't quite say what. I did make sure, though, to have a firm grasp of the railings and not to rely solely on his assistance as I climbed back aboard.

"Sorry, old man," Frank said, as we stood on the little observation platform together, and he made a show of brushing some snow from my coat. "Just a stupid accident. You won't mention it to anyone, will you? I do feel rather foolish."

He gave a sheepish grin, then, and shuffled back inside the boxcar.

What the hell...?

━━━

After the first day's shows at the Unique we decamped to a bar – not Irish for once, but a Scandinavian establishment – a smoky wood-panelled place, with a roaring fire in the fireplace, and a moose's head on the wall with an expression half surprised and half stunned, for all the world like the creature had just charged the outside of the building at full tilt.

Mike, Freddie, Stan and I were already on our second beers by the time the ladies of the company spilled through the doors giggling and smirking over some shared secret. Tilly walked across to our table, and placed her hands on her hips.

"Hey, boys," she said. "You'll never guess who we found waiting at the stage door."

"Who?" Freddie said.

Emily and Muriel stepped aside, and there, in all her voluptuous glory, was Lucia, the burlesque girl who had made such an impression on Mike.

"Lucia!" Mike cried, and Freddie and Stan peered at the door like a pair of faithful hounds, hoping no doubt that it was about to swing open again and provide a similarly pleasant surprise for them.

"Ah, Maieek, *mi amor*!" Lucia said, bustling over and kissing the lad on both reddening cheeks.

"So," I said, as we shuffled along to allow Lucia and Tilly to join us in our booth. "The burlesque show is in town, eh?"

"No," Tilly said.

"No?" Mike said, looking at Lucia with a puzzled frown.

"They are in Des Moin-ez," Lucia said, nuzzling into his neck.

"But isn't that miles away?" Mike was beginning to look panicky.

"Hundreds of miles, actually," Tilly said. "Hundreds and hundreds."

"It's in a different state altogether, isn't it?" I said, and Freddie and Stan nodded, enjoying Mike's growing discomfiture.

"But, Lucia..." he said. "I don't quite... understand."

"I have left the burlesque show," Lucia said dramatically. "I have left them to be with you."

━━━━

A little later I was over by the bar negotiating for some refills when suddenly Mike Asher was at my elbow.

"What am I going to *do*?!" he hissed.

"I do have one suggestion," I said.

"Yes?"

"When you sneak her into our lodgings later..."

"Yes? Yes?"

"Give her a piggy-back, then the landlady will only hear one set of footsteps on the stairs."

"Very funny. You're hilarious."

I picked up a couple of pints and headed back to the table, where to my intense irritation I spotted Frank Melroyd making his usual sly dart to snag the seat beside Tilly. I put down the drinks, took half a step towards him and shoulder-barged him in the chest, knocking the wind out of him.

"Sorry, Frank," I said. "Clumsiness."

He looked at me, and if looks could kill, well, he could have just looked at me without bothering to try and pitch me off a train in the middle of nowhere.

"I think Mike needs a hand," I said, jerking my thumb over my shoulder, and he slunk off, mumbling to himself.

However, it wasn't Frank Melroyd I was chiefly concerned about at that time.

───

The previous few weeks, ever since our conversation at the Aviation Meet in Chicago, had been a little peculiar where my relations with Tilly were concerned.

I had somehow managed to appear critical of her moonlight visit in the guise of the burlesque girl, even though I thought of little else other than a repeat performance. Maybe I was unsettled by her Parisian attitude, her desire to fly free, her unwillingness to be tied down. Of course, as the only single girl in the troupe, there was naturally always going to be an abundance of lads for her to socialise with while we were riding the rails, that was perfectly understandable. But even if she was willing to have a number of 'gentlemen friends', that didn't mean that one couldn't aspire to be her favourite, did it? To the ultimate exclusion and/or possible destruction of all others?

I resolved to try and get a clearer sense of how things actually stood between us, and so one morning that week I strolled over to Tilly's hotel, meaning to take her out for a pre-show constitutional. If I'd been a couple of minutes later I would have missed her altogether, though, because as I entered the lobby I met her coming the other way, arm-in-arm with Chaplin.

"Arthur!" she beamed, not at all perturbed to see me. Charlie, however, looked less than pleased.

"Good morning, both," I said, trying to conceal my own dismay.

"We are going to a nickelodeon, aren't we, Charlie?"

Chaplin sourly nodded a confirmation, with an insincere teeth-clenched smile, and I wondered whether he was fully aware of Tilly's philosophy.

"Join us!" Tilly said, hooking her free arm into mine, and leading us jauntily down the steps three abreast as though we were in a musical number.

"Yes," Charlie said, recovering himself. "There is one a little further along we thought we might try."

"I didn't think you were that interested in the moving pictures," I said to him, over the top of Tilly's hat.

"Oh yes," he replied. "I am sure there is something to be said for them."

Yes, I thought. An opportunity to spend an hour in a darkened room with Tilly, whispering in her ear about how very much funnier he was than the fellows on screen, and how very much more attractive she was than all the women.

We came to the nickelodeon, paid our five cents and went inside. It was a spartan theatre set up in a converted shop, small, fetid and airless, smelling quite strongly of its clientele. We stumbled in the darkness over to a small round table with three hard-backed chairs, which scraped noisily on the stone floor as we settled in, Tilly in the middle. They didn't want to let the light in, you see, because it outshone the pictures, and they couldn't open a window, because the screen would waft around all over the place in the cooling breeze, as it was just a sheet hanging in front of the back wall.

A handful of other customers were scattered around the room. One or two of them had beer, or at least that's what I thought I smelled in the murk, and I squinted into the corners trying to work out where they had got it from.

Now we were all used to seeing moving pictures as part of a variety bill, both at home and here in the States. Usually these would be naturalistic subjects, such as the Royal Family passing along the Mall in their fancy carriages, and if you were a comedy turn waiting to go on you would know that nothing dampened an audience's inclination to laugh more than the sight of old bearded Bertie solemnly parading past in his finery.

The flickers on show at the nickelodeon were different, though. They were short films, shown over and over again all day long, and many of them were attempts at comedy. But were these the pioneers of a new sort of mirth-making? Or were they just no-hopers who would never make it onto the big time, or even the small time, or any time at all?

The first film that we saw that day was called *The Bachelor*. It featured a fat fellow trying to sew a button onto his trousers. Well, do you know, he couldn't manage it, and in the end he decided instead to use a safety pin, gave the camera a big grin, and walked off. The End.

"What?" Tilly said. "Is that it?"

"You know," Charlie said. "I could have done so much more with an opportunity like that."

"I know you could," Tilly said.

112

"Yes," I said, "but why would you want to? Look around, there's hardly anyone watching. We'll have two thousand people watching us later."

"They show flickers to those big audiences too, though, don't they?"

"They do. And that's when everyone goes to the lavatory."

The next film was a biblical subject called *Pharaoh, or Israel in Egypt*, and depicted the plagues that were visited on the Egyptians, with unpleasant pictures of dead children, and a few ropey-looking camels walking around in the background.

Anyway, it turned out that the back wall of this particular nickel-priced entertainment emporium had a door in it, concealed by the screen hanging in front of it, and midway through a plague someone took it into their heads to try and enter by this entrance. This let in a great burst of sunlight from outdoors, which completely washed out the tribulations of Egypt and replaced them with the back-lit silhouette of a man.

We watched this, entranced, as the man stood in the doorway, taking out a pipe and casually packing some tobacco into it. I got halfway to my feet, intending to go and close the door, but Charlie grabbed me by the arm and we continued to observe the shadow play. The fellow struck a match, we could see it as clearly as anything, and we could even make out the plume of smoke once he had lit up.

Then, having got nice and comfortable, he waved at some unseen passer-by and called out to him: "Hey there, Vic? Come and have a beer!"

A second shadow joined the first, starkly back-lit by the bright autumn sunshine. The two figures shook hands, and then turned to enter the room we were watching in. This was the first moment that they were aware of the white sheet hanging down in their path, and perhaps dazzled by the transition from the brilliant

113

outdoors to the seedy interior, they were completely confounded by it.

They walked right into the screen from behind, and still appearing to us as shadows, they tried to wrestle through it. The effect was pretty comical, I have to say, and by the time they disentangled themselves and made their way in, they found that they were the subject of some mirth. They were indignant at first, but there were three of us and only two of them so they put their heads down and passed on through to the counter to seek refreshment.

"Well!" said Tilly once they were out of earshot. "Those guys ought to be in flickers, they were screen naturals!"

"Certainly more interesting than the plagues of Egypt," I agreed.

"And funnier than that fat fellow with a button off his trousers," she said, still chuckling.

"Mm..." Charlie agreed, distracted.

We left shortly after that and made our way to our own theatre, with Charlie trailing along a few steps behind, lost in thought.

━━━━━

AT the end of that week we were heading for the Empress in Duluth, on the tip of Lake Superior. Alf set up his office at the mid-point of the boxcar and got on with the business of paying everyone, while George Seaman had his cards out at the ready, preparing to arrange a redistribution of the workers' wealth, his tongue flicking wolfishly out of the corner of his mouth.

Before the card game could get under way, however, Charlie stood up and called a company meeting. He began by describing the fellows we saw at the nickelodeon getting caught up in the screen, their antics illuminated by the light from the street beyond.

"It was pretty funny, wasn't it?" he said, looking to me and Tilly for support.

"It was," I conceded, and Tilly nodded too.

"Well it gave me an idea," Charlie went on. "We could do a whole sketch in shadow play. It would be like watching a moving picture, except it wouldn't be silent, you could have sounds, and music, and dialogue even. What do you think?"

"It sounds like a marvellous notion, Charlie," Tilly said, her eyes sparkling.

"There's a bit of shadow play in *London Suburbia*, do you remember?" Stan said, his brow furrowed in thought. "In the windows of the tenement, on the blinds?"

"Exactly!" said Charlie.

From the murmurings around me, it seemed that not everyone was convinced. One person was, though, that was for sure.

"Brilliant!" said Tilly, "I think it would be absolutely brilliant."

The look she gave Charlie then was so admiring, so luminous, and Charlie's smile in return so winning and... toothy, that I couldn't bring myself to like the idea at all.

"I don't know," I said. "If people wanted to see folk larking about on a screen, they'd go to the picture house, or just wait till there was a flicker on the bill, wouldn't they?"

"Oh don't mind him, Charlie," Tilly said, shuffling closer to Chaplin along the bench seat. "What would be the story?"

"Well," Charlie said, holding a pause to build up our anticipation of his brilliant notion. "I was thinking... a harlequinade! There, how about that!"

This didn't go down quite as well as Charlie expected. We had all endured a harlequinade at one time or another, a tiresome

115

bit of stylised clowning tacked onto the end of a pantomime, featuring the traditional figures of the Italian commedia dell' arte. It had almost died out entirely, actually, and it was somehow an utterly typical Chaplin idea to try and revive it. He wouldn't have to come up with anything new, he'd just have to devise some bits of business within an established framework. And it was also, of course, insufferably pretentious.

I snorted. "A harlequinade? Really?"

Stan was a little more supportive. "That could work... I suppose..." he murmured.

Even Tilly seemed a little deflated, I was pleased to notice.

"Now, I shall be Harlequin, naturally..." Charlie began, and as Harlequin was a manipulative sprite of a character, I supposed it was natural enough. "Tilly? You shall be my Columbine." Tilly beamed and stood to give a little curtsey, and I felt a lurch in my guts. I didn't like the sound of this at all. Columbine is traditionally Harlequin's love interest, and so this new project was clearly going to involve much pitching of woo. I needed to make sure that I was on hand to keep an eye on this... "Frank, you can be Policeman, Stan will play Clown, Mike – where is Mike Asher? Ah there you are, you will be Pierrot, and... let me see... Albert, Albert Austin, you will be Pantaloon."

"What about me?" I asked.

Chaplin's look of innocent surprise reeked of insincerity. "Oh, but Arthur, I didn't think you were much interested in the idea. Right-o everyone, that's a plan then."

I watched, seething, as he jumped in beside Tilly, and the two of them began chattering about this new scheme. I knew what he was up to, of course, he was making a fresh move on her.

But what could I do, but watch and stew?

116

I was pretty fed up for the rest of that week. Rehearsals for Chaplin's shadow harlequinade took up most of everybody's spare time but mine, and I found myself visiting saloon bars to occupy myself. Many of the smaller saloons were so functionally dedicated to the solo drinker that they did not even have chairs and tables or stools at the bar. There would be a rail at your feet to lean on, that's all, and we like-minded strangers would stand in a line, all facing forwards, concentrating on the booze before us like nothing so much as a herd of stupid cows being milked.

I barely got to speak more than a handful of words to Tilly as she was so wrapped up in the new show, and at the end of the evenings she was too tired to linger, whereas I was decidedly in the mood for more drinking. So that's what I did.

By the end of the week I was heartily sick of Charlie taking Tilly's hand in the dressing room and kissing it, sighing in a lovelorn fashion and murmuring "Ah me alas, my beloved Columbine!" And so, by the look of him, was Frank Melroyd, which meant at least I was safe from his dangerous attentions for the time being.

Then we struck out through more thickly-forested snowscapes for Canada, where we were due to play Winnipeg.

As was usual, now, we eventually decamped stiffly from our carriage and headed for our accommodations, leaving the hands from the Empress Theatre to take care of unloading the set and carting it across town to the venue. We shambled in some time later for the band call, only to find poor Alf tearing out what remained of his hair. A quick glance around backstage told us the reason: there was no sign of any of our stuff. No set, no costumes, no props.

"What's up, Alf?" I said with a puzzled frown.

"It's the boxcar," Alf wailed. "The Karno boxcar."

"What about it?"

"It's gone!"

12
SHADOWS ON
THE BLIND

"GONE? What do you mean it's gone?"

"The Karno boxcar was not detached from the train at Winnipeg," Alf fumed.

"So where is it now?"

"On its way to the bloody Klondike, apparently. Mr Montague the theatre manager has been on the line to the manager of the railroad station, and it seems the car cannot be turned around until it reaches Edmonton in Alberta, and cannot be returned here until tomorrow morning at the earliest. So as for today's shows, well..." He slumped, overwhelmed by the calamity that had descended upon us.

"So?" Charlie Griffiths said brightly. "A couple of nights off, then. Could be worse."

"Although," Alf said, "if we don't play then that will be reflected in our pay."

There was a discontented murmuring at this. Then Tilly stepped forward. "But isn't this the perfect opportunity?" she said.

"For what?" Alf asked.

"Why, to launch the *Harlequinade in Black and White*, of course."

Charlie stepped forward and took both her hands in his. "Could we?" he said. "Can we be ready?"

"Of course we can," Tilly said, gazing into his peculiar purple eyes. "I believe in you."

I felt sick to my stomach.

―――――

I had no part in the new piece, so I slipped around front of house to watch the thing debut that very afternoon.

A bright light came on behind the white screen, the same one used for showing moving pictures, and here was Chaplin as Harlequin, his precise movements showing up sharply in silhouette. He remained sideways on, like an Egyptian hieroglyph, as the shadow technique rendered foreshortening confusing. He was joined then by Tilly as Columbine, beautiful even in black and white, and they danced a pantomime of romantic love, which I didn't particularly enjoy, although they did it well enough. I could sense Tilly's exhilaration at finally being at the centre of things even though there was a screen between us.

The lovers were separated then by a policeman who was knocked cold and then gradually relieved of his internal organs in a gruesome sequence, mostly using sausages, I think, which drew some very vocal expressions of disgust from the audience, particularly the children who were in for the matinée.

I did observe with grim satisfaction that the audience seemed to get bored of the novelty after five or six minutes, and began to behave much as they did when a short film was shown, talking amongst themselves, getting up and walking about. Because after all, if a performer isn't going to look at you, why should you look at them?

The finale was a fight, and I had to admit that Charlie had devised some clever effects. Moving towards the light, or away from it, had the effect of dramatically altering the size of your shadow on the screen, so Harlequin was first a small figure facing a giant, and then suddenly turned the tables. Then all the characters made a leap which gave the effect that they had all leapt up to the Moon, or out over the heads of the audience, and there was a gasp, followed by admittedly warm applause.

I dawdled round backstage again, not particularly keen on witnessing the aftermath of Charlie's success. When I eventually made it back to the green room he was still full of it, whirling Tilly round in his arms triumphantly. I was pleased that she'd had a taste of the limelight, but I must admit that my fervent hope then was that the boxcar would reappear as soon as possible.

There was no sign of it the next day, though, and I considered staying away from the theatre altogether. In the event, however, I found a box unoccupied, and I slunk in there to watch and drink a beer or two on my lonesome.

As the Harlequinade got under way again, however, I was joined by three newcomers, who took the remaining empty seats. I glanced over and recognised them at once – surely these were the enormous guys I had seen parting the crowds in Times Square on New Year's Eve? Big Tim Sullivan, no less, and his two cohorts?

Sullivan was frowning at the shadow play, as though he couldn't quite grasp what was meant to be happening.

"Say, feller?" he hissed at me. "Is this the Fred Karno outfit, do you know? From England?"

"Oh yah, that's right, eh?" I replied, putting on the Canuck accent we had been hearing everywhere and trying to master, not wanting to let him know I was attached to the show.

"Well, this don't make any sense at all," he muttered to his sidekicks. "How are we supposed to see what's goin' on?"

"Dey should pull da curtain up, dat's what dey should do," one of the big fellows said. "Den we could *see* 'em."

"You know what, Brick, you're right at dat," Sullivan said. Put the curtain up, that would do the trick..."

I realised that they simply didn't get the shadow play at all, which amused me. Just then the shadow Policeman gave the shadow Harlequin a resounding crack on the head with his truncheon that made the audience wince to hear it. I was just thinking that I didn't remember that gag from the day before, when Sullivan leaned over to me.

"'Scuse me, sir, do you mind me askin'? What do you make of this here entertainment before us?"

And there it was. It landed right in my lap. The chance to give Charlie Chaplin the slap down he so richly deserved. And here was Big Tim Sullivan, ready to deliver it for me.

"To be frank, sir," I said, in my best Canadian. "I don't know what this is all aboot. I am seriously thinking of askin' for my money back. I can't see a thing, eh?"

"There!" Sullivan said, sitting back and gesturing to his companions as if to say: "Did you hear that?"

———

At the end of the evening I slipped round to the green room eager to see how things would play out. Charlie was nursing a lump like half a hard-boiled egg on the side of his noggin, and waving away Frank Melroyd's protestations that it had been an accident. He was in ebullient mood, despite the bump, and was laying down the law to Alf.

"I think, in the light of the success of the *Harlequinade in Black and White*, we should consider alternating it with *Mumming Birds*, if not replacing the old show altogether."

"Oh, I don't know about that..." Alf began.

"I'm sure there would be considerable savings," Charlie said. "Well, we can think about that, can't we?"

One or two of us, myself included, were already beginning to think about that, as we surely represented the considerable savings he had in mind. Chaplin's beady little purple eyes sought me out then, and an unpleasant half-smile came to his lips.

Just then, right in the middle of the backslapping, the green room door flew open, and we had company. Big Tim Sullivan had arrived, and the room suddenly seemed darker. Behind him were the other two brawny sons of toil, both wearing placid expressions on their massive plug ugly faces that belied the air of physical menace exuding from them like an odour. One of them had a fistful of the collar of the theatre manager, Mr Prenderville, who seemed to be joining this conversation very much against his will. I shrank behind a coat-stand so as not to be spotted.

"Gentlemen... and ladies," the leader of this extraordinary group began. "My name is Sullivan, and I am the partner of Mr John Considine."

"Ah," said Alf Reeves, stepping forward, hand outstretched. "A pleasure, sir. I am..."

Unnervingly, Sullivan carried on talking as though Alf was not even there. "Mr Considine has contracted you to appear upon our circuit and so, as a businessman, I took it upon myself to come along and size up my investment. You foller?"

Everyone held their breath, it seemed, as we suddenly got the unmistakeable whiff that the whole tour was in the balance all of a sudden.

"I can only apologise on behalf of this great country," Sullivan went on. "What must you think of us, eh? You come all this way, you perform your comedy for us, and we haven't the decency to lift the screen and let the audience see what you are doing. It's an insult, so it is."

Charlie frowned, perplexed. "No, you see..." he began, but Prenderville was shaking his head vigorously from side to side, and the message was clear. Don't cross this man, and especially don't tell him he's wrong.

"I have had a little parley with our friend here, and he understands that this is not to happen again." He turned to Prenderville, and prodded him firmly in the chest with a huge meaty finger. "Or I'll get to hear about it, and we'll be back. You foller?"

"Yes sir, Mister Sullivan, I understand perfectly," Prenderville gibbered, sweat bursting from his brow.

"Good." Sullivan gave a little nod, and the bruiser let go of Prenderville's collar, letting the theatre manager flop down, his heels clacking onto the floor. It was only at this moment that we realised that he had actually been suspended in mid-air by the creature's massive paw.

"Well, then I shall bid you all good night, gentlemen and ladies. And I look forward to a long and fruitful partnership. Boys?"

Big Tim slapped his hat onto his great head, and he and his bodyguards were gone. The room seemed lighter again, and Prenderville slumped onto the arm of a chair and loosened his tie.

"Whew! That's that, then," he gasped. "No more shadow play."

"What?" Charlie cried indignantly. "Surely you don't mean to pay any attention to *that...?*"

"*That*," Prenderville cut in, "is the most powerful man in the whole of New York City. You can cross him if you like, but not in my theatre. Perhaps you'd like to find another engagement?"

"No, no," Alf said, stepping between them. "That will not be necessary. The boxcar has been rerouted, and we can play our main show tomorrow, all being well."

And that was the end of the *Harlequinade in Black and White*.

———

I was gleeful at this setback for my rival, but if I thought I would start seeing more of Tilly again I was to be sadly disappointed.

Charlie tumbled into one of his periodical black depressions, as usual the tragic hero of his own melodramatic life story, and Tilly devoted herself to bringing him out of it. She was falling for it, in other words, but I could hardly say that, could I?

So every night after we finished work at the Empress the two of them would ensconce themselves in a corner of the bar, he sipping port and moaning about how the world was against him, she nursing gin and sympathising.

It was hard to watch, but what could I do about it? Any hint that I might be about to tell him to snap out of it was met with a glare from both of them, and in any case I was the one who hadn't believed in him, wasn't I? Who hadn't supported his genius? I couldn't win.

So I didn't really get the chance to be alone with her – well, as alone as you can be with fifteen of your colleagues knitting, reading and playing cards just a few feet away – until we were all back on the Karno boxcar heading West.

As the train climbed up into the Rocky Mountains I was glued to the window. We rode up richly forested slopes, clinging to the side of gorges, eventually looking down on waterfalls and rapids, until we were up among the snow-capped peaks themselves. The contrast to the hours – the days – we had spent chugging across the prairies could hardly have been more stark, and for a boy from Cambridge, the jewel of the millpond-flat Fens, it was an unending banquet of geographical features.

There was a light rustle of skirts, and Tilly was beside me, having extricated herself from the sewing circle.

"Look," she said, nodding her head towards the far end of the boxcar, to where Charlie was sitting with his knees drawn up to his chest, wallowing in his misery for everyone to see. Not that most were paying him any attention. Tilly, though, was clearly moved.

"He'll get over it," I said.

"Yes," Tilly sighed. "It is a terrible shame, though. He put so much into creating the shadow play, and it was so much *fun*."

"Really?" I said.

"Oh yes. It was the first time I really felt I was *doing* something, you know. I even think I felt a little of what you call the Power, you know?"

"Well," I said, "that's good going, to feel that from behind a sheet."

"Yes, but that's the whole point, don't you see? The audience were laughing – they were laughing, weren't they, I'm not just making it up?"

"Oh yes, they were having a whale of a time," I admitted.

"Exactly, and they were laughing at what I *did*, enjoying my actual performance. It wasn't just about what I look like, for once, or what I am wearing, because they couldn't even see that, I was just a silhouette to them, and it really made them laugh."

"That's right," I agreed. "And you were brilliant."

"Oh? Thank you, Arthur, that's nice of you." She shot me such a radiant smile at this that I was encouraged to lay it on even thicker.

"I always knew you had it in you to be a great actress," I said. "In fact, wonderful though it was, I don't even think it was your best performance."

"Is that so? Well then what, pray tell, was my best performance?"

"I think your turn as Clara the burlesque girl will take some beating."

"Yeeesshh!" she said, glancing furtively around to see if we could be overheard. The card game was reaching a climactic moment, though, with Stan seemingly poised to trounce old George Seaman, for once, and a little crowd was gathered there, leaning over the seat backs to see.

"Has Clara got any friends?" I dared to say.

Tilly sighed, smiled. She put her hand on mine, and was about to say something more, but just then Stan let out a howl and there was an accompanying roar from the crowd of onlookers over at the card game. Stan leapt to his feet and pushed over towards us, a grin on his face as always, but there was anguish there too.

"Every time I call his bluff he turns out to have an even better hand than the one I thought he was only pretending to have!" he cried.

"Next time," I said.

"Next week, more like. He's completely cleaned me out!"

George Seaman was still shovelling the pot towards his pile, a predator's grin on his chops.

I turned to Tilly, but she had slipped away during the commotion. At the far end of the carriage I spotted her, nestling in alongside Chaplin, trying once again to cheer him out of his gloom. How could she be buying his performance? It seemed so transparent to me.

I gazed blankly now at the scenery, my mind churning with resentment.

I'd had the ammunition, the evidence, to prevent him from making the trip. I could have gone to Karno and exposed the dirty tricks Charlie and his brother had played to wangle him that top spot. The heckler that they had paid to disrupt my performance, the footballer that they had paid to break my leg. He knew I could have finished him.

And yet here he was, lording it over me as though I had no hold over him whatsoever. Wheedling his way into Tilly's affections, knowing my feelings for her. Playing on her ambitions to push herself forward as a performer.

And I didn't like the look he'd given me when he mentioned that replacing *Mumming Birds* with the *Harlequinade* would mean savings. I hold your future in the palm of my hands, that is what that look said to me.

Where was the gratitude? For the second chance I had given him?

Where was the deference to my feelings that was my due, for not shopping him to the Guv'nor and ending his career?

I needed to have a word...

13
A LITTLE IDEA
OF MY OWN

OUR next destination – Butte, Montana – was like nowhere we had been so far. We had sampled America's cities, with their tall buildings, their mighty bridges and their elevated railways, and enjoyed the hustle and bustle and energy of those places. We had visited smaller towns, slower-paced, more genteel, and we had nipped across into Canada, where our audience had seemed so predominantly English that it had been much like playing Nottingham, say, or Bristol.

Butte was the largest city for a hundred miles in any direction, one of the largest cities west of the Mississippi, and it had a reputation as a place where anything goes. It nestled in a natural bowl high up in the Rockies, on what the locals styled 'The Richest Hill on Earth'. Originally it had been a prospectors' camp, for miners trying to winkle silver and gold from the hard rock, but then Mr Edison had jump-started the age of electricity, and suddenly what the world needed more than anything else was copper, for making wire. And there was copper in them thar hills.

And if it was boom time for copper, and boom time for Butte, then it sure as hell fire was boom time for vaudeville. There was the Majestic, where we were to spend the week, then there was the Orpheum, the Lyric, the Princess and the Empire, not to mention the Broadway, 'the largest auditorium between St Paul and Spokane', which prided itself on bringing attractions from New York all the way to the Rocky Mountains.

Each of the different nationalities of miners that had pitched up there from all corners of the globe was catered for by its own brewery, making beer the particular way its drinkers liked it, and just about the only respite from the choking smoke constantly spewing from the smelting works' chimney stacks was wandering into the cloying yeasty orbit of a mash tun. Nonetheless, everyone was so determinedly having a rambunctious good time *all* the time, hard rock miners from around the world, living hard, playing hard, that it was an exhilarating place to be.

We would walk along the main strip late at night, past the end of Venus Alley, the red light district, where hundreds of girls were waiting in their cribs to relieve cowboys and miners alike of their spare dollars, and every saloon would have light and noise spilling out onto the street. An Irish fiddle playing on one side, a concertina or even a balalaika on the other, and the signs reading 'Please spit into the spittoons provided' were in sixteen different languages.

Walk along that same strip at lunchtime, however, and it was like a ghost town. Half the population were sleeping off the night before, the other half were underground earning the money to pay for it. The saloons were open, though, and would offer a free-lunch counter to tempt in what passing trade there was at that time of day. This was mostly, in truth, the artistes from the many shows.

We took to spending the time before our three-a-day at Mack and Carey's Orpheum bar, where for a nickel you could get a glass of beer and your pick of a delicatessen counter. There we'd find pigs' knuckles, sliced ham, potato salad, sardines, macaroni cheese, all kinds of sliced sausages, liverwurst, salami and hot-dogs. On our wages, the place was a Godsend.

One lunchtime that week I barrelled in there with Freddie, Mike and Stan, eager to fuel up for the day, and saw that Charlie was in there on his own, sitting in a corner. Tilly and the girls were nowhere to be seen, and I spied my chance.

So, once I'd piled my plate up high with goodies, I headed over to join him. As I crossed the floor the barman sang out: "Hey! Where the hell are you going with that load – the Klondike?"

I paused guiltily mid-step, my food mountain teetering in my hands, but he waved me on. Michael O'Neill, his name was, and he had come over from County Clare with more than enough funny stories to take to the boards if he'd a mind to do it.

Anyway, I sat myself down opposite Charlie and began to chomp on a Cornish pastie. He looked up from his book for a moment, then down again.

After a mouthful or two I began.

"Charlie?" I said. He looked up again. "I wanted to ask you for a favour."

"A favour?"

"Yes. In return for the considerable favour that I did you, you will remember, when I permitted you to continue your career and come along on this trip."

Charlie slowly turned down the corner of the page he was reading, closed the book, and placed it on the table in front of him.

"When you *permitted* that," he said, savouring the word.

"That's right. I could have gone to Karno, you know, and told him what you and Syd got up to, around the time of that contest we had over *The Football Match*."

"You could have," he acknowledged. He was not at all flustered by this conversation. In fact, if anything, he was irritatingly serene, as if he had expected this to happen sooner or later. I, on the other hand, was getting more and more wound up.

"But I didn't do that, did I, and so..."

"Why didn't you?"

"Why didn't I?"

"Why didn't you go to Karno? I would have."

"That doesn't matter..."

"Then you might have been the number one, instead of me."

"I would have. I *should* have. Karno would have chosen me, if it hadn't been for the fact that you paid a footballer to break my damn'd leg!"

"Well. I suppose we'll never know that, will we?"

"Oh, I know it."

Charlie sat back in his chair and regarded me curiously. "What is this 'favour' to which you believe you are entitled?"

"I want you to stop... monopolising Tilly, that's what I want!"

"*Monopolising*," he smirked.

"Yes, monopolising her."

"Do we know what the young lady in question has to say on the matter?"

"Leave her out of this." He laughed, and even I realised it was a ridiculous thing to say, but I was steaming.

"Well, it occurs to me that she might have her own thoughts, regardless of anything we might agree on between ourselves. She is a bright girl, and very talented. Perhaps she would like to see that talent expressed, developed, enjoyed? Perhaps she sees that the best way to achieve this is to consort – for want of a better word – with the number one of a company, rather than a mere supporting artiste such as yourself."

"All it takes is one wire to the Guv'nor," I snarled, pointing a finger in his face.

"Oh, d'you know what? I think that ship has sailed, my friend!" Charlie smiled.

"That's what you think, is it?"

"Yes, it is, I'm sorry. I can't imagine Karno bothering himself with a parochial little matter such as that. So far away, and so unimportant? Perhaps when we were right on his doorstep, and it wasn't something that happened well over a year ago, he might have felt strongly enough to intervene, but now? I'm not too concerned. So wire away if you feel you must."

"Remember what happened last time you stepped on my toes," I said, menacing, leaning closer across the table. Charlie smiled again, but I saw in his eyes that he did remember.

We'd been in Paris, playing the Folies Bergère. He had found Tilly, when I'd been looking for her for a year or more, but he hadn't said anything to me, and had begun courting her behind my back.

I'd confronted him in a crowded restaurant, and swung a furious haymaker at his head. He dropped to all fours and scuttled between my legs, popping up behind me. I swung again, and he did the same dodge, this time kicking me unceremoniously up the backside. Enraged by the hoots of laughter from the other patrons I tried to grab him in a bear hug, pinning him from behind. He ran up the white shirt front of a fat gentleman with a walrus moustache – yes, ran up him – and twisted out of my grasp. Then he planted a kiss on the end of my nose and sprang to freedom.

We'd both been tipped out onto the street then by burly waiters, and had continued our dispute back at our lodgings, where our fight had been refereed by our Karno colleague Ernie Stone, an ex-professional pugilist, and Maurice Chevalier, and we had gone hard at one another. By the time they'd called "Enough!" there was blood on the walls, blood on the ceiling, Chaplin's eyes were swollen shut and his perfect white teeth were rattling loose in his jaw. I had been awoken the next morning by the screaming from a *première danseuse* at the Folies who'd thought Charlie was dead...

Abruptly our conversation was over, because Tilly herself came in, followed by the panting Frank Melroyd.

"Hello, you boys," she said. "We've just been sight-seeing, working up a bit of an appetite for our lunch. We've seen the headframe of a copper mine called the Never Sweat, and the chimneys of the smelting works. It's been terribly romantic."

Frank laughed dutifully, and the pair of them went to inspect the nickel buffet. I stood up and glared back at Charlie, as if to say: "Remember what I said!" even though the discussion hadn't been a tremendous success. He didn't seem chastened at all. He just looked smug.

I brooded on the misfire of my attempt to keep him in line for the next couple of days. It was eating away at me that he was still persisting in making a play for Tilly, and if our rivalry had been put to one side for a time it was now very much back centre stage.

I found myself determined to try and get back at him, take him down a peg. Or even two pegs, two pegs would be good. I knew, of course, that the best way to really get under his skin was to outshine him, steal his limelight. But how was this to be achieved?

A solution presented itself quite out of the blue towards the end of that week. I was in Mack and Carey's bar after the evening's shows, a much busier place than at lunchtime, with a line of miners at the bar taking it in turns to hawk black phlegm into the silver spittoons, and a stocky, muscle-bound fellow with curly hair approached me.

"Excuse me," the man said with a familiar hint of an Eastern European accent. "But you are the English Magician, no? The Prestidigitateur?"

"That's right," I said. "Did you enjoy the show, Mr Houdini?"

"Ah so," the great man nodded. "I was not sure you would remember our brief conversation in New York."

"Indeed," I said, pumping his hand enthusiastically. "It is a great pleasure to meet you again, sir. My name is Dandoe, Arthur Dandoe."

"Pleasure is mine," Houdini said. "I feel I must own up to something. You see, I came to your theatre this evening, after my own performance was completed."

"That's right," I said. "You are at the Broadway, are you not? The large theatre at the far end of the strip?" Houdini nodded in acknowledgment of this, and continued.

"I came principally because I heard that your turn featured a performance by a magician."

"Oh, I am really just an actor pretending to be a magician," I said.

"All magicians are just actors pretending to be magicians," Houdini replied. "Or do you believe that magic is real?"

"Um…"

"There are many so-called magicians on the circuits and I make it my business to see as many as I can, and if possible to deter the unworthy from queering the pitch for the rest of us. There is a society, now, based in New York, and we wish to make it impossible for a magician to perform unless he is a member. In this way we hope to maintain quality and standards."

"We?" I asked.

"The brethren, the brotherhood of, if you like, prestidigitators." Here he gave a little nod, acknowledging the title my character insisted upon in the act.

"I see," I said, wondering where this was leading.

"Naturally I realised early on that you were not a true magician, but merely a comical stooge."

"Well, I'm a little bit more than that..." I started, but he waved my objection away.

"Nonetheless, it sticks in my throat to see a brother conjuror, even a fake one, fall foul of a drunken imbecile such as the tumbling dolt in your show."

"That's Charlie Chaplin, of course, you remember him?"

Houdini grimaced, and I could see that he remembered our number one very well. Suddenly I recalled something I had read not long before, and I asked: "Hey? How the hell did you escape from the belly of a beached whale, for God's sake?"

Houdini tapped the side of his nose. "It's all about preparation, my friend."

"Really?"

"Oh yes. Where do you think the suggestion really came from? Eh?"

Houdini had claimed he could escape from any location suggested by a member of the public, but I saw what he was getting at. "You?"

He shrugged. "Who do you think beached the whale in the first place?"

I looked at him. Surely that was a joke... wasn't it? But he was giving nothing away.

"Anyway," he went on, "as I was saying. Perhaps I have an uncommon perspective, but I did not like to see the drunken spectator get the better of the magician, I did not like that at all, and I wondered if something could perhaps be done. Within the act, I mean. And for the sake of the act. A twist no humourist of your standing could resist."

"A twist?"

"Well, your tricks are all, of course, intended to go disastrously wrong, but what if one, just one of them, were to suddenly... astound?! Wouldn't that create a moment? Wouldn't that get people talking? Would that not be... magic?"

"I guess it would at that."

"And would it not also confound that wretched persecutor of yours?"

I kept a straight face, but I was grinning inside. "Did you not find Chaplin funny, Mr Houdini?"

"Funny? Pah! I wanted to climb up onto the stage und shove him back in his box with my bare hands!"

To my great amusement Houdini seemed to have developed quite a grudge against Charlie, and did not, apparently, believe the little man was a genius. As you can imagine we hit it off handsomely.

Within a short while he was proposing effects, tricks, things he could teach me, things that it would take time and dedication to perfect of course, but things that would most definitely upstage our number one comic, and no mistake.

"In the end, you know, if you think you could pull it off, the best thing would be to work on the dove pan segment, do you agree?"

The Prestidigitateur would proudly claim that he could produce a dove from thin air. With great pomp and moment he would produce a silver platter with a matching lid, which he would dramatically whisk away to reveal... a small cloud of white feathers, and no bird. He would then rampage around searching for the escaped creature, while the Swell (Charlie) pelted him with fruit and other detritus. It was very much the climax of the Magician's humiliation, and his lovely assistant (Tilly, of course) would then usher him into the wings.

"What if...?" Houdini began.

And as he explained what he had in mind, I felt a huge smile cracking my drunken chops.

14
HOG WILD

AFTER Butte we hopped around the North West corner of the United States. Mercifully the boxcar journeys there were shorter and not so gruelling. Spokane we visited next, then Seattle, Mr Considine's home town, with Vancouver, Tacoma and Portland to come before heading down South towards California.

While we were in Seattle my friend Mr Jobson, Considine's butler, presented himself backstage at the Majestic. His boss had expressed a desire for a chat with some of our company, and would I like to visit him for morning coffee the very next day?

Alf Reeves was particularly keen that I should oblige, as he was busily angling for further Sullivan and Considine dates once this tour was finished. So I talked Stan into coming along, and the two of us strolled up a luxurious curving driveway towards a pretty fancy-looking double-fronted mansion the following morning.

Jobson relieved us of our coats and hats, and showed us into a library, where John W. Considine, theatrical entrepreneur, was sitting by a fireplace chomping a cigar and reading a hefty-looking leather-bound tome. Actually, I wasn't sure that he was reading it, because as he put it onto a side table it looked like it was upside down, but anyway.

"Hey fellas, great to see ya!" Considine said, standing and shaking us warmly by the hand. "Tell me, how are you enjoying your first tour of the Sullivan and Considine circuit?"

"Very much, Mr Considine," I said.

"Grand, that's grand. It's going to be the first entirely trans-continental vaudeville circuit, you know, West Coast to East Coast, once Sullivan lines us up some theatres in New York, which he assures me he will most certainly do. The railroad is a marvellous thing, a marvellous thing," Considine barrelled on. "Why Mr Sullivan himself was able to visit me just this last week."

"Really?" I said.

"Yes, and he told me the darn'dest thing. I asked him about your show, see, and how did he like it, and he said there was a white sheet hanging in front of the whole thing."

"Ah, yes," Stan said. "He saw our shadow play."

"But I was under the impression that I had booked the world-famous *Mumming Birds*," Considine said, and there was an angry edge to his voice all of a sudden.

"Well, ah, yes," said Stan, a little flustered. Clearly he had picked up on the tone too. "The thing is, you see, our boxcar, with all our set and costumes in it, went missing from Winnipeg, and so we were obliged to improvise something quickly, d'you see, to fill in?"

"Your boxcar went missing?"

"Not missing exactly, it just was not uncoupled at Winnipeg, so..."

"And who was responsible for that?" Considine growled.

"I'm sure it was just a mistake at the switching yard, sir," I said.

"Mistake my corn-fed backside!" Considine raged. "You know who's behind this, don't you?"

I had been wondering whether Charlie might have been behind it, actually, so as to have an excuse to put on his shadow effort, but Mr Jobson, returning with a coffee pot and cups, was already nodding in a long-suffering fashion.

"It's that king Greek!" Considine exploded.

"I beg your pardon?" I said.

"Winnipeg is his home town, he's always hated that I have a theatre there too, he'll stop at nothing to close me down. Sabotaging my headline act! The nerve of the man!"

"I'm sorry," I said. "But what man? Who are you talking about?"

"Why Pantages, of course! Pantages! Tell them!" he pulled out a handkerchief and waved it at his butler, who took up the explanation.

"Mr Alexander Pantages is a rival of Mr Considine's. He too has a circuit of vaudeville theatres, in many cases in the same towns, even the same main streets."

"King Greek, he calls himself! King Greek! Fancies he's going to run me out of business with his low-down tricks. Well he doesn't want to go up against me, let me tell you! A fella came for me once with a gun, wearing a bullet-proof vest he'd made himself by sewing silver dollars all over it. Know what happened to *that* crazy bastard?"

Stan and I gulped, and shook our heads.

"I took his gun and shot him in the neck, that's what happened!" he shouted, mopping at his forehead with his handkerchief.

Jobson eased between us. "Gentlemen? Mr Considine is becoming a little overwrought – perhaps another time...?"

Stan and I nodded gratefully, and got the hell out of there pronto.

On the way back to the Majestic, we talked about how affable and friendly the man seemed at first, but how tightly wound he became when we were discussing his rivalry with Pantages,

Funny – it reminded me of something.

———

In the green room we found Charlie deep in conversation with one of the other artistes. Ralph Lohse was one of a gymnastic double act, Lohse and Sterling, which had joined the bill in Spokane and now seemed likely to be travelling with us for the foreseeable. They were billed as 'European Gymnasts', even though both of them were blonde and well-built Texan farm boys. Charlie and Lohse had become friendly, and I noticed that both seemed to be recovering from recent exertions. They were flushed, their hair was damp, and they had towels casually slung around their shoulders.

"What ho," I said. "What have you two lads been up to, eh?"

"Sparring," Lohse said, genially.

"Really?" I said. It was a strange mental picture, as Lohse must have stood almost half as tall again as Charlie.

"Charlie wanted to learn, and I used to box when I was a boy. Great way to keep limber, eh Charlie?" Lohse gave Chaplin a cheerful clap on the shoulder, which almost knocked him over.

"Did he stand on a chair?" Stan said, deadpan, and I saw Mike Asher trying not to laugh.

"Ha ha ha!" Lohse laughed. "He got some good shots away, actually. I'll make a fighter of him yet!"

The big Texan left in search of some running water to wash himself down. I turned to Charlie, and saw that he was looking at me with a challenging half-smirk on his chops.

Very well, I thought. You have your plan, and I have mine.

In the mornings I had been pursuing my project, which was to locate a pet shop with a decent stock of white doves. This was not as easy as it sounds, as there were a number of other – I say 'other', I mean 'actual' – magicians plying their trade in the city, and several times I got into rather heated arguments, right there on the sidewalk, with curly-moustachioed fellows demanding to see some credentials, perhaps even a membership card for Houdini's special society.

Nonetheless I was able to secure a basket with half a dozen specimens cooing away merrily inside, and I managed to sneak them up to the roof of the hotel. There I made my first stumbling attempts to perfect the illusion that Harry Houdini had suggested would steal the show from under the over-rouged nose of the celebrated Drunken Swell. The great man's instructions were plain enough, including the techniques (which I had to swear not to give away) for rendering the birds docile enough to manhandle. Even so, whenever I reached the final step, the grand finale of the illusion, my reluctant co-star would take off like a (white) bat out of hell itself, streaking away over Puget Sound never to be seen again.

Still, if at first you don't succeed, as the old saying goes, then buy more doves.

──────

Charlie and Ralph Lohse became constant companions, keeping up a regimen of sparring every morning, lunching together, and then walking over to the theatre. Then when we travelled down to Portland, Oregon, the big Texan was invited to ride in our boxcar. What Sterling, his trapeze partner, must have made of it all we could only imagine. As I watched the two of them chatting away together I couldn't decide whether Charlie was using Lohse as a fighting coach or a bodyguard. Or both.

Suddenly they let out a great cheer, and jumped to their feet to press their noses to the window, jabbering excitedly and pointing. I looked out of the window too, but struggled to spot anything that would have justified such a reaction – maybe a circus, or perhaps a flying elephant.

Freddie slipped along the aisle and joined me, leaning in conspiratorially. "Hogs!" he whispered.

"What?"

"Hogs! That's what they're talking about, Charlie and the Texan feller. I've been earwigging, and that's all they've been going on about since we left Seattle."

"Shut up!"

"I promise you. His family are farmers, the Texan, and he reckons that he has his grandfather's secret method for making sausages. The two of them are going to go into business together. They are going to buy two thousand acres of Arkansas and become hog farmers!"

Well, as you can imagine, this was startling news. The idea of Charlie giving up the business of show, which had been his life ever since he was three (if you believe his story about entertaining the troops at Aldershot with a little song and dance when his mother became too ill to perform) was pretty far-fetched, but to give it up to raise hogs? It beggared belief.

I realised that I must have really put the wind up him, if he was prepared to carry on this lengthy charade just to keep the big blond lad close at hand.

Hogs!

I was at the theatre, the Portland Grand, later that same week going through the daily business of preparing for the day's shows, curling the Prestidigitateur's fancy moustache, wondering where Tilly had got to. She wasn't out with Chaplin, at least I knew that, because he was studiously applying his drunk red nose make up just a few feet away.

I sauntered nonchalantly into the corridor on the off chance that I could get a squint into the girls' dressing room – just to see if she had arrived without my noticing. I heard footsteps on the stone staircase, and Tilly appeared round the corner, followed closely by Frank Melroyd. He was flushed, and looking pretty pleased with himself. She was white as a sheet.

"Tilly?" I said. "Whatever's the matter? Are you...?"

She gave a tiny shake of her head, and her eyes flashed "Not now." Then she disappeared into the girls' room, closing the door behind her.

Frank watched her go, then squeezed past me into our dressing room, raising an eyebrow with a provocatively smug smirk as he did so. Then he began to whistle.

Well, as I'm sure you can imagine, this eloquent little pantomime conjured all sorts of unwelcome scenarios in my imagination.

The very next moment I had to pursue inquiries was when the two of us stepped into the wings after the Magician segment. Onstage, *Mumming Birds* was still in full flow, and the Inebriated Swell was shaping up to tackle the Terrible Turkey in the Wrestling Match finale.

My lovely assistant was scurrying away from me towards the dressing rooms when I grabbed her by the elbow.

"Tilly?" I hissed. "What on earth happened between you and Melroyd?"

"Nothing," she said, and tried to move away, but I held her there.

"Don't give me that," I said. "I saw how you looked when you arrived."

"We went for a walk, that's all."

"That's all?"

"And a cup of tea."

"And?"

"And nothing."

"Has he hurt you?" I said. "Because if he has, so help me I'll..."

"No, no, nothing like that, he's not like that."

I had a quick flash, then, of Melroyd looking down at me as I dangled off the back of the boxcar. "Are you sure?" I said.

"Just... let me go," she said.

"Tell me what happened to make you look so shocked," I insisted.

"Oh!" She gave an exasperated glance to the stage, where *Mumming Birds* was reaching its climax. "If you must know, he proposed, didn't he?"

"He proposed?!"

"Yes, he proposed. Now, you're not to tell *anyone* I told you, do you understand?"

"Ha! Maybe it's not such a grand idea to string several gentleman friends along all at once, eh?"

"Thanks Arthur, that's very helpful!" she hissed.

"What did you say to him?"

"Well, I'm thinking about it, aren't I, obviously? Taking some time to think about it. He took me completely by surprise. I mean, we are friends, that's what I thought, but then I am friends with all you boys, aren't I, it doesn't mean... Oh, I don't know!"

I was stunned by this revelation, and Tilly took advantage of my bewilderment to yank her arm free from my grasp and scuttle away down the stairs, while I sat down heavily on a prop box, vigorously scratching my scalp.

The Karnos finished to a good solid round. I could have gone on and taken the curtain call with them, but I didn't, and then my colleagues began bustling past me on their way to the dressing rooms. I glanced up at them as Frank Melroyd went past, with a triumphant little grin on his fat face.

Frank Melroyd? Tilly would never seriously consider tying the knot with a dullard like *Frank Melroyd*.

Would she?

15
LET ME CALL YOU SWEETHEART

I stewed on this new development for the next few days. Well, there was nobody I could talk to about it, since Tilly had told me not to tell anyone, and she herself remained elusive, avoiding another conversation on the matter.

At the weekend we embarked for one of the longest boxcar hauls of the whole tour, a gruelling eighteen hours down to Sacramento, with a 6am start. Plenty of time to think.

Tilly was soon deep in conversation with Amy, Muriel and Emily, married women all, of course. I figured she hadn't announced that she was contemplating marrying herself, or else that corner would have been a whole lot noisier, and I didn't spot a single furtive sidelong glance at Mr Melroyd either, so I didn't think she had sworn them to secrecy.

Charlie had his unofficial bodyguard beside him, and the two of them were already on the lookout for hog farms. The card game was not yet under way, and most of the other lads were dozing, trying to catch up on lost kip.

Frank was snoozing, his hands clasped over his paunch, and

he didn't look to me like a man whose hopes had been dashed.

What to do? Should I be making a counter proposal? Was that what Tilly wanted? Was that what *I* wanted? What would that mean to my ambitions? I couldn't be sure, and turned it over and over in my mind as we trundled down through Oregon.

It was a good couple of hours before Tilly got up to stretch her legs, and I followed her out onto the observation platform. She was lost in thought, the wind tossing her blonde curls this way and that, the chill bringing a lovely pinkness to her soft cheeks. I stood and watched her for a long moment before she realised I was there.

"Oh, Arthur, it's you," she said with a little start. I leaned on the railing next to her.

"That was a good long talk you were having with the girls," I said.

"Well, it's a long trip, this one, isn't it, so I had to kill off some of it somehow."

"What were you discussing?"

"Oh, they were just telling me about married life, the practical things. Usually they don't talk about that when I'm with them. In fact if they start up with their moaning it's usually me who changes the subject. But today I was interested."

"What were they saying, then?"

She laughed. "You would have expired from boredom hours ago."

"No, tell me, I want to hear."

"Well, George and Emily have been working as a couple for Karno for donkey's years, you know? Touring fifty-two weeks a year, no home, no family, but they love it, it's the life for them. I think Muriel Palmer rather fancies giving it all up sooner or later and having children, but Fred thinks George is his hero just at the moment and wants to be like him, so there's a storm a-brewing there. Amy and Alf, well, they've got it made, haven't they? As long as he is working, she is working."

"Tilly? You're not actually thinking about accepting Frank's offer, are you?"

"Frank is a gentleman, and he has done me a great honour."

"Oh my God, you *are* thinking about it, aren't you? What happened to not being tied down? What happened to flying free?"

"It's a serious proposition, don't you think it deserves serious consideration?"

"I suppose so, but..."

"Well, that is what I am doing."

"Tilly, listen, there's something I want to ask you..."

She closed her eyes, put a hand up to stop me. "No, Arthur, don't."

"You don't know what I'm going to say."

"Yes, yes I do, and I don't want you to say it."

"Well... Why not?"

"Because I couldn't accept you, could I? I'd always be thinking you had only asked me to keep me from marrying Frank, and that I'd trapped you, put you on the spot. And you'd always be wondering whether your career was being held back because you were part of a pair."

"No, I wouldn't."

"Yes, you would. Do you think George Seaman is ever going to be a number one?"

"No, but he's not funny enough, it's nothing to do with..."

"Emily hanging round his neck like an albatross."

"Tilly..."

"Please, Arthur, don't. Just don't. And if you don't mind, I'd like to be alone for a little while."

"But..."

"Please, Arthur."

There was nothing to do but traipse back through the props to the seating compartment and my thoughts.

Melroyd was still asleep, and I watched him bitterly. I should have seen it before, of course. I wondered briefly whether telling him about Tilly's, shall we say, unconventional morality might put a spanner in the works, but I decided that wouldn't put him off. He was smitten, smitten to the point of obsession.

I remembered walking with Tilly in Central Park, thinking I had spotted Frank before he disappeared behind a fountain. Was he following us? Watching us? I remembered now Frank grabbing that heavy oar from Stan during the *Wow Wows* and swinging it furiously at my head. Maybe that wasn't a new bit of business, maybe it was jealousy.

Then in Chicago he had seen a burlesque girl leaving my room in my coat, and then later Tilly handing me my coat back, and had put two and two together. And it was shortly after *that* that his 'clumsiness' had almost catapulted me off the back of the boxcar. At high speed, and in the middle of a frozen wilderness, probably teeming with bears and wolves and what have you. Good God, I suddenly thought with a chill creeping into my bones. That could have been the end of me, and was that really an accident? Or had he really tried to shove me off the back of the boxcar?

Surely not, I thought, that would be craziness. But then, during the *Harlequinade*, he'd walloped Charlie with a truncheon, hadn't he? Charlie was the one spending all his time with Tilly then, swooning over her, pitching woo as Harlequin to her Columbine, with Tilly lapping that stuff up. God knows I'd felt like thumping Charlie then myself. Perhaps that wasn't an accident either.

It hit me like a thunderclap. The fellow was off his rocker!

He had to be stopped.

And the more I thought about it, the more I realised there was only one man who could help me.

━━━━━

At various times during the journey we would make our way, one or two at a time, through to the Southern Pacific California Express that was hauling us southwards in order to take advantage of the restaurant car.

Stan and Freddie got peckish early and beckoned me to join them, but I had other ideas and bided my time. Eventually I saw Ralph Lohse nudge Charlie and suggest that it was time to eat, and he agreed. I got to my feet as well, and followed them, falling in behind Charlie's big Texan bodyguard. As we reached the restaurant car I tapped him on the shoulder.

"I say, Ralph?" I said. He turned and loomed over me. "I think I heard your fellow trapeze boy, Sterling, say he wanted a quick word with you?"

"Oh?" he said. "Right," and he squeezed past me and lumbered back the way we had come.

I found Charlie had already taken a seat at one of the tables by a picture window, and was gazing out at a wide river we were riding alongside, the track raised up above the bank on a sort of trestle viaduct. I slipped smartly in opposite him.

"Charlie," I said.

He jumped so violently I thought he was going to fall off his chair. His expressive features registered his shock, and his inward cursing at having allowed himself to be taken by surprise, followed by resignation, and a grim determination to give a good account of himself. I had to suppress a snigger – as if I would start a fist fight in a restaurant car, really.

"Arthur," he said, managing to collect himself. "Where's...?"

"He'll be along in a minute," I said, and Charlie visibly relaxed. "I told him there were hogs in one of the other carriages."

Charlie absorbed that. "So, are you joining us for luncheon?" he said.

"Thank you, no," I said. "I just wanted to let you know something, something you should be aware of, as the number one."

He frowned. "And what is that?"

"You remember when Frank Melroyd gave you that whack on the head?"

"Yes. What of it?"

"An accident, you think?"

"Of course. It was only our second performance of the *Harlequinade*, naturally there were one or two bumps we would have ironed out, given a fair chance. What about it?"

I decided to cut right to it. "He has proposed to Tilly."

"What?!"

"Frank Melroyd has proposed marriage to Tilly."

Charlie gaped at me in open astonishment. "What? But... I had no idea they were..."

"They're not."

"They're not?"

"No."

"But he still...?"

"Between you and me, I think he might be crackers."

Charlie's fingers crept up to the bump that was still visible on the side of his head, and he nodded thoughtfully.

"What has she said, do you know?"

"She is considering. I guess she doesn't want to hurt his feelings, but sooner or later the situation will need to be resolved, and there will likely be consequences to company morale, one way or another. So I thought you should know what was happening, so that you are prepared. As the number one."

"Thanks. Thanks, Arthur," Charlie murmured, frowning. "Decent of you."

Just then Lohse appeared. "Say," he said. "What gives? Sterling didn't want to speak to me. He was fast asleep."

"My mistake," I said. "I'll leave you two to it."

I made my way back to the boxcar with a little bit of a spring in my step for the first time in days. Maybe the two of them would kill each other off and save me the bother.

And I didn't have too long to wait. The next morning when we assembled for the band call at the Empress in Sacramento Alf Reeves gathered us together for a little announcement.

"Some of you may have noticed," he began, "that Frank Melroyd is not with us today. He has left the company to pursue opportunities elsewhere, and left town this morning heading for Salt Lake and then the East. He wanted me to pass on his very best wishes to you all, and apologise on his behalf that he was not able to say his goodbyes. This means some reorganisation, of course, to cover for him, so let me see..."

He got on with moving people around, reallocating parts and bits of business, but I wasn't really listening. I was watching Tilly, who was staring at Alf with a look of sand-bagged astonishment, and Charlie, who was looking serious, but barely managing to hide a satisfied half-smile.

That was bloody quick work, I thought.

Relieved though I undoubtedly was at the departure of the problematical Melroyd, the speed and efficiency of his dispatch did make me acutely aware that Charlie was not only ruthlessly wielding his power as the number one, but also making very clear his own ambitions where Tilly was concerned.

Time, I reckoned, to press on with my scheme to put him in his place. Time to let him know that *I* would not be so easy to shove aside.

To that end, I spent every spare minute that week practising with a trio of doves that I managed to acquire from a pet store, and by the time we moved on to San Francisco, with my dove basket cunningly concealed in the boxcar, I felt I was ready for Mr Houdini's trick to make its debut.

16
THE SIGH OF A DOVE

SAN Francisco. Gateway to the Orient. It was only five years after the Great Earthquake had destroyed more than three quarters of the city, and yet the reconstruction had been so energetic that, apart from a couple of alarming cracks in the roads here and there, you would hardly know anything had happened.

In point of fact the locals referred to the catastrophe as 'The Great Fire', as far more damage was done by flames than by the tremors. The city burned for four days as the quake ruptured gas pipes all over the place, and the rumour was that many conflagrations had been started on purpose by people who found that their property insurance did not cover earthquake damage but did cover fire. No one you spoke to would admit to having done this, but all reckoned they knew someone who had.

We were at the Empress Theatre, a new building (of course) recently opened by one Sid Grauman and his father. The big sign out front proclaimed it was the city's first 'Completely Fireproof Theatre'. When I remarked on this to Grauman on our arrival, he was matter-of-fact about it all. "We lost the Unique and the Lyceum in the disaster, but we set up business again right away

154

in a big tent, using the pews from a collapsed church for the audience to sit on, and the sign we had then said: 'Nothing But Canvas to Fall on Your Head if There is a Shake'".

He was a character, Sid Grauman, a little clown-haired livewire. He and his father had made their pile in Dawson City during the Klondike Gold Rush, not actually striking gold themselves but providing entertainment for those who did. Now they were riding the vaudeville wave, with two other new theatres in San Francisco – the Imperial and the New National – and further interests in San Jose and Los Angeles.

"So which one of you guys is Fred Karno? That's what I want to know. Where's the star?"

Charlie explained that Mr Karno was back in London, at his base, the Fun Factory. Grauman frowned.

"In London, you say? So why was I told to put his name on the poster? Who wants to know who the producer in London is? People want to know the name of the star."

"We've got Fred Karno Junior with us," I said, pushing Freddie forwards. "The great man's son."

"A cowboy act?" Grauman said, peering at the hat Freddie had been given by Considine.

"*I* am the star," Charlie said then, stepping forwards and shoving Freddie and me back into the ranks. "Charles Chaplin, at your service."

"Now, you see, that's good to know," Grauman said. "Next time you come let's make sure it's *your* name on the poster."

"Grand idea, Mr Grauman," Charlie beamed.

"Oh, Sid, call me Sid! Mr Grauman's my father!"

Grauman chattered away about the ins and outs of entertainment in a big cosmopolitan city, and then disappeared to keep his finger on the pulse of activities in his other two theatres. One gem

I picked up from his chit-chat, however, was that the reviewers from the newspapers would be attending the second show, and so I decided to keep my powder dry until then.

So after a routine first performance for a warmly appreciative audience, and a couple of quick stiffeners in the saloon next door, I slipped up to the roof where I had stashed my dove basket. I aimed a kick at a local moggy who was taking an unwelcome interest in my co-star, and opened the lid.

Now I don't know if it was the presence of the cat, or the stress of the journey, but the birds were unusually skittish, and whichever one I had been rehearsing with had managed to kick off the little band I had placed around its ankle to mark it out from the other two, the understudies. I wondered momentarily whether to abort the whole thing, but the memory of Chaplin pushing past me saying "*I* am the star!" drove me on.

I grabbed the dove which looked the least stark staring mad, shoved it under my jacket into my armpit, fastened the basket lid, and scampered back down the stairs.

Houdini had assured me that once a dove was in position, as it were, it would be placid, but I seemed to have chosen one with advanced stage fright. As I took my place alongside Tilly in the wings, the creature kept digging its claws into me.

"Do be still, Arthur!" Tilly hissed.

"Sorry," I whispered, trying to calm the wretched bird, but what made matters worse was that the act onstage, standing in front of the tabs as our fake boxes were quietly moved into place and populated waiting for curtain up on the show-within-a-show, was a monologist and whistler. Every time he whistled my hidden companion wanted to join in.

"Whatever is the matter with you?" Tilly hissed again as I wriggled uncomfortably. "You'll disturb the turn!"

I nodded, but my inside pocket would not keep quiet.

"Jack Goldie, the whistling monologue guy," Tilly whispered.

"What?" I whispered back.

"It's Jack Goldie."

"I know it is."

"Oh, I thought you said 'Who?'"

Mercifully, Goldie reached his whistling climax and exited to warm applause. The curtains rose to reveal the set for *A Night at an English Music Hall*, and we were under way. Amy was on first as the Saucy Soubrette, then Bert Williams reciting the *Trail of the Yukon*. Waiting in the wings we could hear the laughs punctuating these items as the Naughty Boy tried to bounce a bun off Bert's head, and the Inebriated Swell tumbled from his box. It was going well, sounded like Chaplin was on good form.

Albert Austin, the Numbers Man, raised his voice over the chaos onstage to announce: "And now Dr Bunco, the celebrated *prestidigitateur par excellence...!*"

"Woooh!" went the crowd.

"... accompanied by the lovely Selina!" and Tilly and I strode out onto the apron.

I saw Tilly giving me a funny look, and I must have been unusually hunched over, trying to keep the damn dove from breaking loose, but I managed to foul up the first couple of tricks in regulation fashion, and the audience were enjoying the scornful derision of the Inebriated Swell, as he sidled up to me and tweaked my moustache.

The joke, of course, was that I was a terrible Magician, but the business was delivered with a pompousness and self-regard that the Swell and the Naughty Boy could prick. We had done it so many times that the act ran on greased rails.

Soon enough we reached the climax of my act-within-the-show-within-the show, and Tilly, my glamorous assistant, presented me with the dove pan. It was like the sort of platter you might be served in a fancy hotel, with a silver lid to keep the food warm.

I showed it to the audience, as I had a hundred times, demonstrating that it was empty, then with a bit of hocus-pocus and abra-cadabra whisked the lid away right in front of the Swell's nose. The trick was a vaudeville standby, of course, and the audience were well aware that a bird, or perhaps a rabbit, some sort of wildlife anyway, was meant to appear, so when a cloud of white feathers blew out of the lid they knew perfectly well that something had gone wrong and laughed heartily.

This was then the cue for the Swell to go into a sneezing jag, on account of the feathers, and his sneezing would blow some of the feathers up so that they would get inside his shirt and he would wriggle and twist around as they tickled him, and the poor Prestidigitateur and the lovely Selina would bow and scrape their way from the stage.

Not tonight, though.

Charlie had unleashed a sneeze or two, and was just beginning to work his comedy wriggle. Tilly was beaming a fixed smile and beginning to back away towards the wings, and Stan, the Naughty Boy, was trying to hit my top hat with an orange from the topmost box.

I stepped forward, centre stage, and in a voice of unusual command I bellowed:

"Wait!"

There was a hush.

Charlie looked startled, and also, in that moment, stone cold sober.

Tilly looked at me as though I had gone mad.

Stan was poised, wide-eyed, another orange clutched in his hand above his head.

I knelt down on the stage, and very slowly, very gently, gathered all the feathers I could into a little pile. No one else onstage with me moved a muscle, not even Chaplin, and after the raucous racket that had gone before the audience could tell that something unexpected was happening, and they hushed.

Carefully I scooped the white feathers into my hands and gazed sorrowfully at them, before clasping my hands together tightly and pulling them into my chest.

"Wait!" I said again. "Look!"

I felt the Power then, that feeling that you have the audience, everyone in the room, hanging on your every move. The Power makes you feel like you have all the time in the world.

I took a moment to glance at Charlie, and he wrinkled his nose contemptuously, clearly having concluded that I was trying to wring some cheap sentiment out of the moment and waiting to shoot me down.

I looked at the audience, opened my hands, and released the dove exactly as Houdini had shown me.

It was a special moment.

The dove, making its stage debut, did not merely sit tamely on my hands, but opened its wings and soared around the auditorium above the heads of the crowd, who gasped in wonder.

And when it finally returned to sit perfectly upon my finger the place erupted in such cheering as I had never heard before.

Best of all, though, was Chaplin's face, a picture of the frankest astonishment. I reached a hand out to the baffled Tilly so she could bow with me and share in the limelight, but she didn't seem to know where to put herself.

As I bowed again and again, Chaplin suddenly came to himself and re-inhabited the Inebriated Swell. He came over to usher me from the stage – and the audience began to boo! They booed Chaplin! This was delicious, more even than I had hoped for!

He turned to look at them, and his bewildered expression clearly said: "But... don't you know who I am? I am the *star*!"

I bowed once more, and then again, and then the dove and I departed the scene to more tumultuous applause.

"Well, thanks for telling me you were going to do that!" Tilly grumbled as we passed in the wings. "I'm only supposed to be your assistant."

"Sorry!" I mouthed with a grin, and gave her a quick peck on the cheek as I slipped by on my way to returning the dove to the basket on the roof.

In the green room afterwards there was a good deal of merry backslapping. To begin with, anyway.

"However did you *do* that?" Stan cried.

"Sorry, old son, sworn to secrecy by the brotherhood of presti-digitateurs," I smirked.

"It was incredible! I knew I was supposed to throw an orange at your hat, but I just wanted to see what was going to happen next! What a surprise!"

A couple of the older seen-it-all hands were affecting indifference, but by and large the whole company was buzzing. After all, when you've played the same show twenty-five times a week for five months straight, as we had, you welcome any little change just to break the monotony. Then Charlie came in. He – surprise-sur-blinking-prise – was furious.

"Dandoe! There you are! Unbelievable! What on earth did you think you were doing?"

"Just a bit of fun," I shrugged.

"Incredible! Incredible lack of professionalism!" he spluttered.

"What do you mean? You try new bits all the time!"

"Not like *that*! Not something that completely changes the nature of the sketch, and without telling anyone beforehand!"

"I thought it would be a nice surprise," I said.

"And if I try something new it is because *I* am the number one, *I* am the prime source of laughter out there, and anything *I* can do to enhance that is for the good of everyone. Maybe I'll try something on the spur of the moment, but always in character, and always little touches, grace notes, not this... premeditated... sabotage! I mean, how long have you been practising that little stunt for, eh?"

I held up my hands. "Sworn to secrecy, I'm afraid."

"It was unbelievably unprofessional!"

"Hah! Unprofessional am I? Well, at least I didn't take a night off to go to the opera while the company manager was out of town. Not to mention persuading another member of the company to sneak off with you, in the hope of stealing her away from me."

A sneer formed on Charlie's face, but before he could retort we heard:

"What's this?"

Everyone had been concentrating on the argument between me and Charlie, but now the company turned as one to see Alf Reeves in the doorway, a look like thunder on his face.

"Alf!" Charlie said, breaking the stunned silence with bluster. "We were just talking about Dandoe's irresponsible behaviour, completely messing up tonight's performance."

"Oh come on," said Stan, sticking up for me. "It was a bit of fun, that's all. And you have to admit it was pretty incredible."

There was a low murmur of agreement, but nobody else wanted to pop their head above the parapet until they saw which way the wind was going to blow.

"It was remarkable," Alf conceded. "But perhaps you should have cleared it with me first."

"Cleared it with *you?* What about *me?* I was on stage with him at the time! I am the number one of this company! He should have cleared it with me!"

"Yes, well, what's done is done, isn't it?" Alf said, trying to pour oil on troubled waters, but Chaplin was practically frothing at the mouth.

"He should be punished! He should be reduced to the ranks! He should be a super, that's all, no more than that!"

Alf stiffened. "Now, look, there's no need for that sort of talk," he said. "I'm sure Arthur won't be pulling that stunt again, now will you, Arthur?"

"Whatever you say, Alf," I said, holding up my hands, reasonableness itself.

And that might have been an end of it if only little Sid Grauman hadn't come in to the room at that moment, practically quivering with excitement.

"Fantastic!" he cried. "Fantastic! I've never seen anything like it! First you make the magician seem like an incompetent boob, and then suddenly boom! He's a genius! So unexpected! Brilliant! I can hardly wait for tomorrow night. I'm telling everyone I know!"

"Well, in point of fact," Alf said, uncomfortably, "... that was by way of being a one-off performance."

Grauman blinked at him. "What do you mean?"

"That's not what we normally do, that's not what's supposed to happen... um... at that point."

"It was a mistake? Why, whatever is supposed to happen? Is the bird meant to be dead? What?"

"No, no, it's just... Arthur here took everyone by surprise, that's all. We didn't actually know he was capable of producing a dove like that."

"Ha ha, that explains the looks on your faces! But he can do it again, surely? You can do it again?"

Alf looked at me, raised his eyebrows. I shrugged, nodded. Grauman beamed happily.

"Perfect, then that is the show for this week. Can't drop an effect like that, you know, especially not if it gets a mention in the *Chronicle* and in *Billboard*, which I am absolutely certain that it will. Excellent!"

The little theatre owner with the clown hair-do buzzed off then about his business, leaving Chaplin glaring at Alf Reeves.

"So we are decided, then?" he said, coolly. "No more doves."

Alf grimaced. "Ah, but, well, you heard Mr Grauman just now, and the Empress is his theatre after all. I think Arthur is going to have to keep doing the dove trick for the rest of this week, and then maybe after that we'll have a think about what's best."

Chaplin seethed, but he was in a corner, and there was really nothing for him to do but grab his hat and coat and storm out, so that's what he did.

Alf stared down at the floor and let out a heavy sigh. Then he looked straight at me and shook his head slowly, before turning to look at Amy, his wife, and Tilly, who were both looking mightily apprehensive.

I felt bad for making Alf's life difficult, and I probably shouldn't have blurted out about Charlie's illicit operatic excursion, but as Freddie, Stan, Mike and the rest of my jovial colleagues swept me off to the next-door saloon bar to toast Dr Bunco's magnificent success, I was in celebratory mood.

After all, what was the worst that could happen?

17
CONTINENTAL DIVIDE

THE next day, between the second and third shows, I was up on the roof of the theatre feeding the doves. It was important to keep them well fed, Houdini had told me, because if you produce a hungry dove it is more likely to fly off and look for something to eat, so you need to "weigh zem down". There was a great view down Market Street and out over the bay from up there, and I was keeping the basket tucked behind a chimney so the beaky little fellows didn't notice the enticing vista of freedom.

I chuckled to myself at the thought of Charlie's impotent fury. Unsurprisingly he wasn't speaking to me at all. Suddenly I heard the metal fire door at the top of the stairs clang, and I was not alone. I hurriedly strapped the basket lid down and peered around the brickwork to see who it was, and it was Tilly, wearing a long coat over the top of her magician's assistant costume.

"So this is where you've been hiding," she said as I emerged. I nipped over and opened the door a crack to check that no one was coming up the stairs behind her. The coast was clear.

"Don't tell Charlie," I said. "If he finds these beauties he'll like as not let them out."

"Yes, that's what he'll do. He's a monster."

I looked at her. She didn't seem her usual bubbly self, somehow. "Is something the matter?" I asked.

"You told Charlie, didn't you? About Frank?"

"About...?"

"You told him that Frank proposed to me, and Charlie told Alf to let him go. It had to be you, I didn't tell anyone else."

She was beginning to get tearful, and I tried to put my arms around her, but she pulled away.

"I would have let him down gently, you know? I could have done that! I didn't need any help from you. And Frank didn't need to lose his job, just because he liked me. How do you think that makes me feel? Did you even think about that?"

"Listen," I said. "He had to go. He was..."

"What?"

"Well... dangerous," I said.

"Nonsense!"

"He was. He tried to brain me with that oar."

"That was a joke."

"He beaned Charlie as well."

"An accident."

"And he shoved me off the back of the boxcar. I could have been killed."

"Rubbish!"

"He did. I went flying over the railing and was hanging on by one hand, and he was looking down at me. And did he try to help me? No, he did not."

"I don't believe it. Frank was kind, and, and, and... thoughtful."

"Frank was a jealous nutcase. I'm glad he's gone. I'd do the same thing again."

Tilly said nothing, just shaking her head in disbelief. I decided to change the subject. "Have you seen the *Chronicle*?" I said. She didn't answer, so I took the folded clipping from my inside pocket and read it out loud:

"'Fred Karno's *A Night in an English Music Hall* kept the audience in continuous roars of laughter. This sketch is almost a whole show itself, and the star turn is undoubtedly Arthur Dandoe as Dr Bunco the Magician, whose finale took your reviewer's breath away.'"

"Congratulations, I'm sure."

"I was just talking to Sid Grauman, the owner. He says they're actually turning people away for the first time since he opened the place."

"Well, that's marvellous, isn't it? And all down to your efforts, too, nothing to do with the rest of us."

"Hey, hang on, I didn't mean..."

"Nothing to do with Charlie, at all."

"Well, he's had his fair share of attention, hasn't he?"

"Maybe he'd have helped you get even more laughs last night if he'd been given fair warning. Did you think of that?"

I was definitely feeling the frost in the air now. "You're taking his side, is that it?"

"Not at all. But perhaps it's time you realised that there aren't sides, that everything isn't a contest between the two of you."

"What's the matter? Has something else happened?"

She turned away and looked out over the rooftops, over the bay. "Do you know how I spent this morning?" she said eventually.

"No. How?"

"Listening to Alf Reeves telling me how very disappointed he is in me."

166

"Ah."

"And how very disappointed he is in Amy, too. She has had a terrible time, you know? Because of course she knew all about Charlie and me taking that night off back in New York, she could hardly have missed it, could she, however good Stan was at covering? But she didn't tell Alf a word about it when he got back. He was absolutely raging."

"Perhaps he's got a point."

"What?"

"Perhaps she should have told him."

"What, and dropped me right in it, you mean?"

I shrugged. "Well..."

"Like *you* did yesterday. You couldn't stop yourself, could you? You saw the chance to score a cheap point off Charlie, and you never gave a thought to *me*, to what it would mean to *me*?"

"I didn't think..."

"And this ridiculous business with your silly magic trick. You were so busy trying to put Charlie down, get your nose in front of Charlie, humiliate Charlie, whatever you think you are trying to do, but what about *me*? I was there onstage with you too, you know? Why did you not tell me what you were going to do? Or don't you care if you make me look foolish as long as you put Charlie's nose out of joint?"

I tried desperately to come up with something to say, but she had me there, and I knew it.

"Alf has given me one last chance, you know. I can't afford to put so much as a little toe out of line from now on, or I'm out."

"Really?"

"And since it is my dealings with you that have caused me the most difficulty, I think it would be for the best if we didn't spend any more time together."

"What?"

"We shall remain colleagues, of course, and I shall try my best to anticipate and play along with any further inventions of yours designed to spite any other members of the company, but as for anything else, I will thank you to keep your distance."

I was stunned. "But... Tilly?" She wouldn't turn to look at me, kept her gaze in the far distance.

"I'm sorry, Arthur. That's how it is going to be."

There was a lump in my throat now, and I could hardly get the words out, the only words I could think of to say. "But, Tilly, you know, I... love you."

"I know," she said, unmoved. "I'm sure you do, but I have begun to realise that however strong your positive feelings are for me, your negative feelings for Charlie are stronger. I have to come first, I can't play second fiddle to... all *that*."

I was numb, and just stood there like a useless lump of meat. She turned to face me. "Well," she said. "There it is." She gave me a peck on the cheek, a very sisterly one, and then turned to leave, her blonde hair brushing lightly across my face.

"Wait," I said, "Tilly, I can change...!"

At the top of the stairs she turned and gave a melancholy little shake of the head, then the door clanged shut behind her and she was gone.

━━━━

I slumped against the stone parapet and slid down it onto my backside, staring into nothingness until my buttocks were numb. When the discomfort in my bones finally made me move myself, I realised I had no idea how long I had been up on the roof.

The lid of my dove basket was flapping open, and my feathery co-stars were nowhere to be seen. I forced myself to concentrate, forced one foot in front of the other until I was heading down the stairs back into the theatre. As I reached the wings I heard the tell-tale tones of Nellie Sherman, 'fascinating soubrette', and realised it was still only the first half and I had missed nothing.

I wandered on into the gentlemen's dressing room, absent-mindedly accepted a cigarette from Mike Asher, and watched the lads idly milling around, ties undone, sleeves rolled. I found myself marvelling that things were so utterly normal, despite the earth-shattering catastrophe that had just occurred in my world.

Alf Reeves passed busily by and I grabbed his arm.

"Alf," I said, struggling to form words. "Can't do dove trick."

"What's wrong, Arthur? Are you unwell? You look terrible."

"Birds... flown..." I said.

Alf sighed, and his shoulders slumped. "Right. Right. I'd better tell Grauman. Leave it to me. Charlie? Do you hear this? No more dove trick."

Charlie looked over from the mirror, where he was refreshing his make-up. "So, you've come to your senses, have you Arthur? Realised the importance of being a reliable little support artiste, eh? Good."

———

The next few weeks passed in a miserable drunken haze. I went through the motions onstage, and then retired to whatever bar was nearest to the stage door to take the edge off. Tilly and I barely spoke, and she seemed to spend most of her time, as far as I could tell, either chumming up with Amy Reeves, or listening to Charlie telling her how the company should really be making more of the female talent at its disposal. She and Amy both lapped that stuff up like kittens with a saucer of warm milk, of course. You could practically hear them purring, even across a crowded hostelry.

I was spending a lot of time with Stan in those weeks, and got to know him a little better. We were friends, of course, but it had always been the sort of easy companionship you fall into at work when you find someone of a similar age, with a similar view of the world, and similar leisure pursuits. He was very easy company, Stan, and he laughed easily and generously, not like some in the world of comedy who would rather give you a pint of blood than acknowledge that you had said something funny. Not thinking of anyone in particular...

Stan was so easy-going, and seemed to enjoy the touring life so much, that I was surprised to discover that deep down he was becoming restless.

We were in the Karno boxcar for one of the longest hauls of the whole tour, 750 miles up to Salt Lake City. In the middle of the day, in the middle of summer, passing close to somewhere calling itself Death Valley, it was a bit of an endurance test. Fortunately we had our carriage to ourselves, so most of the gents had their shirts open to the waist, and modesty gave way to comfort – or survival, actually, that's what it felt like.

Alf, stout fellow, had had the foresight to acquire a large slab of ice, which sat in the middle of the carriage on a trolley dripping rivulets across the floor, and every now and then someone would limply drag themselves over to it to chip off a piece and press it to their forehead or chest. Lucia, the lovely burlesque girl who had faithfully followed Mike all the way to California, was riding with us, and she was due to continue on to Chicago having finally been persuaded to try and get her job back. She allowed a substantial piece of ice to melt away to nothing on her sun-browned bosom, her head back, and her eyes closed in a state of ecstatic relief. Most of the men in the carriage were sitting with their tongues out panting like dogs, I can tell you, and not just because of the heat.

"Charlie never seems to get ill, that's the thing," Stan complained. "It's all well and good understudying the lead part if I never ever get to go on. I need Alf to see me, and for the good word to get back to Karno, but Charlie is simply never going to let that happen."

I sympathised, of course, with a grunt, and opened a couple of bottles of beer.

"It's not just that it would be more enjoyable to have more to do, I could use more money. What Karno pays is barely enough to live on, once I've paid for basic necessities like food."

"Beer is food," I said, raising a bottle, which Stan clinked with his own. "Perhaps you need to stop handing so much of your earnings to George Seaman."

"I know, I know," Stan sighed. "I'm trying, but it is *so* tedious in this boxcar, and the card game does while away the hours."

"To the boxcar," I said, and he clinked me again.

"You know, the rumour is that we'll be booked to do another six-month circuit on the Sullivan and Considine time?"

"Siberia time," I said, pantomiming the chill.

"I have been wondering whether I can stand the thought of it," Stan said, suddenly serious.

"You're thinking of leaving?" I asked.

"Well, to be honest, I was really looking forward to going home, and the money goes so much further there, and maybe the Guv'nor would put me in a show where I could actually show him what I can do."

"Maybe we should go back to England," I said.

"Maybe we should."

"Tell the Guv'nor what he can do with his pittance, and his Siberia time."

"Ha ha! Yes, that's exactly what we should do!"

It was just the beer talking, of course, the beer and the heat. We were just venting our frustrations between ourselves, not formulating anything like an actual plan of action. We'd never have gone that far.

═══════

When we arrived in Colorado Springs, a sleepy little place that would have needed to acquire a horse to be called a one-horse town, we received a message – which is to say, Alf Reeves did – confirming that we were indeed to continue around the Sullivan and Considine circuit once again, as soon as the current tour finished in Kansas City (which seemed to be in Missouri for some unexplained reason).

"Six more months of that blasted boxcar," Mike Asher grumbled.

"Hey, lay off the boxcar," Alf said. "You wouldn't like the alternative any better, believe you me."

"So that means we'll be going back to Chicago?" Freddie Junior piped up, brightly.

"We start in Chicago," Alf said, glancing down at the schedule. Mike did perk up a bit at that, and the thought of maybe meeting up again with the luscious Lucia, but the general mood was mixed, I'd say, at best.

Alf tried to whip up a bit more enthusiasm. "Come on, everyone, let's see some smiles. This is good news!"

He was fretting about company morale, and the next day chivvied us all into a walking trip up into the foothills to a place called 'The Garden of the Gods'. Here enormous red boulders perched on top of one another in bizarre formations created by the eroding power of the wind, some like clusters of church spires, others for all the world like strange booby-traps, seemingly ready to topple at a moment's notice on top of some unsuspecting coyote. The hot breeze whipped dust up into our faces, and it was easy to imagine that we ourselves were being eroded into odd shapes even as we stood there.

The backdrop was the sunlit ridge of the Rocky Mountains, with a wooden sign indicating the location of the Continental Divide on nearby Pike's Peak. This was the rough geographical line to the West of which water would flow towards the Pacific, while to the East it would naturally head towards the Mississippi, the Atlantic, and home.

We gathered together in little clusters by this sign, with a massive slab of red rock balancing unfeasibly behind like some enormous head on a tiny spindly neck, all waiting for Albert Austin to prepare his camera for some commemorative snapshots. Charlie, Stan, Mike, Freddie and myself made up the first group. Charlie and I ended up with our arms around one another's shoulders, and the sudden thought that history would record that we were the best of chums meant that I completely forgot to smile.

And then we made way for the married couples. By chance this meant I found myself standing over to one side close to Tilly, for the first time in what seemed like an age, apart from the minutes we would spend together nightly onstage, of course.

"So," I said. "Six more months, then."

"So it seems," she said, coolly.

"Stan and I were talking about it," I said then. "We are finding it pretty hard to make ends meet."

"Well," she said.

I don't know why I said what I said then. Perhaps I simply wanted to provoke a reaction. I wanted to see if the thought of me leaving altogether would betray itself in her face. I wanted a hint as to whether our current estrangement was a temporary thing, whether deep down she was thinking she would one day soon forgive and forget what a fool I was, give me another chance.

"So we are thinking of leaving, Stan and I," I said, "unless the Guv'nor stumps up more cash, that is."

Her face was a mask of disinterest. "Is that so?" she said.

"Oh yes," I said. "Definitely."

"Well, how about that?" she said, flatly. Then it was her turn to join in with a group photograph under the looming red rock, her and Amy, with Muriel and Emily, and I was left standing there alone as she skipped over with a broad beam on her lovely face.

What did that mean? Was she disguising how upset she would be if I left? Or did she really not care?

━━━━

Before the first show the very next day Alf Reeves came into the green room, his face serious, a beige-coloured slip of paper in his hand.

"Your attention if you please," he said, raising his voice only slightly. Heads turned towards him. "Stanley? Arthur? Step forward."

Stan and I took a couple of strides into the middle of the room, a little unnerved by the ominous atmosphere all of a sudden.

"What ho, Alf?" I said. "Something up?"

174

"This wire just came from Mr Karno." Alf gave a little cough and began to read. "'PLEASE PURCHASE BIG HAT AND WEAR IT WHILE READING OUT THIS WIRE STOP.'"

Stan and I looked at one another, not sure what was happening. The big hat was an old trick of Karno's for keeping his performers in line. Whenever a comic would have the temerity to suggest that he was worth another bob or two a week, the Guv'nor would reach into the cupboard behind him and bring out the big hat, as a none-too-subtle visual hint that the supplicant would be requiring more spacious headgear. There was also a tiny pair of boots which he could imply, with equal subtlety, that you were getting too big for.

"We can take the big hat as read, I presume?" Alf said, still serious. We nodded. "The Guv'nor goes on: 'NO PAY RISE FOR JEFFERSON AND DANDOE STOP.'"

"Pay rise? We haven't asked for a pay rise."

"Oh, I'm sorry," Charlie said then. "I thought you said you would leave unless the Guv'nor came up with more cash?"

"What? We never did, did we?" Stan said, frowning at me.

"Yes," Charlie insisted. "Definitely, you said."

I suddenly realised that the one time I had said something similar was to Tilly, back in the Garden of the Gods. And she must have mentioned this to Chaplin, who'd seen his chance to make his move.

"I might have said we were thinking about it, that's all." I mumbled.

"Is there more, Alf?" Charlie said.

Alf glanced down at the wire, and nodded: "'REPLACE-MENTS ON THE WAY STOP.'"

"Replacements?" I said. "What do you mean, replacements?"

Alf took a moment to interpret the remaining money-saving shorthand. "Evidently Ted Banks and Charles Cardon will be joining the company in Chicago."

"What?" Stan cried. "Tell them not to come!"

"I can't very well do that, can I, even if I wanted to. They are probably already halfway to America."

"But..." Stan and I gaped at one another, struggling to take this in. "So that's it? We're out?"

"I'm sorry lads, but there it is."

And just like that, for me and for Stan, our highly promising Karno careers were at an end.

We were out.

PART 2

18
HIS LUGGAGE
LABELLED 'ENGLAND'

STAN and I travelled back to England on the *Lusitania*, the very liner on which we should have travelled out to America in first class splendour nine months before. Alf had managed to slip us just enough petty cash to make the crossing in steerage, and we had a few days with nothing to do but watch the waves, eat, drink and think.

Uppermost in our minds, of course, was what the hell we were going to do when we got back. We were out of the Karno company, booted out ignominiously, without that safety blanket, and without the glittering prize of attaining number one comic status to drive us on. I could still hardly believe the sheer calamity that had befallen us.

Stan wasn't a man to remain cast down for long, however. "It's an opportunity, don't you see Arthur? A great opportunity. We could actually create something ourselves, create a turn, a sketch. Put all our own ideas into it, make it the funniest thing ever."

And he would pace happily up and down the deck as the Atlantic foamed and spumed by, with gags and slapstick ideas fizzing out of his comedy brain, every now and then ducking inside out of the wind to jot something down.

My time watching the waves was given over to brooding and resentment. I had to hand it to Charlie. He'd stitched us up good and proper, telling Karno we wanted more money. But had he overheard me talking to Tilly, or had she told him about it? Later? In a private moment?

Stan wasn't having any of it. "It was just a misunderstanding, that's all," he insisted. "Not Tilly's fault, and not Charlie's either."

"Ha!" I snorted derisively.

"I know you have a bit of a thing about him, and you reckon you should be number one in his place."

"I beg your pardon. *He* is number one in *my* place!"

"But I have roomed with him for months, and we are good friends. He wouldn't do anything bad or underhand. Not to me."

After a while Stan's blithe sunniness began to get on my nerves a bit.

"You do see, don't you, why Charlie wanted to get rid of us?" I said one day on deck. "We are a threat, both of us."

"A threat? No."

"You know he saw you, don't you?"

"What do you mean?"

"You know he saw you, when you stood in for him? When he took his night off?"

"No, why on earth would he do that?"

"I don't know, because he has a screw loose. He came and watched you, and ever since then he's known that you are every bit as good as he is. And that is why you had to go."

For a split second I thought I'd made a chink in his benevolence, but then:

"Charlie wouldn't do that. Not to me."

Finally the two of us stepped off the boat train at Waterloo Station, and shook hands solemnly.

"Where will you go?" I asked.

"You remember I told you about my brother Gordon? The theatre manager?"

"At the – what was it? – Metropole? In Glasgow?"

"That's him. He's to be the manager of a new theatre on Shaftesbury Avenue called the Prince's. It's not opened yet, but he's fitting it out, and he has himself a little place on High Holborn. I've invited myself for a visit," he grinned. "Indefinitely. You?"

"Charley and Clara Bell are minding some of my belongings, and I will see how the land lies there. They will know how to reach me, whatever happens."

Stan nodded. "Well then, this is it," he said, hefting the handle of his trunk.

"See you at the Corner," I said.

"See you at the Corner."

A short tram ride later I found myself sitting at the kitchen table of the Bells' house in Streatham. Charley Bell, a long-established Karno number two and my landlord when I last lived in London, sat opposite me lighting up a pipe, and his wife Clara stood at the stove pouring boiling water into a large teapot.

"So you've left the Guv'nor's employ, then?" Charley said, between puffs.

"Yes, I'm afraid so," I admitted.

"How did that come about?"

"Long story short, it was about money."

Charley grunted. "Yep. That'll do it."

Even though Charley had worked for Karno for many years, the two of them didn't really get on. He and Clara were friendly with Edith Karno, the Guv'nor's first wife, and as a result were privy to far too many tales of domestic cruelty to have a good opinion of the old bastard. They had installed Edith in the house next door so they could keep a protective eye on her.

Clara brought the pot of tea to the table. "So where will you be living?"

I coughed. "Well, I was hoping..."

"I'm sorry, dear," said Clara. "Your old room is let out, of course. Well, you've been gone nine months."

"I understand."

"It's one of the Guv'nor's, name of Billy Crackles. I'm afraid the house is chock full of Karno's boys at the moment. We've even got a fellow on a cot in the back parlour. But we'll keep your bags until you find somewhere. And I'll ask around. There are quite a few theatrical landladies in this neck of the woods."

"Thank you, that would be very kind."

Charley waved this away. "So what will you do now, then, to make your way?"

"I don't really know," I said. "I suppose I could go on up to the Fun Factory and throw myself on the Guv'nor's mercy."

I was half joking, but only half. Charley sucked in a breath, shaking his head.

"No, you don't want to do that, don't give that man a hold over you, eh Clara?"

Clara nodded. "He's quite right. If you want to get back in, you need to make Fred Karno think he's made a big mistake."

"Come up with some sort of turn, you mean?" I said, apprehension knotting my bowels at the very thought of this.

"Yep," Charley Bell nodded, sitting back in his chair and jabbing the thin end of his pipe in my direction. "And make it a good 'un!"

———

With nowhere to lay my head I was bereft of ideas. I finally decided to make my way up to the Fun Factory, Fred Karno's base of operations in Camberwell. Maybe I would see a friendly face or two there, someone who could help me out.

I arrived just as the company's omnibuses and carriages were leaving, carting dozens of performers to various music halls the length and breadth of the capital, as they did every late afternoon. I caught fragments of happy chatter on the breeze as they parped away past me, and it was hard to think that I was not going with them.

The street emptied, and I was on the pavement alone, standing outside the big double doors of the Fun Factory's scene dock, where the sets for the Guv'nor's hit sketches were constructed. I peered inside, remembering the first time I had done so, when the *Wontdetainia* was being built there. The hours I had spent painting that ocean liner set, before Karno had elevated me onto the lower rungs of the comedy ladder – who'd have thought I would ever feel a pang of nostalgia for those days of slave labour?

There was no one around. I could either head into the city and see what I could find, or wait for them all to come back at the end of the night and hope for the best. My feet drifted me down the road to the pub on the corner, The Enterprise, where I had so often mingled with my Karno colleagues on pay day. I bought myself a pint I could ill afford, and made it last all evening as I sat by the window looking back at the Fun Factory, waiting for signs of life.

Finally I saw the lights of the first carriage returning, and I hustled back up the road. My luck wasn't in, though, as one conveyance after another tipped its inhabitants out without me spotting a single friend I could latch onto.

The only person I saw that I even recognised was Syd Chaplin, Charlie's half-brother, who was braying his noisy goodnights to his subordinates as they set off for their various homes. We had worked together a couple of years previously, but I would have bitten my hand off before I held it out to him for help. Quite apart from the fact that he'd been involved in numerous underhand schemes to do me down and advance his brother, I wouldn't have wanted to give him the satisfaction, nor the opportunity to write to his brother with the news that I was on my uppers.

I stood shivering in the street, by myself once again, and watched one of the Karno omnibuses reversing up the little slope to park inside the scene dock for the night. On a sudden impulse I followed it in, keeping out of sight of the driver, and once he'd gone and locked up I tip-toed up the curving staircase to the upper deck and lay down on the big bench seat at the back.

It was cold and uncomfortable, but at least it was indoors. I lay awake, thinking to myself that the Fun Factory had never been less fun, and trying to come up with a plan of action.

Could I devise some kind of solo routine for myself? Certainly no brilliant inspiration struck me that miserable night, and even if it had there was no way I could have translated it into paid work any time soon. I needed something right away, and so as soon as I heard the big doors being opened the next morning I slipped down the stairs and out, and made my way to the Corner.

The Corner was near Waterloo station. If you were working the halls, if you were a turn of any kind, you would do almost anything to stay away from the place, for it was where the unemployed of our business went to... well, not to die, we went onstage to do that. We went to the Corner just to hang around waiting for something, anything, to happen along. And we called it the Corner for short – its full nickname was far more dispiriting: Poverty Corner.

You could pick up work at the Corner, of course you could, or else nobody would be there, would they? No less a figure than Fred Karno himself had got a big break there years before, when a producer had wandered by looking for an act to fill in for some tumblers called *The Three Carnoes*, who he'd double-booked. Karno had grabbed a couple of similarly desperate ruffians and rustled up an acrobatic act, and it had gone so well that he kept hold of the name (after changing the spelling slightly) and before too long outshone the originals.

There must have been upwards of forty people, gentlemen and ladies, huddling together in groups of two or three at the Corner that chilly morning. All were smartly dressed – peacocks almost, some of them – hoping to catch the eye of... well, they didn't really know. Anyone.

I leaned against a wall, hands in pockets, to try and get the hang of how this worked. What was going to play most attractively, a sort of superior aloofness or outright fawning? I supposed that the approach to use would depend on how many days you had been waiting, waiting, waiting...

Hang on, though... there was a familiar face, surely?

"Bill?" I said, strolling over to its owner. "Whatever are you doing here? Down among the dead men?"

Billie Ritchie, a small and wirily pugnacious Scot, took my outstretched hand and pumped it up and down.

"Arthur Dandoe, well, well!" he said with a grin. "I heard you were in America with young Chaplin. What happened, eh?"

"Asked for more money," I shrugged, cutting a long story short. Ritchie nodded. "Aye, that'll do it," he said.

"But what about you?" I said. "You're a Karno number one. You've got it made, haven't you?"

"Ach!" Ritchie hawked and spat into the gutter. "No' any more!"

"How come?"

"Of course, ye've been away, ye havenae seen the Guv'nor lately."

"Not for months."

"Well, he's let things slide a bit up at the old Fun Factory. It's no' just me that thinks it, neither, that's what everyone's a-thinkin'. Sayin', too, when he's out of earshot. See, he's got himself this fancy new houseboat, the swankiest one on the Thames if you please, and he's spending all his time over there. It's all he thinks about these days, and the comedy company can go to hell, apparently. There's no' been a new sketch in ages, and he hardly ever goes to see what's goin' on. Well, somebody had to tell him, and that somebody it turns out was me. And so ah'm oot!"

"No!" I said, disbelieving. If Karno could let Billie Ritchie go then no one was safe from his whim, it seemed. Billie had played all the top parts – the Drunk, Stiffy the goalkeeper, Archibald Binks – it was unthinkable that he would be on his uppers, and yet here he was.

"He'll come roond, I'm sure of it, but till then I'm making ma own way. I was thinking I might give America a try, actually."

The nearest fellow to us gave a little whistle of warning. "Uh-oh! Look out, here he comes."

"Who?"

"See the fellow there in the coat with the Astrakhan collar? With the silver-topped cane?"

"Yes, I see him."

"That's Whimsical Walker."

"Whimsy... what?"

"The original Drury Lane ham."

A portly chap in his sixties was walking across the cobbles in our direction, wearing an expensive-looking black coat and a dark fedora jauntily offset atop his brick-square head. He had a companion with him, a skinny old fellow, bowing and scraping along in his wake. Billie Ritchie regarded the approaching pair with a sardonic smile.

"Now then. Let's have a little respect, lads. There goes one of the great clowns, as I'm certain he'd be only too happy to tell ye himsel'."

"Really?"

"Oh aye. Took over from Grimaldi, y'know, back in the day. Eyes down, boys."

Whimsical Walker stopped in front of us and gazed sadly down his nose, an expression of tired disappointment on his jowly face. He tutted to his companion.

"Dear-oh deary-me! Look at this sorry bunch!"

"Indeed, indeed."

"I am prepared to lay odds that not a one of them could tell you what a harlequinade is, let alone play one."

"I'm sure you are right, Tom," his companion said, shaking his head sorrowfully.

"Oh well, let's move along."

Something snapped inside me, and despite Ritchie grabbing at my arm I stepped forward. And besides, any port in a storm, as they say, or any crust in a famine, more accurately. I wished I hadn't had that thought – now I desperately wanted some port...

"Excuse me?" I said. "I can tell you what a harlequinade is."

The pompous fellow turned and squinted at me. "Pray do so," he said.

"It is traditionally seen at the end of a pantomime, and is a knockabout comedy routine in which the main performers are transformed into or sometimes joined by the stock characters of the *commedia dell'arte*, to wit Arlecchino the harlequin, Columbine, his love, Pantaloon, the Policeman and the Clown."

Walker had turned and was strolling back plumply towards me, a half-smile upon his lips.

"Well, well," he said, weighing me up. I held my breath. Was I going to luck into some work on my very first morning at the Corner? And if so, what might it be...?

"This one, Tom?" the clown's elderly companion said, his pencil poised over a blank page in his notebook for a long moment.

"No," Whimsical Walker decided. "Too tall."

And the two of them strolled away.

"Narrow escape that, trust me," Billie Ritchie murmured.

In any event, that was the closest I came to a spark of interest down the Corner all week.

I dutifully headed down there first thing each morning, and then spent the days hanging around, occasionally trying to look bright-eyed and bushy-tailed if some prospective employer hove into view. I relied on Billie Ritchie to identify them for me, but after a day or two he stopped showing up, so maybe something had landed on his plate.

At nights I was returning to the Fun Factory. I told myself I was still looking for a friendly face, but in truth I'd had no better idea than sneaking in there and kipping on the top deck of the company omnibus. At least it was indoors, so it was better than dossing down under a railway arch.

There were a few hairy moments though. One morning a stage manager I vaguely knew called Wilf Wainwright bumped right into me as I was trying to slip out, but I managed to pretend that I was in fact just arriving to see the Guv'nor, and he made me a cup of tea, after which I nipped out while his back was turned.

Another time I was so wretchedly tired that the opening of the big doors, my usual alarm call, failed to wake me, and I came to myself halfway to the garage where the bus was to be cleaned and refuelled.

My closest call was the morning Karno himself came to work early. I heard his voice, and his unsettling little cough, right below me, and when I looked down I could almost see my own terrified reflection in his shiny shoes, peeping over the back rail.

By the end of the second week I was thoroughly discouraged, and beginning to wonder whether this was really the life for me. Perhaps I should swallow my pride and make my way back to Cambridge for a job and my mother's cooking, which would be sure to come with a heady dash of my father's smug "I told you so" sauce.

On the Saturday the Corner was deserted. Clearly the rest of London's theatrical unemployed knew something I didn't, so I walked all the way down to Streatham to visit the Bells again. Partly this was to raid my trunk for a clean shirt – cleaner, anyway – because nights spent sneaking into the Fun Factory omnibus were giving me something of a vagrant aspect. Partly also because I was pretty much guaranteed to be offered tea and cake, and that would keep me going for a while.

I didn't even get as far as the Bells' front door, though, because as I approached I saw a familiar figure walking towards me.

"Stan!" I cried.

"Arthur? Whatever has happened to you?" Stan said, looking at me with concern. I suppose I looked even rougher than I felt.

"Oh, just... life," I said. "How are you?"

"Me? I'm in the pink," he said. "I just left a message for you with your former landlady. She said you would drop by sooner or later."

"Sooner it is," I said. "What was the message?"

"Well..." Before he could enlighten me, however, I was hailed from the next door front garden.

"Arthur? Is that you? How lovely to see you!"

"Edith," I said to the smiling lady on the other side of the low wall, who was peeling off some gardening gloves as she walked towards us. "I trust you are well? This is Stan Jefferson, who was with me and Freddie in America, Stan this is Mrs Edith Karno."

"Delighted," Stan said as they shook hands.

"Freddie's mother," I explained, just in case Stan hadn't twigged. He raised an eyebrow.

"I am surprised to see you," Edith said. "Freddie's last letter said that the tour was continuing for another six months at least. Is he back, too, then?

"No, no, the tour continues, and Freddie with it," I said. "But as for the two of us, we are..."

"Embarking on a new and exciting passage in our careers," Stan cut in.

"And is that going well?" Edith said, squinting at me rather as Stan had just done.

"It's new," I said. "And... different."

"So I shall be seeing you around the place again, that's nice."
I didn't say anything to that, just looked a bit glum, I expect, and

she gathered the state of play at once. "Are you not staying next door with the Bells?"

"They have no room, unfortunately, and anyway they are committed to housing Karno players."

"You are not sleeping rough? Oh Arthur! Why did you not simply knock on my door? You can have Leslie's room, and he can come in with me, like he does when Freddie comes to stay. And *that's* not going to happen, is it, while he is still in America?"

"You're sure Leslie won't mind?"

"Not a bit."

I was overwhelmed, suddenly. It felt like weeks since I had slept in a bed in a house. In point of fact it *was* weeks. "Well, if you are quite sure?"

"Of course," Edith said. "Bring your things right over and I'll pop the kettle on."

"Perhaps a little later, if you don't mind, Mrs Karno," Stan cut in. "I am sorry to have to drag Arthur away, but we have important business. A pleasure to make your acquaintance."

Edith waved a farewell as Stan trotted briskly up the street with yours truly in his wake, thinking wistfully of tea and cake.

"Important business?" I said. "Where are you taking me?"

"Islington."

"Islington? What's in Islington?"

19
THE RUM 'UNS
FROM ROME

WHAT there was in Islington, it emerged when we arrived an hour or so later, was a small warehouse, at the end of a narrow cobbled alley running along the side of a pub. The door was opened, eventually, to Stan's knocking, by a stocky little fellow with discoloured teeth, who blinked at us as though he hadn't seen the daylight for some weeks.

"Good morning. Mr Goodger?" Stan said.

"Who wants to know?" this Goodger replied, peering at us with his piggy eyes.

"I am Mr Jefferson, Mr Stanley Jefferson, and this is my colleague Mr Dandoe. You should have received a communication from Mr Gordon Jefferson alerting you to our visit?"

"Well, maybe I have, maybe I haven't," Goodger said, with an air of gnomic suspicion. We looked at one another without saying anything further, until I could stand it no longer.

"Well? Which is it? Have you or haven't you?" I said.

"I have," this creature conceded.

"So...? Can we come in?"

Goodger peered at us a little longer, until he finally seemed to realise that this was not going to result in us paying him any kind of a tip and he stepped back inside. Stan and I followed into the building, which was essentially a cavernous single room piled high with furniture and bric-a-brac. What light there was streamed in diagonally through skylights, and there was a good deal of dust suspended in those sunbeams. The whole place had that sort of musty damp-but-not-actually damp odour that all theatrical costumes seem able to acquire after only a night or two. It was the smell of old show business.

We squeezed in through a gap which was just about wide enough for us to pass one at a time, between a pile of dining tables and chairs on the one side, and what looked like the furnishings for some kind of harem on the other.

"What is this place?" I asked Stan.

"It's a storehouse for various West End theatres, stuff from old productions. They keep it here in case it can be used again."

Goodger coughed and spat. "What was it you gents were looking for?" he enquired.

"We shall know it when we see it, Mr Goodger," Stan replied, clambering over a couple of interlocked chaise-longues to see what lurked in the deeper recesses of this Aladdin's cave.

"I'll leave you to it, then," the watchman grumbled, and waddled over to a corner in which he had installed the most comfortable of the many available chairs for his own personal use.

"What are we looking for?" I asked.

"Something... anything... that will give us a brainwave..." Stan opened a trunk, peered inside, then moved on.

"What sort of a brainwave?"

"Well, I feel that our abilities, such as they are, lie in scenarios. Singing? Well, if required. Dancing? At a pinch. Telling stories? Possibly, but I'd much rather come up with a scenario, a sketch. Then we can use the skills we have honed with Karno, action and interaction, to and fro, give and take and double take. What do you say?"

"I'm with you, my boy!" I cried, with an enthusiasm fuelled by the raw relief that I mightn't have to go back to the Corner for a while. "What about this?"

I pointed out a sort of silk palanquin. There was a little pile of curved wooden scimitars on top of the cushions, and an assortment of brightly-coloured baggy pantaloons.

"Hmm..." Stan mused. "Possibly... The Terrible Turks, we could be, something like that."

"That's the name of the wrestler in *Mumming Birds*, of course," I reminded him.

"Yes, true, perhaps not then. Let's keep looking..."

Stan burrowed further into the warehouse, sliding some baskets aside, while I swished a scimitar from side to side. All of a sudden he let out a gleeful shout.

"Hey! What about this lot?"

I hurried over, and saw that he was holding up what looked like a Roman soldier's helmet, with a maroon-coloured plume on the top, and in the other hand a gold-painted breastplate.

"Look!" he cried, his eyes bright. "We can be gladiators, I haven't seen that before, have you?"

I had to admit I hadn't. "Romans," I said, trying it out.

"Rum Romans," Stan said with a grin. "The Rum Romans. The Rum 'Uns..."

"The Rum 'Uns from Rome," I finished, and we both knew that was it.

"Let's see what else we can use," Stan said, and we set to burrowing into the shadows for more bric-a-brac from the same production, whatever that had been.

Eventually we made our way back to the exit and apprised Mr Goodger of our requirements: the Roman helmets (2), the gladiator breastplates (2), tunics, Roman (2), sandals, Roman, two pair, short broad swords, Roman style, (2), free-standing ornate columns, Roman style, (2), a chariot, small, Roman, for one passenger, a burlesque horse costume (possibly not from the same enterprise as the rest of the items), and a moth-eaten lion skin which may have been used as a rug in some hunting lodge scene.

As we'd discovered and set aside all these things, the sketch we would eventually perform had sparked to life there in the dusty darkness. We marched around planning this effect and that routine, until we could hardly wait to get the props home and start work properly. The stolid Mr Goodger wasted no time taking the wind out of our sails, however. He listened to us describing what we needed to take, and he sucked his teeth dubiously.

"The Roman stuff," he said, shaking his head. "That's not just any old junk, you know. That's from Mr Shaw's *Caesar and Cleopatra* at the Savoy back in '07. Played by Mr Johnston Forbes-Robertson and his lovely wife Gertrude Elliott. It was a great success, could be revived at any time."

"Oh," Stan said, disappointment showing clearly on his face. "Really?"

"Yes, oh yes," Goodger said sorrowfully. "I couldn't possibly let those go."

Stan slumped, but something in Goodger's seedy, beady little eyes made me suspect that that might not be quite that.

"You couldn't let them go?" I said.

"No, sirs. Not possibly..."

"For less than...?"

Goodger blinked up at me, sucking at his teeth, and said: "Five pounds."

I whistled. I was expecting the old chiseller to try it on, but that was way out of our reach. 'Well, so much for *that*', I was thinking, but then Stan stepped forward. "I'll take care of this," he murmured.

"Please add it to the account of Mr Gordon Jefferson at the new Prince's Theatre," he said to the old watchman in a commanding tone. "And that includes delivery, of course, at your earliest opportunity."

I boggled at him. Goodger grumbled and fumbled around for a stub of pencil to make a note of this, with a surly grumpiness that made me suspect that he'd really been hoping for a cash transaction that he wouldn't have had to put in his books.

Outside I grabbed Stan by the sleeve. "Your brother is paying for this?" I said.

Stan shrugged, with a rather mischievous smile.

"You mean he doesn't know he's paying for it?"

"Well, not yet. By the time he finds out we'll be able to pay him back, won't we?"

"How?"

"Why, from the proceeds of our new sketch, of course. *The Rum 'Uns from Rome!*"

———

I was a little anxious about the debt we now owed Stan's brother Gordon, even if the man himself didn't know it. And Stan taking charge of our affairs was a source of further trepidation, for I had hardly ever known anyone less well suited to looking after financial matters. Week after week on tour he'd surrendered his wages to the boxcar poker circle and had to scrounge cents for food and drink.

I felt a nagging certainty that the watchman would have taken a lot less money for all those props and costumes. He'd struck me as a man preparing to haggle, but then Stan had stepped in with his grand gesture, which probably cost us a couple of quid we could ill afford.

However, I was relieved to be doing something at last, and put that concern to the back of my mind as our rehearsals began in a bare room in the as yet unfinished Prince's Theatre. I wondered whether Stan's brother Gordon knew anything about that, either, but Stan was able to breeze confidently past the stage doorman, and as long as we were prepared to ignore the noise of the building work we could get on with things.

As *The Rum 'Uns from Rome* took shape we made some modifications to our props. We chopped the floor out of the chariot – well, we were never really going to give it back to Mr Johnston Forbes-Robertson, were we? – and we cut a trick compartment into one of the columns.

Stan was a veritable sparking power-house of invention, and the two of us laughed and laughed that whole time up at the Prince's. My fondest memory of that period is of the two of us falling on the floor helpless with mirth at some new piece of slapstick business, our clothes covered in plaster dust and bits of brick.

Edith Karno helped out by making papier-mâché facsimiles of my head, a skill she fondly remembered from a show of her husband's back in the day, and Leslie, Freddie's much younger brother, delighted in splattering every inch of their kitchen with paste.

In order to carry off the effect we had in mind – and I shall come to that in just a moment – I was required to wear particularly heavy make-up and a false beard, but it was worth it.

I was glad to see how much Edith enjoyed being involved, as I felt it was some small recompense for her kindness in putting me up. I kept trying to promise to pay her for board and lodgings, but she insisted on waiting until I was solvent, bless her.

"It is our pleasure to have you here," she said. "Especially considering what we owe you, Leslie and I."

The debt to which she alluded was from the time when Charlie and I were climbing neck and neck up the Karno ladder, vying for a coveted number one spot. The Guv'nor let me know that the job would be mine if only I would help him with a little problem. He was living in sin with an athletic Amazon of a chorus girl called Maria, who he was passing off as Mrs Karno, but in point of fact he was still married to Edith who was refusing to divorce him.

Their marriage had been a tempestuous one. It had produced two children – Freddie, my friend and sometime roommate, and Leslie, whose room I currently occupied. There had been others in between, at least half a dozen, but none had lived beyond young infancy, and on each sad occasion Karno had forced Edith straight back to work immediately without any consideration for her feelings. Increasingly he had become violent with her, beating her, and openly taunting her with his many mistresses. She bore a half-moon scar on her cheek that had come from a vicious stamp of his shiny heel. Finally her friends, who included Charlie and Clara Bell, and Alf Reeves, and Marie Lloyd, too, had intervened and rescued her, setting her and Leslie up here in Streatham where they could keep a close eye on them.

Despite all this she still loved the old monster, and slept every night on pillows with 'Fred' and 'Edith' embroidered upon them. She would never agree to divorce him, never, it went against everything she was, so Karno was stuck, unable to marry again and resentful of his obligation to provide for her and his sons.

So he'd asked me to 'compromise' her, and provide evidence he could use to get his divorce, an unpleasant proposal that I angrily rejected – but I considered it, oh yes I did, to my secret shame. My anger was fuelled, truth to tell, by the nasty suspicion that the Guv'nor was employing his famous casting couch to audition Tilly, and it turned out she was much too canny to let him get away with that. In any event, I had been fêted as a kind of hero by Edith and her friends, deservedly or not, and was still, it seemed, reaping the benefit.

Now for *The Rum 'Uns from Rome* we needed someone to join us to double as a horse's backside and a lion, and we hooked up with a young fellow by the name of Ted Leo – an oddly appropriate name given what we were asking him to do (George Horse-arse was unavailable) – down at the Corner. Ted was a lugubrious South London chancer, who had just been playing a supporting part in Charles Baldwin's *Wax Works*.

"What did you have to do?" I asked.

Ted shrugged. "Waxwork, wasn't I? Just had to stand there. Got knocked over at one point, but forbidden to put me arms out to break me fall, it was bloody murder. Then I go along to see agents, and they've all seen the show, didn't even realise the waxworks was real people! I mean, what's the bloody point of it all, eh?"

He fulfilled our requirements well enough, but he would keep grumbling about how nobody could see his face.

We had one booking, at the Royal Victoria Hall, but were confident that once people knew about the *Rum 'Uns* then more would follow. When the day came it suddenly dawned on us, almost at the last possible minute, that our funds were so depleted that we would not be able to get all our props and bits and pieces over to the Hall by van. Thanks to some shameless begging we were able to borrow a pushcart from the greengrocer around the corner, and we loaded it up and galloped through the streets of Soho and over Waterloo Bridge to Lambeth, with hordes of children hooting at us and our strange-looking load.

Outside the theatre we paused for breath, sweating like the pair of over-worked pack mules we were, and I glanced at the bill poster on the wall.

"Hey...!" I rasped. "We're not on there! What's happened?"

"Yes we are," Stan wheezed. "There, look... that's us. The Barto Brothers."

"Barto Brothers? When...? When did we become the Barto Brothers?"

"Just thought... whew!" Stan said, leaning heavily against the side of our cart. "Just thought we'd best not use our own names... just in case..."

"Just in case what?"

"Just in case... we stink!" Stan grinned.

"That's good thinking," I said after a moment's consideration, patting him on the back.

Our third member was waiting anxiously just inside the stage door.

"Ah, Mr Barto!" Ted said when he saw us, "and you must be Mr Barto, pleased to meet you. The name's Barto."

━━━━

A short while later the three of us silently erected the twin columns alongside a little platform, listening to a jaunty coster singer getting the bird on the other side of the curtain. Most of the acts we had seen so far had been greeted with derision from the crowd, which was beginning to get a bit too big for its boots, in my opinion. Stan and I shared an apprehensive look, and I tried to quieten the butterflies in my stomach by pressing my hands against my abdomen – that never works, by the way – as we retreated into the wings.

All of a sudden the curtain went up, without the customary warning ripple of applause for the unfortunate fellow preceding us, and *The Rum 'Uns from Rome* was under way.

Stan and Ted, as the burlesque horse, pulled the chariot onto the stage and up to the platform, with me as a self-important and pompous Roman dignitary riding inside. Although not actually riding, as we had removed the floor so that I could walk. I disembarked, as it were, and called for my junior colleague.

"Barmicuss?" I cried. He was Barmicuss, I was Sillicuss.

I looked around in all directions, as did the audience. Suddenly, thanks to a brilliant little trick he had devised himself and executed perfectly, Stan appeared alongside the horse's head in his full Roman gladiator costume. He had been the front of the horse, and the way he held the head up it appeared to be exactly as it had been moments before, and yet now it was empty. The audience actually gasped, it was so well done. Even I, who knew it was coming, took half a step back.

Then Ted Leo reached his arms forward inside the horse suit and took over, pulling the chariot off towards the wings. Now the horse did seem somewhat... floppier.

"What on earth is that?" I said, pointing at this strange sight.

"That is Brutus, sir, the only filleted horse in existence," said Stan with his trademark beaming grin.

Leo managed then to make it appear that the horse's boneless front legs were dancing, and we were off. The place was roaring.

I unfurled a parchment then with great pomp and ceremony, saying: "Gather round!" Stan, seeing that there was only himself there, began to gather round, marching in dumb little circles. My job was to stop this nonsense with a look, but Stan was getting such a good response for his daft little march that he just kept going, and my look built and built into a sort of long-suffering contempt.

The Power was with me, then, that eerie control that takes over when things are ticking along just right for a comic onstage. I knew just how long to hold one expression, before developing it into the next, when to move, when to do nothing, when the audience's attention was on me, when it was on Stan, felt it instinctively all the way to my finger ends.

Stan was feeling it too, I could tell. He judged to perfection how long the 'gathering round' would sustain, and finally noticed me staring furiously at him. His face turned sheepish, then bewildered, and then he tried to win me over with another grin. The audience lapped it up.

My pompous dignitary then whacked the gladiator on the head with the parchment, knocking off his helmet. Stan picked up his battle-axe and chased me around the stage, a classic bit of pantomime incorporating various swings and misses, until I took refuge behind one of the columns (inside the thing, in fact). Stan prowled around, unable to find me, until I tentatively poked my head out from behind the column. With a great roar and a legs-akimbo leap off the platform, Stan buried the axe deep into my head – which was the papier-mâché dummy head, of course.

This horrific violence brought the house down, naturally. I pulled the prop head back inside the column and emerged with a trick axe stuck to my real head, and blood dripping liberally down my white tunic. More gales of laughter.

Now Stan was repentant, and tried to help his victim. With much to-ing and fro-ing he managed to tease the axe out of my skull, and then he set to bandaging the wound, walking round and round in circles once again.

Once I was completely covered, he puzzled over how to attach the loose end. Having no tape or string, he very carefully stuck the bandage in place by tapping a nail into my head. The funniest thing, we agreed, was for me not to complain about this until the deed was done, and then to feel with my hands until I found the nail, whereupon I would become outraged and begin to chase him seeking retribution.

By this time all our business was working so well we wanted the act to go on for hours, but all too soon the finale was upon us. The two scrapping Romans were at one another's throats, seemingly battling to the death, when suddenly with a great roar a terrifying lion leapt on to the stage. Ted Leo in the moth-eaten old lion skin rug it was, of course, but he didn't stand still long enough for the audience to inspect him too closely.

The 'lion' chased us both back and forth, with the audience particularly enjoying Stan's childlike screams of terror, and his cross-legged leaps in the air. Finally the two Rum 'Uns set their differences aside and teamed up to dispatch the creature. Stan's gladiator found a banana in his belt, and it slowly dawned upon him that the lion wanted to eat this, rather than either of us. He tempted the lion this way and that with the fruit, teasing its big head from side to side like a stage hypnotist with a pocket watch, finally leading the fearsome beast into a position where my Roman dignitary could brain it with the pommel of a sword.

Lastly we picked Leo up bodily, slung him over our shoulders – which produced a muted "Oooof!" from inside the lion head – and marched offstage to thunderous applause.

Well, we'd had some good nights with the Karno companies for sure, but nothing to match this. And this was all our own work, of course, not a show we had inherited from previous companies and slotted into like cogs into a slickly-oiled machine.

Ted and I were walking on air, and good old Stan was beaming all over his chops.

"A hit!" he cried. "A massive, palpable, unmistakeable, jaw-dropping, death-defying hit!"

The three of us embraced, and Stan shouted: "Champagne!"

It seemed to us then, as we strolled across Waterloo Bridge towards Covent Garden in search of fizz, too excited to ride any kind of conveyance, that there was nothing we couldn't achieve. Surely this was the start of something? Something big?

20
HARD BOILED EGGS
AND NUTS

OUR high hopes were misplaced, sadly. We discovered the hard way that Dame Show can be a fickle mistress, and those who peek up her skirts do so at their peril.

It turned out neither of us was particularly good at pushing ourselves or our act in the way it needed pushing. We would go and see bookers, or sometimes theatre managers, and when they said "Come back and see us when you have worked it in," we would take them at their word and obligingly take ourselves from the premises rather than badgering them to give us a go. What we needed was an agent working for us, but every time we went to visit one they would say their books were crammed, and we would say our polite thanks and leave rather than insisting that we were better than anything they had.

I think both of us assumed that simply being hysterically bloody funny would be enough, and that everything else would naturally follow from that. That was certainly truer within the confines of the Karno organisation than it turned out to be in the outside world, where other qualities were required to succeed – dogged determination and a self-belief bordering on mental instability – that we did not quite possess in sufficient quantities.

There were bookings for *The Rum 'Uns from Rome* after our triumph at the Royal Victoria Hall, but they were small ones, and few and far between. Odd nights here and there, when we needed whole weeks to survive, and we were all obliged to keep our eyes peeled and our ears to the ground in case something else came along.

One night we played *The Rum 'Uns from Rome* in Brixton – Karno country – and loaded the props onto a handcart afterwards. The show had gone well, but we were pretty fed up as there were no more bookings on the horizon. Ted Leo and I were fed up, anyway. Stan was as relentlessly cheerful as ever.

"Listen, lads," he said once we were settled in the pub. "I got talking to a fellow earlier who is taking a comedy company to Rotterdam. Anyway, he was short, and it sounded like it was too good a chance to miss, so I signed us up. Should tide us over, eh? We leave on Friday."

Ted and I were stunned. "What?" I said. "To play the *Rum 'Uns*, you mean?"

"No," Stan said. "The show is called *Fun on the Tyrol*. The best news is we're staying in a place with a restaurant and a bar, and we get to run up a tab there, on the promoters, like."

"Sounds pretty sweet, if you ask me," Ted said. "Cheers, Stan!"

"And what do we have to do?" I asked.

Stan shrugged. "Dunno," he said. "We'll find out when we get there, I suppose."

Rotterdam was known to be a great town for comedy. We'd heard tales of the warmth of the audiences at the Circus Varieté, where we were due to play, and English pantomime always played well in the Low Countries.

We were called The Eight Comics. I asked our leader, a man called Tubby Reed, whose wife, daughter, brother and sister-in-law made up the rest of the troupe, what he'd have done if he hadn't bumped into Stan. He paused midway through a large pie.

"Well, then I guess we'd have been The Five Comics, wouldn't we?"

We were quartered in the offices of the agents who had booked us, an outfit by the name of Pilcher and Dekker. These rooms were above a pub, no less, and we were indeed invited to run up a tab on the company, so all our food and drink needs were amply supplied. I need hardly say how thrilling this was to hardened music hall artistes used to the traditional doorstep of bread, with jam (if you were lucky) and cup of tea, which was the order of catering traditionally provided by English theatrical landladies. Tubby Reed tucked in with particular gusto, and you could readily believe that this free-food-and-drink arrangement was the main inspiration for setting up the Eight Comics in the first place.

As for *Fun on the Tyrol*, well, it was an Alpine oddity featuring a good deal of nonsense involving milkmaids and cowbells, as you might have expected, but the finale boggled the minds of those of us performing it, so goodness knows what it did to the audience's. We were all on stilts, all eight of us, but it wasn't just ordinary stilt-walking, oh no. It wasn't even the more difficult version where the stilts are stuck up your over-long trouser legs and you can't use your hands. It was stilt-walking with the whole upper half of your body encased inside a gigantic plaster egg.

To be honest, we were all relieved when heavy rain caused the first night to be cancelled. The Circus Varieté had a wooden roof, you see, and the drumming of the torrential downpour drowned out the acts onstage, making the whole thing impossible. We got on with sampling the many varieties of Dutch beer on tap, and practised our stilt walking – not particularly compatible pursuits, by the way.

It rained hard again the next evening, and the grey storm clouds continued to roll in from the North Sea for the rest of the week, leading to cancellation after cancellation. We were content, however, to enjoy the hospitality of Messrs Pilcher and Dekker. Tubby Reed was eating like a king, and the rest of his family were not exactly abstainers.

"Much more of this and we're going to have to start calling ourselves the Nine Comics," Stan said under his breath one lunchtime. "Old Tubby's eating for two."

At the weekend Tubby gathered us together in the bar where we had already spent most of the week. "I have had word from de heer Dekker," he said, a handwritten note quivering in his fat paw. "Our line of credit here at the pub..." here he made a noise a little like a sob, "... will not be extended any further..."

His wife and daughter gasped, and all of us glowered at Tubby as he left the room, frankly suspecting that he was responsible for eating us out of a good thing.

"Well," Ted said. "I'm going to need to get paid, then, pretty quick smart."

"Ah," said Stan, looking sheepish suddenly.

"What?"

"Um... well, you see, the agreement is... no play, no pay."

"What?" Ted and I both shouted together. "You signed us up to a no play, no pay deal?"

"Well, I didn't think it was possible not to... um... play."

Ted spat angrily on the floor and cursed.

"It wasn't just that, of course," Stan said. "There was the free food to take into account, of course, and..." He stopped short.

"And?" I prodded.

"You see, it was such a sure thing, that Tubby suggested that I should buy a share of the production. So we are not just on the straight no play, no pay deal, we are also... on a door split."

"But there's nothing to split!" Ted said, exasperated.

"So we are on a fat share of sweet bugger all," I said, "with no pay, and no food and drink."

"Mmm," Stan agreed. He was looking so forlorn that I had a sudden suspicion that even that was not the whole story.

"Stan?" I said. "How did you buy a share of the production? Aren't we broke?"

"Well, yes, but there was our take from the last couple of *Rum 'Uns* performances..."

Ted let out a loud groan at this.

"... And I... I... hocked the chariot, and the costumes, and the columns. Not the lion skin, they wouldn't give me anything for that. But I got nearly two pounds for the lot."

"Two pounds? But we paid five!"

"Well, Gordon did, technically."

"I know, I know he did, and we still have to pay him back, don't we?" I scratched my head vigorously, trying to comprehend the size of the hole Stan had dug for us. "So you got nearly two pounds?"

Stan nodded.

"Which you invested on our behalf in this misbegotten debacle?"

"Along with our float, remember," Ted put in.

"So how much altogether?"

"Three pounds," Stan said. "It was a pound apiece, you see."

Ted put his head in his hands, and I felt a furious rage building up. "Who the hell told you to do that?" I yelled.

"I thought it was a good idea..."

"You thought? Why didn't you ask me first before you did something so damn'd stupid? We're in this together, aren't we?"

"I didn't want to miss the chance..."

"The chance to be taken for a mug, you mean? Because it's a bloody dream job, this, isn't it? We're stranded in a foreign country, waiting for the rain to stop so we can strut about on stilts dressed as giant bloody eggs, and apparently we've paid every single bloody penny we own for the privilege! Bloody well done, mate! Thank Christ we have you looking out for us!"

"There's no need to be like that," Stan said, looking pretty glum.

"Aarrghh!" I yelled, and kicked a chair, which skittered noisily across the floor and crashed into the far wall.

I couldn't even look at Stan then, or stand to stay in the same room as him, so I stormed out into the street.

———

By the middle of the following week the weather was worse than ever and, ridiculously, the run was cancelled entirely. All because of a wooden roof. Had they never noticed this problem before? Tubby managed to get us a late booking in Liège, and we were obliged to go along as it was the only way we would have even a remote chance to get any of our money back.

Liège was a garrison town, which straddled the Meuse river just a few short miles from the German border. It was surrounded by twelve forts, six on each bank. The intention was that this ring of fortifications should form a formidable obstacle to any potential German army advance towards France, or indeed any French advance towards Germany (much less likely).

Blue-clad infantrymen were everywhere, some marching in formation down the street, others off-duty wandering in and out of bars or shops. It gave the place a sense of foreboding, as though it was in a constant state of readiness for who-knew-what disaster just around the corner. Everyone there seemed acutely aware that if Germany were ever going to make a move on France, then this was the way they would most likely come.[3]

We lugged our ridiculous egg costumes from the station to the theatre, which at least seemed to have a relatively soundproof roof on top of it, trying to ignore the hunger pangs in our bellies. If we could have knocked the top off one of the eggs with a giant teaspoon and all dived in I think we would have done it.

The Eight Comics finally got to perform *Fun on the Tyrol*. We reached the inexplicable finale, somehow, and one by one the giant plaster eggs on stilts made their entrances and lined up. It was pretty hot inside those stupid costumes, and none of us had had a meal for what seemed like days. All of a sudden, I as 'egg-on-stilts number three' heard a low moaning coming from 'egg-on-stilts number four', which contained Stan. Through my sadly inadequate eye holes I caught a brief glimpse of the egg next to me wobbling out of position, and then... Stan fainted.

He fell against me, and bounced away to slump against the egg on the other side, which contained Ted Leo. He fell against Cissie Reed, who knocked over her daughter. Meanwhile I fell against Jim Reed, and he brought down old Tubby at the end with a mighty crash, which smashed his egg,

Humpty Dumpty-style. And there are never any King's horses or King's men around when you need them, are there?

Down we went, like eggy dominoes, and all of us ended up on our backs on the stage, rolling around with our stilted legs kicking pointlessly in the air, unable to right ourselves. It must have looked pretty funny, but was there any laughter? There was a heavy preponderance here, too, of the blue-jacketed soldiery from the garrisons, and perhaps they just weren't in the mood. I strained my ears to hear, but there was nothing, nothing but the echo of my own breathing inside the plaster coffin of my comedy career, until after a moment there was the unmistakeable sound of a boo. The sound grew, and multiplied, until it became full scale jeering, and then, mercifully, the curtain came down.

The run was cancelled even before we unbuckled our stilts.

The eggs had had their chips.

———

We were stranded in Belgium until Tubby Reed managed to get one of his other backers – not Stan, the man was actually a retired Scotland Yard detective with a similar nose for a smart investment – to stump up a little cash for our fares home. By the time we made it back to London Ted and I were not speaking to Stan, and were barely communicating with one another either. We went our separate ways without making any kind of an arrangement to meet up again, and I headed down to Edith Karno's house in Streatham to lick my wounds and try to work out what the hell to do next.

There seemed nothing for it but to loaf around at Poverty Corner once again, hoping for something to turn up, and so that is what I did. At least I had a bed for the night thanks to Edith's benevolence, and she was kind enough to share her evening meals with me.

"You will get a chance soon," she'd say, "and you can pay me something then."

One afternoon I had been at the Corner for hours on end without even the hint of an opportunity coming by. I'd had enough and went for a walk, wandering over Waterloo Bridge, then along the Strand past a couple of steakhouses that set my tummy rumbling, and up into Trafalgar Square.

I strolled across the front of the National Gallery, and lingered by a little knot of pavement artists, who were scribbling away on the stone slabs with little nubs of coloured chalk, their caps alongside them on the ground.

I saw a variety of subjects – scenes of London, Big Ben and Nelson's column (both of which could actually be seen large-as-life simply by turning round), and famous people including Mr Asquith, Mr Lloyd George and the young Prince of Wales dressed as a midshipman – depicted with varying success. A portrait of the arrest of Mrs Pankhurst was bringing one enterprising fellow a regular tinkle of coins from passing ladies. One or two chaps were working away at renditions of famous artworks that resided within the gallery behind them, and I stopped to watch one of these, a young fellow who was putting what looked like the finishing touches to the sky on a pretty impressive paving stone reproduction of Turner's *Fighting Temeraire*.

"Drop a penny in my cap, sir, if you like what you see," he said after a little while, without looking up.

"I like it very much," I said, "but I'm afraid I haven't a penny to my name."

The artist grunted, and continued shading the swirling orange clouds. For some reason it was important to me to let the man know that I was genuinely unable to give him anything for his handiwork.

"I mean it," I said, pulling my empty pockets inside out. "I am a comedian, and I have just come from the Corner, there's nothing doing again today."

The artist stopped and looked up at me for a moment, as if judging my honesty. I shrugged, gave him a regretful smile.

"You hungry?" he said then, which surprised me a little.

"I have not eaten all day," I said.

"All right, tell you what. You sit here and mind my pictures for a few minutes, an' I'll nip round the corner to the ABC and bring us a cup o' tea and a currant bun[4]. Deal?"

"Deal," I agreed readily, and we switched places.

"Just pretend to shade in the sky a bit now and then, don't change nothing," the man said as he stood slowly, flexing his aching knees before trotting off.

He was gone a few minutes, and then returned with two steaming cups and a couple of buns on a plate.

"You can take the china back for me when we're done, all right?"

"Thank you," I said gratefully, taking a bite. "I'm Arthur."

"Donald," the artist said. "Don't mention it. You've done me a good turn. If I leave all this unattended one of those buggers will swipe my pitch." He nodded over towards some vagrants loafing in the square a little way off. "Then it's fisticuffs to get it back. I was dyin' for a cuppa, an' all."

I looked down at the chalk *Temeraire*, cunningly rendered with a few white strokes for the masts, and the dark little tug boat alongside. "How long did this take you?" I said.

"Oh that? I've got that one off. I can do the ships in a few minutes now, and then I spend the rest of the day pretending to

214

be finishing the sky. Now Simon over there," he said, indicating a skeletal youth about twenty feet away, "he studied at the Royal Academy, and every day he attempts to recreate Raphael's *Aldobrandini Madonna*. It takes him most of the day, and it breaks his heart to leave it. Then the street cleaners hose it away and the next day he does it all over again. It's like a performance, people drop pennies in his hat for the entertainment. Others get down here early, finish a couple of pictures nice and fast, and then sit by them with their caps out. Some of 'em don't even do their own drawings. You see the laddo there with the Prince of Wales? I did that for him first thing this morning, an' I get a cut of his take, see?"

"Ha," I said, finishing off my bun. "Maybe I should look into it. I'm not making any money with what I'm doing at the moment."

"Do you draw?" Donald said.

"I have painted," I said. "I did the backdrop for Fred Karno's *Football Match* sketch. It was supposed to look like a crowd of faces."

"Oh well, if you can do faces, my friend, you've got it made. Here..." He scrabbled around, collecting together the odd ends of coloured chalk into a tobacco tin, ushering me along to a bare paving slab. "'Ave a go."

"Oh no, I should be going," I said.

"What? Urgent appointment, is it? Go on, give it a try."

I picked up a little piece of chalk. "What shall I do? I don't know any paintings."

"You were on the 'alls, you say? Draw me a comic, then."

So I began sketching from memory, gradually working out the techniques as I went, and before long I had come up with a decent picture of my old friend George Robey, the Prime Minister of Mirth, who was just about the biggest name in music hall.

"There you go, not bad, not bad at all," Donald said. "Now shade in some background, like a fancy red curtain behind him..."

I did as he suggested, dimly aware that I was being watched, and then my concentration was broken by a metallic clink, and then another. I looked up to see what it was, and a couple of pennies had appeared alongside my knees, and I picked them up, wonderingly.

"Just pop your cap on the floor," Donald said, "an' you're away."

By dusk, to my utter astonishment, I had accumulated a couple of shillings, and had arranged to return early the next morning to secure a pitch alongside my new mentor.

━━━━━

Over the next few weeks and months I became a Trafalgar Square regular. My intention in the early days was to keep heading down to the Corner to look for stage work, but that gradually went by the board. I could make a surprisingly decent amount of pocket money simply drawing on the pavement, enough to keep body and soul together anyway, and enough so that I could finally give Edith a little for my board, while all that awaited me at the Corner, frankly, was humiliation and disappointment.

I missed the thrill of being on stage, of course, but it gradually became a more and more distant memory, and anyway what was I going to do? There was no hope of reviving *The Rum 'Uns from Rome*, it would just cost too much money to retrieve the props and pay off Stan's brother, and in any case I hadn't seen Stan or Ted Leo since our ignominious retreat from Europe.

I told myself I was keeping a kind of connection with my previous life, however thin, by making pictures of scenes from the music halls my specialty. I amused myself by doing a drawing of Marie Lloyd, say, and another of Harry Lauder, and then sitting between them with a collecting cup on either side, thus conducting a rudimentary popularity survey of the personalities of comedy. Little Tich always scored highly, with his great long boots, as did Robey and the great Marie. Others, I think, might have been disappointed by how little they were recognised, although the fault must partly have been mine. I could never quite capture the duality of Vesta Tilley's Burlington Bertie from Bow, for example, and it was pleasing to discover that no one really recognised my portrait of Sydney Chaplin, although it cost me good money to find that out.

My masterpiece, if I say so myself, was a sweeping and detailed representation of the Fred Karno company in *Mumming Birds*. I drew it with Chaplin junior as the Inebriated Swell falling out of the box in such a way that he would be certain to land painfully on his stupid neck. Meanwhile the Prestidigitateur would be enjoying his moment of triumph, as in San Francisco, with the white dove miraculously flying from his hands. I spent most of my time labouring to do justice to his gorgeous assistant, paying attention to every detail of her lovely face and figure.

It always brought a healthy clink of coins into my cup, but I only did the drawing every once in a while, because it broke my heart to do it.

21
THE GUV'NOR AHOY!

ONE warm sunny evening in the summer of 1912 I was walking up and down the garden at Edith Karno's house in Streatham, idly working on a Woodbine which was keeping the midges at bay, when a familiar voice hailed me.

"What ho, Arthur!"

I looked round, and there, beaming from ear to ear and waving his precious Boss o' the Plains hat in the air, was none other than young Freddie Karno Junior.

"Freddie!" I shouted, and strode over to shake his hand warmly. "How splendid to see you! So you're back from the States!"

"Indeed," my young friend grinned. "We sailed last week and I am only just recovering. I didn't get a wink of sleep all the way across thinking about icebergs."

Of course the Titanic had gone down just a couple of months earlier, which had been enough to put a chill into the bones of anyone who had to make that sea crossing.

"Imagine my surprise when I came over to visit Mama and here's you with your feet under the table!"

"She has been very kind. Without her I should have been quite destitute."

"She's a brick," Freddie nodded. "So, you know what I've been doing, but what exciting things have *you* been up to, eh?"

"I am an artist, of sorts," I said.

"Oh stop it. You sound just like Chaplin," Freddie said dismissively. He seemed a good deal more confident these days, I suddenly noticed, more assertive than the young lad who had wanted so desperately to be one of us. "Now listen – what are you doing tomorrow?"

"Not much," I shrugged.

"All the company have been invited onto the Guv'nor's houseboat for the day. You must come along. It should be quite a party."

"Oh, I don't know if I should just invite myself along to a do of the Guv'nor's," I said doubtfully, although a bell was ringing somewhere in my head. That phrase 'all the company', did that mean? Surely it did? Tilly...?

"You're not inviting yourself. *I* am inviting you, and I won't take 'no' for an answer. So it's settled."

━━━━━

And so the next day Freddie and I made our way out of town, past Hampton Court Palace and along the bank of the River Thames towards East Molesey. We passed some houseboats moored here and there, some resembling the longboats that plied the canals, others more like little floating bungalows with the residents taking the sun on the flat roofs between their narrow pipe chimneys. Nothing we saw, though, prepared us for our first glimpse of the *Astoria*, Fred Karno's pride and joy.

It was enormous, two whole storeys high, nestling against Tagg's Island in the middle of the river against a backdrop of tall trees waving gently in the summer breeze. The lower level was very grand, all polished wood and painted ironwork, with alternating picture windows and nautical portholes. At the stern a curving staircase led up to the top level, which was open beneath a sun canopy. Ornate ironwork railings ran the length of the boat, with strings of coloured lights hanging from the upper arches. From the river bank we could hear the merry chatter of dozens of people, the clink of glasses, the occasional popping cork, and there was clearly a substantial event in progress.

"He simply asked them to build him the grandest houseboat ever seen on the Thames," Freddie said, admiringly. "How do we get over there, I wonder?"

A short stroll along the bank brought us to a little wooden jetty, where a wizened old codger was waiting with a row boat. We persuaded him to ferry us across to the island, and he grumbled the whole way about how busy he had been, gasping and gurning the while, exaggerating the effort the job was costing him in the hope of increasing his tip.

"Watch out for icebergs," Freddie chirped, halfway across, but didn't raise even the faintest hint of a smile from our put-upon pilot.

He dropped us on the tip of the island, and we followed a little footpath of trampled grass through the trees until we came to the gang plank connecting the Guv'nor's floating palace to the shore.

"Apparently he wanted room for a ninety-piece orchestra to play on the upper deck," Freddie confided as we stepped aboard. "Now how often do you think a ninety-piece orchestra is going to drop round?"

There were musicians atop the Astoria just then, as it happens, but only a little quartet. The rest of the space was occupied by

220

Karno comics enjoying a sumptuous buffet lunch in the warm summer sunshine.

Fred Kitchen was there, probably Karno's senior number one, getting around the outside of a vol-au-vent or two. There was Syd Chaplin, resplendent in a white blazer and boater, also tucking in, a couple of stray crumbs clinging to his drooping moustache.

Shaun Glenville was there, the first number one I ever saw in action, back when I was a super on *Wontdetainia*, the spectacular sketch about high jinks on board an ocean liner. And George Robey was a special guest, chasing a quail egg around his plate with a silver fork.

Behind them a bevy of lesser mortals waited their turn at the groaning board. I noticed to my amusement that they had arranged themselves according to their place in the comedy hierarchy. A clutch of number twos were ready to serve themselves next, including Johnny Doyle – dressed in a man's garb for once – and then so on down to the also-rans and seat-fillers, who would make do with scraps and leftovers once the giant beasts of the comedy jungle had had their fill.

I spotted the American company grouped together near the river side railings, just as they spotted me.

"Arthur!" said Emily Seaman. "Wonderful to see me, isn't it?"

I slapped a frozen smile on my features at hearing that one again, which amused Bert Williams.

"Sss, sss, ssss!"

Alf Reeves was there, and Amy, and the Palmers, and the Seamans, Mike Asher, Albert Austin, Bert Williams and Charles Griffiths, as well as Ted Banks and Charles Cardon, the replacements for myself and Stan. I greeted them all warmly, and indulged in a little hand-shaking and back-slapping.

No sign of Charlie, though. Nor of Tilly.

But there was Karno himself, proudly showing off the features of his newest toy to anyone who'd listen, sporting a peaked nautical cap adorned with a little golden anchor. When the Guv'nor clapped his eyes on me, they narrowed somewhat. He gave a little cough, which usually meant trouble.

"Hallo Guv'nor," I said brightly, trying to smooth over the awkwardness of the moment.

"Mr Dandoe. Are you a member of this company then?"

"Well... I... um... that is..."

"He most certainly is," Freddie Junior said, putting his arm around my shoulders. "Now let's get you a drink, shall we, Arthur?"

Karno frowned, and I braced myself for some withering remark but it never came. Instead he looked genuinely puzzled, as though he had actually forgotten whether or not I was still in his employ. Maybe Billie Ritchie was right, and he had taken his eye off things at the Fun Factory in recent months.

"Do you want this pork pie?" Amy said to me. "My eyes were bigger than my stomach."

I took her plate from her. "Is... Charlie expected?" I asked.

"Oh, you know young Mr Chaplin," she tutted. "If there's a train to be missed, or a deadline, or an invitation, he'll miss it."

Mike Asher strolled over with a glass and a grin, dapper as ever in his sharply-creased flannels and a straw boater, somehow managing to convey both that he was relaxing and that he was ready for any main chance that might present itself, and we leaned on the railing looking out over the river.

"So Mike, how was the land of opportunity?" I said.

"Ha!" he said, glancing round to see who might overhear, then lowering his voice. "I'm not going back there in a hurry, I'll tell you that."

"Why, what's wrong?"

Mike sighed. "Lucia, that's what."

"That lovely burlesque girl of yours?"

"Yeah, she's not mine, mate. I took a bit of a shine to her, that's all."

"I remember, and she to you, if I'm not mistaken."

Mike's face took on a haunted look. "Yes, well, when we went back to Chicago the second time, after you and Stan had gone home, well, there she was again."

"She got her job back at the burlesque show, then?"

"That's just it. She didn't. She was just there. Waiting for me. Said she was madly in love with me and couldn't live without me."

"Ha ha ha!"

"It's not funny, damn it!"

"What did you do?"

"Well, I felt I needed to be firm, for her own good..."

"Should you be telling me this?"

"Not that, I didn't mean that! I couldn't afford to support her, could I? Well, you know what the pay was, you left because of it, didn't you? But as it turned out she picked up some more burlesque work there pretty easily, so that week or two worked out well enough. Too well, actually, because that led her to believe that..."

"Believe that what?"

"That... we could make a proper go of it, and after that all I heard was about how we should be engaged, and married, and settle down, and in the end I simply had to break with her."

"After how long?"

"Oh, another two months, maybe three. All right, maybe I led her on a bit, but she was so lovely, and it was nice, you know, to have her around even though she was a bit nuts."

"So then that was the end of it?"

"Oh no, no, no, not by a long chalk. *Then* she would turn up at the show, and I would see her in the audience. She wouldn't say anything, or try and see me, but there she'd be, just... watching. Not every day, not every week even, but, you know, pretty regularly. I'd think she'd got over me and then there she'd be again. It started to give me the willies."

"Ironically," I said.

"So by the time we came to leave the States I was really pretty relieved, but d'you know just as the boat was ready to leave New York there Lucia was on the dock, and I was convinced she was going to try to come on board too, but no. She just stood there with a sad look on her face, waving her handkerchief. Can you believe it?"

"You are quite a catch," I said.

"Oh, do shut up!" Mike said, thumping my upper arm with his fist. "Anyway, the hounds of hell wouldn't drag me back there, because she'd know, I don't know how, but she'd know."

He left me then to find more to drink and I paused to take in the view. A little way downstream I noticed the Ancient Mariner was making another crossing in his rowing boat, two passengers in the stern. Nearest me was a dapper little gent in a fancy striped blazer and a straw boater with his back turned in my direction, and his companion was a girl in a green summer dress with a matching parasol.

I watched as they reached the bank, and the little fellow stepped ashore. I couldn't see their faces, but something about the exaggerated courtliness with which he extended his hand to help the girl off the boat let me know with a sudden jolt that he was Charlie Chaplin.

And then the sun struck the blonde curls of his lady friend, and my heart stood still, because it was Tilly.

Of course it was.

The rowboat set off back to the other side, and the two of them started off along the towpath towards the Astoria. She had her arm in his, and they were taking their time, chuckling away at some shared amusement or other.

"They make a lovely couple, don't they?" said a voice at my elbow. It was Muriel Palmer. Like all married women of my acquaintance she could hardly wait to pair everyone else off, as if to validate the choice she herself had made.

All eyes seemed to be on them, and they knew it, as Charlie led Tilly up the gang plank and onto the boat. He brought her hand to his lips and then moved towards the drinks table to fetch them both a glass of something. Tilly stepped across the deck to say hello to the company with smiles and pecks on the cheek here and there.

Then she spotted me, and her eyes widened.

"Arthur, what a lovely surprise to see you, how have you been?"

I was bursting to tell her everything that had happened since I last saw her. I knew she'd have loved *The Rum 'Uns from Rome*, and I could have made her howl with laughter at the plaster stilt egg disaster in Rotterdam, and I had missed that laugh so much. I wanted to tell her too about becoming a pavement artist in Trafalgar Square, but suddenly it struck me that she and Charlie were so tight that telling her about my trials and tribulations was the same as telling him, and I wasn't at all sure I wanted him to know that things had not been going well.

So I said: "Fine, thank you, I have been fine."

"Have you seen anything of Stan?"

"Yes, from time to time our paths have crossed," I said.

"But he's not with you today?"

"No, he's not, no."

"Good Heavens, is that *Dandoe*?" Charlie was with us, a glass of champagne held delicately in each manicured hand. It seemed to me that he had said my name unnecessarily loudly, perhaps hoping that if my presence was noted by the right people I would be ejected.

"Hallo, Charlie," I said. "How's tricks?"

"Oh, life is splendid, isn't it?" he said, handing Tilly a glass, and looking to her for confirmation. She smiled, nodded. "Absolutely splendid. We have completed another two triumphant circuits of America, and now we are off to the Channel Islands for a month. Things could hardly be going better!"

He snaked his free arm around Tilly's waist as if to emphasise the point.

"I'm glad to hear it," I managed to force myself to say.

"After that I am hoping the Guv'nor will send us back to America. England feels so *small-time*, somehow, don't you think?"

I gritted my teeth into a smile, and waited for him to enquire after my well-being in return, but instead I saw his tiny hand pull Tilly closer to him, in proprietorial fashion.

"Now, shall we see if these gannets have left us any lunch?"

"Oooh, yes, let's, I'm starved," Tilly said. As Charlie steered her away from me she shot me a smile over her shoulder, and gave a little helpless shrug.

I leaned back against the railing, dazzled and overwhelmed by seeing her again.

Not only that, though.

Seeing her with him.

22
KARNO'S KARSINO

AFTER lunch Karno led us all off the *Astoria* and onto Tagg's Island. Behind the attractive screen of trees the interior appeared to be a neglected and unkempt little wilderness. He announced that he had something to show us all, and so everyone present trotted dutifully along in his wake as he marched onwards like Professor Challenger exploring the Lost World, the *Strand* sensation at the time.

Tagg's Island was shaped like a boat, and when we reached the prow, as it were, there was a large open area, where some preliminary attempts at clearing some space seemed to have taken place. Karno held up his hand, indicating we should stop and gather round, and wait for the stragglers at the rear to catch up.

I was watching Tilly on the other side of the clearing, sandwiched between Charlie and his brother Syd, laughing as she received oily flattery from both Chaplins at once, so I was rather taken by surprise when Karno himself sidled over to me, an avuncular beam all over his face. It was terrifying.

"Here he is," he said. "*Here's* the man I want to have a word with."

"Really, Guv'nor?" I said, taken aback.

"Oh yes. Something we *definitely* need to discuss, you and I."
He reached an arm around me and clapped me on the shoulder.

"There is?"

"Concerning your future," Karno said, tapping the side of his
nose in a conspiratorial fashion.

"Well, um, er, of course," I stammered. "I'd be happy to."

He seemed to be on the point of saying more, but then all at
once he realised that his audience was now in situ, and he held
a forefinger up in front of my face. "Later," he said, and winked.

I watched his shiny shoes as he stepped up onto an upturned
wooden crate, my heart pounding and the blood rushing in my
ears.

Karno wanted to talk to me!

I experienced a quick moment of alarm when I suddenly
thought he might have found out about me sleeping rough in the
Karno omnibus over at the Fun Factory, but no, surely not, that
was months ago. And anyway, didn't he say it was concerning
my *future* that he wanted to speak to me? A future recalled to the
fond embrace of the Karno organisation? I could hardly breathe.

"Ahem!" Karno coughed, and immediately had everyone's
attention. "Friends," he began. "Thank you all for coming."

"Thank *you* for having us, Guv'nor," Fred Kitchen called out,
raising a glass to the boss, and there was a murmuring of "Hear!
Hear!" from the assembled multitude.

"You are all welcome, I'm sure. Now as you know I have been
spending a good deal of time in this neck of t'woods, since the
houseboat was finished, and the time has come for me to tell you
all what I have been up to."

He paused for dramatic effect, and then he spread his arms
wide and smiled.

"The fact is... I have bought this island."

This bombshell didn't quite produce the sensation he was hoping for. Many of those present had been steeling themselves, I think, for him to announce his retirement, as he had been so distracted lately. And now he had bought an island? What did this mean for the Fun Factory? Everyone there depended upon Karno for their livelihood – except myself, of course, but then maybe I was about to be recalled to the ranks? – and to a man and woman they were all thinking: "What is this going to mean for *me*?" Actually, there was one spectator to this event with no particular stake in developments, and it was he who piped up to break the stunned silence.

"Whatever have you done that for, Fred?" said George Robey, still casually munching the last of an apple pie from his buffet luncheon platter.

"I plan to build here on Tagg's Island a pleasure palace, such as you might find on the continent. A luxury hotel, featuring the finest service, top class West End entertainment, and a casino."

"A *Kar*sino," I blurted, then suddenly bit my tongue. What a daft thing to say! Don't get on the wrong side of him now!

"Hmm," the Guv'nor grunted, not best pleased to be interrupted. "It will be the premier entertainment attraction in London, in England, in Europe, maybe even... the world!"

This messianic announcement jolted the assembled throng into cheering and applause.

"So the hotel will be here, right here, where we are standing now, and all the rest of the island, spreading away behind you there, will be given over to specially designed pleasure gardens, including no less than two hundred yards of lawns."

A spontaneous "Oooh!" went up from the crowd, many of whom turned to try and imagine the jungle of nettles and brambles behind us being tamed and transformed.

"As for the hotel itself, I am having Mr Frank Matcham draw up some designs, but what we are planning is a grand ballroom over there, with a stage for a full orchestra, and the idea is to arrange things so that the proscenium arch is in the middle of the performance area, so that we can play both ways, into the ballroom, and also out onto the lawn on a warm evening."

A smattering of sycophantic applause greeted this vision, and here and there a "Wonderful!" and a "Fabulous!" were heard. The Guv'nor allowed a little smile to reach his lips.

"How are people going to get to this hotel, Fred, if you don't mind me asking?" George Robey chirped up. "Are you not concerned that that old timer with the rowboat could expire on the night of the grand opening?"

There was laughter at this, and even Karno smiled. "Arrangements will be made, of course," he said. "And on the opening night there will be dozens of ferry boats, all piloted by beautiful young actresses."

A little bout of nudging was evident then, as seasoned Karno hands imagined the recruiting process being supervised by the old goat himself, perhaps in the luxurious private apartments that had been glimpsed on the lower deck of the *Astoria*.

"And we'll have none of your *German* waiters – every table will be waited upon by a top London comedian.5" Karno actually winked at this, and the message was clear: I mean you lot!

"Well," I thought. "I'll cheerfully wash dishes all night long if it means getting back in your good books."

Syd Chaplin stepped forward then, and said: "It sounds fantastic, I can hardly wait. I'm sure I speak for everyone here when I say you can count on us for any help you require..." He looked around, and there was a sycophantic murmuring of agreement.

"And allow me to be the first to say 'Congratulations! Another brilliant Karno idea!'"

Everyone started clapping and cheering, and proposing toasts to the new venture.

"Thank you! Thank you!" Karno said, stepping down from his little podium. "Take a walk around, or return to the *Astoria* as you please. Both belong to me now. Afternoon tea at four!"

I tried to catch his eye, but he strode briskly away to attend to something on his boat, and I found myself chatting to good old George Robey as we ambled in his wake.

"So you mean to tell me you are not one of Fred's boys any longer?" he said, frowning.

"Well," I said, thinking nervously of the conversation to come. "Hopefully that's just a temporary state of affairs."

"Let us hope so. Such a waste is not to be tolerated."

I told him about the drawings I had done of him on the pavement in Trafalgar Square, and how he had fared in my rough penny-based popularity contest.

"I should be very happy to give Marie best," he said. "Let battle be joined between me and the audience, not between me and the Queen. After all, are we not all brothers and sisters on the boards? Why should we squabble?"

That struck me as the sort of view someone could freely take when they had already reached the very top of the profession, but still.

———

In the late afternoon tea was served, and with a little flourish the Guv'nor turned on the strings of coloured light bulbs that were draped from the ironwork. It changed the atmosphere from that of a social gathering of work colleagues to a full-blown party, and it must have been a spectacular sight. It certainly caught the eye of one passer-by, anyway, as shortly afterwards we heard a foppish falsetto voice screaming hysterically from out on the water. Everyone moved to the rail to look, and so sturdy was the *Astoria* that it barely tilted. In midstream there was a fellow in white flannels, with a lady reclining in his rowing boat.

"Oh, look at my lovely boat, everyone!" this caricature shouted, showing off to his companion. "Look at my lovely boat! Look at all the lovely lights! Ha, ha, ha!" The two of them then dissolved into hysterical mocking laughter and pointing.

Karno's face turned puce with fury. He gave a little cough, which acted subliminally on the central nervous system of everyone who had ever worked with him. We all turned to listen.

"This young snob," he said, calmly but loud enough to carry above the scornful cackling. "Clearly finds us vulgar. Well *I* say..." Here the great man paused, and filled his lungs, before letting loose a mighty roar. "Let's show him vulgar!"

He grasped the railing and thrust his chest out over it, giving him the look of a lion protecting his territory, and then he unleashed the most violent flow of invective any of us had ever heard. Such crudeness! Such oaths! The air turned blue! We all gaped for a few seconds, then with one will we all turned and joined in, howling and screaming our rage at this idiot and his stupid girl. It was joyous.

The toff's eyebrows shot up into his straw boater, and he began scrabbling around for his oars to propel his lady friend away from this savagery. She was trying to cover her ears and eyes at the same time, but didn't have enough hands to achieve this. One of the oars slipped from its rowlock and began to float away from him, meaning he had to paddle frantically towards the *Astoria* to retrieve it.

Freddie spotted that this brought the rowing boat within range of a decent throw, and knocked the fellow's hat askew with a cream scone. Others quickly followed suit, and before you knew it there was a veritable hailstorm of pastries spattering down on the unhappy pair.

Every heckle line, every abusive shout any of us had ever heard onstage was revisited here with gleeful venom. To my surprise, the aloof Charlie Chaplin was as carried away as anyone, clambering up the railings and leaning out to spit his Rabelaisian contempt at the interlopers. And further along someone else – I couldn't quite see who – had dropped his trousers and stuck out his bare backside like a baboon.

When Karno saw this he raised his hands for quiet, and then led us in a choral salute of raspberries, which sustained as the rowing boat was carried miserably alongside and then away downstream, with its occupants looking like they might never recover from the shock.

Served them right.

The mood after this episode was one of the most glorious camaraderie, and spirits were high. For me this was a bitter sweet pleasure. I was really enjoying seeing everyone again, and realising how much I missed being part of a large team, with the daily pressures of constantly searching for employment lifted from my shoulders.

Naturally my thoughts turned to the prospect of once more calling myself a Karno comedian. Surely that was what the Guv'nor wanted to discuss, and I kept a weather eye out for the opportunity to make myself available for whatever he had in mind.

Of course, I thought with a pang of regret, I knew that it would likely not be with the old company. Charlie would see to that, wanting to keep me away from Tilly, and not welcoming the sort of competition I could provide.

But still, any Karno company anywhere would be a new start, a new chance to get a foot on the ladder, to show what I could do, and maybe one day in the not-too distant future revive my ambition to be a number one in my own right. In the end I could wait no longer, and waylaid him on the top deck.

"You said you wanted a word, Guv'nor?" I prompted.

"Yes! Yes indeed! Let us find a little privacy, shall we? Somewhere where we won't be disturbed."

He led me down to the lower deck, bouncing a little drunkenly from side to side along the narrow corridor, and then pushed open a polished wooden door with gleaming brass handles.

"After you," he said.

I found myself in a luxuriously appointed bedroom, with a quite massive double bed which reached almost clear across the cabin. There was a surprising quantity of frills and flounces, and I wondered whether they were touches provided by Maria, the former chorus girl who had been passed off as Mrs Karno for the last several years, or whether, just possibly, she had never even set foot in the place.

"Sit yourself down," Karno said. I perched on the edge of the monstrous item – there was nowhere else to sit, no room for a chair – and tried not to think of what the old goat might have got up to among these white sheets and pillows. He himself sat down at the other end, and leaned over casually on one elbow, surrounded by cushions like some ancient potentate.

"So tell me this," he said. "How are things going for you?"

"Oh, pretty well," I said, wary of appearing desperate. "I can't complain."

"Ah," Karno said, his eyes narrowing beadily. "So that weren't you I saw t'other day panhandling in Trafalgar Square?"

He'd got me on the back foot there and no mistake. "Well, that..." I stammered. "That is by way of being a sideline."

"Is it?"

"Yes, oh yes. You see I sometimes dabble, as you might say, do some quick pictures for the fellows there, and then they give me a cut of whatever they take in. I can make a pretty packet on a good day."

"Really?"

"Aha, yes. Oh yes. Ahem."

Karno paused, inspected his fingernails. "So you wouldn't be interested, then, in an offer of work?"

"Oh, well, what sort of an offer, Guv'nor?"

"I think I could see my way to finding a place for you..."

"Oh, that would be marv...!"

"...under certain conditions."

"Conditions, Guv'nor?"

"Yes, you know the sort of thing. You scratch my back, I scratch yours."

Perched as we were on his large and flouncy bed, my mind leapt rapidly to some uncomfortable conclusions. I glanced upwards, and caught sight of his reflection in a large mirror bolted to the low ceiling.

"What sort of... scratching do you have in mind?"

"Well, let me see now..." Karno tapped his lips with his forefinger. "Freddie tells me that you are currently residing at the same address as my wife. Is that not so?"

Now I had it. With a flash like a bolt of lightning all my hopes came crashing down upon my head. I knew exactly where this conversation was headed.

"It is," I sighed. "She has been most kind."

"Very cosy, I must say." He coughed his trademark little cough. "So what I propose is this. Simple really. You come back to work for me. Perhaps even a small raise, eh? What d'you say? And then at some point in t' near future, my lawyer will call you as a witness in a little divorce action that I shall be bringing, and everybody wins."

I said nothing.

"You don't need to say owt now. Just present yourself up at t' Fun Factory and we shall see what can be done wi' you, eh?"

He coughed again, and awkwardly pushed himself up from the cushions. "Well, I'd best be getting back to my guests," he said. "So?"

"Right," I said. "Yes. Thank you, Guv'nor."

Somehow I dragged my leaden feet out of there, and I kept going, as if in a trance, off the boat and along the path to where the old codger was waiting to row people across.

As we eased away the *Astoria* twinkled like some fantastical wonderland, like Camelot, with those who, like Freddie Junior, had been afforded an invitation to stay the night in one of the magnificent state rooms on the lower deck, still laughing and drinking and chatting away under the lights and waiting for dinner to be served in the magnificent wood-panelled dining room below. A champagne cork popped, and then plopped lightly into the river behind me.

A chill swept suddenly along the surface of the water, and I pulled my jacket close around me, turning up the collar.

I would have to leave Edith Karno's house in the morning, that much was clear. I would have to tell her why, as well, as I could hardly let her think she had done anything wrong, or been anything other than a good friend to me.

Of course, Karno's lawyer would be swift to paint her kindness in offering me a roof over my head as 'moral turpitude', to use the Guv'nor's own phrase, and our innocent friendship as living in sin.

And Karno had seen me working in Trafalgar Square, evidently, even though I had not spotted him, so he would know where to find me, which meant that I would even have to give up that meagre source of income.

Sitting there balling my fists impotently, thinking of Karno's self-serving and manipulative 'offer', well, it made my gorge rise.

"If that's what it takes to make it in the comedy business," I thought, "you can keep it. It is not worth the candle."

And there and then, in the middle of the River Thames, with the Ancient Mariner's old joints creaking away in time with his gurning and wheezing, I retired.

23
AND IS THERE HONEY STILL FOR TEA?

WHAT will you do?" Edith asked quietly.

"What can I do?" I shrugged. "I suppose I will go back to Cambridge, and see if my father can get me a job in the college. I don't think that will be a problem, he's a fairly important fellow there. I imagine he'll be able to pull a string or two. Of course I shall have to listen to the smug 'I told you so's', but there are worse things than that, aren't there?"

"Will you let me pay for your train ticket?" she said.

"I couldn't," I said.

"I insist," she said. "You are leaving because of me, and I know how hard up you are." She went to a roll-top bureau and I heard the rustling of paper. "Take this." She turned, pressed an envelope into my hand, and then embraced me warmly.

On the tram into London I discovered that she had put four crisp pound notes inside for me, bless her, money that she could ill afford. It got me back to Cambridge, and some left over.

Once there, I presented myself, somewhat sheepishly, at the Porters' Lodge of the old college. My father was there, standing at post behind the counter there. I knew he had been warming his feet by the fire in the back room just moments before, but the cumbersome wooden door had given its hinge-squeaking early warning and its weight served to stall visitors just long enough for him always to appear uncannily ready to serve.

His face betrayed no emotion at the return of his prodigal second son. Or did it? Was I imagining it, or was there a slight tremble to his lip?

"Arthur. Well, well. Is this a flying visit or are we back, now?"

"We are back," I said.

"And your theatrical adventure?"

"It is no more."

"Over and done with?"

"Over, yes, and as you rightly say, done with."

My father nodded slowly, taking this in. He could see I was chastened, and disheartened, and he decided not to press me further just then, for which I was grateful.

"Do I take it that you are looking for alternative employment, then?"

"I am, yes, if you will have me."

"Hmm. I am sure something can be done. We always seem to be short-handed." He lifted the hinged counter and stepped out, guiding me out into the courtyard with an arm around my shoulder. "Why don't I walk you over to the kitchens, and we can let your mother know you are here. She will be glad to see you, I am sure, and there will no doubt be some of her excellent fruit tart left over from luncheon."

"Thank you, father," I said, a lump in my throat suddenly.

He smiled. "You'll have to get used to calling me 'Mister Dandoe', you know, if you are going to be resuming your duties here."

I gave a little laugh. Only a little one, because he wasn't joking.

My mother welcomed me back with a floury embrace in the midst of preparing several great baking trays of scones.

"Hello, dear. You'll have to excuse me, I'm afraid, so much to do. I'll see you at home."

And my elder brother Lance, still a college porter under my father, as he had been since his return from active service against the Boer, passed us in the Old Courtyard as we made our way back to the lodge, a pair of newly-polished shoes clamped in each paw.

"All right, Arthur?" he muttered, without even breaking his stride.

"All right Lance?" I replied.

Two years, I'd been away. And that was that.

There were, unexpectedly, no 'I told you so's', no smugness, no smirking superiority. There wasn't even faint surprise. I was simply reabsorbed into the college serving community as though I had never left, or rather as though this was always going to be my fate sooner or later. Which, in a way, felt even worse.

My old bed remained, made up, in the room I had always shared with Lance in the family home, vouchsafed to us by the beneficence of the college, just off Trumpington Street. I just had to shift some of my brother's boots off the blanket.

Lance showed next to no curiosity about where I had been or what I had been doing. The only conversation we had on the subject was whilst lying in the dark one night, and it went like this:

"So you went to America, then?"

"Yes."

"See any cowboys?"

"I'm not sure. I saw some cowboy hats in Montana, and some fellows with spurs on their boots who might have been cowboys."

"Indians?"

240

"No, no Indians."

"G'night."

"Good night, Lance."

I was given responsibility for three staircases, cleaning and making beds, and as it was out of term time quite a few of the rooms were unoccupied and just needed airing out. It was not particularly taxing work, but I must admit it was good to feel coins jingling in my pocket at the weekends, and to be able to go out for a pint or two without worrying where the next meal was coming from.

Towards the end of the summer the college, indeed the whole city, began to fill up in preparation for the start of a new academic year. The students seemed young, younger than before, and after a week or two I noticed preparations being made for a smoking concert in the Old Reader, much like the one where I had first trod the boards some five years earlier. I saw the young gents' fresh-faced excitement at the prospect of stepping up to try and get a precious laugh from their peers. It reminded me of my friend Ralph Luscombe, the student who had become my friend and first introduced me to the thrills of performing. Like him, though, I thought bitterly, these striplings were doomed to have that joy thrashed out of them by the real world, and like him were probably inescapably destined to spend their adult lives trapped in the family business.

As was I.

I didn't sneak a look at the smoking concert, nor did I venture along to see what the Footlights were about. The students I had known in that society would all have graduated by now, of course, but Rottenburg was still there. The Rotter himself, the *eminence grise* of the mechanics department, who had designed and built the huge dinosaur contraption from wood, canvas and pulleys which had, in turn, attracted a curious Fred Karno to Cambridge and thus started my own adventure in the professional music halls. The show they were doing was called *Cheer Oh Cambridge!*, and had a catchy ragtime title song which I heard absolutely everywhere, not least because they were rehearsing in our college. I would see them coming and going, The Rotter, and Jack Hulbert and the pianist Alan Murray (whose room I was responsible for tidying), but I averted my eyes and bowed my head and was not recognised.

I had no interest in seeing their show – to my hardened professional eye it would have seemed like the sort of scratch nonsense cobbled together by children in their parents' clothes on a Christmas afternoon. I had no interest, either, in seeking out professional entertainment, even though the other porters, even Lance, would often head out to the town's music hall at the weekend and tried to talk me into joining them. The very idea seemed too painful just then, though, and so I stayed away.

In point of fact I seemed to have no great interest in laughing.

I tried not to linger on memories of Tilly arm in arm with Chaplin, but it was not easy. Every pleasant memory I had of being onstage seemed to lead me back to that, and thoughts of defeat, having to give second best to... *him*.

I suppose in my bitterness I was not particularly good company, and after being pretty sociable to begin with the other staff started to leave me alone. I found more and more that when I went to the pub at the weekend it was by myself, and I was probably drinking more than I would otherwise have done. I hoped it would help me forget, but it didn't really. It just made me drunk while I remembered.

Things must have reached a pretty low point for it to have caught Lance's attention. One day he cornered me as I was coming out of the linen room.

"Tonight," he said.

"Tonight what?"

"No argument, I've bought you a ticket."

"For what? What are you talking about?"

"You've been so bloody miserable since you came back, it's time you had a good laugh."

"Oh, no, I don't want to go to the bloody music hall, Lance."

He reached into his pocket for the tickets, and waved them in front of my face.

"Not the hall, little brother. You and me is going to the circus!"

I sighed inwardly, but it was an unusual gesture for him to even acknowledge my existence, let alone show concern for my well-being, so I nodded.

"All right. Thanks Lance."

So that evening we made our way to Parker's Piece, where Hengler's Circus had erected a rather impressive big top. It was going to be packed, as well, as crowds of people were bustling inside, humming with what seemed like more than ordinary excitement. Lance and I perched on a wooden bench, a little puzzled by the air of expectancy.

The orchestra struck up a little fanfare, and then the ringmaster entered the arena, resplendent in bright red tails and a top hat. With a little ceremony he guided a small party of VIPs to their seats front and centre, waving his arms to urge us to applaud. There was the mayor of Cambridge, a beaky-looking fellow by the name of Algernon S. Campkin, looking very pleased with himself and the grand chain of office around his neck, which he fingered constantly. He was followed in by a little group of middle-aged gents in blazers, who we applauded without being quite sure who they were. The last to emerge, however, was an unmistakeably distinctive figure, tall, in his sixties, with a big grey beard and a paunch, familiar from cigarette cards and newspaper reports of his exploits. It was none other than Doctor W.G. Grace himself. I dimly recalled hearing tell of a Gentlemen versus Players veterans match that was taking place at Fenners – presumably these were some of the veterans in question. A great cheer greeted the Doctor, and he waved to the crowd as he took his seat.

Well, despite myself I found the circus diverting. The elephants were astonishingly large close up, the trapeze artists breath-taking, the bareback horse-riding ditto, and midway through the evening my hands were sore from clapping.

Then it was time for the clowns.

The ringmaster strode into the centre of the ring, and bellowed at the top of his voice: "Ladies and Gentlemen! Hengler's Circus is proud to present to you for your entertainment and delight, the premier clown in the King's realm! Mister! Whimsical! Walker!"

Good Heavens, I thought. The very fellow I had met down at Poverty Corner. I turned to Lance. "I know this chap," I said.

"So?" he shrugged, unimpressed.

The orchestra burst into life, and half a dozen clowns ran around the edge of the ring, clockwise and anti-clockwise, bumping into one another, rolling around.

Then Whimsical Walker made his entrance. He was all in white, with a great belly I didn't remember him having before, and a huge beard that covered most of his torso. His nose was bright red, and in his hand he wielded a cricket bat. Plainly he was going to start with a sketch lampooning the evening's celebrity guest.

All heads turned as one to look at the good Doctor. He was not amused.

Whimsical Walker strode around the ring, proclaiming himself the greatest cricketer the world had ever seen. So confident was he in his abilities, he cried, that he would give five pounds to any man who could get him out.

On cue, two of the lesser clowns produced a set of stumps and banged them into the ground in the centre of the ring.

"If only there was someone here, with us this evening," Walker went on. "Someone who could provide me with the sort of challenge that would really test me. Perhaps you sir?" he said, planting himself in front of Grace. "The scourge of Australia, the captain of England, the *second* greatest cricketer on the face of the earth."

With a little sleight of hand he suddenly produced a ball and offered it to the great man.

"Will you oblige me, and everyone here, by bowling at the great Whimsical Walker?"

The audience dutifully cheered at this, but the doctor was unmoved.

"Sir?" Walker said, waving his arms to whip up more cheering, but the old cricketer was having none of it. He folded his arms across his stupendous belly, and growled:

"They've come to watch you capering about, not me bowling!"

Things started to get a little uncomfortable then for the nation's premier clown. He persisted a little while longer, trusting that the crowd would quickly break down Grace's truculent resistance, but he badly underestimated his opponent. He turned then to other members of the cricketing party, but none of them wanted to get on the wrong side of the hero, and all shook their heads.

"Will no one accept my challenge?" Whimsical Walker cried in desperation, and people were beginning to shift on the wooden benches wanting it to stop.

"Here!" a voice near me shouted, and to my astonishment it was Lance. He grabbed my hand and shoved my arm up in the air, pulling me to my feet.

"What are you...?"

"He bowls," Lance called out, and before I could protest further clowns had swarmed from all directions and were dragging me into the ring. Applause rang out, and you could almost taste the relief in the air that the awkwardness was over.

Walker swaggered over to the stumps to take guard. "Now," he said, holding a finger up. "You are a bowler, is that right?"

"I have bowled," I said. In fact I had played just a couple of weeks before for the staff against the professors, and I was reasonably confident I could pick up the cash prize, if there really was one.

"Are you fast?"

"Reasonably so," I said, throwing the ball from hand to hand.

Walker did a little pantomime of apprehension at this, and the audience were beginning to warm back up. "In that case," he said, and snapped his fingers. One of his cohorts quickly galloped over to the entrance and returned with a gigantic bat, almost as big as the clown himself, which completely covered the stumps.

"Now remember," he said. "You must clean bowl me to win the five pounds."

Well, I hammed it up a little, but the task was clearly going to be impossible. As I ran up to bowl Walker pretended to be scared, and hid behind the giant bat with his knees knocking together. Then when the ball arrived he ducked, closed his eyes and scooped it high up into the air. The ball described an eerily perfect parabola and landed right in the meaty paws of Doctor Grace. He could hardly have shelled it if he had tried, and they heard the cheers in Grantchester.

"Thanks for dropping me in it," I said to Lance as we were making our way out later.

"I thought you might win the money," he muttered.

Just then a clown in a conical hat appeared at my elbow, and began tugging my sleeve. "Mr Walker would like a word," he whispered.

"What's that?" I said. "Speak up."

"I can't," he whispered. "I'm supposed to be the silent one. Mr Walker would like a word with you."

I followed this chap, and he led me over to a little caravan. Whimsical Walker was inside, midway through taking off his face paint.

"Aha!" he cried. "There is the young man! Thank you, sir, you quite saved my life!"

"Oh, no, no, no," I said.

"Yes yes yes!" Walker insisted. "The mayor particularly asked me to get up something to spoof the old cricketer, but who knew he was going to be such a cantankerous soul, eh?"

"I'm happy I could help," I said.

"Sit, sit," the old clown said, shoving some over-sized boots and a collapsible bunch of flowers out of the way to make room for me. "Now, tell me, because I am not often wrong. You have been on the stage, have you not?"

"What makes you say that?" I said.

"Your instincts," he cried. "Your instincts are sound. Your perfect double-take when the big bat appeared, and that perfect delivery that just begged for me to send the catch to old misery-guts."

"You give me too much credit," I said. "But you are right. I was one of Fred Karno's comedians."

"I knew it! I *knew* it!" Walker cried, punching his fist into his palm. "I wonder, young man, whether I might interest you in a little proposal..."

24
CHANCE MEETING

MY first suspicion was that I was about to offered a job as a clown, but thankfully that wasn't the case.

"It is just a one-off performance," Whimsical Walker explained. "A benefit, at the Theatre Royal in Drury Lane. A week to rehearse, that should suffice, since we are a pair of old pros, eh?"

"To rehearse what?" I asked.

"I have been asked to give my old *Barber Shop* sketch, and I need a reliable stooge. You come into the shop for a shave, you sit in the chair. I start stropping my three-foot long razor, then I chop a cabbage to show how sharp it is, you make your eyes nice and wide, show a little bit of fear, yes? Feeling your neck, that sort of thing?"

"Right..."

"Then the lathering begins. Lather everywhere, buckets of the stuff, until we can hardly see your face any more for lather. Then – Swish! I swing the razor and off comes your head!"

"You want to cut off my head?"

"Yes, yes, and it bounces around on the floor, and I am talking to it, telling it everything is going to be all right, you see?"

"I see..."

"And the audience are shrieking, because of all the blood, and I tell them it is all going to be fine because we will just get the gentleman a new head. So you come in as my assistant now with a tray of replacement heads to choose from, and then while I screw it on we work you back into the chair for the reveal."

"Aha," I said. "It's a substitution."

"Of course. I'm not really going to cut your head off, I'm not a madman. Now, it's messy, but it's a sure fire hit, I promise you. So what do you say? Eh? Are we on?"

I considered for a moment or two, and then said: "Do you know what? I think I might actually be able to lay my hands on a papier-mâché model of my own head."

———

I thought my father might raise objections to my taking the time off, but he was happy to release me.

"To be honest, Arthur, this is the first time I have seen you with a smile on your face in weeks. It does my heart good to see it, so go with my blessing."

The next morning then I presented myself at Whimsical Walker's caravan, and we rode with the circus down to Hackney Marshes. There we rehearsed his *Barber Shop* routine between his performances, and he put me up on a little divan that pulled down out of one of his cupboards.

As we worked together on the routine I warmed to Whimsical Walker. It was clear that he enjoyed nothing so much as getting a laugh, whether onstage or during one of his many anecdotes.

"A good laugh," he would say, "is sunshine in the house. That's Thackeray, that is."

You could hardly mention anything in his presence without kicking off another story. I didn't mind, to be honest, as his tales were good value, and generally featured him falling over or being locked up for a night in the cells. Or else it would be the one about how he trained a donkey to sing and performed with it for Queen Victoria at Windsor Castle.

The circus was where he had spent most of his illustrious career, travelling the world with Hengler's, or with Barnum and Bailey, and he regarded himself very much as a classic clown, part of a long and noble tradition. In his pomp, he'd been the resident clown at the Drury Lane Theatre, appearing in pantomimes with the great and late Dan Leno and Herbert Campbell. His speciality was, as he never tired of mentioning, the harlequinade, that odd bit of *commedia dell' arte* tacked onto the end of a pantomime which had all but died out. He blamed the music hall for this, as now any Tom, Dick or Harry could call themselves an entertainer without the training or the reverence for traditional techniques that Whimmy – as he insisted on being called – regarded as essential.

At the end of the evening, once he had painstakingly removed his classical clown make-up, we would go for a drink. He would nurse a 'Gaiety mixture' – whisky cold with a slice of lemon – or perhaps a glass of Chartreuse, and as the weekend's benefit approached he began to confide in me.

"This is the last week of Hengler's," he said, "and the echoing void looms large on the horizon. But...!" He held up a finger. "I hear a rumour that they are planning to revive the good old harlequinade at Drury Lane this Christmas, so if we are a hit... well!"

"I didn't realise there was so much at stake," I said.

"Pish posh!" he said. "They will be begging good old Whimmy to return, you'll see!"

"I hope so," I said.

"And I shall take care of you, don't you worry. I will be needing a Policeman, or perhaps a Pantaloon. Someone with good instincts."

I didn't say anything to that, but it was kind, and it set me wondering. Could I? Could I throw myself back into the performing life? Whimmy drained his glass and gave me a sudden reminder of just how precarious a life it could be.

"Between you, me and the doorpost," the old fellow said, "I have lost an awful lot of my savings in a particularly ill-advised investment that went belly up, so if this weekend doesn't work out as I hope I shall be pretty much on my beam ends."

Crumbs, I thought. Nothing like a little bit of extra pressure to spice things up.

On the Sunday I arrived at the Drury Lane Theatre to find him already transformed into his working persona. From the ground up he was every inch the clown. White shoes with black pom-poms, white stockings featuring a leafy design, then great frilly pantaloons bulging out around his backside, a very fancy white silk bodice with frilly sleeves and the same leafy patterns, topped off with full clown make up. His silver-grey hair was teased into three startling spikes and coloured bright red, and the rest of his head was made up white, with his features picked out in red and black. He was just applying a bright red nose when I appeared at his dressing room door.

"I used to always wear a black nose, you know, that is the tradition, but I found the children like the red better. I don't want to scare them, after all," he chattered, nervous as a kitten despite all his years of experience.

"Well, you look like no barber I've ever seen," I said.

Our turn came midway through the second half, and he had absolutely nothing to be nervous about. Goodness me that *Barber Shop* was a riot! How the people loved it, and the old clown milked every lathery moment. For myself, even just standing anonymously alongside him plastered in soap, feeling the crackling electricity of a comedy routine was like a burst of fire straight into my veins.

After four roaring curtain calls I went to the tiny bathroom to clean myself up, and then fairly ran up the stairs to our dressing room, full of adrenalin and energy, to celebrate with the old chap. I found him dabbing listlessly at his white face make up.

"Well, well, Arthur. Things are never quite how we would want them to be, are they, eh?"

I thought about Tilly, somewhere in the world, and about Charlie's smug smirk, and the end of my Karno days, and I had to agree with the poor old soul.

"No, Whimmy, I'm afraid they are not," I said.

The old clown sniffed, and dabbed at his face again. He appeared to be removing his make-up but I saw a glistening tear swept up by his cotton wool.

He had barely had a minute to enjoy his triumphant return to his old stomping ground, the stage where he had enjoyed such successes with Leno and Campbell, before the theatre manager dealt him the cruel blow that there would be a pantomime but no harlequinade this year, and consequently no role for Walker W. It had hit him hard, I could see, and I decided to leave him to change in peace.

"I'll see you in the Albion, shall I?"

"Indeed, dear boy, indeed. I shall be right along." He waved a frilly-sleeved farewell, and I headed out into the October chill of Covent Garden.

I didn't go straight to the Albion, because I only had enough money for one drink, if that, and so I needed to time my arrival nicely. In any case, Whimmy would be an age getting ready, and a bit of fresh air and quiet contemplation was what I felt like, so I set off in the general direction of Leicester Square.

I was just strolling past the front of the Empire, peering idly at the bill matter to see what was what, when who should heave to alongside and tap me on the shoulder but Stan Jefferson?

"Stan!" I cried with delight. "My dear fellow, how have you been?"

We shook hands vigorously, beaming all over our faces, our low points in the Low Countries quite forgotten.

"Mustn't grumble," he said with a big grin. "Oh, all right, maybe I'll grumble a bit in a minute, but how are you? Are you working?"

I explained that I'd just been playing stooge to Whimsical Walker, and his eyebrows shot up with surprise.

"Really?" he said. "And where were you doing that? The eighteen-eighties?"

"Funny. And you? What happened to you when we got back from Belgium?"

"I made my way to Gordon's place in Holborn," he said. "I saw him on the pavement outside, dressed to the nines, obviously waiting for someone. He looked so prosperous, and clean, and I looked down at myself and I was a tramp, a half-starved hobo, and I suddenly felt I could not intrude. So I hid."

"You hid?"

"Behind a lamp post. God knows I was thin enough. Sure enough Gordon's friends appeared, in their finery, and off they went together. And I waited there until he returned at the end of the evening, and just as he was opening his front door I hailed him."

"Did he know you?"

"Not at first, but then he took me in, and gave me a ferocious talking-to about how I would never make it as a comic, how I was wasting my life, and how I needed to get a grip of myself and knuckle down, and if I did then maybe I could have a career in theatre management, like him. And like our father, of course, it is in the blood."

"What did you say?"

"What could I say? It was hard to argue with him, and after all he only wants what's best for me, doesn't he? And I did owe him all that money, still, for the *Rum 'Uns* stuff. So I have been working for him as a script copier, trying to pay him back. It is so hard, by the way, the temptation to improve as you copy is so strong. And I have supplemented my meagre income by walking on in Gordon's production of *Ben My Chree* at the Prince's."

"*Ben My Chree*? Whatever is that?" I asked.

"It's Manx, apparently, if you can believe it. I still think of the *Rum 'Uns*, though. Maybe one day we'll be able to buy the props back, eh?"

"Maybe," I said. I didn't have the heart to tell him I had retired, and would soon be heading back to Cambridge and college servitude. "Come over to the Albion, I'll see if I can't get old Whimmy to stand you a jar."

"Whimmy?"

"I'm sorry, I should use his full name of course. Whimsical. Let's see how Whimsical's credit stands, shall we?"

The two of us set off back towards Covent Garden, arm in arm, two brothers reunited. Before we had gone a hundred yards, however, we were stopped in our tracks by a familiar hail.

"Arthur! Stan! Fancy bumping into you!"

We turned, and there was Alf Reeves, our bow-tied sturdy old company manager, large as life and just as welcome.

"I trust you lads are thriving?" Alf said, once a further bout of back-slapping and hearty hand-shaking was concluded.

"I have just been on with Whimsical Walker at the Drury Lane," I said, "and Stan here is at the Prince's."

"Ha! Starring in the West End, is it?" Alf beamed.

"Starving in the West End, more like," Stan muttered.

"And how about you, Alf?" I asked. "The Guv'nor treating you well?"

"Hmph! *He's* not the problem!" Alf said.

"Why, what's up?" said Stan.

"I am taking a company over to America again. Charlie Chaplin is the number one, and the rest of the personnel is pretty much as before, but the odd two or three have let me down."

"Mike Asher, by any chance?" I asked.

"How did you know that?"

"Oh, just something he said that day on the *Astoria*, remember, back in the summer?"

Alf was outraged. "Well, I wish the beggar had said something to me! He's only just pulled out this afternoon."

"And when do you leave?"

"First thing tomorrow morning!"

"Whew!" Stan and I glanced at one another.

"Charles Cardon the same, the big twit, and the Palmers. They all made their minds up weeks ago, I know it, they just wanted to play the dates we had left over here before they let me know. It's infuriating!"

"Not very considerate, right enough," Stan said.

"But it's providential that I should run into the two of you like this, just now. I don't suppose you'd think of signing up? Stepping into the breach?"

Stan whistled. "My brother would have my guts for garters," he said.

"Oh well," Alf said. "You can't blame a fellow for trying."

"I didn't say 'no', did I?"

"I could probably sort out a bit more money than last time," Alf ventured.

"All right, count me in!" Stan cried, grasping Alf by the hand.

"Excellent," Alf said. "Be at the Fun Factory at seven in the morning, got that?"

Stan was all a-flutter suddenly. "Yes! Going back to America, and tomorrow! I need to get to Gordon's, explain that he'll need another Second Policeman for tomorrow night because I shall be at sea. At sea! I need to pack myself a trunk, good grief, there's so much to do! Arthur, *do* say you're coming too!"

I stood there in agonies, and Stan was so excited he didn't wait to hear my answer, just galloped off, away round the corner and into the night.

"Well, Arthur? How about it?" Alf said.

"I'm sorry, Alf, I can't," I said.

"Is it Whimsical Walker? I can have a word with him if you like?"

"No, no, it's not him. That's finished. In fact, I'm not sure he has anything coming up for himself let alone for me, the poor old sod."

"What then?"

I took a deep breath. "You remember when Karno asked me to... compromise his wife, so he could divorce her?"

Alf's face went hard. "Quite a few people remember that," he said. "And they well remember what you said to him, too, and give you credit for it still."

"Well," I said. "When I came back from America I had nowhere to stay, and Edith put me up, out of the goodness of her heart. Karno got to hear about it, and said he was going to call me as a witness, as though it was... something it wasn't, not at all. And in exchange he'd take me back into the company, or at least into the organisation somewhere. So you see, if I came back to work for him it would be like I'd agreed. To all that. Do you see?"

Alf nodded slowly. "Yes, lad, I do."

"I left Edith's house, left London, left the business altogether, apart from this one single show tonight with Whimmy, so that Karno wouldn't know where to find me."

Alf nodded again. "I understand," was all he said. We shook hands solemnly, and he turned to walk away.

I stood there as the rain began to fall and watched the last chance of ever picking up the shattered pieces of my comedy career, the last chance of ever hooking up with Tilly again, and the last chance of ever putting Charlie Chaplin in his place striding off into the darkness. I couldn't move. The misery felt like lead weights in my legs, in my guts.

A moment before he disappeared out of sight around the corner, Alf stopped under a yellow flickering gaslight. He turned round, cupped his hand to his mouth and called back to me.

"Of course, if you were in America, the Guv'nor wouldn't very well be able to call you as a witness to anything, would he?"

"He'd know, though, wouldn't he, if I was to start working for him?" I shouted back.

"Would he? Only if I tell him your real name... Mr Smith."

PART 3

25
THE STOWAWAY

I stood on the deck by myself to get a good view of our departure from Liverpool. Everything had happened so fast. I thanked my lucky stars that I had bumped into Alf Reeves – was it only the night before?

I did wonder briefly what my family would think when I didn't return to Cambridge, but on balance they probably weren't going to be surprised. Maybe I'd send them a postcard.

It would be hard, I thought, to make much of an impression on the Karno organisation if I was technically using it to hide from the man himself, but it was a big step up on Poverty Corner, that was for damn'd sure.

The aspect of this whirlwind of events that was making me most excited and apprehensive by turns was the imminence of seeing Tilly again. She had been friendly enough on the *Astoria* back in the summer, but I also remembered Muriel Palmer's reedy voice, saying, "Don't they make a lovely couple?"

Would we be friends again? How, if she was always with Charlie? I couldn't imagine *he* was going to be pleased to see me. Or to see Stan either, for that matter.

There was a decent crowd to wave the SS *Oceanic* off, and as we eased away from the quayside I noticed quite a few people laughing and pointing, and nudging their neighbours. I looked down and there, a couple of decks directly below my feet, I saw a head sticking out of a porthole. Some fool was clowning around, pulling faces, pretending that his head was stuck, turning this way and that.

Somehow, while people down below were hooting with glee, he managed to rotate his head right around so that he was facing straight upwards. There must have been a piece of furniture right beneath the window inside his cabin or else I couldn't imagine how uncomfortable he must have been. Suddenly he caught sight of me peering over the rail above.

"Ah, Arthur, there you are, my boy!" Whimsical Walker called out, plaintively. "I wonder could you come down and help me out? I really am most inextricably stuck!"

He was, as well, and it took me and a sniggering steward some considerable time to free him, which we eventually did by squashing his ears flat with a spoon.

"Well, there's a lesson learned!" the old man chuckled.

I looked around at his cabin, where he had begun to unpack several full-scale variations of his clown costume.

"How many pairs of silk stockings have you brought?" I said.

"Two dozen, all colours, some patterned," he said.

"You're never going to use them, you know."

"One never knows what adventures may befall one," he insisted. "And America knows me, I could hear the clarion call at any time."

We had travelled up on the boat train to Liverpool together, without seeing any of our colleagues thus far. Alf reckoned it would be for the best if I didn't meet up with everyone else at the Fun Factory, just in case Karno himself happened to be lurking around there, and I was happy to go along. It had been Alf's idea to offer Whimmy a job as well.

"I've known him for years," he'd said, "and I know he's funny. And if the Guv'nor sees a well-known name like that appear on his roster it's liable to distract him from asking any questions about this 'Arthur Smith' who is also sneaking along for the ride."

"Good plan," I had said. "But do I have to be 'Arthur Smith'? It seems so... ordinary, somehow."

"When we get to America," Alf had muttered, "you can be whomsoever you like."

"I am really most grateful to Alf for this opportunity," Whimmy said as he put on a tie for dinner. "Although I have to say the pay is the worst I have ever accepted."

━━━━

A little later the two of us made our way to the dining room, where we met Alf Reeves near the double doorway.

"Ah, there you are, welcome Whimmy, let's introduce you to the company, shall we?"

Walker inclined his head graciously, and Alf led us over to the little group of tables occupied by our colleagues. "Everyone? This is Mr Whimsical Walker, who is joining us for this tour, and Arthur I believe many of you are already acquainted with."

I stepped out from behind Whimmy, and a roar of surprise went up. Stan leapt to his feet, beaming all over his face, and threw his arms around me. Freddie Junior was not far behind.

"I saw an Arthur Smith on the list, but I never dreamed it was you!" Freddie cried.

'No,' I thought, 'because if Alf'd told you then you might've blabbed it to your dad,' but I grinned cheerfully and then leaned over to hug Amy too.

"That's my wife," Alf explained to Whimmy, "and those excitable young guns are Stan and Freddie. Then here's Bert Williams, Charlie Griffiths, George Seaman and his wife Emily..."

Whimmy stepped around the tables shaking hands, and I followed in his wake greeting my sometime boxcar chums.

"This is Mr Edgar Hurley and his wife Ethel, they are new to the company," Alf was saying, and suddenly I found myself shaking the warm soft hand of a raven-haired beauty, whose deep dark eyes were openly weighing me up in what felt like a rather lascivious fashion, while her husband glowered at me from a couple of feet away. I blushed and moved on.

"Here is Annie Forrester, our new songbird, just wait till you hear her," Alf said, ushering us over to a shy, demure young girl who could hardly have been more than sixteen years old. She seemed like a child, especially next to Ethel Hurley, who was most decidedly a woman. "And there is Billy Crackles..." – this last-named raised a large glass to us, and then immediately got on the outside of it, and it was plain to see that having him along would lead to considerable savings in red nose make-up.

Then we came over to a table for two, a little apart from the ordinary mortals. "And finally let me introduce Miss Tilly Beckett, and our number one, Mr Charlie Chaplin."

"Charmed," Whimsical said, kissing Tilly's hand, while her mouth formed a perfect 'O' of astonishment at seeing me there.

Charlie's purple eyes bored into mine as he shook hands with the pair of us. "Mr Walker," he said, "and Arthur. So you are back."

"I am," I said.

"Well, I trust you will pay more respect to your number one than when you were last with us."

"Believe me, I shall be giving him exactly the respect he deserves," I said, and his eyes narrowed slightly.

"Arthur," Tilly said, standing to kiss my cheek. "What a lovely surprise. I look forward to hearing all your news."

Alf guided Whimmy and me towards an empty table nearby, and Charlie watched me all the way, clearly seething. I suddenly thought I perhaps shouldn't have provoked him so early on.

"You don't think Charlie might try and spill the beans, do you?" I said. Alf thought for a moment, and then led me across the dining room to the captain's table.

The captain himself, a portly bearded fellow in a spotless White Star line uniform, dabbed his mouth with a napkin and got to his feet as we approached.

"Mr Reeves, a very good evening to you," he said.

"Captain," Alf said. "I wonder if I might ask a small favour?"

"If I can be of any assistance at all, just ask," the uniformed gentleman said. "Anything for Mr Karno."

"If any member of my party should think of sending our Guv'nor a wire, perhaps you could let me see it first, make sure they are not bothering him with trivia?"

"It shall be done, Mr Reeves, it shall be done. I shall speak to the Marconi operator myself."

"That should take care of things until we reach New York, anyway," Alf muttered as we returned to our seats for our own dinner. "That's the best I can do for you, and for Edith."

The SS *Oceanic* was a liner of the British White Star line, a distinct step up from our previous converted cattle boat, and we were able to do the crossing directly to New York this time rather than taking that long detour through Canada. It took nine days, which was not quite as fast as it could be done, but nobody in the shipping business had the stomach for full speed that year, preferring to take things a little slower and post plenty of lookouts for icebergs.

There was no frantic need to rehearse our turn *en route*, as we would arrive in plenty of time, so our afternoons were spent on deck. On one particularly lively sea day, I clung to the railings next to Tilly, while all around us our colleagues turned up their collars and tried desperately to hold onto their lunches.

"When I was in England," she said. "I went to Southend to see my family."

"Oh?" I said. "How were they?"

"Gone," she said.

"What?"

"No sign of them. A new family living in our house, no forwarding address."

"Goodness – what do you think happened?"

"I did a little detective work," she said, "and it seems there was an accident one night. You know how Dad had got it into his head that the Germans were going to invade by sea, and they would land at Southend?"

"I remember," I said. "They have been building quite a navy, by all accounts."

"You don't think he was right, do you?"

"No, no," I said. "Their Kaiser is cousin to our King, isn't he, and the Russian Tsar too. If they have any disagreements the three of them can sort it out over a nice cup of tea."

"Well, Dad was 'prepared', he kept saying – well, he told you that, didn't he?"

A brief recollection sprung into my mind of Mr Beckett staring out to sea, a look of grim determination on his face as he said: "When they come we'll set fire to the pier, Mr Punch and me... All that wood, it'll go up like billy-o!"

"I think he must have been keeping some dynamite in the Punch and Judy stand. He must have been going to blow up the pier, if, you know, push came to shove. And where the Punch and Judy stand had been there was just a crater in the ground, with a sad little puddle of seawater in the bottom," Tilly said, becoming tearful.

"So what happened, did you find out?"

"An explosion, that's all anyone knew. At night, thankfully, so at least there weren't any children sitting there watching Mr Punch go up in smoke."

"That's the way to do it."

"I spoke to a bobby, and the prevailing theory is that some fool thought it would be funny to flick his cigarette end in there, a mark of disrespect for the old Punch and Judy man."

"And he got a surprise."

"He got his backside blown through his hat is what he got."

"How awful! Is Mr Beckett in trouble? He must be..."

"They did a moonlight flit, no one knows where they've gone," she shrugged. "And that's that."

"There must be something you can do?" I said, but she shook her head sadly. "Tell you what, when we get back to England I'll help you, we'll find them, you'll see."

"Thanks, Arthur," she said, and gave me such a sad smile that I felt I would do anything to cheer her up.

I glanced around, and in point of fact the whole company were looking pretty fed up just then. The sea was rough, and Bert Williams was using his ventriloquist skills to make muted retching noises appear to come from all over the deck as though we were on some kind of plague vessel. I strongly suspected that he had a bet on with someone, the wolfish George Seaman most likely, about who would throw up next. Charlie was sitting at the prow, hunched and sulking like some sort of malevolent goblin figurehead, and it was obvious he wasn't going to be doing anything to lift people's spirits. For some reason, my sea legs seemed to be more reliable than most, so I suddenly thought hell, I'd do something myself.

So I staggered into the middle of the triangular foredeck where the Karno masses were huddled, and said, raising my voice against the wind: "Come on everyone, chins up! We are English after all, masters of the seas! How about a good old sing-so...?!"

Before I could even finish my spirit-lifting exhortation the boat's bow plunged down into a wave, sending a freak spout of icy brine high up into the air to splash down onto me – *only* me I might add – drenching me right through to the bones and internal organs.

Well, that cheered everybody right up. Stan laughed fit to bust, which set Freddie off, and pretty soon everyone was chuckling away. Even Chaplin managed a smirk.

"Go on, Arthur, you'd best get out of those wet things, you'll catch your death," Alf said, the mother hen of the company, brushing tears of laughter from his cheeks.

As I staggered through the hatch towards the stairs down into the belly of the boat I passed a couple of stewards loafing around sneaking a Woodbine moment or two. One was tall and thin, and the other was shorter and bald – they were rather like Mutt and Jeff[6] – and they sniggered nastily at my misfortune as I splish-sploshed wetly down the steep metal staircase, seething quietly to myself.

Down in my cabin I stripped off every item of clothing I was wearing, and squeezed as much of the Atlantic out of them as I could. I had fresh clothes, of course, in my trunk, but if I wanted to go back up on deck I would have to wait for my overcoat and shoes to dry out. Unless...

I poked my head out the door. The corridor was deserted. I nipped along in my spare long-johns and bare feet and tried the handle on the door of the end cabin, which was where the props and costume trunks were being stored for the duration. Open... aha!

I let myself in, and began to have a bit of a rummage. At first I was just looking for a top coat and shoes, but as I did so, an idea came to me.

It began as a kind of tribute to my friend George Robey. I already had one of his trademark bendy canes, which he had given to me after I broke my knee – or rather, had it broken for me – and a couple of quick dawbs of charcoal make-up gave me his quizzical half-moon eyebrows. Then a get-up consisting of baggy trousers a size or three too large, a jacket that was too tight, the dishevelled dignity of a waistcoat, collar and bow tie, and battered shoes with one sole a-flapping turned me into something halfway between the master Robey and the stock Karno drunk. I jammed a bowler hat on top of my head, and as a last touch glued on a little moustache to disguise my face.

It was the work of no more than a minute or two for a Karno quick-change veteran like myself, and so those two skiving stewards were still finishing off their sly smokes when a strange, shambolic figure began awkwardly clambering up the metal staircase towards them. Several times he seemed about to slip and tumble down again, but he righted himself somehow with his oddly-bowed cane and continued towards them. As the figure neared the top, he whirled about precariously, and the taller steward lurched forward to grab him by the lapels and haul him to safety.

"Careful how you go there, sir," he said, giving a sly grin to his mate as he straightened the fellow up. "Wouldn't want a mishap, now, would we?"

"Thank you, my man," the stranger slurred, summoning up a battered old-world dignity. "Now, I wonder if you gentlemen could assist me?"

"Certainly, sir," Mutt replied, reeling back from a blast of the whisky mouthwash I had given myself moments earlier. "What can we do to...? Sir...?"

I darted through the hatch and out onto the deck in search of my audience, and, as I hoped, both the stewards followed me outside, anxious to make sure that this drunken fellow didn't topple overboard.

My fellow Karnos all perked up as I hove into view, doing the drunk roll that we all knew so well, feet pointing at ten-to-two, leaning heavily on the bendy George Robey cane, suddenly careering off to one side as the boat tipped. The two stewards caught up with me, and I leaned heavily on the second one – Jeff, the shorter and balder of the two – and gave him the benefit of my whisky breath too.

"Ah, there you are," I said, letting my feet slide away backwards, and then forwards again as I pulled myself up by his jacket front (a staple Karno move). "Would you be so very kind as to help me to locate my travelling companions?"

Jeff rolled his eyes at his colleague over my shoulder. "Certainly, sir, if I can. What are their names?"

"Well, let me see. There is a splendid fellow by the name of Mister Johnnie Walker, do you know him?"

"Johnnie Walker? Like the scotch?"

"I certainly do," I said. "You're very kind. Make mine a double!"

"No, I mean..." the man sighed. "I don't think I know a Mr Walker."

"Oh well, no matter," I shrugged. "I'm sure you must know his friend, an American gentleman from Tennessee by the name of Daniels."

"Daniels?"

"Precisely so. First name Jack."

He frowned. "Jack Daniels? Like the whisky?"

I could hardly believe he had served up the same feed line, but I was never one to look a gift horse in the mouth. "Absolutely I do," I cried. "Make mine a double!"

By now Mutt and Jeff were getting flustered by the obvious mirth of the watching Karno comedians, and they each grabbed one of my arms. I, however, was starting to feel the tingle of that particular energy that comes when you are onstage performing, and everything is at your fingertips. The Power was flowing through my veins now.

"Perhaps then you know my Dutch friend," I ventured. "Mijnheer Advocaat...? Or my French colleague, vair, vair splendid chap, goes by the name of Monsieur *Cognac*?"

Hoots of laughter, now, from my colleagues clinging to the railings, their *mal-de-mer* quite forgotten, and I was enjoying myself. The two stewards, however, were getting quite red in the face from all the attention, and decided to assert themselves.

"I think we had better escort you to your cabin, sir," the tall one said, grasping my upper arm quite firmly now.

"My cabin?" I said.

"Yes, I think you could really do with a nice lie down, don't you?"

"Good idea, good idea!" I said, wrestling myself free and straightening my jacket. "I'll tell you exactly where I have had the great good fortune to lay my head these last few nights."

"Where?"

"Why... right here!" I said, raising my cane and tapping the side of the lifeboat suspended above our heads.

"What?" said Mutt.

"Here? You've been sleeping *here*?" said Jeff, his brows knitting as he worked this out.

"Certainly," I said, prodding him in the chest, "and let me tell you, the service has not been all that I hoped for."

"You've been sleeping in the lifeboat!" the taller frowned. "You mean to say you're... you're a..."

As my unwitting stooges finally put two and two together, I confirmed their suspicions with a perfectly executed 'Rumbled!' double take, slapped the bowler down onto my head, and galloped off around the side of the boat, with the cheers of my colleagues ringing in my ears. The two stewards set off after me, of course, shouting "Hoi!" and "Come back 'ere!", which only added to the general merriment.

Not actually being drunk, and being relatively nimble (despite my dicky knee) I completed a lap of the vessel well in advance of my pursuers, and concealed myself behind one of those upturned horn-shaped things that I've never quite worked out the purpose of. I tipped my hat chirpily at my colleagues, all of whom were enjoying the show immensely.

Suddenly, the first of my would-be captors appeared around the corner and skidded straight past me on the wet deck right over to the railings. The ship heaved, and for a ghastly split-second I thought the fellow was going to pitch over the side, but the Power was with me and I whipped my cane around and hooked it in the waistband of his trousers, hauling him back from the brink, and then I used that movement to deliver the momentum for my escape from his clutches once again. The Karno company whooped as one as I careered off on another circuit of the boat.

The next time I came around I skidded to a stop, twirled my cane, and took my applause with a little bow. The bald steward appeared, red-faced and gasping in my wake. I dodged, punted him roundly in the seat of his pants, then kicked my heels in the air and set off again, ignoring the fellow's indignant cries.

Halfway round another lap of the boat I calculated that I had pushed my luck just far enough, and indeed up ahead of me I could see that one of my pursuers had had the bright idea of changing direction to cut me off, so I ducked into a hatch and slipped back to my cabin, where I quickly changed back into my – still horribly wet, unfortunately – previous accoutrements.

I strolled back up onto the foredeck, where I had to hush the cheers of my colleagues lest they gave the game away. Indeed, the two breathless stewards appeared moments later, one from each side gangway, drawn by the racket. As they scratched their hapless heads in puzzlement I said loudly (and in a very different voice): "Well? What did I miss?"

Tilly let go of the railings and skipped over to me, throwing her arms around my neck and giving me a big kiss. I was over-whelmed – what did this mean? Was she letting me know that her feelings for me were rekindling? Then as she broke away from the embrace she managed surreptitiously – and rather painfully, actually – to rip off the fake moustache I had neglected to remove. Ah, that was it.

Once the frustrated stewards had left to scour the ship for their elusive quarry, I enjoyed the congratulatory back-slapping of my chums, their sea-sick misery temporarily forgotten.

"That stowaway character, that's not a bad turn, you know?" Stan said, his eyes still bright with mirth.

"Oh, you know, it was mostly Robey," I said modestly.

"Oh, of course it was, and stock drunk business, but there was a little something else too. You should remember that," he said, tapping his head and then punching me on the arm.

I looked over at Charlie Chaplin, and he wasn't laughing at all, not even smiling.

And that's when I knew for sure I'd hit on something really good.

26
A FELLOW OF
INFINITE JEST

WE arrived in New York once again, and settled into our accommodations. Alf made his speech about 'moral turpitude' once again, and actually it turned out that 'moral turpitude' was given as a reason by the port authorities for denying a person – or presumably a whole theatrical company – entrance to the country, so perhaps Karno had a point.[7]

The next morning we made our way a short walk up Broadway to a rehearsal room to begin knocking our show into shape. While we waited for stragglers to turn up, and knowing how she felt about Karno's weakest offering, I sidled over and muttered to Tilly.

"I can't believe we're doing *The Wow Wows*."

"Oh, but it's quite different now," she said.

"Different?"

"Oh yes, Charlie has transformed it, you'll see. He has devised lots more brilliant business, and there is much more for the girls to do."

Just then the man himself arrived, hair all over the shop in artistic turmoil, and Tilly skipped over to greet him, the light of the true believer in her eyes.

Now a Karno company was a well-oiled machine with parts that worked together perfectly. It had to be. All the versions of every particular show had to be the same wherever they were, because you never knew when you would have to drop in a replacement part at a moment's notice.

For that reason, a rehearsal was usually directed by the company manager, working from a prompt version approved by Karno himself. It seemed, however, that three circuits of the United States had left Charlie with a mighty sense of his own superiority. He was the number one, and the rest of us were nowhere, including Alf.

So Charlie took the rehearsals. He treated us with barely concealed scorn, and dismissed any ideas we might venture as hardly worthy of consideration, and I began to feel – and I am sure I was not the only one – that this company was not so much a Karno machine as a mere support act for the brilliant genius of young Mr Chaplin himself.

Sure enough, though, he had improved *The Wow Wows* out of sight. The main character, posh twit Archibald Binks, was a much closer relative now to the Inebriated Swell of *Mumming Birds*, which gave free rein to Charlie's whole gamut of drunken tumbles and spills, and as Tilly had suggested he had also integrated the female performers much more eye-catchingly.

The *pièce de résistance*, now, was a sequence in which the senior Wow Wows demanded that Binks eat a whole packet of dry cracker biscuits, without so much as a glass of water to help them down. This simple idea had generated a long drawn-out funny spot for Charlie, who sat on a stool front and centre, chomping away confidently at first but then more and more uncomfortably as his mouth filled up and he couldn't swallow.

He insisted on demonstrating the routine in full for us, because he wanted to be sure that we practised presenting a deadpan façade to it. It was all face work, to begin with, but then as he turned to protest to his tormentors that he could manage no more the clouds of crumbs that would fly out into the air were so unexpected, and then so beautifully managed, with such matchless timing, that those of us who had not seen it before were in pieces.

When it came to the rest of the sketch, however, Charlie proved a difficult taskmaster. He became frustrated very easily while trying to explain something, and would always end up demonstrating what he wanted himself, and then saying; "There, just do it exactly like that." No comedy performer appreciates that sort of help, believe me.

And when it misfired Charlie would fly into a rage. "No, no, no!" he would scream, "how can you not be getting this? It is simplicity itself! Again! Again!"

Everyone felt the rough edge of his tongue, even Tilly. Actually, I say everyone – in point of fact he never flew off the handle with little Annie Forrester. She was such a fragile-looking little thing, and sang her song like an angel, and Charlie was often moved to tears, even in rehearsal. He would never fail to compliment her, and do what he could to bolster her confidence and make her comfortable.

Nobody got it in the neck quite as much as Whimsical Walker, though. Time and again Charlie would show him some little bit he wanted doing, and Whimmy would nod genially and say, "Got it."

"Good, let us see it then."

"Oh, no, don't worry. I have it. Up here."

"But I want to see it, now!"

"Oh, I never do a thing full bore until there is an audience."

By now Charlie would be tearing his hair. "Here's your audience!" he'd shout, waving a dismissive arm at the rest of the company, sitting watching the fireworks display.

"Oh, but they all know what's going to happen, it is pointless doing it for them. What will we learn?"

"Whether *you* know what you are doing, you old fool!"

At this point Whimmy's feelings would be hurt, and one or other of the women would come over to comfort him. Meanwhile Charlie would be kicking a chair at the far end of the room, while Whimmy explained: "It's just a different way of working, that's all it is. Everything will be fine, he'll see. You'll all see. Nothing to worry about."

Everything about Whimsical Walker seemed to rub Charlie up the wrong way. The old clown asked to room on his own, saying: "I have particular habits which I would not want to share with anyone." Charlie seemed to take this as a kind of personal affront to his status, even though he himself could easily have afforded to do likewise if he were not so parsimonious. He never put the money he saved towards a round of drinks, neither, let me tell you *that*.

And Whimmy's tales, his jests that set the table on a roar, everyone loved them but Charlie.

Whimmy had been particularly taken with the 'Stowaway' routine that I had done on board the *Oceanic*. It was essentially clowning, of course, but it was also a practical joke, which was his very life blood. 'Spoofing' was what he called it, and many of his anecdotes were concerned with japes that he and his fellow members of a club known as 'The Spooferies' got up to. Dan Leno, the sad, mad genius whose shadow was still cast over music hall, even though he had been dead for more than a decade by then, was one of the great spoofers, according to Whimmy.

It was actually one of Charlie's proudest boasts that he had appeared on a bill with Leno. The implication was that the torch of the great comic's genius had been passed on to Charlie, as the brightest light of the next generation, although this assertion rather flew in the face of the fact that this apparent meeting of the greats had occurred when Chaplin was barely ten years old, and a virtually anonymous member of a boy clog-dancing team called *The Eight Lancashire Lads*.

Whimmy, though, had worked in Drury Lane pantomimes with the great Leno for many years, had known him well, and Charlie was not pleased to have his own singular connection to comic history so comprehensively trumped.

"Well, you all know I have always been a dab hand at training animals to perform?" Whimmy began one evening after work. "I told you, didn't I, how I once trained a donkey to sing, and we performed for Queen Victoria at Windsor?"

"Yes!" we chorused, for he had told us that one many a time.

"Well, the quickest learner I ever had was a gorgeous little poodle. It was my pride and joy, and one time it needed looking after, so Dan said he would take it to his home for me and I could collect it later. So when I went round to Dan's the next morning he gave me the box with the dog still in it, and he hadn't taken it out at all. I said 'Dan, surely you have fed and watered the poor creature?', but he shrugged and said that I never told him to do any such thing, which of course I hadn't, because it was just common sense. I reached in, and the dog was as cold as the grave and stiff as a board."

"Dead?" little Annie Forrester gasped.

"Dead as a doornail, dead as a dodo."

"Dead as clowning," a voice chipped in. It was Charlie, seething by himself over a port on the next table.

Whimmy blinked, and then pressed on. "I was so upset, but then after a little while Dan put his arm around my heaving shoulders and said 'Whimmy? Look here. This is not your dog!'

It was all a spoof, a classic Leno spoof! Imagine going to the trouble to find a dead dog that perfectly matched my pet, but it is the trouble that sells the spoof, you see, because the poor patsy can never believe that you would go to such lengths."

———

At the end of the week we travelled to Cincinnati by train, and I renewed my acquaintance with that Karno boxcar. The newcomers, like the Hurleys, were very taken with the idea of the company having its own carriage. I thought of telling them that it got old hat very quickly, but decided to let them enjoy swanking around for a while first. Whimsical Walker, however, was not so easily impressed, having travelled around in even grander style on previous tours.

"When I was with P.T. Barnum back in the eighties," he said, "we needed three whole trains to move the show around the country. One was for the performers' sleeping cars, one had the tent and all the hands, and then the third was for the menagerie. Did I ever tell you about how I was responsible for purchasing Jumbo the elephant from London Zoo for Barnum and Bailey...?"[8]

George Seaman got his cards out, with that familiar predatory look in his eye, but it seemed as though Edgar Hurley was not going to be drawn in in the way young Fred Palmer had been, and Stan too was keeping his distance.

"I have decided, whatever happens, to try and hang on to my money this time," he confided. "You were quite right about that. I'm going to work on a little nest egg."

"Good for you," I said.

I glanced over to where our number one was glowering moodily out of the window at Pennsylvania rattling by, seemingly sat under a dark storm cloud that could break at any moment.

"Charlie's no happier, then?" I said, wandering over to Alf.

"Well, he thinks the Guv'nor is ignoring him, you see," Alf replied, keeping his voice low.

"Oh? And why is that?"

"Because he thinks he wired the Fun Factory four times from the boat, complaining that you were hired without his approval."

"But he didn't?"

"As it happens, no, his messages were sent directly to the waste basket."

"Aha."

Tilly was keeping Charlie company, and I was having to face the fact that the two of them were pretty thick together these days. I sat by myself, brooding on this, thinking maybe it would be for the best if I could just think of her as a colleague, no more. No easy scheme, since she had dominated my thoughts, one way or another, since I first met her, dazzling me, teasing me, under the gas lamps outside the Fun Factory.

My reverie was interrupted when Ethel Hurley came and took the window seat beside me. She took a moment or two, wriggling to make herself absolutely comfortable, until she ended up sitting right alongside me, our shoulders and thighs touching in a way that made me suddenly very aware of my own breathing.

"That's better," she said. "I could barely see anything out that side, this is much more interesting."

Ethel and her husband Edgar were new to the company, and so far I had not had a great deal to do with them. I had noticed Ethel, of course, you could hardly miss her, for she was a very attractive woman, long dark hair, full-figured, and with mischief and double entendre in her dark eyes. There was something about her, a look, that made you think that she knew every single thing you were thinking, at least where she herself was concerned. What hardly seemed fair was that there was something about that look that made you think things about her that you wouldn't want her to know.

"Well now, Mister Dandoe," she said brightly. "This is a nice chance for us to get to know one another a little better, don't you think?"

"Yes, indeed," I said. "And you must start by calling me Arthur."

"And everybody calls me Wren," Mrs Hurley said. "It's been my nickname since I was a girl."

"Wren," I said. "That's nice."

"Why thank you, Arthur. Yes, I was such a tiny girl. I was a late bloomer."

I thought to myself – well, I could hardly help thinking, could I? – that she certainly had bloomed, and that she was decidedly no longer a girl. She was a woman, and such a woman that she made the other females in the company, even the married ones like Emily Seaman and Amy Reeves, seem like mere girls in comparison. I didn't speak that thought out loud, but I had the impression that she heard it anyway.

She leaned in close to breathe in my ear, and I was suddenly intoxicated by her perfume, her warmth, her closeness.

"These long train journeys are such a bore," she whispered, "but do you know the worst thing?"

"No," I managed to mumble.

"That one still has to dress so decorously, it would be so much more tolerable, don't you think, if one could travel in pyjamas, or a dressing gown?"

Trees continued to flash by outside the window, but all my attention was focused on the firm swell of her bosom pressing against my forearm, which was quite trapped.

"This dress is so tight," she breathed. "Everything is so... squashed up in there."

I stared straight ahead, trying – and failing – to keep from thinking of what was squashed up in there.

"You wouldn't be a darling, would you? And reach behind my back, undo a couple of little hooks for me?"

"You want..." I managed, then had to clear my throat. "You want me to..." my voice dropped to a whisper. "Undo your dress?"

"That's right, be a dear," she said.

I glanced over to where Edgar Hurley was flicking through a newspaper, not finding anything particularly interesting, by the look of things.

"But your husband is *right there!*"

"I want you to undo it a little, that's all, make me a bit more comfortable. I don't want you to undress me entirely!"

"Well, all right then, let me see..." I managed to free my arm, but not without a certain amount of barely appropriate contact. The fastenings behind her back were fiddly, but I succeeded in loosening them without exciting any attention from elsewhere in the boxcar. Wren let out a deep sigh of satisfaction that seemed, to my increasingly fevered imagination, to contain a promise of sharing such sighs again in a more private context.

Her husband was nearby, still grumbling and twitching his moustache at something in the newspaper, but that didn't stop Wren from sitting closer still, easing herself in under my arm, which had nowhere to go but around her shoulders. She chattered away then in a style that was simultaneously totally innocent and inconsequential and yet somehow really flirtatious, and I was sure she must have realised the effect she was having on me.

Suffice to say when the train pulled into Columbus for a fifteen-minute stop over, I was the only member of the company who didn't take the opportunity to get up and stretch his legs.

27
K-K-K-KISS ME AGAIN

Everyone agreed that the new tour had started nicely, but Charlie wasn't happy. The cause of His Majesty's displeasure was our pal Whimsical Walker, who was still finding his feet. You see, he'd never worked with a Karno company before, and didn't quite grasp the rhythms and responsibilities of being a mere cog in a machine. He was used to being the centre of attention, and, what's more, he was used to pacing his performance for audiences composed largely of children. Consequently, whenever it was Whimmy's turn to speak, the whole sketch would grind to a halt as he took his time, and pulled his funny faces, and shook his head from side to side as though he was wearing a hat with bells on, and deliberately got things wrong to try and get an extra laugh. Most of us weren't overly concerned – he was an old hand, he knew his stuff, and he would surely get the hang of how things worked pretty quickly. And he was getting laughs, after all.

Chaplin, though, was still livid at being lumbered with the old man, and harangued him backstage every night.

"For goodness' sake!" he exploded one night. "The phrase you should say is 'ad libitum'. Ad libitum. Say it!"

Whimmy frowned in pained incomprehension. "Ad libitum," he said.

"Exactly! What's so difficult about that?"

"Nothing at all."

"So why, why, *why* must you come out with this 'ablibblibum.... ablobbliboo... addlibibblibobbliboom...'? Gurning away at the audience all the while like some sort of simpleton?"

Whimmy couldn't see the problem. "They were laughing."

"They were laughing *at* you, you old fool, because you were getting it wrong!"

"What difference does that make?" Whimmy shrugged. "They're still laughing."

Chaplin waved his hands in the air in exasperation. "But why, answer me this, why, if the Wow Wows are a bunch of incomprehensible old idiots, why would Archibald be so keen to join them? Why would he not run a mile, and thank his lucky stars for a narrow escape, and perhaps report the whole mob to the nearest lunatic asylum?"

"Does it matter?"

"Of course it *matters*, you are undermining the very premise of the sketch!"

"All right, Charlie, calm down," Stan said. "We're all on the same team, remember?"

Charlie snorted, and allowed himself to be led away, leaving old Whimmy blinking at the rest of us. We knew Charlie had a point, I suppose, but it was the sort of thing that would naturally smooth itself out with practice, and everyone liked the old clown and was prepared to indulge him.

That week in Cincinnati I found myself idly thinking about Wren Hurley quite a lot. She had such a flirty way with her, and the most innocent interactions could suddenly seem laden with sexual import.

Just when I had nearly convinced myself that this was all in my over-heated imagination, I found myself lingering idly in the doorway of the men's dressing room. The ladies were changing in the room opposite, and the door had swung open so I could hear their chatter and see them milling about. Wren was there, and I waited for her to glance my way so I could wave a hello.

She didn't seem to have noticed me, and was looking at herself in the mirror, checking the innumerable details that women do. Suddenly she slipped the robe from her shoulders, and stood there in just a silk underskirt, quite naked from the waist up. Her back was to me, and she was concentrating on her reflection, which was hidden by the door. As I watched, unable to tear myself away, she gathered up her long dark hair in both hands and piled it on top of her head, swaying slowly from side to side. I hungrily took in the line of her lovely smooth back, the curve of her slender waist, the flaring of her hips, the tantalising glimpse of...

Slam!

Emily Seaman had suddenly realised that the door was open, and had darted over to slam it shut, but not before shooting me a withering glance and a loud "Tut!"

Now what was all that about? Was that a happy accident? Or was that meant for me? Whichever it was, it fuelled my daydreams for quite a while, I can tell you.

I turned to make my way along the corridor, and there, standing stock still with a look of thunder on his face, was Edgar Hurley.

"Ah! What ho, Hurley!" I said, flustered, but he didn't reply, and didn't move, just stood there staring darkly at me. I tried to pass him, but he would not yield an inch in the narrow passageway, and I had to press myself tight against the wall to get by.

To escape his baleful gaze I strolled off along the corridor, and happened to pass outside the theatre manager's office. I heard the tail end of a furious rant from inside before the door was flung open and Charlie, red-faced and steaming, stormed out. He shoved past me and stomped away towards the dressing rooms.

I looked into the room and saw Alf Reeves sitting there at his borrowed desk, his head in his hands, having just borne the brunt of Chaplin's fury.

"Shut the door, Arthur, there's a good lad," he said with a sigh. I took a seat opposite him as he reached for a bottle of bourbon and a couple of glasses. It seemed that this was a two-finger problem.

"So what's up?" I prompted.

"Charlie wants me to send Whimsical Walker home," Alf said, shaking his head sadly.

"What?!"

"He says it's not working, says he's a liability, says his timing is all wrong, says he is too old and set in his ways to work at the Karno pace."

"But we've barely been playing for a week, we're still running him in..."

"I know."

"And he'll get it, you'll see, he was making people laugh before Charlie was even born."

"I know, I said all that."

"You're not going to do it, are you? You're not going to send him home?"

I was quite alarmed for the old clown all of a sudden. He was really on his beam ends, as he put it, and had nothing much to look forward to if he was sent packing.

"No, no, not if I can help it. It's just hard to cope with Charlie in that sort of mood, you know?"

"Don't worry, Alf," I said. "We'll take Whimmy in hand, and this will all blow over, you'll see."

Alf nodded, and I left, steaming about Charlie's antagonism towards Whimsical Walker. It was harsh, very harsh, to try and get the old chap booted out, and I wasn't best pleased about it. I hadn't forgotten how Charlie had managed to manoeuvre me and Stan out of the Karno company, and here was another black mark in the ledger.

However I couldn't very well stick my head above the parapet, could I, because if I found my name being mentioned in dispatches then I would be for the high jump myself. So I set about trying to help Mr Walker fit more smoothly into the team ethos of the company. It was a task that needed handling with tact and delicacy.

"I say, Whimmy? Can I have a word?"

It was the break between the matinée and the evening show on our last day in Cincinnati, and the old chap was touching up his make-up in the dressing room by himself.

"Of course, dear boy," he replied. "How may I oblige you?"

"It's this," I said. "You see, the rest of us have played this sketch many times before, and it is a tricky thing to pull off, with fifteen people all onstage at once. It needs to work like... well, the Guv'nor, Mr Karno, always says that a Karno company is like a well-oiled machine."

"No problem there," Whimmy said. "As far as I can see most of us are well-oiled most of the time! Eh!"

"Yes, yes, indeed, ha ha. But you see, the thing that might sometimes gum up the works... I mean, what makes it hard for everyone, is if *somebody*..." – here I mentioned no names but weighted the word significantly enough, I thought. "Insists on dancing to his own tune, as it were. Do you understand me?"

Whimmy stroked his chin thoughtfully, and then nodded slowly. "Yes, I think I catch your drift. You are saying that we are a team, and there is no room for one person to simply indulge his ego?"

I sighed with relief. "Yes, that's it exactly, yes, thanks Whimmy."

"And so, as the senior man, you would like me to speak to him on everyone's behalf?"

I was halfway to the door. "Speak to who?"

"Why Chaplin, of course. Anyone can see he is not a team player. The whole thing has to revolve around him. He stamps on my laughs, flatly refuses to wait for me, and then rages at me afterwards as though I am in the wrong. Yes, it's high time somebody had a word with that young man, and now that I know everyone is with me, I shall..."

"No, no, Whimmy, please!"

"You know, I believe there is the kernel of something good in there, but he needs to learn the discipline that comes of living and working for years in the business, as I have. This will be good for him, you'll see. Learning to respect and accommodate one's elders and betters is an invaluable lesson for a young man starting out. I'll go and find him right now."

I had to take him by the shoulders and sit him back down, as he was ready to go and beard Chaplin at once. I had the distinct impression that he had been thinking about doing so for some time.

"No, listen, Whimmy, for Heaven's sake. The most important figure in a Karno company is the number one. What he says, goes – and that is Charlie Chaplin."

"But..."

"No buts, Whimmy. You have to do what he says, speed it up, find the pace of the sketch, because he wants to send you home. Do you hear me?"

"Charlie wants to send me home?"

"Home. So listen, no more funny faces, no more 'that might be funny let's try that', no more 'look at me I'm the senior man', or it'll be no more *job*. Am I getting through?"

Whimmy frowned. "I see. I see," he mused.

"Good. Thank you."

"I see now what my mistake has been."

"It wasn't a mistake, don't say that, it is just that it takes a bit of time to pick up the..."

"I have been too funny."

"What?"

"Too funny, oh yes. Well, from now on I shall not be funny at all, and we shall see how young Mr Chaplin likes *that*, shan't we?"

I groaned.

"I shall be human scenery, my friend, never fear."

And with that he began scraping away crossly at his white face make-up. As we had another show to do shortly I could only think he was planning to perform without it. I decided to leave him to it. I had done my best, and adjusting Whimmy to fit alongside Charlie was clearly going to take more than one awkward conversation.

That evening Whimsical Walker was less whimsical than I had ever seen him. He performed his part with a downbeat functionality, and anyone who was used to watching his usual exuberant mugging must have thought he was playing some elaborate practical joke, or else he was seriously ailing.

Certainly that is the conclusion most of the company seemed to have reached by the end of that night's *Wow Wows*, and he received anxious enquiries on the way back to the dressing room from Tilly and the girls.

"I am fine, thank you," he replied, tight-lipped. "Please do not trouble on my account."

Charlie bustled in, and made a point of going straight over to the old clown.

"Much better, Walker," he said, patting him on the back with awful condescension. "Now you're getting it."

I watched him strut smugly along to the other end of the room, and thought to myself:

The day is coming. I don't know when, but it's coming.

———

The Karno Karavan rolled on up to Chicago next. On our travel day I sat by myself in the boxcar, still fuming to myself about Charlie's treatment of Whimsical Walker.

There was a gentle rustle of skirts, and Wren Hurley slid in beside me. There was plenty of room for the two of us to share the bench seat, but she pressed right up against me as though there wasn't.

I sat bolt upright, and my eyes darted around for her husband, who was sitting a little way off in conversation with Stan. It looked like Stan was talking him through the *Rum 'Uns From Rome*, actually, and as I was looking at them Stan got to his feet to act a bit out, which was making Edgar chuckle.

Wren slipped her arm under mine and pulled it snug against her bosom.

"So, Arthur," she breathed. "How did you like Cincinnati?"

"A agreeable," I managed. "How about you?"

"Oh, I should have liked it better if there had been a little more *sin*. Do you know what I mean?"

I didn't really, but it sounded saucy so I nodded and smiled. She glanced across at her husband, and then got to her feet, taking my hand in hers as she did so.

291

"I fancy a bit of fresh air. Why don't you keep me company?"

"Um, all right."

She led me through the dark props and costume compartment of the boxcar and out onto the observation platform at the back. There was a guard's van attached behind us this time, so we moved around to the side to look at the view sliding by.

Wren shivered. "Ooh, it's colder out here than I thought," she said. "Give me a little warmth." She burrowed in close to me, and her dark hair blew across my face, filling my nose with her heady perfume. I wasn't cold, not at all. In fact I was quite warm, and sweating rather freely.

"So," she said. "I was wondering what you handsome young lads do about sowing your wild oats?"

"I beg your pardon?"

"Well, the company isn't exactly chock full of single girls, is it? That Tilly is nice, but Charlie has hooked her, hasn't he?"

"Mmm," I said, through gritted teeth.

"And little Annie Forrester is a bit on the young side."

"She is," I agreed. "Well, um, since you ask, last time I was in Chicago several of the lads struck up a rapport, as you might say, with the dancing girls from a burlesque company who were sharing our hotel."

"Aaahhh!" Wren said, shooting me an arch look that made me feel like I was a major Lothario of some kind. "And you? Did you... strike up a rapport?"

An image jumped into my mind of Tilly, pretending to be 'Clara' the burlesque girl.

"It was a good time," I said.

"Just at the moment, though, you are footloose and fancy free, are you not?" This came with a look of such coy suggestiveness that even a clot such as I could not miss it.

292

"I am," I said. "And *you* are a married woman."

I did not mean it as a rebuke, but to my surprise she suddenly looked crestfallen and began to cry. I felt her sobs shaking her shoulders.

"Wren? Whatever is it?" I said, not quite knowing where to put myself.

"I am a married woman, yes," she said. "But Edgar has not been a husband to me for months now."

"Wha...?" I croaked, my mouth dry.

"Back in England we were touring in *Hilarity*, and Edgar was number two to Shaun Glenville. We knew that Glenville was planning to take a role in the West End, and he said he'd put a word in for Edgar, but when it came to it Karno promoted Will Poluski Junior to number one, and we got shunted off on this trip instead. The word we heard was that this was 'more appropriate employment' for a married pair. So you see it is all my fault."

"No, no," I said.

"Yes, he blames me, he does! He thinks that if he were single he'd have achieved his ambition, and now he can hardly bear to look at me, let alone touch me!"

"Oh, come now, I'm sure that's not true," I said, thinking that if I were in Edgar's place I'd be hard pressed to keep my hands off her.

"It is, it is!" she wailed, and buried her face in my chest.

I stood there, embarrassed and awkward, acutely aware all at once of the shape of her, the nearness of her. I patted her shoulder in what I hoped was a comforting fashion, and said: "Perhaps we should go back inside?"

Wren seemed to compose herself a little then, and dabbed at her eyes with a lacy hand kerchief which seemed to have sprouted from her sleeve.

We slipped back into the dark compartment where the props and costumes were stored, and I began to lead the way through to the passenger half of the boxcar, holding her by the hand as I did so.

Suddenly she pulled back and steered me forcefully into a dark recess that lurked behind a rail of costumes.

"Hold me, Arthur," she breathed, clasping her arms behind my back and pressing herself hard against me.

"I... oh!" I said, my shoulders bumping against the side wall of the boxcar.

"I need to feel like a woman again," she murmured.

"We can safely say you are definitely one of those!" I babbled. Fortunately for the standard of the repartee, at least, she turned her face up to me, stood on tiptoes, and kissed me.

Her mouth was warm, and urgent, and soft, and firm, and hungry, and wet. After what seemed like an age and yet, suddenly, not nearly enough time, she pulled back and gasped, worried that she had gone too far. Well, I am only flesh and blood, and I leaned forward and kissed her right back, and this time the kiss went on and on and on. My hands explored the thrilling curves I had glimpsed through the door of the dressing room, and she tugged at my shirt, her hands searching beneath for my bare back.

There was a toot then from the locomotive far ahead, and a jolt when the carriages bumped together as we began to slow into Chicago Union station. Hurriedly we separated, and quickly tried to straighten ourselves and tuck ourselves in. It was dark, though, and when we pushed though the curtain into the sunlit passenger half of the boxcar to rejoin our colleagues, Wren's husband amongst them, we must have looked pretty dishevelled.

I certainly felt dishevelled.

28
A DISH BEST
SERVED COLD

II seemed as though we had got away without drawing attention to ourselves, somehow. Wren seemed as surprised as I was by the turn events had suddenly taken, and she kept her distance for the rest of that day. In fact we barely spoke to one another that whole run in Chicago, although I did catch the occasional flirty glance in my direction. I thought about her a great deal, though, you can count on that, but she was not the only person of a female persuasion to preoccupy me that week.

One night at the Chicago Empress I peered lazily out across the footlights during one of Chaplin's interminable bouts of showboating, and my eye was suddenly taken by a spectacular vision, sitting majestically in the middle of the front row, like a proud galleon in full flow breasting the waves.

It was Lucia, the burlesque girl, there to see Mike Asher. Of course, the sap was skulking in cowardly fashion back in the old country so as to escape her clutches. Anticipation had not yet turned to disappointment, but she kept glancing anxiously at the wings, waiting for her beloved to make his appearance. I couldn't help feeling sorry for the poor girl, gazing sympathetically at her cleavage as I did so, and I almost missed my own cue as a result.

Afterwards the theatre manager, a bearded fellow by the name of Baggust, popped his head into our dressing room and said: "There is a young lady at the stage door who wishes to speak with one of your company."

I knew straight off who that was going to be, so I sighed and went to do my friend's dirty work for him. Sure enough, there in the alleyway outside the stage door was Lucia, pacing agitatedly up and down, brandishing a large fancy white handkerchief in much the way you might if you were trying to communicate by semaphore.

"Hallo there," I said. "It's Lucia, isn't it?"

"Yes," she said, making it sound like 'chess'. "Please can you tell me – where is Mike?"

"I'm very sorry," I said. "But I'm afraid Mike is no longer with us."

"Aieee!!!" she screamed, clutching her heart. "*Madre de Dios!* Maieek! *Mi amor!*"

"No longer with the company, I mean. He's not dead. Please, calm yourself!"

"Aieee!!!" she wailed again, and began tearing at her handkerchief. It was quite alarming to see, especially as a number of passers-by had gathered at the mouth of the alley to watch – thereby no longer qualifying as passers-by, it occurs to me – and seemed to be more than ready to blame me for the lady's distress.

"Um..." I stuttered, looking around for help, and then, miraculously, Tilly appeared in the doorway.

"You've got this all under control, I see," she said, tartly. I waved my hands helplessly.

"Lucia?" Tilly said gently. I remembered then that they were friends, of course, and that Tilly had borrowed Lucia's burlesque outfit that night back in Chicago. The memory distracted me for a minute or two, and by the time I began paying proper attention again Tilly had got Lucia's heaving bosom under control.

"I'm sure Mike's quite well," she was saying. "He was the last time I saw him, anyway. But I'm afraid he's in England – Inglaterra. I'm sorry."

Lucia, tragically downcast, walked slowly away down the alley, and Tilly and I watched her go.

"Ah," I said. "The perils of romance, eh?"

"You do all right for yourself, by all accounts."

"Eh?"

"That's what I hear, anyway."

And she turned with a prim little flounce and went back inside.

She was referring to my encounter with Wren, of course. How did she know about that? And if she knew, who else knew? Would any of them let something slip in front of Edgar Hurley? Or Alf Reeves, for that matter, because it would be hard to think of a more flagrant example of moral turpitude than carrying on with another player's wife.

What I really wanted to know, though, was what did *she* think? Was she relieved, presuming that I was no longer pining after her? Or was she regretting the fracture of our own romance, wondering what might have been?

As I was...

———

After Chicago the boxcar headed for Winnipeg in Canada. I spent several anxious hours wondering whether Wren was going to come and sit beside me, but she didn't even so much as glance in my direction. She was clearly regarding our heated kiss and fumble as an aberration, and perhaps that was for the best, all things considered. I couldn't help feeling a pang or two of disappointment, though, even so.

This time when we got to Winnipeg our boxcar was uncoupled from the train without any drama. It would have been hard for the Pantages crew to have pulled the same stunt twice, because Alf Reeves was wise to it this time and he was not alone. Mr John W. Considine himself was at the station to oversee our arrival, accompanied by his English butler, Mr Jobson, who ghosted over and invited me and Stan to join his master for a little chat.

"I wonder what he wants," I said to Alf.

"Whatever it is, you just say yes," he said. "He's the boss. If he's got an idea for the show, say yes, he'll forget about it soon enough. If he wants help with something else, you do it. Got that?"

A little later I found myself in the palm-filled conservatory of the grand hotel where Considine was staying. The man himself was holding court, Stan was opposite me, and Whimmy had come along too, partly because he fancied a cup of tea and partly because I was toting his bags for him.

"I'm mighty pleased to make your acquaintance, Mr Walker," Considine said. "I met these two boys on their first go-around for me, didn't I fellers?"

Stan and I nodded.

"That was when we had that bit of trouble with your railway car going missing, remember?"

"What's this?" said Whimmy.

"Mr Considine has a rival," I explained. "A Mr Alexander Pantages."

"Calls himself King Greek. Hrrmph!" Considine snorted derisively.

"Well, when we were in Winnipeg before, this fellow Pantages, or maybe someone who works for him..."

"Oh, he knew all about it, you can depend upon that!" Considine cut in. "He arranged for that boxcar of yours with all your set and costumes in it to remain coupled to the locomotive, and sent it off on a little expedition of its own to the Klondike."

"Ha ha ha!" Whimmy laughed. This sort of thing was right up his street, he liked nothing better than a good practical joke. "I wish I'd thought of that. What a terrific spoof!" he cried.

"It wasn't a spoof!" Considine protested. "It was sabotage! Well, that's why I'm here now. It's payback time!"

"Payback time, Mr Considine?" Stan asked.

"That's right. Let me tell you what I have in mind. This, you see, Winnipeg, this is the Greek's home town. He's been building the showcase theatre of his whole circuit here, brand new, grand opening tomorrow night. He's invited me along just to rub my nose in it, not really meaning for me to come, but I have turned up, just to rub *his* nose in it."

"Ha! Excellent!" said Whimmy. "Do please go on."

"Now he's been trumpeting this place all over the mid-West. It has the latest new-fangled air cooling system. The idea is to make the theatre tolerable in the summer months, when we simply have to close some places down altogether because it gets so hot. There are these great blocks of ice from the Hudson Bay tucked away in the basement, and these great electric fans blow the cool air across them, and up through big vents and into the auditorium. I've seen the designs, same feller designed a place for me in Spokane few years back, he showed me them for... a consideration."

"But it's November," I said. "He'll hardly need to switch them on tomorrow night, will he?"

"Oh, he will do, don't you concern yourself about that. He wants the world and his wife to know he has the very latest doo-dad right here in Winnipeg. All the ladies will be wearing their furs in any case, he's planning quite a shebang, by all accounts." Considine looked off into the middle distance and began grinding his teeth.

"So what can we do for you, Mr Considine?" said Stan.

"I need your help, boys. I need your help taking the wind out of the Greek's sails. Can I count on you?"

"Sure, Mr Considine," I said with a go-getter's grin, and Stan nodded along obligingly.

"I need you to break into the morgue."

"The...?" I spluttered.

"Morgue. The morgue. You limeys have those, don't you? I need you to steal a dead body, and stick it in one of those there vents of his, and then on his opening night he'll start up those great fans, and blow the stench of icy death right up the nostrils of Winnipeg's finest. Yes, by God, that'll do it, and that's what I want you to do."

"A dead body?" Stan gasped.

"If only I'd thought of this sooner, I could have got Sullivan to send one from New York, he always seems to have a couple he's tryin' to get rid of."

Stan and I gaped at one another, and gulped at this sudden terrible insight into the man we were dealing with. It didn't seem like a good idea to disappoint him, that was for sure. Meanwhile Whimmy was lost in thought, seemingly considering this lunatic plan.

"Just to be clear," I said. "You want us to get hold of a dead body by breaking into the *morgue*?"

"Yes, of course. Don't think of killin' someone just for this. That'd be crazy."

"Crazy," Stan agreed.

"No, they'd be too fresh, see? You want a corpse that's really *ripe*."

Considine rubbed his hands together with glee, as Mr Jobson glided alongside with a tray of drinks and began dispensing them.

"If I might suggest, sir?" the butler ventured. "A dead person would be found sooner rather than later, and identified, and questions would be asked. The same might not be true of, say... a cat?"

"That's right," Whimmy cried, snapping his fingers. "A cat might have wandered in and dropped dead without anyone thinking it was anything other than a tragic mishap."

Considine's brow furrowed. "But then... will Pantages know it was me?"

"No," Whimmy said. "But it's the *not* knowing that will eat him up, d'you see?"

Considine brightened. "That's right! He'll wonder, but he won't *know*! Boys, I think we're onto something!"

―――

The grand gala opening of the new Pantages Theatre was the following evening, and we had three shows of our own to do that day so the only time we could really find what we needed was late at night, after the evening's shows were completed, and before we allowed ourselves to crawl into our beds.

Whimmy was surprisingly bright and breezy as we set out through the darkened streets with an empty carpet bag apiece. "The night-time," he insisted, "is the perfect time for spoofing. At the Spooferies the fun seldom began before midnight and rarely finished before the milk."

We shortly decided to split up to look a little less suspicious, and to be honest Stan and I both felt that if there was trouble of any kind we had a better chance of a clean getaway without Whimmy to worry about.

"Happy hunting, boys!" cried Whimmy, and we watched him head towards some woods at the edge of town with a spring in his step that had been missing since his performance had been adjusted, shall we say, in Cincinnati. In truth, some of the old mugging and scene-stealing had been creeping back into the show, but not enough yet to provoke a reaction from Charlie, who was going through a period of not having anything much to do with any of us. A shame, really, as I'm sure he would have enjoyed scavenging in the alleys behind the restaurants of Winnipeg looking for dead cats.

Stan sighed. "Why ever are we doing this?" he muttered.

"Would you rather be breaking into the morgue?" I said.

With a grim nod, then, Stan went one way and I another.

Over the course of the next few hours I searched every back alley in Winnipeg, or so it seemed. I dodged every patrolling police constable, not wanting to explain why I was creeping about the place in the middle of the night with an empty carpet bag and the shovel from the landlady's coal scuttle, and I should think I startled pretty much every grizzled hobo in town.

As the night wore on, desperation forced me deeper and deeper into the darkest recesses of the place, following the hint of foul stinks that I would ordinarily cross the road to avoid, and by the time I slunk back to my bed I had acquired not only a decomposing dog but also the rather fresher corpse of the raccoon that had been eating the dead dog, which I brained with a rather stylish off-drive from the shovel when it came at me snarling. Nice high elbow, four runs all the way, I'd say.

Back at our digs I met up again with my comrades to compare spoils. Stan had managed to locate the reeking corpses of a matching pair of alley cats, while Whimmy the woodsman opened his bag with a triumphant flourish, unleashing a stink that made both our heads kick back involuntarily.

"Meet my good friend the late Mr Skunk!" he cried.

———

Well, that was only the half of it, of course. The next day we had only a brief opportunity, between the second show and the third, to get the dirty deed done, and so as soon as *The Wow Wows* came down that late afternoon the three of us high-tailed it quick-smart over to the Pantages.

Preparations for the grand opening were in full flow, and the new building shone with golden lights in the gathering dusk. We had seen many new vaudeville venues in our time in America, indeed it seemed that they were springing up everywhere all the time, but of all the sparkling new pleasure domes we had played there was none to quite match the splendour of this new Pantages building in Winnipeg. All three of us pushed our hats back on our heads and whistled approvingly.

The headline act for this special night was a sketch called *Johnny's New Car*, a perennial favourite of the time. A character called Johnny Flat-tire was at the mercy of a little red trick automobile with a mind of its own. It would stall as soon as it drove onto the stage, and then with every effort of Johnny's to get it going again something would come off or explode or otherwise go awry. Flames would shoot from the exhaust, a geyser of steam would spurt from the radiator, and there'd be an explosion in which bits of the engine and the steering wheel would catapult into the air and come crashing down all around the hapless Johnny and his date, Katie Speedington, who would harangue him non-stop for his mechanical incompetence.

The comedy was heightened by the blank countenance of the lead comic, whose name was Harry Langdon,[9] and he got his laughs by reacting as little as possible to the chaos around him. We were looking forward to sneaking a peek at this turn later in the week. For now, though, we had a job to do, and so we hustled around to the stage door with our carpet bags and their stinking contents. We had agreed that Whimmy's role would be to distract the stage doorman, so that Stan and I could slip inside to wreak our reeking havoc.

The doorman was actually standing in the doorway looking out, and we ducked back round the corner. The stage door was halfway along the narrow alley, and at the far end we could see a portion of the queue waiting to be allowed in for the gala evening itself.

Whimmy smiled to himself. "Perfect," he said. "Leave this to me, boys."

He shoved his hands into his pockets, and strolled with extravagant pantomime nonchalance towards the doorman. As he passed by he raised his hat and bowed rather hammily, and I fretted that he was overdoing it. On he strolled, up the alleyway beyond the stage door, until he came within range of the queue of theatre-goers. He bowed to them as well, ensuring that he had their attention, then something seemed to catch his eye. He moved over to a door, set in the wall of the theatre, and bent to peer in through the keyhole. This was all done in the most eye-catching and over the top style you could imagine, and yet people were transfixed.

"Good Heavens!" he expostulated, stepping back in amazement. "Who'd have thought it?"

"What is it?" someone called out, but Whimmy waved the inquiry away, and moved forward to peer through the keyhole once again.

After a moment or two, a few curious souls made their way up the alley to take a look for themselves, at which point – glory be – the stage doorman felt he should be taking charge and left his post unattended.

Stan and I darted over to the door and nipped inside. We had been in enough theatres in our time to find our way around, and we quickly slipped backstage, where we tiptoed around a little red automobile parked there, not realising that it was Langdon's prop motor. Stan must have leaned against a hidden button of some kind, because the hood suddenly rocketed up into the air and came crashing down – CLANG! – with a racket that would have awakened the dead. I whirled around to see if anyone was coming, and my bag brushed the side of the car, whereupon the exhaust exploded with a double BANG! BANG!!

Stan and I were screaming now, and promptly abandoned all attempts to sneak around quietly, we just pelted hell for leather towards the steps leading down into the basement. Halfway down we were challenged by a stagehand, who asked what we were looking for, but we pretended to be acrobats from the Ukraine with very poor English and he quickly left us to our own devices. I think the odour emanating from our overcoats may have deterred further questioning.

Downstairs we paused to get our breath back and slow our galloping hearts, then managed to locate the room with the electric fans in. They were enormous, and looked quite capable of blowing the pair of us right up into the theatre. Even though they were quiet just then, the room was freezing, like a gigantic meat locker. Two gigantic slabs of ice, each the size of a hansom cab, lurked in the dark. They must have been slip-slid into place through two large doors to our left, having originated, if the pre-publicity was to be credited, in the Hudson Bay.

Shivering suddenly, both with the cold and the terror of being caught, we located the slanting vents leading up into the auditorium itself. Stan, being narrower in the frame than I, climbed up onto my shoulders, removed the protective grille from the front, and disappeared up into the first of these passageways. I then passed up one of the bags so he could wedge the animal corpses into place. He quickly moved to the second vent and did the same, looking somewhat pale, I must say, as the smell was unbelievably foul, and seemed to be permeating our clothes, our skin, our hair, our eyes.

Outside in the alleyway once again we found Whimmy and the stage doorman surrounded by a little crowd. Whimmy was saying loudly: "What luck, finding the door to the dancing girls' dressing room like that. Quiet, everyone, lest they hear!" Some chump stepped forward to take a peek while the stage doorman smirked and slyly shook hands with our friend – another fish hooked!

As we scuttled back to our own theatre, Whimmy was full of his successful spoof. "You see, you get someone to peer through the hole, and when they see that there is nothing there they first feel cross at being diddled, but then you persuade them that the joke is to see how many more can be made to fall for it. And thus the stage doorman became my accomplice as we spoofed the crowd, it was priceless! I once got the Mayor of Dublin with the very same trick, and then he helped me to get Sir Randolph Churchill to squint through a hole for an absolute age, desperate to see what we said we had seen. Ha ha!"

We hustled up to the dressing room, and in the corridor outside bumped into Wren Hurley, who sidled over in her most flirtatious mood.

"Hello boys, whatever have you been up to?" she said, batting her gorgeous eyelashes. Then she caught a strong whiff of whatever we had been up to, turned on her heels and quickly sidled away again.

Stan, Whimmy and I changed our clothes, and scrubbed and scrubbed at the sink, but try as we might we couldn't quite get the lingering aroma of late raccoon to leave us, and the staging of *The Wow Wows* that evening developed some interesting innovations as our colleagues tried to create as much space between us and them as possible.

By and large we all managed to hold it together, though, until we reached the point in the scenario where Charlie was sitting on a stool stuffing dry crackers into his mouth one at a time, filling his cheeks with dry crumbs and dust. The longer this sequence went on, of course, the more he was required to breathe through his nose, and try as he might he could not ignore the foul stink that was assailing his poor nostrils.

Suddenly he retched involuntarily, and a great cloud of biscuit crumbs flew from his mouth. This got a big laugh, as it usually did of course, but ordinarily Charlie was in control of these eruptions. He convulsed again, and again, until finally even he had to give best to circumstances and move on with the rest of the piece.

As soon as the curtain came down, Stan, Whimmy and I grabbed our things and fled the building.

"I hope we did manage to sabotage that Pantages fellow's evening," Stan said. "Because we sure as hell sabotaged ours."

29
A LITTLE OF WHAT YOU FANCY

WE didn't find out the true extent of our success until John W. bought us a slap-up lunch in his hotel the next day. Stan and I had spent most of the intervening time scrubbing and dousing ourselves in what perfume we could lay our hands on, and we were now just about presentable for polite company.

Considine was gleeful, and even the self-contained Mr Jobson was having difficulty concealing a smirk. While Whimmy, Stan and I tucked into our celebratory steaks, the entrepreneur talked us through the previous evening at Alexander Pantages' grand opening.

"King Greek himself came out onto the front apron to make a speech, all puffed up and full of himself, and all the swells of Winnipeg were there to see it. The mayor was there, the state governor. He even had the British consul and his wife there, front and centre in all their finery."

Whimmy nodded approvingly. All his best practical joke stories featured persons of note, of course. Considine went on:

"The little snake spoke proudly about how this theatre would be the jewel of the Pantages circuit, and a source of pride and joy for the good city of Winnipeg itself, the place he was proud to call home. He described the innovative new cooling system that he had installed especially for them, his people, and then he gave the signal for it to be turned on. We could all see the stage manager smiling proudly as he threw the switch, and we could just faintly hear the fans starting up down below. People began to applaud, and then suddenly – augh! The stench! It wafted up as if from the very bowels of hell itself! Women screamed! Grown men gagged! Everywhere people clamped handkerchiefs to their faces! It was horrible! Horrible!"

Stan and I shared a look across the table. We could quite believe it. Whimmy was hugging himself, chuckling. Considine spread his hands wide, acting out the finale to his story.

"Pantages stood before them, holding his hands out for calm, and he was getting the worst of it, you could tell. He was going green! His eyes rolled up into his head, and all of a sudden he fell to his knees... and vomited into his own orchestra pit!"

Tears of laughter sprung to the big man's eyes. "I'll tell you boys, I won't forget this in a hurry. No sir!"

I turned to Mr Walker, who was chortling away too. "It's a shame you didn't see it, eh, Whimmy?"

"Don't worry, my boy," he said. "When I tell it back at the Spooferies, I shall have done!"

———

The next weekend the Karno boxcar rattled along through the wide open spaces of Montana towards Butte and its all-you-can-eat buffet. Most of the Karnos were dozing, except for those seated near to Whimsical Walker, who was reminiscing about making this very trip with some circus or other by wagon train before the railway was even thought of. He'd had some fascinating encounters with Red Indian tribes along the way, and reckoned his performances had made a big impression on them.

I looked across at Chaplin, who was one of those trying to snooze rather than listening to old Whimmy's circus memories. As I watched he slid slowly along the back of his seat until his head was resting on the shoulder of the person snoozing next to him, who was Tilly. She shifted slightly, and Chaplin's head dropped further until he was nestling in her lap. She stroked his hair maternally, and I saw a half smile appear on his chops. He was awake, of course he was, and I ground my teeth with jealousy. I was so preoccupied that I barely noticed the delectable Mrs Hurley slipping over to join me until she was right alongside.

"Arthur," she said softly.

"Oh. Hello Wren," I said.

"We haven't really spoken, have we, for the last little while?"

"Four weeks," I said. "Apart from 'hello' and 'good evening'."

"Exactly. Since... well, since."

"Since."

"Yes, that's right. I wanted to say... well, I can only imagine what you must think of me."

"No, please, don't worry, nothing bad, I promise you," I said. In fact I had been thinking of her often, of course, and in particularly glowing terms. Just having her sit close to me again was reminding me quite forcibly of one or two of those intoxicating daydreams.

She leaned in close, squashing herself against my arm, as was her way, ignoring – trampling, even – the expected decorum of a married lady sitting with a single gent.

"We can't talk here, not properly, not while everyone's within earshot," she whispered.

"Most of them are asleep," I said.

"Yes, but not all, not all. Come on." Wren stood and swayed nimbly through the curtain into the props and costumes compartment. I sat where I was for a moment or two, trying to see if anyone was watching, but then I risked it and followed her through into the dark.

At the far end of the storage section I could see the daylight streaming in through the door that led to the outside observation platform, but Wren was not silhouetted there waiting. While I peered into the shadows I felt her hand on my arm, and she was beside me.

"It's too cold out there," she whispered.

"Yes," I said. "You're probably right."

"I wanted to apologise, really, for throwing myself at you that time."

"No apology necessary," I said, with what I hoped was appropriate gallantry.

"I was feeling lonely, and rejected, and..."

"Well, quite, me too actually."

"... And the feel of a strong young man's arms around me, after so long..."

"Me too. That is, I mean to say, the sweet-smelling, soft, yielding form of... a beautiful woman."

"I just got..."

"Quite understandable..."

"Carried away." We both said the last two words together, and then stopped. We looked into one another's eyes for a moment, then that moment became longer, and longer, and finally it became unbearable.

With a moan and a gasp we flung ourselves together. Her arms flew around my neck, pulling me down to her, and

I clasped her around the waist lifting her up onto her toes. Our mouths met hungrily, our tongues explored and danced together, and I realised that she had been imagining this every bit as much as I had.

Part of me was aware that this was an incredibly dangerous thing to be doing. All the others were just beyond a single curtain – her husband (who would take a dim view), our boss (ditto), Tilly (how would I explain?), Chaplin (who would be simply *gleeful*), not to mention the best part of a dozen of the biggest gossips you could ever hope to be stuck in a boxcar with. Wren knew it too, and yet we clung to one another, sliding fingers inside clothing, feeling for warm skin, kissing...

Suddenly with a wet smacking smooching sound she pulled her mouth away from mine, gasped, and quickly put a finger to my lips. Then I heard what she had heard – footsteps coming our way. Quickly she ducked down behind a piece of scenery. I made to follow but there wasn't room for us both, so I hurriedly tucked my shirt back in and made as though I was just returning from outside.

The curtain was tweaked back, and big Charlie Griffiths eased through the gap.

"Ah, Dandoe, is that you?" he said when he caught sight of me. "Just going for a cigar. Is it brisk out?"

"Yes, somewhat," I said, hoping that in the dark he couldn't make out how much I was sweating.

"Windy, anyway – your hair's all over the shop."

"Ah, thanks," I said, smoothing it down, straightening my tie. "Well... I'll be getting back, I think."

"Good-o..."

I regained my seat, and a couple of minutes later Wren came through and sat beside her husband without catching my eye.

A good couple of minutes more and my heart finally stopped racing.

That had been a close run thing.

———

If I'd been searching for a metaphorical representation of the state of my career in the Karno organisation if Wren and I were ever caught out, then I could hardly have done better than the scene that greeted us when we arrived at the theatre in Butte.

It was nothing more than a smouldering ruin, a pile of ashes. Evidently it had burned down a few days before, and nobody had thought to tell us not to come. Here and there we could see some desultory scavenging going on, either stage hands trying to see what might be salvaged, or else emboldened chancers seeing what they might get away with. It was clear that nobody was going to be doing a show there this week, next week or any week in the near future.

Stan sidled over and murmured out of the corner of his mouth. "You don't think, do you...?"

"What?"

"Well, that this is part of the feud between Considine and Pantages? Maybe retaliation for our little stunt in Winnipeg? Payback for our payback?"

"It's a bit much, don't you think? Burning a whole theatre to the ground?"

"I agree," Whimsical Walker said, behind us. "It's beyond a practical joke, so to speak, but well... you never know what people will do when pushed too far."

Not far away from where we were standing, Charlie was shifting a small pile of ashes from side to side with the shiny toe of his shoe.

Some of the other acts on the bill were also hanging around, looking pretty gloomy, and it was not hard to guess why. No play, no pay, that was the reality of vaudeville, and it was hard enough to get by as it was without a blank week for the old pocket book.

"Hey Stan!" I sang out. "Remember that time in Middlesbrough?"

"Oh, not Middlesbrough again..." Charlie muttered.

"What happened in Middlesbrough?" Whimmy asked.

"The theatre gave my old dad's company top billing," Stan grinned, "so the Karnos took over a church hall and stole our audience away. It was quite a thing!"

I remembered it well. It was a time when Tilly and I had been particularly close, an exciting time, a happy time. I looked over at her and she smiled, clearly remembering it too.

"Well, what do you say, Alf?" I said. "Shall we find ourselves a church hall?"

Alf thought for a moment, tweaking his bowtie this way and that. "Why not?" he said. "Why not indeed?"

———

We found a meeting hall that would serve well enough, and were able to secure its use once we had persuaded an organisation called the Industrial Workers of the World[10] to move a rally they were planning in the hope of persuading the Anaconda Mining Corporation to improve pay and conditions for its cosmopolitan army of miners. Their bold threats of organising industrial action were undermined, to my way of thinking, by the fact that they gloried in the nickname 'The Wobblies'. In any case, it appeared that their rally, such as it was, would fit comfortably into a corner of Mack and Carey's Orpheum bar, so we had a clear run.

314

The hall was not so well furnished for a theatrical presentation as it might have been, of course, but there were no complaints as everyone was so relieved at the prospect of some earnings for the week. And it was a little out of the way for the town's entertainment seekers, being in a residential area, wedged between two headframes for the copper mines beneath our feet and a large smelting operation with a handful of narrow chimneys belching black smoke into the sky, but Alf managed to get small handbills printed in double quick time, and the whole company was pressed into walking the main strip handing them out, letting people know that the new temporary vaudeville venue was in business.

Whimmy couldn't believe the transformation in the town since his first visit a couple of decades before. "This was just a mining camp," he said, "with a few grizzled prospectors and panhandlers, and we barely found enough people to fill the circus tent. Now look at it!"

He waved his hand at all the entertainments on offer on the main strip, and at the great copper works buildings visible in the near distance. A bout of coughing overtook him then, and he seemed to be having a bit of trouble getting his breath. Perhaps it was all the smoke from the smelting works. A kindly shopkeeper hurried out with a glass of water for the old boy.

"Why don't you take a rest, Whimmy?" I said. "We can manage this."

"Nonsense, dear boy, I shall be fine. And this is part and parcel of my working life, you know. Get the word out! The show must go on, all that! Madam, can I interest you in an evening of prime entertainment?"

We never found out whether King Greek or his people had anything to do with the conflagration at the Sullivan and Considine Empress, but if they did then the stunt backfired on them, as while we were turning people away, the acts on the Pantages bill were performing to rows and rows of empty seats.

The extra work and the harsh environment took a heavy toll on some of us, however, and we were alarmed to find Whimsical Walker slumped in a corner of Mack and Carey's bar one night towards the end of that week, his drink untouched, and a trickle of blood leaking from one nostril.

"Whimmy? Are you all right?"

"Wha...? Ah, yes, fine, dear boy, fine!" The old clown wiped the blood from his nose with a handkerchief which, we could hardly help but notice, was already streaked with blood.

"Are you quite sure?"

"Just a little nosebleed, boys, nothing to worry about. Now who's for another? Eh?" Whimmy tottered uncertainly to his feet, trying his best to convince us that all was well.

"Sure, the air is terrible here in the winter," Michael the barman said. "The clouds keep all the smoke in, y'see. I've seen this a hundred times."

"Exactly," Whimmy said. "I'm sure I shall be quite recovered when we reach Vancouver and the Pacific Ocean air."

The next evening, however, Whimmy staggered into our impromptu dressing room.

"Hey! Who did your make-up?" I said. His nose was bright red and much larger than usual, and there were two equally brightly coloured patches on his cheeks.

"I haven't got my make up on yet," Whimmy said, sitting down heavily.

"Well, you look like a clown, my friend," Stan said, passing over one of the few hand mirrors we had about the place.

"Oh dear!" Whimmy said when he clocked his reflection. "Oh dearie me."

I took a closer look, and there seemed to be angry patches of swelling erupting all over the old man's face.

"Does that hurt?" I asked, concerned.

"No, I hadn't even noticed. Oh my!"

"We should fetch a doctor, don't you think?" Stan said.

"No," Whimmy cut in quickly. "No doctors. I will be fine, I'll just cover these patches with white face, no one will know anything is amiss."

"If you are sure you feel well enough to do the show...?" I said.

"Oh yes, I've performed with far worse than this," Whimmy assured us, then muttering barely audibly, "... whatever this is..."

Stan and I conferred in the corridor outside the dressing room.

"What do you think?" Stan said.

"If he says he can go on, then I'm sure he knows best."

"Right. He'll probably be just fine, won't he?"

And that is what we both thought for about another hour, until smack bang in the middle of *The Wow-Wows*, Whimsical Walker walked out onto the stage, and collapsed.

30
NOOKSACKS

A few days later I found myself driving a horse-drawn buckboard southwards out of Vancouver. I trundled slowly past a row of logging yards, smelling of fresh sawdust and sap, and then out of town and into a lushly forested snowscape stretching ahead for miles into the distance. I was looking first for the Nooksack River, and then I planned to head inland in search of the Nooksack Indians.

Whimsical Walker was lying on the flatbed behind me, swaddled in as many blankets as I had been able to find, his eyes flickering as he slept fitfully. This trip was his idea, a last-ditch hare-brained plan to save his Karno career.

Twenty years before he had ridden out this way with the circus wagon train, and he had befriended a chief of the local tribe. The natives had been enchanted by his capering, apparently, and particularly taken with his brightly-coloured variegated stockings. The chief had tried them on, and Whimmy had left him some pairs as a gift, thus cementing what we hoped would prove to be a lasting friendship.

Now while he was visiting the tribe he had apparently experienced a remarkable example of healing by their medicine man, and he was staking everything on this fellow, or possibly his successor, working some magic for him.

"He gave me some medicine made from fish oil," he said, "nasty stuff, but do you know I was right as rain in no time."

The old man's desperation had got to me, and so I had agreed to borrow this cart at the crack of dawn, and get directions, and sneak him out from under the noses of the nurses and bring him out here into the wilderness to see what could be done. I was beginning to get anxious, for we had already been on the road for hours, and I didn't much like my chances of getting back in time for the matinée.

I shook my head, and pulled my coat tighter around my chest against the cold. "What the hell are we doing?" I muttered to myself, my teeth chattering.

As the horses clopped along through the snow I thought back over the events of the past few days.

Back in Butte the doctor who had attended him had said that he thought Whimmy was exhausted and just needed to rest.

"He does look awful pale, though," he'd mused with a frown. "And I don't much like the look of that red nose."

"That's his make-up," I'd said.

So we had pulled down the camp bed from the wall of the boxcar and let Whimmy sleep on the long haul up to Vancouver. Everyone was very solicitous, checking on him, bringing him drinks of water when he woke. Even the ongoing poker game had kept the noise down.

Only Charlie grumbled at the inconvenience of turning the boxcar into a hospital ward.

"You know, it's my turn to have the bed, actually," he'd muttered as we helped Whimmy aboard, but he'd been roundly told to hush by all the women in chorus.

A couple of hours into that tedious journey I looked up and saw Wren swaying along the carriage towards me. Behind her I could see Edgar reading a book, and he had only to glance up to see where I was sitting. Alf Reeves and Amy were also facing me directly, deep in discussion about something, presumably our invalid. And at the far end, nearest the door that led to the rest of the train, Tilly and Charlie were also wide awake and talking.

There was simply no way she could come and snuggle flirtatiously next to me, as was her wont, without everyone seeing. I signalled her 'No!' with my eyes but she kept on walking down the centre aisle. Thankfully she didn't join me, but kept straight on past and through towards the observation platform out back. As she passed, however, she indicated with a pointing finger that was shielded from everyone else's view by her marvellous figure, that I should follow.

I waited several minutes, trying to spot whether anyone was keeping an eye on me, but I saw only boredom, nonchalance and indifference on my friends' faces. They could have been putting it on, of course, but I knew them all and they weren't that good at acting.

So I stretched and got to my feet, and strolled out to get some air. My intention was to say to Wren that this was madness, but I only managed to say "This is mmm...!" before she clamped her delicious mouth to mine.

"Mmmm...!" she agreed, and we were off again. She took my hand and guided it to her breast, and ran her fingers feverishly through my hair.

Then, though, we heard footsteps, and as before she ducked down out of sight and left me to face the music. Not genial Charlie Griffiths this time, but none other than Edgar Hurley, the hornèd husband himself.

"Ah, ahem, hullo Hurley," I said.

"Hmmph," he grunted. "Did you see my wife outside just now?"

"Your wife?" I said. "No, I think she went to the restaurant car a little while ago."

"She definitely came this way," he frowned.

"Well, perhaps you're right, I haven't been out there yet, let's take a look shall we?" I said, guiding him through to the open air. Behind me I could just make out the rat-scuttling footsteps of my partner-in-crime making good her escape, all the way to the restaurant car if she had picked up my heavy hint.

As I almost managed to say – madness.

When we pulled into Vancouver, it was plain for anyone to see that Whimmy's condition had deteriorated still further. He was struggling to get his breath, the rashes on his face were so bright red they seemed almost to shine, and you could feel his fever radiating off him from a foot away.

"Straight to the hospital," Alf had insisted. "No arguments."

Once the patient was installed in a bed in the Vancouver hospital, a conference had taken place in the corridor outside between me, Charlie and Alf.

"He'll have to go home," Charlie said. "Wire Karno for a replacement."

"Hang on," I said. "We don't know how long he's going to be in here. He could be fine in a day or two."

"Is it worth waiting? Even if they let him out of here, he's going to be recuperating for who knows how long. The workload is too great for the old man, and he was too slow at the best of times. I'd rather just move on."

"Listen Alf," I said. "We can cover for Whimmy until he's fit again, like we did in Butte the last two shows."

Alf was wavering, trying to be fair, but Charlie was insistent.

"He's dead weight," Charlie said. "A liability."

"You've been pushing that all along, haven't you?" I said, squaring up to him. "You've wanted to get rid of him since we first set out, well, I won't let you do it, do you hear me?"

"It's not up to you, though, is it?" Charlie sneered, and I felt myself lurching towards him to wipe the smile of his face, but Alf interposed himself.

"All right, let's calm down," Alf said. "We have to do what's best for Whimmy, and if he's not going to be able to work, then perhaps the best thing is for him to stay here in Vancouver until he is recovered, and then make his own way back to England."

"But...!"

"I'll see that everything is paid for, but if he's not ready to work by the time we move on, we'll have to leave him behind."

A doctor came to speak to us then, and he seemed quite perplexed.

"A most puzzling case, most puzzling," he said, looking down at his notes. "Tell me, has your colleague been handling any deceased wild animals?"

"No, of course not," Alf said. "He is a comedian."

"Well..." I said.

"Well what?"

"Well, he's not really a comedian," Charlie butted in. "That's what you were going to say, isn't it, Arthur, and I must say I concur..."

"Will you shut up?" I snapped. "I was going to say there might have been a skunk."

"A skunk?"

"Yes. Just one, dead one. Is that what has made him ill?"

"I really don't know," the doctor said. "But it was a possibility I was hoping I could rule out. A skunk, you say?"

We opened at the Vancouver Orpheum, filling in for our absent colleague as we had done towards the end of the run in Butte. The matinée was a good lively house, and the sketch was very slick and well received.

Afterwards Charlie was full of himself, telling anyone who would listen: "That is how it *should* be, d'you see? We have been held back on this trip, weighted down, hobbled, but now at last we are free to fly."

"Oh hush!" Tilly snapped at him. "Have you no tact at all?"

Charlie looked around for support, and found little Annie Forrester. "You think it was better, don't you, Annie?" he said, giving her his most brilliant simpering smile.

"Yes, Charlie, I do," she said, blushing shyly.

In the break between shows I nipped along to the hospital for visiting hour. Whimmy was sitting up in bed. The rashes on his face were glistening with some sort of unguent, and his eyes were wide and panic-stricken. As I stepped alongside he grabbed my wrist. "Arthur!" he hissed. "Don't let them send me home!"

"You need to get well," I said.

"They want to send me home, I know they do. Don't let them do it!"

He was quite agitated, and it dawned on me how much this job mattered to him. There was nothing for him to go back to, and the important thing for the old clown was the dignity of being employed, and the opportunity to make people laugh, to exercise the Power. I looked into his pleading eyes, and was struck by the sudden certainty that sending the old fellow home would be the end of him.

I felt responsible, I suppose. If he had not met me, and I had not met Alf Reeves, then Whimmy would not even be here. And the antipathy Charlie felt towards the old fellow, well, I had a sneaking suspicion it sprang from his feelings towards me. He had tried to get shot of me a second time, and had been unable to do so (thanks to Alf), so he was trying to get at me through my friend.

I wasn't about to let him get away with it.

Which is how I came to be freezing my backside off on this particular fool's errand. The borrowed horse nodded and plodded along through the snow-burdened trees, with no sign yet of the Nooksack River, or any human habitation.

"Bloody Charlie Chaplin!" I muttered, pulling my coat closer and a sort of fur trapper's hat that I had found in the theatre wardrobe further down over my ears.

Up ahead now I saw a little group of wooden shacks. Smoke curled out of the chimneys, and despite the cold we could see that there were figures sitting on the verandahs taking the air. As we drew alongside the first of these dwellings I lifted my hat in greeting to a couple who were watching our approach, the man in a dark suit with a waistcoat and his wife in a long frock of dark blue.

"Good morning," I said. "We are trying to reach the Nooksack Indian tribe."

The man got to his feet, leaving his wooden rocking chair, and raised his hat, a bowler.

"We are Nooksack," he said.

"Aha." When I got a closer look at him, I could see there was a native American cast to his features which I hadn't noticed at first, wrong-footed by the sheer ordinariness of his little homestead. Looking around, I saw now that all the curious faces peering at us from in front of the other little houses had the same dark weathered skin, dark hair and narrow eyes.

I must admit I was a little disappointed. So much of my youth had been taken up with reading penny bloods, tales of cowboys and Indians, and I had been expecting wigwams and feathered head-dresses, war paint and rain dances. Yet here was a very ordinary-looking bunch, dressed much as we ourselves were, living in a little village, just watching the world go by.

I explained that our friend was unwell, and that he hoped a Nooksack medicine man might be able to make him better, but my little tale was met with blank indifference. I jumped down from the cart and led the fellow round to see the patient for himself. I was, however, beginning to feel sure that we were on a wild goose chase, chasing after a wild goose, what's more, that had left a couple of decades before never to be seen in these parts again.

Whimmy tried to sit up to speak, but as it turned out no words were necessary. As soon as the Indian clapped eyes on our friend he let out a gasp, and then cried to his neighbours, waving them over to see for themselves.

"It is Mr Whimsy!"

The whole population of this little outpost clustered around our cart to see, and then hastily concocted a plan of action. Before we really knew what was happening, we were surrounded by all the men on horseback, and our cart was being led first down to the river, and then along the bank, heading inland towards the distant Rockies.

"You must have made quite an impression when you were here before," I said.

"Yes," Whimmy croaked. "And I look like I'm wearing my clown make-up, that probably helps."

After another half an hour, maybe more, we reached a larger habitation which seemed to be more of a centre for the community. There were two long buildings side by side, fashioned from planks of cedar wood. There were no windows and just a single door on each, and central chimneys from which dark smoke curled lazily.

We were left to wait outside while the Nooksacks who had guided us here went in to announce our arrival, and I looked over the front wall, which was covered in paintings, red, white and black representations of hands and eyes, and fish, and a totem pole of carved wood thrusting up into the sky.

"This tells the history of our tribe," one man said earnestly to me, and I nodded, interested. Suddenly something about two thirds of the way up the pole caught my eye and I gasped. That face, that carved face, with its peeling paint and the weathered cracks beginning to split the nose, the round red nose, was that meant to be... Whimsical Walker?

Just then the chief of the Nooksacks emerged from the main cedar plank longhouse in a state of high excitement. He was a man of perhaps sixty-five years of age, and was far more exotically dressed than the fellows who had brought us there, but still not quite in the fashion I was expecting from my boyhood reading. No, if anything you'd have to say he was dressed like a clown.

The costume had seen better days, certainly, and had been patched and mended here and there, but this had unmistakeably once belonged to Mr Whimsical Walker. This chief came over to our cart at the gallop, and his delight on beholding its cargo was plain to see.

"Mr Whimsy, old friend! You promised you would return one day, and here you are!"

"Good heavens!" Whimmy gasped. "Is that my old capering outfit? Hasn't it lasted well? Arthur, in my bag, here, here..."

I opened his case for him, and together we presented the chief with a brand new silk costume from Whimmy's collection, and several new pairs of coloured tights. The man was absolutely thrilled to bits, and skipped back indoors to get changed at once.

"I told you they would come in handy," Whimmy whispered.

When the chief returned, preening in his new silks like Grimaldi reborn, I stepped forward.

"We were hoping you could help us," I said.

"How?" said the chief.

"How," I said, bowing deeply.

"No, I mean, how can we help?"

I explained again that Whimmy was ill, and a veritable whirlwind of activity ensued. An almost naked chap took the lead, and I took him for the tribe's medicine man. His modesty was barely preserved at the front by a sort of sporran arrangement fashioned from cedar bark, but his buttocks were exposed to the winter chill. Rather him than me, I thought.

We were led down to the river, where there was a fishing party set up on the bank. This was a little bit more like it, actually. A large fire in the middle of a clearing, surrounded by triangular teepees, made from poles and animal hides, and canoes pulled up out of the water, and behind us a massive white peak looming up from untold acres of forested foothills.

The chief saw me admiring this magnificent view, and proudly declared "Kweq' Smánit!" – which I took to be the name of the mountain[11].

Whimmy and I were seated by the fire, and plied with bowls of a sort of tea with a lingering taste of soil. Meanwhile the Nooksack Indians busied themselves plunging into the freezing river and bringing great handfuls of mud up onto the bank, where slowly but surely they constructed a small lodge arrangement.

The chief took the opportunity to show Whimmy what I took to be an approximation of the clown's performance from twenty years before, hopping nimbly from one foot to the other, while the sick patient smiled benignly from under a pile of patterned rugs and clapped a rhythm with his hands.

I thought: "Imagine your performance making such an impression, that it is still remembered twenty years later, and talked about, and re-enacted, and carved onto a totem pole. That's success, however you cut it. Charlie Chaplin can only *dream* of something like this."

Once the mud dwelling – unnervingly tomb-like, actually – was completed, the Nooksacks lit a fire in there, and then slid good old Whimmy reverently inside. The medicine man pranced about a bit, making incantations, and the chief sidled over to me in his new clown costume.

"Heat good," he said, nodding encouragingly. I nodded back, crossing my fingers.

Whimmy's head was sticking out of his muddy tomb, and the sweat was pouring freely from his fevered face. The old man winked up at me encouragingly – clearly this was precisely what he had been hoping for.

At a signal from the medicine man, Whimmy was then pulled out of the heat and lifted to his feet. He swayed from side to side as the Nooksacks unwrapped the various rugs and blankets he was swaddled in, until he was standing there in just his long combinations, shivering uncontrollably.

The clown-chief turned to me. "Cold good," he said.

"Are you sure...?" I began, but then Whimmy was picked up bodily by four Indians, who then ran down to the river and pitched the old man into the icy water.

"No! Wait!" I shouted, and galloped down to the shore. The medicine man and the chief smiled and nodded as though everything was going according to plan, but I could no longer see Whimsical Walker. I peered hard at the icy depths flowing hard right to left, trying to make out the shape of the patient, not wanting to commit to plunging in until I was sure of his whereabouts.

Suddenly the clown-chief pointed away to our left.

"There!" he said, and sure enough Whimmy's pale head had bobbed to the surface a little way off. He was being carried off by the current, and we raced frantically along the bank trying to keep up with him. He disappeared under the surface again, and re-emerged even further away, picking up pace. Something about the panicky way the Nooksacks were running for their horses made me suspect that this was not part of the treatment.

"If they don't catch him soon he'll be heading out to sea," I panicked, as the Indians thundered by, their horses' hooves kicking up clods of earth in our faces.

I lost sight of old Whimmy then, as his big white head glided around a bend in the Nooksack River, and we crashed through some bracken and ferns trying to cut off the corner. I was starting to think that we had lost him.

When we emerged out of the trees again, though, it was to see a more encouraging sight. Several of the Nooksacks were inching along a fallen tree trunk that was thrusting out into the current, and there, lodged in the branches at the far end I could see the limp figure of my friend. They hauled him up out of the water and manhandled him to the shore, where I could see he was coughing and waving his arms around, so at least he was still alive, for now.

Our hosts didn't wait for me to catch up, but slung Whimmy over the back of a horse and thundered back to the encampment. By the time I scrambled back there Whimmy was back in the muddy sweat coffin warming up again, and after a warming bowl of the soil-flavoured tea the Nooksacks helped me wrap him up as snugly as possible and load him back onto the buckboard. Time was getting on, and I was desperate to get back to Vancouver, not only because I had a matinée to do, but also to return the old man to some proper medical attention.

We thanked the Nooksack chief, resplendent and beaming in his new costume, and the medicine man, still not wearing very much at all, and headed back to the city.

On the way back Whimmy and I were subdued, although we did discuss the possibility that the efforts of the Indians might actually have had an efficacious effect.

"You never know," the old clown murmured. "It might be just what the doctor ordered. Stranger things have happened."

"Yes, indeed," I said. "But not many."

31
QUITE CHOP-FALLEN

FORTUNATELY we were only playing two-a-day in Vancouver, so I made it to the Orpheum with minutes to spare for our tea-time performance.

"Have you been to the hospital?" Tilly whispered as I arrived in the wings during the preceding turn, still doing buttons up. "How is he?"

I remembered the doctor confronting me angrily as nurses unswaddled the patient and returned him to his sickbed. "Where in the name of all that's holy have you been?!"

"I thought the fresh air might do him some good," I'd said.

"Oh you did, did you? Well, let me disabuse you of that notion right away. This man is very much worse. He has a serious pneumonia, and the bacterial infection has spread to his jaw. We shall have to remove all of his teeth!"

I shook my head. "Not too good," I said.

"Poor Arthur," Tilly said. "You look exhausted. Have you been sitting with him all this time?"

"Kind of," I nodded.

Back down in the green room after the performance I fielded solicitous enquiries from just about everyone – not quite everyone, though, young Mr Chaplin managed to contain his curiosity – and assured all Whimmy's friends that he was comfortable and in good hands.

Alf Reeves was leaning against the doorframe, his arms folded. "Funny thing," he said. "I went to visit Mr Walker myself this lunchtime, and the hospital said they had lost him."

"Lost him?" I said, not liking the sound of this.

"Yes, he'd disappeared. I didn't say anything because I didn't want to upset you all, with shows to do. But then I went again just half an hour ago and he was back. Back, and in very much poorer shape, I'm sorry to say."

"Where had he been?" Freddie said.

"I don't know. Perhaps you can enlighten us all, Arthur?"

I sighed, took a deep breath, and explained about the Nooksack expedition. Got a fair few laughs, as well, which I noted carefully to tell Whimmy about in due course. I felt sure he would already be looking forward to making merry with that little anecdote.

"Well," Alf said, shaking his head. "I'm sure you meant well, but that sounds incredibly irresponsible to me."

"It does," a voice chimed in. "Unbelievably irresponsible." Charlie had perked up, having spotted a fresh stick to beat me with.

"Yeah, like *you* care," I muttered, turning to square up to him.

"All right," Alf said, a mother separating two squalling brats. "Let's leave it at that, shall we?"

As the company milled about I noticed that Wren was not there, and now that I thought of it she had not been among the well-wishers asking after Whimsical Walker either.

I wandered out into the corridor and caught sight of her through the open door of the girls' dressing room. She was sitting by herself, staring into a mirror. Her hair was different, somehow, let loose and falling over one half of her face so that I could barely see her left eye. As I watched she swept the hair up and let it fall again, and I thought I saw redness there, swelling, and even the beginning of a bruise. She reached for some make-up and was about to make a start on covering up when she saw me reflected in the mirror, looking at her, and she hurriedly hopped up and slammed the door on me.

I felt a chill. Had Hurley hit her?

And what did that mean? Was the cat out of the bag?

I couldn't think clearly, though, couldn't focus on that, because all I was thinking about was thumping Edgar Hurley.

I needed to know the truth of the matter, of course, first, and it was not easy to envisage a way of engineering an opportunity to talk to Wren alone, especially if we desperately needed to be discreet. As it was we barely had anything to do with one another between those frenzied bouts of grappling in the dark of the box-car, and I certainly couldn't wait until the weekend and the ride down to Portland.

In the end, I lurked behind as Freddie, Stan, Charlie and the others all made their way up to the wings for the evening turn. Edgar Hurley gave me a look like thunder as he pushed past, or was I imagining it? The girls filed out of their dressing room, Emily, Tilly, Annie, Amy, and bustled away up the stairs, but Wren was lingering behind, perhaps still putting the finishing touches to her camouflage. I stepped in, and shut the door behind me.

"Arthur!" she gasped, her hand flying to her mouth, a make-up brush clattering on to the table top.

I reached out and slowly lifted her hair from the left side of her face. She had covered up well, but she was clearly going to have quite a shiner.

"He did this?"

"Listen..."

"Because of me? Because of us?"

"Listen Arthur, there is no 'us', it was just a bit of foolishness, just foolishness, that's all."

"I'm going to knock his block off!"

"No! No, Arthur, you mustn't! Then we will all be out on our ears, don't you see that?"

"Be worth it," I grumbled.

She put her hand on my arm. "It was just... one. One punch. And I had asked for it, hadn't I, really? I had. And he was so sorry afterwards. He wept, Arthur. Edgar wept, I have never seen him do that before. And he blamed himself, for driving me away, and promised faithfully that things would be different from now on, said it had made him realise how important I was to him, suddenly faced with losing me. Do you see? So we are going to make a fresh start, Eddie and I, and forget this ever happened, so you must not confront him, or speak to him, or ever bring the subject up again, do you understand?"

"I... um..."

"And now, look, we must hurry, chop-chop, or they'll be starting without us, come on!"

━━━━━

The next morning I went along to the hospital to check on the patient. I was looking forward to seeing his face – albeit sans teeth, I remembered with a shudder – when I told him how many laughs the Nooksack story had garnered the previous evening, and checked off the salient points as I walked – totem pole, Indian chief in clown tights, mud hut, 'heat good!', Whimmy's head bobbing out to sea amongst the ice floes.

I made my way up to the room where the old boy was quartered, and found Alf Reeves in the corridor outside.

"What ho, Alf," I said, with early-morning jauntiness. "How is the old bean?"

Alf looked at me, and his expression froze my heart.

"He's gone, Arthur," Alf said bleakly. "He's gone. He didn't make it through the night."

I sat heavily, and Alf slumped beside me.

"Charlie'll be pleased," I said.

"Now then," Alf scolded. "That's not fair, is it? Not fair at all."

"No, you're right, sorry. I'm just.... It's a shock."

We sat there, staring blankly at the tiled floor.

"I suppose I shall have to make arrangements," Alf said, after a minute or two.

"A funeral?"

"Well, not here. We shall have to send him back to England, to his wife."

"I didn't even know he was married."

"Oh yes, for years. They had a home in Hull. Sons, too, I think."

"He never spoke of them to me."

"No?"

"No. Just that bloody donkey he trained to sing, and performed with in front of..."

"Queen Victoria at Windsor Castle," Alf joined in, and we laughed. A sad laugh, a hollowed-out empty laugh, but a laugh all the same.

━━━━━

I went for a long, long walk. Nothing else would do. My feet took me into a large square with a grand new building down one side, columns on the front, a union jack fluttering from its flagpole. It was a courthouse, and I gave it a wide berth – I was feeling guilty enough as it was.

I was blaming myself, of course. If I hadn't let those half-baked Nooksacks chuck the old fool into an icy river he might still be with us. If I hadn't met Whimsical Walker at all, hadn't gone to the circus that night with Lance, then he might be capering still in his variegated tights, maybe on the stage of the Drury Lane theatre...

I couldn't settle, couldn't sit still, couldn't stop to eat or drink anything. I just wanted to punch somebody. That half-naked idiot of a medicine man, I wanted to land a good one on him. And Edgar Hurley, too, kept flashing before my angry eyes, that self-satisfied little smirk on his face. I thought about wiping that away, giving him a black eye to match the one he'd given Wren.

Most of all, though, I thought about thumping Charlie Chaplin. It was down to him, actually. If Charlie hadn't been so hostile to old Whimmy, put so much pressure on him, agitated for the old fellow's removal, then he wouldn't have been panicked into trying the Nooksack cure in the first place, he'd just have sat there getting over whatever had been wrong with him on the first place, whether that was down to the filthy air in Butte or his encounter with the late Mr Skunk, or both.

Oh yes, I blamed myself. But I also blamed Charlie.

———

The bad news travelled faster than I did to the theatre that afternoon, and when I arrived our number one was standing on a chair making a little rallying speech to the troops.

"The show must go on, that's what dear old Whimmy would have said," Charlie was saying.

"Surely, though, as a mark of respect?" Charles Griffiths muttered grimly.

"We'll raise a glass to him later," Charlie said. "But for now we have a job to do, and he would want us to do it. So come on, everyone, let's get our heads up and do our best."

He jumped down and got on with his own preparations, but no one else seemed to share his business-like mood. Everyone was very down, naturally enough. And judging by the way the others started avoiding me, it was apparent that no one else shared my opinion that Charlie was to blame.

No, I was carrying that particular can all by myself.

It was a thoroughly miserable week, that week in Vancouver. One of the worst. And the mood didn't show any signs of improving when we all boarded the boxcar once again for the trip down to Portland.

After a while I couldn't bear the baleful looks and sidelong glances any longer, and took myself through the storage section of the car and out onto the observation deck for a bit of privacy. I had no thought that Wren would follow me. She and Edgar had been sitting together holding hands since we left the station, occasionally pecking one another on the cheek in a faintly nauseating fashion. At least the spectre of discovery seemed to have been lifted, that was one good thing, but I couldn't help thinking back to the excitement of those frantic encounters.

The observation deck was freezing cold, and I couldn't stand it out there for more than a few minutes. I couldn't face re-joining the company, and so I ended up burrowing into a space behind where the set was stacked up. There was just enough room to lie down, and I pulled a couple of big coats off the costume rail to stretch out on.

I suppose I drifted off. I hadn't slept much for the previous few days, what with Whimmy on my mind, and Wren, so I was pretty tired.

I awoke after who knows how long to find Tilly leaning over the stack of set panels and looking down at me.

"So this is where you are hiding yourself," she was saying.

"Tilly...?" I said, half-wondering if I was still asleep.

"Looks rather cosy, actually. Room for another?" she said.

"Another what?" I said, dopily.

"Move over." She clambered round into my little cubby-hole, over my shins, and laid herself alongside me, propping herself up on one elbow. "Hello, there," she said.

"Well, hello."

"Is this where you had your little liaisons with Mrs Hurley?"

"No... you know about that?"

"My dear, everybody knows about that."

"What? What do you mean?"

"Wren wasn't particularly secretive about it. She practically hung a signpost out."

I was appalled. "*Everybody* knows?"

"Well, certainly all the women do. Maybe some of the fellows are a little more dense."

"Well, whatever it was it is over now," I said. "She and her husband have had a big reconciliation."

"Of course they have," Tilly said breezily. "That was what it was all about, wasn't it? That was why she was so brazen about it. She wanted him to notice, wanted him to do something."

"He did do something, he hit her."

"Yes, and then grovelled for forgiveness, no doubt, and now everything in their garden is hunky dory. She used you, my friend."

"I see," I said. "The scales are falling from my eyes."

"Has she broken your poor heart?"

"No! I'm relieved, really, more than anything. I've been afraid that at any minute Alf would be obliged to call 'moral turpitude' and chuck me out of the company once again."

"Well, quite so."

"I didn't enjoy life outside the Karno organisation that much."

"Did you not?"

I told her then about sleeping rough at the Fun Factory, about *The Rum 'Uns from Rome*, and how Stan's rather happy-go-lucky business sense had done for it. I told her about the plaster eggs on stilts and being stranded in Belgium, about Poverty Corner, and my brief career as a pavement artist in Trafalgar Square.

As I talked, and she laughed and prompted me for more details, I realised just how much I had missed exactly this. Talking to Tilly, sharing the stuff of life with her. I felt as though nothing was real until I had told her about it, and in recent months I had even caught myself going over things in my head in conversation with an imaginary Tilly, just to get them straight in my head. Now, at last, here was the real Tilly again, and I poured it all out to her.

I told her about how I had retired from show-business to get away from being dragged into Fred Karno's divorce against my will, about going back into service in Cambridge, and finally my chance association with Whimsical Walker.

"Poor Whimmy," she said sadly. "Such a terrible thing."

"They all seem to be blaming me," I said, nodding in the rough direction of the passenger cabin.

"Well, in fairness you did allow some Indians to parboil him then chuck him in a river."

"Ah yes, but if Charlie hadn't..."

"I don't think it was Charlie's doing," she said, and I didn't press the point.

"Charlie," I began. "He has been monopolising you rather."

"Charlie is very attentive. It's really very attractive, actually. He makes a girl feel like the Queen of the May. All dressed in white, flowers in her hair, with everyone dancing round her, paying homage to her beauty and her innocence, her purity. Trouble is it's a hard act to keep up day after day, and speaking as the girl in question, one always feels like there will be another Queen along next year, even purer, even more innocent, and... well, younger, not to put too fine a point on it."

She looked away. There was something on her mind, and I waited for her to tell me but nothing was forthcoming. In the end I broke the silence by concluding my own tale.

"Anyway," I said, "it was only the merest chance that I happened to bump into Stan, and then Alf as well, just the night before this tour sailed, and if I hadn't then old Whimmy would never have come to America, would never have..." I stopped, a lump forming in my throat.

"Don't," Tilly said, putting her finger on my lips.

Her touch was electrifying. I didn't speak for fear she would move and break the contact. I looked up into her eyes, her lovely green eyes, brimming with kindness and tenderness.

"Why did you come looking for me?" I said when she finally moved.

"I was worried about you. I care about you. I was afraid you were brooding all by yourself with no one to turn to. I thought you might need a friend."

"Always," I whispered.

With aching slowness we moved closer and closer, with minute pauses as we each seemingly sought confirmation from the other that this was really what we wanted to happen.

And then our lips met, and we were kissing, tenderly, gloriously, overwhelmingly.

When we finally broke apart we both seemed to realise that either we became covered with embarrassment, scrambled awkwardly out of our hidey hole, and tiptoed back to our seats as though nothing had happened, or we went on.

We went on.

No one disturbed us, no one found us, we lost ourselves in the rhythm of the train, in each other.

At one important juncture she whispered; "Is this what you and Wren did, then?"

"Shh," I said.

It was as different to the frantic fumbling that Wren and I had indulged in as chalk is to cheese.

Because that was lust, a means to an end for her as it turned out. Not even lust, it was play-acting.

This was love.

32
MONKEY BUSINESS

HEY fellas, I tell you, this guy is the greatest comic I ever saw!"

"This? This is the guy?"

The San Diego dressing room I was sharing with Charlie, Freddie and Stan was suddenly invaded by four energetic lads, all – mystifyingly – waddling around doing an imitation of Chaplin as Archibald Binks in his over-sized shoes. They stopped after a minute, dissolving into laughter, shoving one another around. They looked like they couldn't keep still for a moment, even if you paid them to do it.

"Sorry about that," said one of the lads, the leader, stepping forward. "Julius Marx. I caught your act in Winnipeg, haven't stopped talking about it since. I had a stopover, couple of hours to fill waiting for a train, so I didn't have time to introduce myself then. And these are my brothers, here's Arthur, and Leonard, and that's Milton."[12]

We launched into introductions and hand-shaking that quickly became a chaotic eight-handed routine, during which the brothers managed to tangle all their arms together into a knot.

"Say, are you guys on the bill this week? That's swell!" Julius turned to his brothers. "Wait till you see this guy, he's hilarious. In fact, fellas, the whole act is a hoot, every one of you. But especially this guy. Catch you later!"

And they were off. It was like a whirlwind had paid us a visit. Nothing in the room seemed to be exactly as it had been before.

━━━

The previous six weeks had seen us play Portland, Tacoma, Sacramento, Oakland, San Francisco and Los Angeles.

I still marvelled at what had happened in that boxcar. Perhaps, I thought, it had been an affirmation of life in the shadow of death, Whimsical Walker's last gift to me.

Earth-shattering though it had undoubtedly been, it had not wrought a massive change in our circumstances, but I knew it wouldn't. Tilly had continued to spend all her spare time with Charlie, but of course she had to. She couldn't just bring her relationship with him to a sudden and dramatic close, because she knew what that would mean – a one-way ticket back to Blighty. And if she had happened to mention that I was the reason, then that would have been my reward as well, and both of us would have been on the outs.

Clearly Charlie needed handling. Tilly and I hadn't talked about it, but I felt we had an unspoken understanding. I had to leave it to her, and let things play out. After all, there was still plenty of time left on this leg of the tour, and the promise of another circuit to follow, so I could afford to play a long game.

The important thing was that her feelings for me were surely clear, so for the first time in an age I could permit myself to hope.

The brothers Marx were appearing in a sketch entitled *Mr Green's Reception*, along with a couple of male singers, and a chorus of fifteen pretty girls in short skirts, blonde hair and pink stockings. It had grown out of a previous offering called *Fun in Hi Skule*, in which Julius played the role of a Germanic teacher organising a school concert, and the others were his "Dumbkopf!" students. There was something of a fashion in those days for putting on a funny German accent, and those that did were known as 'Dutch' comics, either because they sounded Dutch, or because the word 'Deutsch', the German word for German, did. That fashion would die out entirely in a couple of years' time, as I'm sure you can imagine.

We went to see it at the first available opportunity, the Monday matinée. Charlie sat in the middle of the front row, as he would often do, especially when assessing a rival. The better the act, the less likely he was to laugh, or even break into a smile, but the Marx brothers didn't know this – how could they?

I saw Julius spot Charlie almost as soon as he came onstage, and from then on his performance was directed right at the middle of the front row. Every gag that Charlie failed to respond to drove him into more and more manic excesses, no matter how well the sketch was being received in the rest of the auditorium.

The other Marx boys, too, began to be driven mad by Charlie's stone face, until the final curtain came down on their act and they sailed offstage in a boat on rollers, wistfully casting a last uncomprehending glance his way across the orchestra pit.

For my part their antics had me in stitches. Leonard was a very nimble pianist, Arthur played the harp, and all of them could sing, but I would have happily skipped some of the musical numbers to see more of the boys in full flow.

"Pretty good, eh?" I said to Charlie as we slipped backstage during the interval.

"Hmmm..." Charlie replied, distracted, and I knew that meant it had been very good indeed.

In their dressing room, though, Julius and the boys were downcast when I stuck my head round the door to congratulate them.

"It's just his way," I said. "He never laughs at anything."

"Is that right?" Julius said, his eyes narrowing.

"Sure," Leonard said. "He's like that guy, remember, who locked himself in his dressing room and turned the taps on full so he couldn't hear anyone else getting a laugh."

Julius nodded slowly. "Here's what we're going to do," he said. "We'll take a box for this evening's performance, and I'm ready to bet he can't get any one of us to crack a smile. You tell him that."

"Good luck," I said, and went along the corridor to our dressing room.

"You upset those Marx boys," I said to Charlie.

"What do you mean?" he said, looking up from tying his tie.

"Sitting right at the front, not giving them anything. They say they're taking a box for the evening show, and they're betting you can't get a laugh out of any of 'em."

Charlie smiled. "Oh, really?"

A little extra interest in a particular performance was always welcome, and so I'm sure I wasn't the only one to sneak a peek at the boxes when the curtain came up that evening. This particular Empress had only two. The one stage right was empty, while the one stage left was occupied by four nuns – black and white habits, wimples, the whole kit and caboodle.

Our act got under way, and I caught a quick smirk from Charlie as he noticed the occupants of the box. Clearly these nuns were the Marx brothers in costume trying to throw him off his game. He began confidently enough, but once he was into his sure-fire dry cracker routine, the one that had so convulsed Julius when he saw it before, you could see that the lack of response – or even a vague flicker of interest – from the sisters was beginning to get to him.

Despite their best efforts, he was going to get a laugh out of them. He cranked the business up a notch, and then another, and by the end he was giving it everything he had, all directed at the stage left box. The house was howling, but in the box all was still. One of the nuns actually yawned.

To top the act off, Charlie threw himself into a stage fall of such extravagant violence that I felt sure he must have broken something, perhaps even his neck, but the slapstick met with the same blank disinterest as everything else from the sisters of no mercy.

He hauled himself into the wings, exhausted, emotionally wrung out from the effort of trying – and failing – to make his rivals respond. And there they were, all four of them, standing in the dark waiting for him to come off.

"Well done, my friend!" Julius said, clapping him on the back. "Sorry we didn't get to see the whole thing, maybe tomorrow."

"But..." Charlie gasped. "Weren't you... in the box?"

"I bought some tickets, but in the end I gave them away to some sisters, they do such marvellous work don't you think?"

And that's what Charlie got for not laughing at the Marx brothers.

After this prickly beginning we became firm friends with the Marx boys, even Charlie did. For the rest of that week we spent a lot of time together, frequenting the local pool hall during the day, and drinking into the small hours after work. Leonard affected an Italian tough guy accent when playing pool, and he was a dab hand at the game, taking considerably more than loose change off Freddie and me.

One evening Stan and I were in the bar waiting for the boys to show when Charlie and Tilly came over to join us. He was bright as a button, but she seemed to have the cares of the world upon her shoulders.

"Evening fellows!" Charlie chirruped. "What are we drinking to? The future?"

"Whatever happened to that idea of yours about going into hog farming," I said.

"Oh! That nonsense!" Charlie snorted. "What was I thinking?"

"So that dream bit the dust, did it?"

"Bit the mud," Stan chipped in.

"To be perfectly honest I was reading in one of the manuals about the method for castrating the creatures, and it put me off my food for a good couple of days. I may never eat another sausage as long as I live!"

He nudged Tilly, who gave him a brief, mirthless smile.

"No, it's another spin around the old Sullivan and Considine carousel, guaranteed work for another six months at least, and we shall all make our fortunes."

"Huh," Stan grunted. "Not on what Karno is paying, we won't."

"I'm serious," Charlie insisted. "I went to a fortune teller, back in San Francisco. Little shop on Market Street, your future told for a dollar. The seer was a little round Chinese woman, and I think she was halfway through her dinner when I came in."

"So she didn't foresee your visit, then?" I said. "That should have told you something."

"Ha!" Charlie cried, good-naturedly. "She shuffled some cards and laid them out on the table, then she had a good old squint at my palms. You know what she said?"

"I'm afraid my psychic powers are at a low ebb today," I said.

"She said that I had money-making hands. Yes! She also said that I will make a fortune in a different business to the one I am currently in, but she was wrong about that, of course."

"Otherwise she'd have said you had hog-castrating hands."

"Well, ha ha, quite! Also I can look forward to at least three marriages, and any number of children, apparently."

Tilly looked down at her own hands, her lips pursed tightly together.

Charlie shrugged. "So you see," he continued brightly. "The future's rosy."

"Excuse me, boys," Tilly said, standing up quickly. "An early night for me, I think." Before Charlie could get to his feet and accompany her she hurried over to Amy, and the two of them grabbed their coats and hats and disappeared arm-in-arm into the night.

"Well," Charlie said. "What was that about?"

"Perhaps it was the talk of all these marriages of yours," Stan said. "You surely didn't need a fortune teller to tell you how well *that* would go down, did you?"

Charlie frowned, and I smiled inwardly. Cracks were appearing.

———

On the Friday I happened to glance into the ladies' dressing room, where I saw, unless I was seriously mistaken, Tilly being comforted by Amy Reeves. It was just a glance, because Amy reached over and pushed the door to when she saw me outside looking in, but I was suddenly thrilled. Was something finally happening between her and Chaplin?

I paid close attention to Charlie that evening, and although he was capable enough onstage he did seem distracted, somehow. Interesting...

I was keen to pump Stan, his perennial roommate, for the inside track, but the two of them raced off together at the end of the show without coming for the customary drink or five, and so I was left to my own fevered speculations.

The next morning I was up and about bright and early for once. In truth I hadn't really slept, my mind buzzing with curiosity. As early as I thought decent for knocking on a theatrical hotel room door I strolled along the corridor to tempt Charlie and Stan to join me for breakfast. I was keen to try and glean whatever titbits I could to feed my growing optimism, but both were already up and out and about somewhere. Curiouser and curiouser.

Then at the theatre I noticed to my private glee that the only time Tilly and Charlie spoke to one another was onstage, and then afterwards neither they nor Stan lingered long. Even more interesting.

On the Sunday we boarded the Karno boxcar one more time for one of the longest hauls of the whole tour, 750 miles up to Salt Lake City. It was a gruelling ride, though undeniably spectacular, as we crossed deserts peppered with strangely compelling red-brown rock monoliths, clung to the sides of towering gorges, skirted the Grand Canyon itself, and finally emerged onto the flatlands of Utah. Despite the breath-taking primeval scenery, however, most of the time I only had eyes for the far end of the carriage, where Chaplin glumly gazed out of one window, while Tilly stared fixedly out of another.

I was in agonies wanting to go over and talk to her, and find out how things stood, but I forced myself to bide my time and leave it to her.

We arrived in Salt Lake City at sunset. I went for a stroll among the lengthening shadows and a sort of shimmering heat haze, even though it was January. It made the whole place seem like some bizarre mirage, plucked from an Arabian Night, and for the first time in weeks I smiled to myself as I thought that my fairy tale, mine and Tilly's, might just have a happy ending after all.

The next day, our first at the Salt Lake Empress, Charlie seemed a little more chipper, which put a little dampener on things for me. I tried to catch sight of Tilly, but the ladies' dressing room door remained closed, and their timing was so precise that I didn't see any of the girls in the wings before our sig music began, and it was time for Freddie and me to bustle onstage. Charlie appeared as Archibald Binks soon enough, but the audience didn't seem that impressed. There was an odd aloofness about the Utah people, none of the friendly fun of San Francisco, say, or the lively vivacity of Butte.

We went through the motions of Archie's initiation into the society of Wow Wows, until we reached the sequence in which the girls would come along and tease him. I glanced over, and there was Amy, there was Emily, there was Wren and Annie Forrester... and that was all. Where was Tilly?

I peered into the wings, thinking she might be there in the shadows, hastily buttoning herself up, having left it just too late, but no...

Was she unwell? She'd have to be feeling pretty poorly to risk missing another show after the wigging she got from Alf for taking that night off in New York.

There was a silence, suddenly, that grew and grew until I realised I had missed a cue, and blurted out my line just as Stan started busking something to cover for me, so we both spoke at once. I flashed him an apologetic look, and then tried to concentrate as I stumbled through to the end curtain.

A trio of trick cyclists bounded past me in their red and gold leotards as I caught Amy by the elbow.

"Amy," I hissed. "Where's Tilly? Is she ill?"

Amy turned to me, her face a picture of sorrow and pity. "Oh sweetheart, she's gone."

"What?" I said, far too loud. Amy hushed me, and dragged me over to the stairs.

"What do you mean she's gone?" I said, holding both her shoulders tight.

"She's gone, she's quit, she's left the tour, left the company."

I couldn't take this in. "But I saw her, she was on the train."

"Yes, and she stayed on the train all the way to Chicago. She'll be practically in New York by now. I'm sorry, Arthur."

"But she didn't say anything."

"No, nor to me neither. She left a letter for Alf, she said she'd just had enough and was going back to England."

I slumped down onto the hard stone steps, and Amy laid her hand against my cheek. "I'm sorry, darling, really I am," she said, and then left me alone.

PART 4

33
MR CHAFFIN'S
OPPORTUNITY

SIX months later we found ourselves in Philadelphia with a few days off before the start of yet another Sullivan and Considine circuit.

Charlie was bigger and bigger news everywhere we went. Theatre managers were using his name as the draw on their posters, twice as large and twice as often as the name Fred Karno, and if the Guv'nor ever got to hear of it he'd no doubt blow his top.

This time around we would be playing a show called *A Night at a London Club*, which was a sort of hybrid of *Mumming Birds* and the new stuff that Charlie had added to *The Wow Wows*, which allowed him to combine the Inebriated Swell and Archibald Binks.

I was his chief antagonist, a character called Mr Meek, who is continually prodded to complain by his wife, played by Wren Hurley. We had some good moments, but there wasn't much for anyone else to get excited about. Little Annie Forrester was the only one, really, who had anything like a star turn, a lovely showpiece song. Charlie had seen to that, and, by the way, anything else Annie's heart desired.

Charlie was over Tilly, that much was crystal clear.

My own feelings were a little more complicated.

At first I had been distraught. At the end of that week in Salt Lake City it was all I could do to force myself aboard the boxcar, so fierce was the memory of being there with her. As soon as the train was under way I stumbled through to the prop compartment, but it was unbearable to be in there now. I pressed on out to the observation platform at the rear of the train, banging my shin on something hard on the way. Once outside I looked back at where we had come from, at the rails carving across the plateau back to Salt Lake, with the mountains on the horizon beyond the Great Salt Lake Desert.

I climbed up onto the roof of the boxcar so I could look in the direction we were heading, in the direction Tilly had already travelled. I stood straddling the skylights on top of the car, looking along the train, along the carriages ahead of us, all the way to the locomotive at the front, the smoke pouring from the funnel.

And I wondered: should I try and stand up here as long as I could, being battered by the cold dry gale, until my feet went numb and a friendly gust whipped me away to oblivion? Or perhaps there'd be a bridge to sweep me off, were there bridges on this line? Should I ride the roof into the mountains ahead, looking for a scenic gorge to throw myself into and end it all?

I glanced down through the skylight between my feet, shuffling forward a foot or so to make sure no one inside could see me standing up top. This manoeuvre gave me an angled view into the car below, and down there, framed by the skylight window, was Charlie Chaplin. Where in the height of summer there had been a block of ice, Alf had organised a tureen of hot vegetable soup on a candle burner to take the edge off the January chill. Charlie had ladled out a cup and was presenting it as a token to little Annie Forrester, and she was smiling shyly, accepting it two-handed.

Then he sat, thinking to himself, and he smiled a smug, self-satisfied smirk, as though something had gone his way. I imagined him smiling just that very smile at the news that I had disappeared, taken myself out of his life, out of our personal competition, handing him the victory.

And I couldn't, I couldn't give him that. That, believe it or believe it not, was what made me turn and crawl back to the rear of the boxcar, shin down to the observation platform, slip back inside past all the props and costumes, and carry on with my miserable life.

"Smashing hairstyle, Arthur," Ethel Seaman sang out when I reappeared. "That will definitely catch on."

As the weeks went by after that I struggled to explain Tilly's departure, and often copious amounts of alcohol assisted me in that struggle. Usually after the evening's performances, but increasingly before, and occasionally during.

Had she really, as she said in her note, simply decided that the life was no longer for her?

Had she become so concerned about her family's disappearance from Southend after the explosion of the Punch and Judy stand that she had decided to go back to England at once and search for them? It was possible, I supposed, but she would have told me that, wouldn't she?

I went back to that explanation from time to time, gnawed away at it, but I couldn't escape the suspicion that the true reason had something to do with me and with Charlie Chaplin.

The powerful rekindling of our affections that day in the boxcar must have had some effect, mustn't it? Must have set her thinking about what she wanted? Had she told Charlie that she wanted to break with him, and he had promptly dispatched her back to England as he had the hapless Frank Melroyd?

Or had she been unable to choose between us? Had she simply thrown up her hands and refused to do it? Whatever, it seemed she'd found herself unable to go on travelling the United States of America with me, or with him.

And she was gone, gone for good. No way of finding her, contacting her, no sense in giving everything up to try.

So in those days I was just numb. Stuck there going through the motions night after night, week after week, town after town with Charlie bloody Chaplin, my ambitions to supplant him as number one a long distant memory.

I couldn't see how anything was ever going to change.

Then, one morning, we were all in our dressing rooms at the Nixon-Nirdlinger theatre in Philly waiting to be released to look for a couple of days' entertainment. A small boy wearing shorts with braces, a white shirt and a peaked cap came marching along the corridor and into the dressing room, bold as brass, shouting at the top of his breaking adolescent voice: "Western Union! Western Union, looking for Mr Alfred Reeves!"

"I'm Reeves," Alf said. The boy stepped smartly over to our manager and held out a tan coloured envelope.

"Cable for you, sir."

Alf frowned and took the envelope from him, and in a flash the lad was off down the stairs on another errand. The ladies came through from their dressing room, curious, and we all watched as Alf tore open the message and read it, and then scratched his head.

"What do you make of this, listen: 'IS THERE A MAN NAMED CHAFFIN IN YOUR COMPANY OR SOMETHING LIKE THAT STOP IF SO WILL HE COMMUNICATE WITH KESSEL AND BAUMAN 24 LONGACRE BUILDING BROADWAY'."

"I know that building," said the manager of the Nixon, a Mr Linighan. "Stuffed with lawyers' offices. Quite fancy ones, too."

"Well, quite clearly the message is intended for me," Charlie pronounced. "Chaffin – Chaplin, see? There's the 'Cha', and the 'in', and these Keppel and Booboo figures have just made a mistake in the middle."

"Yes, I suppose it could be that." Alf said.

"Wait a minute," Freddie Junior piped up. "Why should it not be for Stan? 'Chaff' is closer to 'Jeff' than it is to your name."

"What? No, no, it is clearly meant for me," Charlie frowned, unable to grasp a scenario in which he wasn't the centre of attention.

"Fred's right," I chipped in, enjoying the moment. "Chaffin is much closer to Jefferson than it is to Chaplin. Don't you think, Stan?"

"Oh, I don't know," Stan said. "Why would fancy lawyers want to see me?"

"Exactly," Charlie said. "It's far more likely that they would want to see me."

"All right, all right!" Alf said, raising his voice to quell the increasingly boisterous discussion. "Here's what I am going to do. I will reply saying that our Mr Chaffin will call on Messrs Kessel and Bauman tomorrow."

"That's good," Charlie interrupted, "and then I shall go and see what's what."

"And both of you will go, you *and* Stan," Alf said firmly.

Chaplin blinked, surprised not to be getting his own way. "Both of us?"

"And I will come with you," I said, putting my arms around both their shoulders. "Let's have a day out in New York City, eh?"

Spending one of our precious days off riding a train did feel a little bit like a busman's holiday, but at least we were travelling like regular members of the public and not in that Karno box-car.

"So what do you think these fellows want to talk to you about, Charlie?" Stan asked as we rattled over to New York early the next morning.

"Or you, Stan," I insisted. "It still might be you."

"I have a wealthy aunt somewhere in America," Charlie said. "Maybe she has died and left me a fortune."

We gaped at him – this was an astonishing thing to drop into the conversation. "You have a wealthy aunt?" I said. "Why have you not mentioned this before?"

"I don't know, I..."

"How wealthy? Where does all her money come from? And how are you related? Mother's side? Father's side?"

"Well, I can't quite..."

"And where in America does she live? Why have you not visited her?"

"I'm not sure. I'm wondering now whether I may have dreamed the whole thing..." Charlie frowned and looked out of the window, and he genuinely did seem to be puzzled as to the existence or otherwise of this aunt.

"What about you, Stan? Do you have any rich relatives tucked away anywhere?"

"Ha ha, no, that's the stuff of a penny blood, isn't it?" Stan laughed. "Rich aunts!"

"There was something, though, you know?" Charlie said, still worrying away at it like a dog with a bone. "I seem to recall my

360

mother talking about a distant connection of some sort, possibly even a minor royal..."

Well, that pretty much put the tin lid on that. Everyone knew his poor mother was crackers.

"We'll find out soon enough," I said.

———

24 Longacre Building on Broadway was indeed a hive of lawyerly activity, as Mr Linighan had suggested, and we found our way to the reception room of Messrs Kessel and Bauman. Their receptionist disappeared for a minute or two, leaving us to twiddle our thumbs in the wood-panelled leather-seated finery of our surroundings, before returning with a pot of tea, some cups, and a plate of biscuits on a silver tray.

"Mr Kessel will see you now," she said, and led us through to a plush office with a view out over Times Square below.

A tall, lean, moustachioed figure was standing by the window with his thumbs in his waistcoat pockets as we entered, and he turned to greet us with a welcoming smile.

"Mr Chaffin?" he inquired, peering at the three of us, left to right and then back again.

"Well, that remains to be seen, doesn't it?" Charlie said, stepping forward.

"I beg your pardon?"

"My name is Chaplin, Charles Chaplin, and my colleague here is Mr Stanley Jefferson. We believe that the Chaffin you seek is one or other of us, but it is for you to solve the conundrum, Mr Kessel."

"I see, I see. And your name, sir?" he inquired of me.

"Dandoe. Arthur Dandoe, pleased to make your acquaintance, sir," I said formally.

"Oh no. No, no, no, that is not it at all," Kessel said, looking blank. "Not even close."

"Mr Dandoe is merely an interested observer," Charlie said airily. "Please feel free to ignore him entirely."

Kessel moved to his seat behind a handsomely-appointed desk. "Please be seated, gentlemen. Some English tea?"

Clearly we were expected, then. Charlie breezed on, while Stan busied himself being mother.

"So, Mr Kessel. What can you tell us about the man Chaffin?"

Kessel was somewhat flustered by this directness, and picked up a page on which some handwritten notes had been made.

"Ah, oh, well, yes, let me see now. The man I am charged with contacting, who may or may not be called Chaffin, is a comedian..."

"As we both are," Charlie said, indicating himself and Stan.

"Quite so, yes, yes. A comedian... let me see... who plays a notoriously inebriated character for the Fred Karno comedy company."

"Ha!" Charlie cried triumphantly. "Yes! It *is* me! I knew it was me!"

Stan shrugged amiably, as if to say 'Fair enough!', and poured some tea.

"So what is the matter at hand, Mr Kessel? What is it that you wish to impart?"

"So to be clear," Kessel said, "I am addressing my remarks now to you, is that correct?"

"Just so."

"Very well. I represent the interests of the New York Motion Picture Company, who would like to engage your services as a comic actor. I take it you would be agreeable?"

"Er... what?" Charlie was flabbergasted. "Motion pictures, eh? Well, well, well."

Stan and I looked at one another, eyes wide. Charlie's head tilted to one side, pantomiming thoughtful consideration.

"I won't deny I have long been intrigued by the motion picture art form," he said. "The notion of capturing one perfect performance for posterity, rather than trotting out twenty-five variously flawed versions every week, it is interesting. We know all about the slog of vaudeville, don't we lads?"

"Indeed we do," I said.

"And based where? Here in New York? It is my understanding that motion pictures are made in various centres. Here, and also in New Jersey, in Chicago, in Florida, and even in Los Angeles. Particularly those who are trying to get as far away as possible from the Edison patent enforcers, eh?"[13]

"That is certainly true," Kessel agreed. "And although we are called the New York Motion Picture Company, in point of fact we are the parent company for a number of smaller outfits, including one specialising in comedies, which is called Keystone Pictures, and they are indeed based in Los Angeles."

I was dumbstruck. From nowhere had come the sunny prospect of Charlie being tucked away in hot, dusty Los Angeles, one of the least appealing of all the stops we made on the Sullivan and Considine circuit, leaving us – leaving *me* – free to tour on bigger and bigger time without him, well, it was intoxicating.

Charlie was thinking. "Hmm. How has this offer come about, as a matter of interest?"

"Does the name Mack Sennett ring a bell, Mr Chaffin?"

"Chaplin. No, I am afraid it does not."

It rang a bell with me, though, a distant one. I padded through the house of my memory in my old slippers and dressing gown, trying to locate the tinkling.

"Mr Sennett witnessed a performance of yours at the American Music Hall right here in New York City."

Sennett! There he was! I had him! The big straw-haired fellow with the huge hands and the beetling brows. I remembered his lithe and lively friend Mabel, the Gibson girl, and his lugubrious companion D.W. Something-or-other, and then I remembered him saying: "When I set up my studio *that's* the sort of guy I'm gonna be talking to."

Lord above! That was the night, the night that Stan pretended to be Charlie and had such a stunning success! And they asked me his name and I was so very drunk, and I got stuck between saying 'Jefferson' and saying 'Chaplin', didn't I, just in case they might be scheming to whisk Charlie away.

Which meant that Chaffin actually *was* Jefferson, after all!

"Wait!" I said. Kessel turned to me, as did Stan and Charlie.

So this offer, this offer from Mack Sennett was actually intended for Stan. My mind was twisting every which way all of a sudden. Because on the one hand this might be a great opportunity for my friend, and yet on the other it might represent the best chance for me to get shot of Charlie Chaplin for good and all.

I had a mere second to think, as they peered inquiringly at me.

"Nothing," I said. "Carry on."

"Hmm," Charlie mused. "Aspects of the proposal do have appeal. Working out in the open air, for one thing. Cutting down on all the travelling that my life seems to consist of these days. That blessed boxcar, eh?" He cut us a smile, then scratched his chin. "And creating material for new pictures would certainly give my creative muscles a lot more exercise than they presently enjoy."

"Good points," I said, sitting now on the edge of my seat. "Very good points."

"Excellent," said Kessel. "Well then, I shall communicate the good news to Mr Sennett, and we will begin making the necessary arrangements."

Charlie was looking very confident, however. "Whoa, whoa, whoa," he said. "Hold your horses. First of all I am under contract to Mr Fred Karno for another tour."

Kessel paused, his pen poised. "I see, so when would you be available to start?"

"Not so fast, Mr Kessel. I do not believe I have yet heard an actual offer."

"Ahem, oh yes, well, Mr Sennett has authorised me to propose the sum of one hundred and twenty five dollars a week for a deal to make twelve moving films a month."

Stan turned to me behind Charlie's back and mouthed the word "Wow!" Charlie meanwhile took this stupendous offer in his stride. "Of course you would have to better my current salary with the Karno company," he said.

"Which is?"

"Two hundred dollars a week."

There was a spluttering noise to my left, as Stan was taken by surprise halfway through biting a biscuit.

"Two hundred dollars a week?" Kessel said, frowning, stroking his moustache with a finger and thumb.

"Vaudeville is big business, you know," Chaplin said.

"Indeed it must be," the lean lawyer said, getting thoughtfully to his feet. "I shall need to consult my colleagues. Gentlemen, thank you for coming to call. The listings pages of *Variety* and *Billboard* will enable me to follow your itinerary, Mr Chaffin, and I dare say we shall be in touch."

Out on the street Charlie was beaming fit to bust. "Well, that was fun!" he said.

"Pretty exciting stuff," Stan said.

"Yes indeed," Charlie said. "Of course, I'm not actually going to *do* it! Lunch?"

He led the way down Broadway into Times Square, while I came crashing down to Earth in his wake. I glanced briefly down 43rd Street towards the mouldy old brownstone with the laundry in the basement which had been home on our first visit to the big city. It was gone, demolished, and in its place a new Times Building was taking shape.

Over a plateful of steak and potatoes, Stan and I pressed Charlie for his thinking.

"So you're not interested?" I said.

"Oh, dear me, no," Charlie said, rather smugly. "What? Work in Los Angeles, that horrible airless dump? Give up all the groundwork I have done in vaudeville, for what? Some anonymous running around in the dirt? You know most film comedians don't even get credited by name?"

"So why didn't you tell them you weren't interested?" asked Stan, always the straight shooter.

"I am in the last year of my contract with Karno."

"Who is paying you two hundred dollars a week, apparently!" Stan scoffed.

"Oh, of course he isn't. He pays me seventy-five, but if these fellows will double my money? Well, Karno is going to have to dig deeper into those miserly pockets."

I chewed on my steak as the dream of Charlie leaving to make pictures receded before my very eyes.

"Have you seen any Keystone flickers by the way?" he went on. "I think I have, just some harum-scarum scrambling around in the muck. They have a bunch of characters who are cops, I think, who fall over and bump into things, but it's not for me. Vaudeville, that's the place to be. It's booming, anyone can see that. New theatres opening all the time, pages and pages in the newspapers. And we have just been swimming in the shallows, you know, with old Considine. There are still peaks to conquer, believe you me."

As if to demonstrate the point, that very afternoon Charlie took us to a matinée of the *Ziegfeld Follies of 1913*.[14] Sure enough it was a very different world to the hardscrabble provincial touring we were used to. A lavish Broadway revue, in residence at the New Amsterdam Theatre, it featured breathtakingly expensive sets and ticket prices to match. The Ziegfeld Girls were an eyeful, and no mistake, and it would certainly have been no great hardship to share backstage corridors with them and their feathered headdresses. I inspected them all closely, wondering if Tilly might have found her way to Broadway, but no such luck. And glamorous though they were, none of them could have held a candle to her.

As well as the luxurious musical numbers there were comedians, who had all graduated from the world of touring vaudeville. Frank Tinney, known as 'The Funbeam', for instance, whose routine consisted of deliberately corny jokes, and an overgrown schoolboy of a comic called Ed Wynn, who styled himself 'Joe King the Joke King'.

There was Nat Wills, who was a celebrated tramp comic with the jaunty little walk and the cheeky outlook that was the stock in trade of the type. He did a musical skit, a take on the popular hit *The Trail of the Lonesome Pine*, that Stan was particularly taken with.

And best of all was a cantankerous comic juggler called W.C. Fields, who did a routine with a pool table. He had any number of bizarrely-shaped cues, with which he would attempt a variety of trick shots, and his table was specially constructed for a number of genuinely surprising visual gags. I greatly admired the selfish world-weariness of his persona, and the many ways he found to scoop his hat off his head with a cue tip.

Charlie sat through all of these acts without cracking a smile, as was his wont. Afterwards, though, he had plenty to say. "See? These guys are at the top of our game. This is where it is possible to end up if you keep pushing on in vaudeville. Some of these chaps are on the best part of a thousand bucks a week. A thousand! And all it takes is getting spotted."

That evening Charlie announced his intention to spend the night in New York, so Stan and I rode the evening train back to Philadelphia, and our digs, while he, if you can believe this, booked himself into the Astor. He must have been feeling pretty full of himself.

All the way back I brooded on what had happened that day. Charlie seemed pretty determined not to risk going into the motion picture business.

But perhaps he could be persuaded.

34
BOMBSHELL

A𝒮 those hot summer weeks rolled slowly by I was preoccupied with working out what Charlie was thinking. If he would only take the plunge and leave Karno – how marvellous would that be?

When we arrived at the theatre in Minneapolis there was a letter for Charlie from the office of Kessel and Bauman. I was on pins to know what was in it, but Charlie was keeping things close to his chest.

"Negotiations are ongoing," was all he'd say, tapping the side of his nose.

To read the pages of *Variety* you would hardly know that a burgeoning film industry existed. Tucked away on an inside page you might find a small column of titbits such as: "Roscoe Arbuckle[15] has just finished his first Keystone film", something like that. Compared to the acreage given over to vaudeville gossip, however, this was next to nothing at all.

There were, however, some new publications springing up devoted solely to the moving picture business, items such as *Motography*, for example, or *Motion Picture World*, and I would pick these up whenever I could in the hope that I would find ammunition for my war of attrition on Charlie's resistance to the Keystone offer. The best time to fire a shot across his bows was when he was a captive audience, sitting across from me as the Karno boxcar devoured another couple of hundred sweaty miles.

"Listen to this," I said, with all the casualness I could muster. "'John Bunny, the popular Vitagraph comedian, says he has received fan mail from as far afield as France and Italy following the release of *Pickwick Papers* earlier this year...'"

"Really?" Charlie said, admiring his fingernails.

"Yes, France and Italy, it says. 'The portly star revealed that he has never visited Europe, and despite numerous invitations to appear there he regrets that he is now committed to filming fifty-two weeks a year'."

"Imagine that," Stan chipped in. "A roaring success in France and Italy, and he's never even been there."

"Interesting." Charlie murmured, looking out of the window, not interested at all.

The trouble was that so many so-called comedy films then featured a gang of anonymous buffoons running around like headless chickens, tumbling over entirely imaginary obstacles in stories that made no sense whatsoever. If motion pictures were ever really going to grab hold of Charlie's attention, it would be because he saw something half-decent that he could *improve* with the application of his genius.

That's how the happy accident of sharing a bill at the Empress in Winnipeg with a Keystone film entitled *Barney Oldfield's Race for a Life* made such a valuable impression. Stan and I persuaded Charlie to come round front of house and watch it. You could always get a seat when the flicker screen came down, because a significant number would take the opportunity to go and relieve themselves, or refresh themselves at the bar, or both in a kind of self-perpetuating cycle.

The film was a comic melodrama, in which a lovesick rube tries to save his sweetheart from the clutches of a moustache-twirling villain. It began with the young Romeo shyly offering the girl a flower, with the kind of nauseating display of simpering that Charlie himself so excelled at. He was not impressed with this, sitting in the seat beside me, and I distinctly heard a scornful "Pffft!"

In truth the lead in this flicker was not a traditionally-built romantic hero, being a big clumsy lump with huge hands and an outsized face, and with a start I recognised him – it was Mack Sennett himself. The girl, once I got a good look at her, was none other than sparky Mabel Normand. She didn't have a great deal of opportunity to show what she could do, because once she had rejected the overtures of the roguish villain, played by Ford Sterling, she was promptly kidnapped and tied to a railway track.

While Sterling and his cohorts go off to commandeer a locomotive to finish her off with, Sennett the lovelorn lump gets wind of Mabel's predicament and rushes to her rescue. Fortunately he bumps into Barney Oldfield, the celebrated racing driver, who has his name painted on the side of his car just in case you don't recognise him.[16]

Oldfield and Sennett career wildly along in a desperate race with Sterling and co on their murderous train, and true to form the famous racer begins to pull ahead, and then puts in such a turn of speed that he overtakes the camera and disappears, leaving Sterling shaking his fist in impotent fury. Sennett and Oldfield reach Mabel, and start chipping away at the chains holding her with some puny-looking chisels. At this rate it will take hours to free her, and yet... oh no!

Here comes the train, bearing down on them, and it approaches so fast, getting larger and larger on the screen, and they are taking so long to free Mabel that surely they must all be destroyed. At the very last possible instant, Barney Oldfield picks up her legs, Mack Sennett her shoulders, and they dash aside with literally a split-second to spare.

The engine loomed large on the screen and flashed past, and to a man, woman and child the audience flung their hands up in the air in shock. Even Charlie, the most impassive and mirthless spectator you'd ever sit next to anywhere, flinched and gasped along with the rest.

Deep down I guess we all knew that if the comedians had been killed then we wouldn't be seeing these pictures, but it was still a terrific coup. There was genuine terror on Mack Sennett's face as the train brushed by his sleeve, the thought "Hurry it up for Christ's sake Oldfield!" writ large upon his over-sized features.

Perhaps this was the first film to stir some ambition in Charlie. He saw first-hand the dramatic impact a properly-crafted cinematic moment could have on an audience, and he also saw, in Sennett's lumbering boob of a lead, a performance he could easily better.

———

In Winnipeg we found ourselves once again sharing a bill with the Marx brothers. In the bar late one night Charlie was showing off, and inadvertently confided some indication of his thinking about Keystone. Julius, in his brash and forward way, asked him outright what he was making working for Karno, and Charlie said: "Seventy five bucks a week."

From the looks on the Marx brothers' faces I guessed that this was better money than they were on.

"I have been thinking over an offer from a movie mogul, as it happens," Charlie went on.

"Really? A mogul? An honest-to-goodness mogul?" Julius said. "Fancy!"

"I am being offered five hundred dollars a week to make movies."

Stan and I shared a glance. *How* much?

"Congratulations," Julius said, deadpan. "When do you start?"

"I am not going to take it," Charlie said.

Julius was astonished. "Why not? You're only getting seventy five now. Don't you like money?"

"Of course I do," Charlie replied. "But look, boys, I can make good on what Karno is paying. If I sign up with the pictures and they find me out, they'll fire me. Then where will I be? I'll tell you where I'll be. Flat on my back!"

He shook his head, took a thoughtful sip of port. The Marx boys' jaws had hit the floor – one, two, three, four – at the very idea of knocking back that sort of dough.

I puzzled over this conversation later, lying awake in my bed, with Freddie snoring away in the other berth. Was Charlie really being held back by a fear of failure? And had he really managed to drive Keystone up so high? Surely not. It was almost as if he wanted people to talk him into it, wanted people to tell him he would be a fool to pass it up.

━━━

There was a tradition at the theatre that the madam and the girls from the local sporting house would always be in the upper box for the Wednesday matinée of any week, and if they liked what they saw, they would not be shy about inviting an act over for some further entertainments of their own devising.

That week the Marx boys were flushed with success. They had fired a preening tenor who had got above himself, and their show was going better than ever before. On the Wednesday afternoon they looked up at the top box, and the girls were waving a piece of paper with their address written on it, trying to attract their attention. It was too high for them to reach, though, and the girls didn't want to just throw the paper down in case it fell into the wrong hands.

After taking several curtain calls, and a number of failed attempts to jump up and grab the note, blond Arthur stayed in front of the curtain when it came down, and when it went up for the start of the next act, up he went with it and landed in the box right amongst the ladies. Problem solved.

That evening there was quite a party over at that sporting house. Freddie, Stan, Charlie and I accompanied the Marx lads over there, and those girls were mighty pleased to see us all.

The motto of the place seemed to be 'Why have a chair when a chaise-longue will do?' The walls were covered in thick velvety flock wallpaper in maroon and cream, decorated with framed nude photographs of the girls themselves. The pictures seemed stark and unappealing compared to the genuine articles, which were available wherever one looked. Girls wearing candy-striped stockings and little else, others wearing elaborate flouncy under-garments that it would have taken Houdini a good few minutes to extricate the girl from.

Everywhere the girls' overpowering perfumes competed to assault your sinuses and sting your eyes. There was a dog, an English bulldog, and I found myself imagining him going stark staring mad after being asked to track one particular girl in that place. The booze flowed, and gradually a pairing-up process began to happen.

Freddie was the first to disappear, then the Marx boys one by one, and finally I found my eye taken by a tantalising pair of pink stockings and began to follow them up the staircase that led up from the large and luxurious salon to a balcony with various doors leading to who knew what delights.

At the top of the stairs I looked back, and there was Charlie, all by himself. The madam herself had taken quite a shine to him, but he had politely fended her off, and none of the highly attractive younger girls seemed able to arouse his interest. Instead he sat on the piano stool, tinkling away at a little melody with his left hand, while his right scratched the ear of the madam's English bulldog.

I stopped. What was this? Shyness? It seemed almost wilful, and if he was trying to avoid any awkwardness, surely it was more difficult to continually reject these obliging ladies than it was to take up with one of them and join in the party. That was the line of least resistance.

No, it almost looked like innocence.

That thought struck me like a thunderbolt, and I froze at the top of the stairs and leaned on the balcony for support. The girl I was following disappeared into a boudoir across the landing, beckoning with an alluring finger, leaving the door invitingly open.

I glanced back down at Charlie playing with the dog. His relations with women, as far as I had observed them, had always been far more romantic than lascivious.

He'd pursued that very young girl, Hetty Kelly, back in London, and seemed utterly besotted with her, waxing nauseatingly lyrical about the divine smell of the soap she used. You would have said it was an idealised romantic infatuation, though, rather than a physical one. He ended up driving the poor girl away, I remembered, by demanding a declaration of undying love after just a couple of meetings, and he spent more time pining wistfully for her than he ever did actually enjoying her company.

Recently he had been paying plenty of attention to little Annie Forrester in our company, another very young girl who was a picture of fresh-faced innocence.

And his pursuit of Tilly, that was highly romantic too, wasn't it? He certainly enjoyed casting himself as the romantic hero, a knight errant, and wooing her away from me seemed to be the most appealing aspect of the whole affair to him.

When the other lads in the company, like Freddie K Junior and Mike Asher, had chased hotly after burlesque girls, or the dancers in the other acts on the bill, he had never, not once, joined in, or even shown any particular interest in their bragging afterwards about their adventures.

Was it possible, I wondered, that he didn't actually know what to do? Was it?

This thought was still intriguing me at the end of that week when the boxcar headed West towards the Rocky Mountain Empresses once more, with Stan sitting opposite me.

I was always wary of having a dig at Chaplin in front of Stan. For one thing, they were pretty matey. They'd shared a room on tour, and inasmuch as Charlie knocked around with anyone in the company it would be with Stan. For another, Stan was such a sunny individual, always prepared to see the best in everyone, it made it difficult to try and discuss the darker side of my rivalry with Charlie, so I had grown used to biting my tongue.

However, this was too juicy a titbit to keep to myself, so I beckoned him closer in order that we wouldn't be overheard and told him what I'd seen in the Winnipeg sporting house.

Stan just laughed.

"What's so funny? It's possible, isn't it?"

"No," Stan chuckled. "It's not possible."

"You can't possibly know for certain, though," I said.

"Can't I?"

"What, you mean you've seen him... in action?"

"Of course not, no, but I do have pretty conclusive proof that our friend is a man of the world."

"What proof, you can't possibly have proof, what are you talking about?"

Suddenly Stan caught himself, and seemed to realise he'd said too much. "Listen, let's drop it, shall we?"

"Drop it? You're joking, aren't you? Tell me what you know, Stanley."

Stan was getting flustered now. "I can't, all right? Just leave it at that."

"All right," I said. "I'll tell you what. Either you tell me what you are alluding to so coyly, or I'll march over there and ask Charlie myself."

"No, don't do that."

"I'll tell him that you have personally vouched for his experience and expertise, and demand the details."

"You wouldn't."

"Oh, wouldn't I?" I got up halfway to my feet, and Stan shoved me back into my seat. I smiled – he was such a pushover.

"Listen," he said, suddenly serious. "I'll tell you. I should probably have told you before now, but you're not going to like it much."

"What on earth are you talking about?"

Stan took a deep breath, glanced over his shoulder to make sure no one was earwigging, and began.

"It was in San Diego. I came back to the room I was sharing with Charlie, and found him in a terrible state. The curtains were

377

drawn, and he was lying on his bed, with his knees drawn up to his chest, clutching his shins. His hair was all over the place, and there was an empty bottle of bourbon rolling around on the floor."

I remembered seeing Charlie in one of these self-indulgent depressions back in 1910, when he thought he wasn't going to America and his Karno career was in tatters.

"I asked him what was the matter," Stan said. "And he groaned, said it was all over, all his work, his career, ruined."

"What? How the...?"

Stan held his hand up to stop me, and dropped his voice to a whisper. "He'd got a girl pregnant, that's what it was, you see."

I whistled softly.

"And he was fretting about what the Guv'nor said about 'moral turpitude', and he couldn't see any way that he wasn't going to get the chop, even though the theatre managers loved him."

"That's him talking?" I said.

"Yes," Stan admitted. "So I said why didn't he pay the girl off, give her some money to, you know, take herself out of the picture, but he said he didn't have any."

"Ha!" I scoffed. "Did you not hear him bragging to Julius about how much he's getting paid?"

"Apparently, though, all that goes into a saving scheme, at a bank in Manhattan, and he can't just access it whenever he wants. So anyway, I had built up a little bit of a nest egg, you know?"

"Since you stopped playing poker with George Seaman, you mean?"

"Exactly. And I gave it to him, to help him out. And he gave it to her, and that was that."

"Whew!" I said. "You're a good mate, Stan. But why did you not tell me all this before? I mean, obviously it's a secret and everything, and I suppose you were worried that I'd try and use it to get Charlie kicked out, but still..."

Stan said nothing, just sat there looking at me, waiting for me to catch up.

Then, with a bump that shook my world and rattled my teeth, I did.

The boxcar seemed to retreat, and all I could hear was the rushing of the blood in my own ears.

"Arthur...?" Stan was saying, but he sounded like he was half a mile away.

Tilly. The girl was Tilly.

Blonde ringlets and sparkling green eyes.

Skin like warm silk.

That first kiss under the street lamp outside the Fun Factory.

"Oh Arthur, such a silly thing has happened!" when we were mistakenly allotted married accommodation on tour in Blackburn.

Her head on my shoulder as the *Cairnrona* pulled away from the dock, leaving for a new start in the New World.

A New Year's kiss in Times Square that went on and on and on.

Lying together watching the lights of the elevated train on the wall of my room in Chicago.

Tilly on Charlie's arm, laughing at something he said with those big, white teeth.

Tilly and Charlie, together.

Tilly gone in the night, travelling alone, who knows where.

Tilly. Pregnant.

Tilly. Taken, and ruined, and discarded, paid off by Charlie Chaplin like a common whore.

It was too much to take in all at once. I was going to need hours, days, *weeks* to think this one through, to come to terms with it. My fists couldn't wait that long, however, and they were already clenched, and pushing down on the arm of the seat as I staggered to my feet, rocking from side to side with the motion of the train.

Stan stood also, and planted the palm of his hand in the centre of my chest.

"No," he said. "Don't."

I was breathing heavily, and wouldn't have been surprised to see steam bursting from my nose like a bull ready to charge. I took half a step forward, pushing Stan aside, but he grabbed me firmly and wrestled me back into my seat, a pleading look on his face.

"Think!" he said urgently. "You have it out with Charlie, what will happen?"

"I'll bust his nose, maybe knock out some of those lovely white teeth," I growled.

"And then what?" Stan hissed. "You'll be out, that's what. And once Charlie realises that I have let the cat out of the bag, well, I'll be for the high jump as well, won't I? Alf won't be able to save us, not the position Charlie is in nowadays. He *is* the company, like it or not."

"Not," I muttered.

"I should never have told you," Stan said shaking his head.

"Yes, you should," I hissed back. "You should have told me six months ago, and a hundred times since."

"I was in an impossible position, you must see that, caught between two friends."

"One of whom has never let you down, and stood by you in the hardest of times, and the other of whom went behind your back to get you the sack because he was worried that you were going to be every bit as good as him."

"I am sorry, you know?"

I looked at my friend's earnest, pleading face, and I knew it wasn't him that I was really angry with. In fact the anger was already draining away, and being replaced by an awful feeling of desolation and impotence.

Chaplin was still snoozing away at the far end of the carriage, all unaware of the storm clouds gathering on his horizon. His mouth seemed to twitch into a little smile at something he was dreaming.

Or maybe it was the utter completeness of his victory over me.

35
CAUGHT IN
A CABARET

HEY! You'll never guess who's here!" Freddie threw open the curtains and let Seattle's September sunshine stab my eyes and pierce its way through to my hangover.

"What? What the hell time is it?"

"Breakfast time. Now come on, I'm dying to tell you. Who do you think I saw last night?"

"I dunno..." I sighed, pulling a pillow over my face to block out the day and Freddie's inappropriate early morning exuberance.

"I'll give you a clue. I went along to a burlesque house with the Hurleys, and this person was there. Running the place, actually."

"Burlesque house?"

"Yes, come on Arthur, you are not usually this dull. Who do we know who loved the burlesque? The burlesque girls? One burlesque girl in particular...?"

"Asher, you mean? Mike Asher?"

"Bingo!"

I sat up, suddenly wide awake. "Mike Asher is here, in Seattle? And he's *running*, did you say, a burlesque house?"

"I know, it's amazing, isn't it? You wait till you see the show he's got playing there. Unbelievable! We'll go tonight – they start right after we finish."

"What's so unbelievable about it? Filthy, is it?"

"You'll see. Right-o, I'm off to tell Stan," Freddie said, and bounded over to the door.

"Fred. Close the curtains, there's a good fellow."

"Of course, yes, sorry," he said, springing across the room to do so. "Hey, this is exciting, isn't it?"

"It is, but it would still have been just as exciting if you'd told me all about it in three hours' time."

━━━━

That evening, just after eleven o'clock, Freddie led a little group of Karno troupers - myself, Stan, Edgar and Wren Hurley and Charlie Griffiths - over to the burlesque house he had visited the night before, gambolling excitedly in front of us like an over-active puppy in a cowboy hat. Chaplin was having one of his anti-social days, mumbling something about having to meet somebody about something or other in order to get out of the evening's entertainment.

We turned a corner, and Freddie bowed like a circus ringmaster and cried "Da-daaah!" There, on the other side of the road, was 'Mike's Place'. It hadn't been open long, that much was clear, as it had just had a lick of paint, and the fixtures and fittings looked new.

Freddie led us inside, and said confidently to the hat-check girl: "Friends of Mike's." She gave a little signal to the bar tender, who nodded at a waitress, who scuttled over to a corner table, and then, quick as a flash, Mike Asher was amongst us, smart as a new pin and twice as prosperous, having seemingly snagged that opportunity he'd been on the lookout for.

"My friends!" he cried, embracing us all one by one. The Hurleys hadn't been on the earlier American tours with him, but it turned out he knew them well from a tour of *Hilarity* some years before so they got their hugs too. He led us all through to a table and waved over some free drinks.

"Mike," I said, when I caught my breath. "How has this come about? Last time I saw you, on Tagg's Island, you were swearing never to return for fear of being snared by your burlesque girl from Chicago."

"Yes, that's right. The lovely Lucia," he said. "Now *Mrs* Asher, and the principal choreographer at Mike's Place." Mike gave a little finger wave to a statuesque girl at a nearby table, and she blew him a kiss back. Lucia. There was no mistaking that magnificent embonpoint, barely encased in a strapless black lace number that seemed held up by sheer determination.

"Turned out I couldn't live without her."

"Well, that's marvellous, marvellous news, congratulations!"

"Thanks, old man. And you? Back with the Guv'nor? Not many get a second go there."

"That, my friend, is a story for another time," I said. "A gripping tale of chance, fluke, and false identity. But what about this place? Spill all."

"Oh, well, you see, Lucia was working here, and I was given charge of the comedy, which can be a trial in a place like this, because people come to see a bit of glamour rather than to laugh, but I thought: 'Surely there must be a way to do both?' And well, what with the years working for Karno, you know, I contrived to pull off a bit of a hit, and then the manager suddenly had a heart attack and died, simply the most tremendous bit of luck, really."

"Not for him," I said.

"No, indeed, ha ha, not for him, but Lucia and I were able to step into the breach, and well, here we all are!"

"Cheers!" I said, and a fiesta of glass-clinking rippled around our table.

Onstage a saucy soubrette with a decent set of pipes was warbling her way through a song that nobody was paying much attention to, being far more absorbed in the lines of her voluptuous figure.

"So, what about this comedy of yours, then?"

"Oh, you'll see," Mike said with a smirk, whisking a watch from his waistcoat to check how soon. "You'll see."

The thriving manager of Mike's Place left us then, to circulate and make sure the evening was proceeding smoothly.

"Good old Mike," I said to Freddie and Stan. "He's being very mysterious about his comic turn."

"Oh, I think you'll enjoy it," Freddie smirked. "Sssh! Here we go!"

The singer ended, and left the stage to hoots and whistles of approval, and the lights changed. Where there had been a single following spotlight on the girl, now the whole stage was lit up. Mike Asher himself, now a Master of Ceremonies, appeared to one side and announced:

"Ladies and Gentlemen, welcome to... *A Night at the Show!*"

The lush red curtains rose to reveal the set behind. Stan, Charlie Griffiths and I gasped, while Freddie and the Hurleys sniggered away, watching our reactions.

Onstage there was a fake proscenium arch, flanked by two sets of boxes. There was no mistaking it – it was the very spit of the set for *Mumming Birds*.

"The cheeky beggar!" Stan murmured.

The boxes were populated with fake audience members, as in

the classic Karno routine, but they were not quite the same as we would have played them, being intended to parody the patrons of a burlesque house rather than a vaudeville venue. So single men and sailors rather than uncles and naughty boys. The acts, too, were different – where we would have introduced a dull recitation of *The Trail of the Yukon*, this show-within-a-show featured a shapely soubrette very similar to the one who had actually just left the stage, and some cooch dancers. In short, what Mike had achieved was a burlesque of a burlesque show, and I had to admit it was a clever idea, even though he had quite brazenly stolen the format.

The clinching piece of luck-pushing came, however, a couple of minutes into the routine, when a late-comer arrived in the lower box, stage right. He clattered in, dressed to the nines and drunk as a lord, and promptly toppled out onto the stage amongst the dancers.

Mike Asher, as the M.C., rushed to intervene, and wrestled this drunkard – well, this Inebriated Swell – back into his box, with much achingly-familiar comedy business.

"Oh my goodness...!" I whispered to Stan, who was chuckling away more in disbelief than anything. "Imagine if the Guv'nor ever found out about this!"

With a start, then, I suddenly recognised the man playing the Swell.

"Isn't that Billie Ritchie?" I said.

"Good God, d'you know, I think it is," Stan said.

Ritchie had played the Drunk countless times, of course, in his time as a Karno number one. Last time I saw him he had been planning to try his luck in America. How utterly amazing to find he'd pitched up here. I looked forward to hearing all about it after the show.

Something about the shapely soubrette then drew my attention, maybe the particular timbre of her singing voice, or a familiar throw of the hip. Whatever it was, suddenly the burlesque house seemed to retreat into the distance, and she was all I could see or hear. I rose halfway out of my seat, trying to get a clear view of her face beneath a pile of dark curls, a wig. I had been fooled that way before, in Paris, when she was right under my nose at the Folies Bergère. It couldn't be. Could it?

Tilly.

"Hey Fred!" I whispered, grabbing my friend by the arm for support. "Isn't that...?"

Freddie wasn't looking at the stage. Even by the low light of the single candle on our table I could see he had gone white. I followed his shocked gaze to the back of the room, as did Stan, sitting beside us.

There, standing by the exit, watching on, was a familiar stone-faced figure. *Our* Drunk.

Charlie Chaplin.

Next to him, also very far from amused, was Alf Reeves.

Beside him, one of the very last people I would ever have expected to see there, so very far from home. Sydney Chaplin – himself a man who had played the Drunk on many occasions of course.

And beside him... oh my good Lord! A dapper little figure, in trademark shiny shoes.

The Guv'nor.

Fred Karno himself.

Seething.

"Dad...?" Freddie breathed, not quite able to believe his eyes.

We turned to look back at the stage, where *A Night at the Show* was rollicking along, all unaware. Mike Asher and Billie Ritchie were engaged in another piece of stage contretemps as the Drunk tried to get past the M.C. to chat up the tasty cooch dancers, while Tilly gave it a spoonful of the good old "show must go on" spirit.

There was nothing we could do to warn them of the impending storm. All we could do was watch with appalled fascination as this catastrophe broke upon our friends.

Karno had seen enough. I heard the click of his impeccable footwear approaching before I saw him, and then there he was elbowing his way past waiters, weaving around the tables, driving determinedly towards the stage like a bull at a matador. When he was perhaps a dozen feet away, surging forwards with a face like thunder, a vengeful Fury in full flight, Billie Ritchie caught sight of him.

Instantly the Drunk was quite sober. "Christ! It's the Guv'nor!" he gasped, lapsing into his Scots accent.

Mike Asher, who had his back to the audience at that moment, whipped around to see for himself. "Shite!" he yelped, with equal professionalism.

I saw Tilly, eyes wide, turning and pushing through the dancers, disappearing backstage as quickly as she could.

Karno meanwhile leapt up onto the apron and grabbed the two miscreants by the scruff of their collars.

"Ladies and gentlemen. This unauthorised performance of my lawfully copyrighted material is at an end!" the Guv'nor bellowed.

"It's a burlesque!" Mike protested.

"What?" Karno roared, turning to him. Billie Ritchie took advantage of the distraction to wriggle free, and he fled the stage in double-quick time. Poor Mike, however, was now well and truly trapped. Karno had his head in a lock, and was waving a fist in front of his nose.

All I could think was that Tilly was there, backstage somewhere, and I was on my feet, pushing forwards, making for the stage myself.

Karno gave me an approving nod as I clambered up alongside him, no doubt thinking that I was driven by a righteous desire to see Billie Ritchie brought to justice, but then he frowned, as if he was trying to place me. I looked wildly around, trying to work out where Tilly had gone.

Karno turned his attention back to the hapless M.C. "What did you say, you pitiful worm?"

"I said it's a burlesque," Mike choked out. "It's fair game! Copyright doesn't apply."

"We'll see about that!" Karno shouted. "You will all cease and desist! You will hear from my lawyers forthwith!" He punctuated these points by planting a hefty punch on Mike's helpless nose, which began to pour claret. Mike's eyes pleaded for me to pull Karno off him, but I had other things on my mind, and I charged into the darkness of the wings.

I barrelled down the stairs into the belly of the building, kicking open dressing room doors, but Tilly was nowhere to be seen. One door that I booted off its hinges was the principal star's dressing room, and I saw the panic-stricken Ritchie halfway out of the window, dragging his clothes in a bundle behind him, trying to do a bunk.

"Arthur!" he squealed when he saw me. "Ye wouldnae thump an old pal, would ye?"

"No, Bill," I said, distracted. "How are you, how have you been?"

"Oh, not so bad, y'know, musnae complain."

"I'm looking for Tilly, do you know her?"

"Aye," Billie said. "Lovely girl. She was away and gone even faster'n me, like she'd seen a ghost. Sorry."

"I see," I said. "Well, you'd probably better... you know?"

389

"Aye, I will. Thanks lad. Aw the best!" Billie wriggled the top half of his body out of the little window and dropped down out of sight. Then I heard his footsteps fading away as he made good his escape from the Guv'nor's wrath.

Mike was not so lucky, though, as I found when I ran back up to the stage. He was kneeling groggily, dripping blood from his nose, amid the ruins of his enterprise, as Karno stood centre stage and announced firmly: "Ladies and gentlemen! This performance is over!"

Karno was right, of course. The performance was very much over, considering the leading actor had fled as though his pants were on fire, most of the other participants had also made themselves scarce, and the producer/M.C. was swaying helplessly, drifting in and out of consciousness.

"Come on, we're leaving!" Karno said, marching towards the exit through the stunned crowd, with Alf Reeves and the two Chaplins in his wake. He didn't so much as glance at our table, where his own son was cowering alongside Stan, Charlie Griffiths and the Hurleys, all shocked by the suddenness and violence of what they had just witnessed. And although they were all entirely innocent bystanders, each of them shrank from the gaze of our old Guv'nor.

I was a driven man by this time. I grabbed Mike by the shirt-front and hauled him up onto a chair. There was a loud murmur of shocked protest from the audience at this, most of whom were already getting to their feet preparing to leave.

"Hey, fella!" one uniformed sailor said, stepping up to intervene. "Let him be, he's had enough!"

"It's all right," I said, holding up a hand. "I'm his friend, I just want to clean him up."

I grabbed a napkin from the nearest table and then hopped back up to where Mike was slumped. I began to wipe away some

390

of the blood from his face, and the sailor-boy calmed down and went back to his table.

"Mike?" I said urgently. "Where's Tilly? How do I find her?"

"Thanksh for your help, by the way," Mike slurred bitterly, testing his teeth for soundness.

"Where is she living, Mike? I just want to see her, talk to her." Mike sighed. "I'll have to ashk her firsht."

"Why?"

"In cashe she doeshn't want talk to you."

"What? Why wouldn't she?"

"I'll leave you a messhage at the shtage door. Thatsh if I remember in the morning. I'm going to be drinking thish night clean away..."

———

The next morning I was up and about early, having not slept at all. Seeing Tilly again had brought a lot of emotions back to the surface, and I was in turmoil.

Mike Asher seemed to think she might not want to see me. Embarrassment, I supposed. I still wanted to see her, though, even if only to put those feelings behind me once and for all.

And then there was Karno to worry about. I'd been reckless to show myself the night before, and I knew he had seen me, but I couldn't tell if he had recognised me. If he realised that I was in his employ then it would be a simple matter for him to order me back to England to help him out with that blasted divorce of his. Which would be awkward, to say the least.

I made my way to the theatre around midday to see if Mike had left me a message, as he said he would, but there was nothing yet. I presumed he was still asleep, or possibly over at the hospital having his nose realigned.

There was, however, a familiar figure waiting patiently by the stage door. It was Mr Jobson, Considine's English butler, and it was me he was waiting for.

"Good day, sir. Mr Considine would like to invite you to join him for luncheon," he said.

"Oh?" I said. "Well, that's very nice of him. Lead on."

Jobson and I walked a couple of blocks, and I wondered what Considine could want with me. Perhaps I would have to talk him out of some madcap scheme or other to shoot 'King Greek' in the family jewels, but he was good for a decent steak, I reckoned. Maybe even a pudding.

So I had my most charming smile on my face as the maître d' led us through a rather swanky silver service restaurant to the table where Considine was already getting to his feet to greet me. That smile froze in place, however, when he stepped to one side and I saw who our lunch companions were to be.

Mr Fred Karno and Mr Sydney Chaplin.

"Arthur! Come in, good to see ya!" said Considine warmly, steering me into the conclave. "Have a seat, join us. Mr Karno and I just wanted a little chat. You know Sydney, I take it?"

"I do," I said, nodding at Charlie's half-brother, who tried his hardest to offer me a smile but didn't quite manage to get it to reach his lips.

The three of them looked at me, Karno gave a little cough, and it struck me that they didn't quite know how to begin. Clearly they wanted something from me, or wanted me to do something for them. I decided to get busy ordering the biggest slap-up meal I could find on the menu in case it was to be my last.

"Say, listen, I was real sorry to hear about your friend, old Whimsical. He was quite a feller."

"Thanks," I said. "He was."

While we waited for the food to arrive, the Guv'nor talked a little about the success of his latest preoccupation, the pleasure palace on Tagg's Island, the Karsino.

"Wait," I said. "You really called it that?"

"Yes," he said with another little cough. "It's a cross between 'Karno' and 'casino', you see?"

"I know, yes."

He clearly did not recall that I had coined the name on the day he showed us all the site of his would-be Xanadu. Sydney took up the story, sycophantically supplying details of the gorgeous young actresses who had piloted the boats, of the top comedians who had waited tables, and of the thousands of onlookers lining the banks of the river opposite.

It was not until we had eaten, and were sitting back with our hands on our full bellies, that the conversation turned serious.

"Well," said Karno, dabbing at his mouth with a napkin. "It is always pleasant to see an old colleague in a far-off town."

"I'm sure Mike Asher and Billie Ritchie would agree," I said, perhaps emboldened by a glass too many.

Karno flexed his bruised fingers with the hint of a snarl. "I were surprised to see you here, actually," he said. "I suppose you replaced that feller Smith, did you?"

He fixed me with a knowing eye, and I flushed.

"Anyhow, I was under the impression that you would be able to do me a good turn back home a year or so back, but then you were nowhere to be found."

"Ah, well, Guv'nor," I said. "I, er... this was a last-minute opportunity, too good to miss."

Here it comes now, I thought. I steeled myself to show a bit of backbone, to refuse to return to England to fake a testimony against his wife's character, to face the consequences of that, which would be certain unemployment, exile, vagrancy...

"Well, what's done is done," he said. "The fact is, you are in a position to do me a good turn now."

"I am?" I said, taken aback.

"You are," he said. "We want to talk to you about Charlie."

"Charlie? Charlie Chaplin?"

"That's right," Considine chipped in eagerly.

"What about him?"

Sydney leaned forward. "We understand, that is to say, he wrote me a letter, in which he said that he had received a lucrative offer from a motion picture company."

"Yes, that's right. Keystone Pictures, I believe they are called," I said.

"Oh, so you know about it? You know, then, that he is giving it very serious consideration, is in fact minded to *accept* their proposal?"

My heart skipped a beat. "It is a handsome offer, as I understand," I said.

Karno coughed, another of his trademark coughs. Something was coming now, and Syd held himself in check.

"Arthur," the Guv'nor began. "I know that you have wanted to be a number one comic, like old Sydney here, that's right, isn't it?"

"Well, perhaps not exactly like," I said.

"And if that footballer hadn't broken your leg that night at the Oxford, well, I'm sure you would have been a number one before this."

Ha! I knew it! I would have been number one of the *Football Match* company, if only the Chaplin boys hadn't had me nobbled! I looked across at Chaplin major, who was wriggling uncomfortably in his seat.

"I think I can promise you that you *will* be a number one, my boy, and soon," Karno said, leaning forward. "But in return I will need you to do summat for me."

I froze, like a rabbit hypnotised by a cobra. This was almost too much to take in all at once. Everything I had wanted since I first joined Karno all those years ago. And all I had to do was... well, what? I realised they were all looking at me, Karno, Chaplin and Considine.

"What?" I managed to stutter.

"I need you to convince Charlie that this film business is all stuff and nonsense, that his future lies with the Fred Karno comedy company. Do you think you can do that for me?"

I almost laughed. "What? What makes you think he'll listen to me? Especially with Syd on hand?"

"This is just a flying visit," Karno said. "Syd and I have business to attend to in New York. You're Johnny on-the-spot, as it were. And you are a resourceful chap, I'm sure if you put your mind to it, you'll think of something."

I pulled a rather dubious face. "Well, Charlie's his own man, you know."

"But you'll do what you can, eh, Arthur?" Considine said eagerly. "That's all we can ask, eh, Fred?"

Karno looked as though he felt he could ask a good deal more of me than that, but he solemnly offered his hand for me to shake, and after a moment I took it. This understanding having apparently been reached, suddenly they seemed anxious to be rid of me. Karno took a pocket watch from his waistcoat, and raised a meaningful eyebrow at Considine, who got to his feet.

"Thanks for coming by, Arthur," the big promoter said. "Always a pleasure."

Well, that was one question answered. There was to be no pudding. Mr Jobson ghosted alongside, and he walked with me outside and the two blocks back to the theatre.

"I'm afraid Mr Considine is particularly anxious at the moment," he confided. "I am sorry to say that his partner Mr Sullivan..."

"Big Tim Sullivan?"

"Quite so. Big Tim Sullivan has been committed to a sanatorium suffering from paranoid delusions, brought on, I am afraid to say, by tertiary syphilis."

"Good Heavens."

"Mr Considine's whole vaudeville enterprise depends heavily upon Mr Sullivan's investment, which is uncertain now to say the least, and so the loss of a big draw like young Mr Chaplin might just prove the final straw."

"I see. Well, I'll certainly see what I can do, old man."

"Thank you, sir."

In point of fact I couldn't see how Charlie would pay a blind bit of notice to anything I had to say, especially where his precious career was concerned, but what could I do except show willing?

When I got to the stage door there was a message for me from Mike Asher. It was cryptic, to say the least. It read:

"Miss Matilda Beckett walks out by the Hoo Hoo House every day at midday."

36
THE HOO HOO HOUSE

IT took a bit of doing, and I had to ask a lot of people, but I finally found the Hoo Hoo House the next day with nine minutes to spare.

It was a two-storey prairie-style wooden building on the lushly manicured campus of the University of Washington, built – according to a carved wooden plaque – by the International Concatenation of Hoo Hoo, if you please, for the Alaska-Yukon-Pacific Exposition of 1909. The entrance was guarded by two matching statues of black cats, their backs arched and their tails in the air, and eyes that lit up at night.

I sat and waited by one of these black cats, looking out at the view across Lake Washington. I was very jittery about seeing Tilly again.

I couldn't help imagining her walking towards me, up the path there, smiling her lovely smile, greeting me with a kiss on the cheek, then saying: "Look, Arthur, I want you to meet little Charlie…" before turning her bassinet to reveal a baby with those unmistakeable violet eyes, and enormous perfect teeth.

I shuddered, and tried to think of something else. Across the campus a clock began striking twelve.

Then, suddenly, there she was.

Tilly.

She was every bit as beautiful as I remembered. All the more so, for being here in front of me at last. There was something new – she seemed a little more grown up, somehow – but she was wearing it extremely well.

She stopped a couple of paces away, a smile on her face, uncertainty in her bright green eyes. I found myself hoping, stupidly, that the baby had inherited them, rather than Chaplin's idiosyncratic colour, which was why the first thing out of my mouth, my stupid, clumsy mouth, was this:

"Did you not bring the baby with you?"

Her face fell and she sighed. "So. You know about that," she said quietly.

"Yes, I know about that," I said. "Is that why we are meeting here, rather than where you and the child are living? So you could keep it a secret?"

"No, I thought you would be amused, that's all. This house was built by the Hoo Hoo, they're like an exclusive secret society of lumbermen, if you can imagine such a thing. They reminded me of the Wow Wows."

"Maybe the Guv'nor was right after all, and America is riddled with secret societies."

"They chose the black cat as their symbol, and they revere the number nine, because of the cat and his nine lives. So this clubhouse was opened on the ninth day of the ninth month in '09, and it was paid for by every member making a donation of $9.99. Isn't that crazy?"

When she ran out of nervous chatter I offered her my arm and said: "Let's walk, shall we?" After a moment she took it, and we headed down a path which led through a bank of Douglas firs to the shore of the lake beyond.

"So Charlie told you then," she said, once we had strolled in awkward silence for long enough. "I really didn't think he would."

"No, he didn't tell me, we have not spoken about it."

"Amy, then. I swore her to secrecy. I should have known."

"Stan told me," I said. "Eventually."

Tilly was puzzled. "Stan? But how did he...?"

"The money that Charlie gave you?" I said. "Borrowed from Stan."

She raised her eyebrows at that. "Ah."

We walked a little further, and soon we had the path to ourselves. "So?" I said. "After you left without a word, and up the spout, apparently."

"Charming."

"What did you do? Where did you go? Back to England?"

"No. At first I was going to, to see if I could find out what happened to my family. I was sitting on the train by myself for hours after they unhooked the boxcar at Salt Lake City, feeling pretty fed up, I can tell you, with not much to look forward to except turning up on my mother's doorstep, wherever that may be, with a baby on the way, and my performing career as good as over. Then a girl sat opposite me, such a pretty girl, and she asked me why I was so miserable. And then, just like that, we realised we knew one another, because she was Lucia."

"Mike Asher's burlesque girl, you mean?"

"Exactly. She was on her way home from a stint in Denver. She is so sweet, such a kind girl, and so funny. And really stuck on Mike Asher, that silly booby. Anyway, by the time we reached St Louis she'd persuaded me to come to Chicago with her, and I got a job with her in that burlesque show. And there I stayed. All the girls were really kind, and welcoming, and when I became too...

obvious, shall we say, to prance about onstage in tights any more I worked as a hat check girl."

"You should have joined Billy Watson's Beef Trust, you'd have fitted right in there."

She smacked my forearm. "I wasn't that big! Anyway, then the baby came, and he was so beautiful, Arthur, and..."

"Yes, yes, all right!" I said, the vision of a purple-eyed mini-Chaplin returning to swim before my eyes, simpering and showing off his perfect teeth.

"Well, all the girls helped out, and they would make such a fuss of the little man, it was like he had a dozen mothers."

Just like his father, I thought sourly, landing on his feet.

"Then out of the clear blue sky old Mike turned up at the burlesque house. He swept Lucia off her feet, and they were married a fortnight later. It was so romantic."

"Well, well," I smiled. "I'm glad it has worked out for them."

"Yes," Tilly said, and I wondered if she was thinking if only, if only it had worked out as well for the two of us. No chance of that now.

"So then. How did you fetch up in Seattle?"

"Oh, well, Mike and Lucia had the chance to come here, and they didn't want to leave us on our own, so they pretty much insisted on us tagging along. We did wonder whether we had made the right decision, coming here. We get a lot of sailors in at Mike's Place, of course, and they can be quite rough."

"Almost as rough as old Karno," I said.

"Did you know he's broken Mike's nose?" Tilly said. "He must have been so cross."

"You could say that."

"I suppose that's the end of this little engagement. Shame, I was enjoying it."

"It was a brilliant idea, actually, I have to say. Burlesquing a burlesque."

"Do you think so?" Tilly said, with a sly smirk.

"Brilliant, but naughty."

"It was my idea. Karno should have broken *my* nose."

"Ha! No wonder you scarpered!"

"I wonder what's going to happen. It's all a bit of a mess, isn't it?"

"I suppose it is," I said.

"But anyway. What has been happening with you? Are you still doing well with Karno?"

I thought about the conversation I'd had with the man himself just the day before. It had left me feeling pretty vulnerable, truth to tell.

"It's complicated," I said. "But I'm not out just yet."

"Good," she said. "That's good. I'm sure it will work out well for you, just like it has for Charlie."

Not a good idea, mentioning Charlie like that, talking about him doing well. Suddenly I had a vivid mental picture to deal with, of Charlie and Tilly together, of him kissing her face, stroking her hair, sliding a perfectly manicured hand up a smooth-stockinged thigh...

We strolled on a little further, until the trees gave way to an open grassy area. Finally I couldn't help myself, and blurted out:

"I still can't believe Charlie did what he did to you."

"He gave me the wherewithal to get home."

"He gave you the bum's rush, that's what he gave you, my dear! What sort of a scoundrel gets a girl in the family way, and then pays her to go away? Eh?"

"Let's not," she said. "It's so nice to see you again, and looking so well. I have missed everyone, missed you, Arthur."

"He should have stood by you."

"Well…"

"That's what I would have done."

"Yes."

"And you, how could you leave without a word?"

"What could I have said?"

"Goodbye, for a start. I mean, I know I made it difficult for you to… to return my feelings for you, and I know you had a certain… rapport with Chaplin. I mean, obviously you did, for reasons that escape me, but I did care for you, Tilly, and I thought you cared something for me too."

She was quiet.

I was suddenly angry. With Tilly, with the situation, and – as usual – with the man who had caused it. I flipped out my pocket watch, glanced at the time.

"Well, I am going to have to go," I said stiffly. "Matinée to do, you remember the drill."

Tilly looked up at me, shyly. "You didn't ask whether the baby is a boy or a girl."

"You said he was a little man, didn't you? Anyway, I don't want to know about it."

"Don't you want to know his name?"

"No!" I turned on my heel and started to walk back up the path the way we had come.

"Arthur."

"I said 'no'." I covered my ears with my hands as I walked away. After twenty punishing paces or so I turned, and she was standing there in the middle of the path, a wistful expression on her lovely face.

She called out: "I will be here, at the Hoo Hoo House, every day at midday."

Then I turned and strode away from her.

I didn't bother returning to the Hoo Hoo House to see Tilly again. What would have been the point? I'd seen her one last time, now I had to put her behind me and move forward with my life without her.

On the Sunday morning, around eleven, we all trooped onto the boxcar once again to ride down to Portland. I was in no mood for conversation, but Amy came and sat next to me, a knowing smile on her face.

"Hello Amy," I sighed. "Something I can do for you?"

"So-o-o...?!" she said, drawing that one little word out impossibly long.

"So? So what?"

"So how was your time in Seattle? Interesting?"

"You could say that."

"You bump into any interesting old friends?"

"Well, there was one around every corner, it seemed to me."

"Yes?"

"Yes, Fred Karno, Syd Chaplin, Billie Ritchie, Mike Asher. It was like a Fun Factory reunion."

"And?" she said, nudging me with her elbow.

"And? What do you mean, and?"

"Oh, Arthur, don't tease me! You know what I want to know. Did you see..." she glanced around to make sure we were not being overheard, and then whispered, "... her?"

"Who?" I said.

"Arthur Dandoe, I will swing for you, I swear I will! Why, Tilly, of course! Did you see Tilly?"

"Did you?"

"Oh, very quickly. I saw her for a cup of tea, but I had to

403

be so careful. She didn't want Alf to know she was there, or Charlie, but I did so want to see the baby."

"Ah," I said, shaking my head quickly to rid myself of the mental image of the miniature Chaplin.

"So?"

"Yes, I saw her," I said.

"And?"

"And we talked, and that was that, and now it's finally over and done with."

Amy frowned, puzzled. "What do you mean, over and done with?"

"Well, you know, she left without saying anything, and she had Charlie's child, didn't she, so all I really wanted to say was goodbye and, and, and good luck with... all that."

"Arthur Dandoe!"

"What? She's made her bed, hasn't she?"

"You mean to tell me...? Oh, you chump!"

"What's the matter with you?"

"Surely you didn't leave without...? Ohh!" Amy was exasperated with me for some reason.

"Without *what*?"

Amy turned and looked me in the eye. "I'm not supposed to... But I can't just sit here and let you just..."

"Let me just what? Whatever are you so cross about, Amy?"

"Oh, it was all for you, don't you see? You cloth-headed buffoon! Can't you work it out?!"

"All for me?"

Amy sat there, her lips pressed together defiantly. She wasn't going to say any more, but she wasn't going to leave until I put it together for myself.

So I thought about what she could possibly mean.

At that moment a picture popped into my head.

Tilly, on the path outside the Hoo Hoo House.

"Don't you want to know his name?" she'd said.

"No!" I'd shouted, hadn't I, angry, turning to walk away, out of her life.

"Arthur," she'd said, softly.

Arthur.

Not speaking to me. Not calling me back.

Telling me the name of the child, her child.

But why would she call the boy Arthur, of all things, if he was Charlie's? That didn't make a lot of sense, did it?

She'd only have called him *Arthur*, if...

The blood was rushing in my ears.

"Got it now?" Amy tutted, hands on hips.

The Pacific Express pulled out of Seattle station and began to pick up speed. I leapt to my feet, barrelled out through that dark baggage compartment of happy memory, pushed through the back door and vaulted over the observation platform, landing heavily on the sleepers between the tracks.

The boxcar pulled away towards California, but I was already running in the other direction.

Running back to the Hoo Hoo House.

———

I didn't know if she would come. Did she walk here every day? Was that what she meant? Or was she here every day this week because she knew I was in town, and now that she thought I was heading South might she not bother to come, give it a miss?

I had no clue how to find her otherwise, short of haunting Mike's Place, trying to bump into the battered Asher, or Lucia.

The clock chimed, and midday came and went, and I slumped, head in hands.

I stood up, pushed myself away from the statue of the arched black cat with the illuminating eyes.

Suddenly, there on the path, a little way off, I saw her. She was pushing a bassinet, and as I spotted her she leaned in with a smile to adjust a blanket or maybe to chuck the little chap's chin.

"Tilly," I called.

She stood up, startled, and looked around.

"Arthur! I thought you'd be on your way by now."

"I should be. I jumped off. Jumped off the back of the train."

"You...?"

She frowned a little, and then seemed to realise why I would do such a thing, and she looked down at the floor.

"He's called Arthur?"

"Come and say hello."

I walked over to the bassinet and stooped to peek inside. There was a bonny little pink boy lying in there, snoozing away, a white woollen cap on his head tied under his chin with a ribbon. So tiny, and yet, somehow, overwhelming.

"Well. Hello there, Arthur," I said. "I'm Arthur."

"Would you like to walk with us?"

"I think I would like that, yes."

We set off down the path, me pushing the baby's carriage. Tilly walked beside us, one hand resting on the edge. The wind rustled the tops of the tall trees.

"Why didn't you tell me?" I said at length.

Tilly sighed. "I thought about it. Too much, probably."

"I mean, you are sure?"

"Of course I'm sure!" she said, indignantly.

"But Charlie must believe... differently?"

406

"I'm not particularly proud of that."

We walked on in silence for a little while, and I let her gather herself to spill all.

"When I realised I was with child," she said, finally. "And it was that time in the boxcar with you, obviously, no other explanation was possible. I tried to think what to do for the best. If I stayed with the company, and I started to show, and it was known that you were the father of the child, then we would both have been booted out together for moral turpitude, or whatever Karno's ridiculous phrase is."

"I would have stood by you," I said.

"Of course you would," she said, without sounding entirely convinced. "But for ever after I would feel that I had ruined your most cherished dream, and that's no way to live a life."

"But..."

"I thought about coming to you, and offering to leave to have the baby alone. But if you'd chosen that, chosen to reject me, and stay with Karno, how would you have been able to live with yourself?"

"I wouldn't have done that," I said, but I was wondering.

"Wouldn't you? I couldn't make you choose between comedy and me. I was afraid of what choice you would make. And whichever choice you'd made would have been the ruin of you. I know you. I couldn't have done that to you."

"So what did you do?"

Tilly walked along for another moment or two.

"You have to understand what my relationship with Charlie was like," she said then. "He is very attentive, he makes a girl feel adored. There's no other word. And it is very attractive."

"Huh," I said.

"He puts the girl on a pedestal, and he woos her. What appeals to him is an ideal of innocence, purity, youth, freshness, a sort of first flowering, I think. You remember I said I felt like the Queen of the May? So you see, our relationship was never allowed to sink below an elevated level, shall we say?"

"I see," I said.

"I began to feel my days were numbered in any case, especially when that little Annie Forrester arrived."

"Well, you were right about that," I said. "He has hardly left her side these past few months, or let her open a door, or carry anything."

"Hmmm. But you see he was still wanting to spend all his time with me, because we were friends, and good companions, and because..."

"Because what?"

She paused, but then decided the conversation might as well go all the way. "Because of you, I think. I began to feel that he thought of me mainly as a kind of trophy, to be brandished in your face."

I nodded. Tilly took a deep breath, and then plunged right in.

"So I decided to seduce him. It was kind of awful, in some ways, because he still wanted to idolise me, but in the end nature took over, and it was all a little embarrassing. It was all I could do to make sure he'd... done enough, to convince him later that he was responsible for my condition."

"Really?"

"They'd never have sacked him. Not him. He's far too import-ant now. Everywhere·we went, remember, it was his name on the posters, not Karno's, not any more. He's bigger than Karno, he's the one all the theatre managers want to see. And we were going back to places we'd been before, and he's the one the audiences remember, and come to see again and again."

"Yes, all right," I said. She was laying it on a bit thick, I thought.

"So he'd have been safe, that's the point, he'd have been all right. And he'd have been able to protect me, and the baby when he came along. And at least that would have been something."

We walked along in silence for a little while. I saw clearly enough that she had tried to protect me, to take the burden entirely on her own shoulders. I thought of Tilly wanting to be the next Marie Lloyd. It must have crossed her mind that getting Charlie to stand by her was the only way to hang onto her own ambitions.

"Did you think he would marry you, when you told him?" I said finally.

"I suppose I thought it was possible," she said.

"Did you love him then?"

"I think I did, a little. But those feelings died a death."

"They did?"

"Oh yes. When he handed me a fistful of dollars and told me to leave at once without speaking to anyone."

"He didn't think he was safe," I said. "Stan told me. He was in a blind funk."

"Yes. It was a lot to ask, I see that now. At the time it seemed to make a kind of sense to me. When a baby is on the way you feel like you have to make plans, even if they're not as well thought out as they might be."

"Here's a plan," I said. "I will leave Karno, leave right now, and take care of you and the baby."

"You will not! I don't want that. It would be the same thing, the very same thing that I feared, don't you see that? You would feel good about your choice for a while, virtuous even, but soon enough you would start to think, start to regret, start to wonder if you could ever have been a number one, and whose fault would it be then for holding you back? My fault, mine and the child's."

"I would never blame you."

409

"You would, my dear, you would. You wouldn't mean to, but sooner or later you would. And then what would become of us all?"

"We could go back to England."

"And what would we use for money? I can still remember how you talked about the time you were out on your own. Imagine that but with a family too."

We walked on through the trees, the bassinet's wheels crunching the gravel. Was she right about me? Perhaps she was. Part of my mind was already calculating how much time I had to catch up with the company in Portland, whether there would be trains.

Suddenly I stopped dead. The little baby carriage rolled on a couple of feet before Tilly grasped the handle.

"Listen," I said. "Listen. Why don't you come back to Karno?"

"Ha ha!" Tilly laughed. "He's not likely to welcome me back, is he? Not after this week."

"He wouldn't need to know."

"I feel like I really let Alf and Amy down," Tilly said.

"Nonsense, they love you. You know they do."

"I could hardly bring a child on tour, could I?"

"Why not? We are a company just like those burlesque girls of yours, do you think we wouldn't help out? We are a family."

"A baby? In the boxcar? Really?" Tilly was musing, unconvinced. "Besides, it would mean leaving Mike and Lucia in the lurch, and I couldn't possibly go back, not while..."

She stopped, but not while Chaplin is the number one, that's what she meant to say.

"Ah, but things could be changing soon," I said.

"Really? Changing how? You're not going to do anything stupid, are you?"

"No, no. Charlie could be leaving us to go and make motion pictures."

410

"Shut up! Why on earth would he do something as daft as that?"

"I know, I know, it's craziness, but he's got a pretty decent offer and he is seriously considering it."

"And then... you?"

"Maybe. Why not? Why not me? Then I could have whoever I asked for."

"Don't tell him you saw me."

"Who?"

"Charlie, of course."

"So will you?" I pressed.

"Will I what?"

"Come back to Karno's, when Charlie's gone and I am the number one?"

"If that happens..."

"When, *when* it happens."

"When... all right. *When* that happens, you come and find me, and ask me again."

"Now that is what I call a plan," I said.

I took her hands and clasped them in mine. Then I took her properly in my arms and kissed her.

Then I set off running to the railway station.

All I had to do now was get rid of Charlie Chaplin.

411

37
KEYSTONE KAPERS

CHARLIE, Stan and I sat in the back of a limousine driven by a chauffeur in a peaked cap and watched suburban Los Angeles flicker past the windows like a moving picture, bungalow after bungalow, palm tree after palm tree, all dusty and bright in the autumn sunshine.

We were on our way to visit the Keystone Studios in Edendale, at the invitation of Mack Sennett. He had come to see Charlie at the Empress the night before, and afterwards in the bar he had made a beeline for me and Stan – the *real* Mr Chaffin – before Charlie had quickly made himself known and elbowed his way into the conversation. Sennett cheerfully invited all three of us over to inspect his facilities, hoping of course to impress Charlie into signing a deal, and the opportunity for me to maybe give the little man a nudge in that direction was too good to miss.

Because that was my plan now.

Ever since the emotional upheaval of that week in Seattle, a month ago now, I had been perched precariously on the horns of a dilemma. What to do? What to *do*?!

On the one hand, Karno had promised me a number one slot if I could persuade Charlie to stay with the firm. It was a tantalising prospect, I had to admit, something I had dreamed of ever since I had first stepped onto a music hall stage. But supposing I did that, put all my eggs into that basket. It would have to be with another one of the Guv'nor's companies, more than likely back in England, where I would be thousands of miles away from Tilly and the baby, and perilously on hand to get entangled in the old goat's divorce proceedings. And even that was presuming I could trust Karno to keep his word. Aye, there's the rub, as some fellow once said.

The more I thought about it, the more it seemed to me that if Charlie stayed on board, which seemed pretty likely, it would be damn'd difficult to demonstrate that it was any of my doing, so I might not actually be able to take any credit at all, and where would that leave me? Stuck in the blooming boxcar with Charlie for ever and ever amen, that's where.

On the other hand, though, on the other hand... if I could somehow persuade Charlie to abandon vaudeville to make Mack Sennett's idiotic motion pictures, well, then there would be a sudden vacancy as the number one of our American company, with bookings to fulfil, and I felt sure I could convince Alf Reeves of my merits ahead of Charlie Griffiths or Edgar Hurley, or even Stan, especially considering the company manager's desire to protect our friend Edith Karno. Then, you see, *then* I could return to Seattle in triumph, collect Tilly and little Arthur, and everything would be rosy on Dandoe Street.

And so, after many sleepless hours of deliberations, that was the course I had chosen.

How was this to be done, though? How to manipulate the arch-manipulator? How to be more devious than King Devious himself? How to have less ruth than the most ruthless person I knew? And how to do that, moreover, whilst letting Karno – perhaps the

413

second most ruthless person I knew – believe that I was doing my very best on his behalf?

Now Charlie claimed to be merely using the Keystone offer to screw more cash out of the Guv'nor, and it suddenly struck me. What if Karno found out – from a concerned and loyal employee – that Chaplin was trying to play him? What would he do then?

I decided it would be well worth finding out, and sent a wire by the Western Union which would be waiting for him when he returned to the Fun Factory.

Edendale, when we got there, was not a particularly glamorous part of the world. There were a few small lumber yards, and a junk yard or two, and then some farms which seemed to be pretty much deserted. A handful of general stores fronted onto the dusty road, and they were little more than shacks.

We arrived at the Keystone lot, and the limousine rolled up to the entrance, which was up a garden path to a rather unprepossessing bungalow. I could have wished it were a little more impressive, actually, for there was a dilapidated feel to the place, with its shabby green fence. I tried not to let my disappointment show, however, and smiled approvingly at everything as we stepped from the motor car.

The three of us walked up and into the building, not really knowing what to expect. Mack Sennett himself was waiting inside, and greeted us warmly. "Let's go straight onto the lot," he said. "Then you can really see what we've got going here."

Out the back of the bungalow we followed him to the stages, where that day three movies were being made at once, on three adjacent sets. A soft even light pervaded everything, thanks to broad streams of white linen that diffused the bright sunlight to provide the very best conditions for photography in the California daylight.

That first glimpse of the world of motion pictures was overwhelming. You never saw anything so busy. You never stood in one place with so much to look at all at once. The three films were being shot on interior sets, but none of the buildings had ceilings, they were all open to the sky and the sunshine. In the distance you could see the mountains, and the ramshackle farms that made up the neighbourhood. The Keystone lot must have been a farm itself, and the building that housed the dressing rooms looked very much like an old barn.

All around there was hustle and bustle as people hurried hither and thither with planks of wood on their shoulders, or furniture, and on the sets themselves everyone seemed to be shouting all the time to make themselves heard above the general rumpus and racket.

On the first set Mabel Normand was banging on a door, shouting "Let me in!" Then the camera stopped and that was it. We stared – we had no idea that movies were made piecemeal like this. We assumed that they were filmed like stage sketches, all at once.

On the next set, which butted right up against the first, Roscoe Arbuckle, a baby-faced clown who gloried in the nickname 'Fatty', was evidently paying court to his sweetheart. It was an intimate little scene, but there was no thought of anyone asking for silence. The actors were expected to perform while wooden beams were being hammered for another construction just a few feet from their heads, and the director was shouting his instructions over the constant racket; "Look left... sad face... now to me, to me... all right, get up now, and fall at the bottom of the stairs... great... and let's go again..."

Sennett made a little speech, talking constantly as he showed us around. It didn't seem to occur to him that he might be a distraction to the work in progress, and in point of fact he wasn't, he was simply ignored like everyone else.

"Movies are the fastest growing business in America," he shouted as we traipsed along in his wake. "Folks can't get enough of 'em. Anything you can get on film will make money, that's why there are companies springing up all over town, like Comet, Imp, Thanhauser, Lux, Majestic, Gaumont, Champion, Éclair..." He counted these off on his fingers as he went.

"Let me tell you something – all those guys are making big bucks, all of 'em, if they know what they're doing. The key thing – the Keystone thing, if you like – is to specialise, and we specialise in what you guys specialise in. Comedy. Comedy, comedy, comedy!"

He waved a hand to encompass the whole operation surrounding us, and with perfect timing Ford Sterling, the leader of the Keystone Cops, fell out of a window right beside him.

"OK, cut it there. Mack, you were in that shot."

"Ha ha ha! Sorry fellers, sorry Ford!"

Sennett patted Sterling amiably on the backside, and then explained their method of working: "We have no scenario. We get an idea then follow the natural sequence of events until it leads up to a chase, which is the essence of our comedy."

Charlie turned to me and mouthed: "No scenario?" All I could do was shrug.

On the middle set the director was waiting for his leading man, Fatty Arbuckle, to be ready to shoot again. Sennett grabbed him by the elbow and pulled him over.

"Fellas, this here's Henry Lehrman. We call him 'Pathé' because he used to work for them in France, but now he works for us. Pathé, this is Charlie Chaplin, he's going to be joining us."

"Well, I..." Charlie began, as Lehrman looked him up and down, weighing him up like a piece of meat.

"Can you fall off a step-ladder?" the director said, in an indeterminate European accent.

"What?" Charlie said, taken aback.

"I mean, can you do a funny sprawl off a stepladder wizout breaking of your bones?"

"Sure he can," Sennett cut in. "Here, look..." and he grabbed a stepladder from the third set, the Keystone Cops headquarters, and set it up right there in front of us. Charlie looked helplessly at me and Stan, but there seemed nothing for it but to give it a go, and so he did, tumbling down off the ladder into the dirt in his smartest suit, then dusting himself off. We laughed dutifully, and Lehrman seemed satisfied, turning back to his work. Meanwhile a stagehand was hanging off the top of the third set by his fingertips, feeling with his toes for his missing stepladder, finally falling noisily into a pile of paint cans.

We stood and watched the great Ford Sterling shooting his scene for a while. He was a very popular comic, and plenty of people were gathered round just to watch him work. He was playing his character in the 'Dutch' style, ad-libbing all the while in a heavy Teutonic accent, which got lots of laughs from the guys standing around watching, but which would be useless on film, of course.

"Ford Sterling, he started in vaudeville, you know?" he said. "And Chester Conklin, there, the fella with the walrus moustache, and Mack Swain, the big lad at the back? Spotted both of them in vaudeville shows. They both love it here, you can ask them. Ask them if they'd ever go back to the twenty-five shows a week grind. Not right now, of course, the camera's rolling."

It was, as well, not four feet away, but nobody thought to tell the boss to keep quiet. They probably couldn't even hear him over the rest of the banging and crashing that was going on. The cameraman was hand-cranking the film with a handle on the side of the camera, keeping a steady pace. Sennett nudged me.

"Tell you a secret. You see that handle there?"

"Yes?" I said.

"You have to turn that at a particular speed, the guys learn that, it's part of the job. We had a Russian guy called Sergei when we first started, and it turned out he was cranking too slowly, undercranking we call it, and we'd tell him to speed up, speed up. 'Why does everything have to be such a rush?' he'd say, old Sergei, and he'd just carry on the same lazy way. Anyway, we noticed that cranking slow, like Sergei did, made the fellas on screen seem to be racing around like mad things, and sometimes – in a chase sequence, say – that's just the ticket, so now we do it on purpose. But we found out entirely by accident. How about that?"

Just then there was a loud cry of "Lunch!", and suddenly all the action stopped, tools were downed, and people poured out towards the entrance, heading for the general store over the road, which did a roaring trade in hotdogs and sandwiches, evidently. A blessed silence descended gradually upon the lot, and Sennett watched with a benign grin on his big face as eight or nine chaps in police uniforms galloped away from us to get the nosebags on.

"Another thing I like to do," he said, "especially with the cops, is I get them to pretend to bang into imaginary obstacles, bounce off 'em, so they're always changing directions. Works, too."

Sennett clapped his hands together. "Say, why don't you boys take a look around by yourselves, while it's quiet, and when you're done come up to my office. It's up there."

He pointed out the tallest building on the lot, and a picture window looking down on the mayhem from on high, and then with another beaming grin he strode off.

"Well," I said to Charlie. "What do you think? It's pretty exciting, isn't it?"

"It's a madhouse," he muttered. "A madhouse..."

"I like Mack," Stan said. "Seems like he'd be a lot of fun to work for."

"Hmmph," Charlie grunted.

We strolled around the sets, and noted how flimsy they seemed compared to some of our stage builds.

"They only need to use it once, I suppose," Stan said, applying logic to the chaos. "It's not like they have to pack it into a boxcar and put it up again in the next town, week after week."

Charlie was wandering ahead by himself, lost in thought. He was fed up, and it could hardly have been more obvious if there had been a large black cartoon cloud hovering over his head.

"Whatever's the matter?" I asked.

"Oh..." Charlie wondered for a moment about keeping things to himself, but the desire to vent won out. "It's Karno, he's digging his heels in over the next contract. He's offered me a tiny little raise – pitiful really, considering that I am the marquee name – and he wants to stick with the Sullivan-Considine time, won't even *consider* trying to break an East Coast circuit."

"Disappointing," I commiserated.

"I've a good mind to go with Keystone just to put the old bastard's nose out of joint!"

"Yeah," I said. "He'd hate that, true enough."

One thing at least seemed certain – the Guv'nor had got my wire.

We came to one of the whitewashed bungalows, perhaps once a farm building of some kind. The sign on the door read 'Costume Dept'. There was no one inside, so we went in to get out of the midday heat.

Charlie slumped into a wicker chair. "I don't know," he sighed. "It's just not my style of thing, is it? No scenarios, did he say? I can't abide chases. And this stop-start way of working. How would you ever build anything worth a damn?"

"I'm not sure," I said. "But once you got used to it I'm sure you'd find a way of getting the most out of it."

"Thanks for the vote of confidence, Arthur," Charlie said. "But I can't see what I would even do here."

"Oh come on," I said, looking to Stan for help, and we both started rooting around in the piles of clothing strewn around haphazardly on tables. "What about...?"

I found a jacket with a sort of battered grandeur, a couple of sizes too small, and quickly slipped it on, doing the buttons up with difficulty across my belly.

"Here," Stan said, chucking me a pair of over-sized baggy trousers, which I pulled on over my own, then I stepped straight into a pair of long, flappy shoes which were tucked under a table. By now I was looking around for a hat, and found a rather shabby derby, which I jammed onto my head, and another comedy standby, the springy cane, I chose from about a dozen stuffed into in an elephant's foot umbrella stand behind the door.

"There," I said, turning just as Stan slapped a small toothbrush moustache onto my top lip to complete the whole effect.

"Ha, excellent!" Stan said. "It's our old friend the Stowaway."

I turned out my toes and did a shuffling walk up and down the costume room, twirling the cane as I went. When I reached the far end I hooked the cane around a hat stand and used it to change direction, with one foot up in the air. Then I waddled back, doffing my hat with an exaggerated gentility, and swaying from side to side as I had on the *Cairnrona* all those many moons ago.

Charlie muttered: "Nat Wills, more like."

Stan guffawed and clapped his hands. "No, no, it's the Stowaway all right. All you need now is some ship's stewards to chase, and there you are, that's a scenario right there!"

"No scenarios," Charlie grumbled. "Remember?"

"Oh come on, Charlie, cheer up," I said. "Look how quickly I put this together just from what's lying around here. It'll be a piece of cake for someone with your skills, and your music hall nous. And look at all the vaudeville players he's got on the strength already."

"Yeah, not exactly the crème de la crème, are they?"

"What do you mean?"

"Well, you don't see Ed Wynn or W.C. Fields hurrying to appear in movies, do you? These fellows are strictly second rank."

I didn't know what to say to that, and an awkward pause ensued, which Stan broke by getting to his feet.

"Let's go up to Mack's office, shall we?"

D.W. Griffith was just leaving Sennett's room, wafting his face with his straw hat, and he was introduced as "the celebrated film director".

"I saw your show at the Empress," Griffith said. "Not this week, but the last time you were in town. I really liked the costumes you wore for that initiation scene."

The costumes he was referring to were the long robes we used in *The Wow Wows*, topped off with the conical masks with two holes cut for the eyes, the costumes that we hated to wear, because they were baking hot inside for one thing, and for another they rendered us totally anonymous. Still, it was nice to hear that somebody liked them.

"Take a seat, fellas," Sennett said, ushering us in.

We could hardly help noticing at once the room's most unusual feature, a large claw-footed bath tub over by the window.

"Ah yes, I get some of my best ideas soaking in that tub," he said proudly. "I get a good cigar on the go, and look down on everyone from Mount Olympus."

Sennett sat in his big chair, and plonked his huge feet up on his big desk. "So, fellas," he said. "Whaddya think to Keystone?"

Charlie looked lost for words, so I jumped in. "It's fascinating," I said. "I don't know what I was expecting, but it is amazing to see everything so squashed together."

"Oh yes, we need more space, no doubt about it," Sennett said. "But we don't shoot everything here on the stages, you know. Sometimes the place is deserted. No, we are out and about, out on the streets, or we'll go to the park, say, if we decide we simply have to throw Fatty into a pond, for example. And sometimes we'll take a camera out and see what we can find. I remember one day there was a Shriners parade in town, and we busked together a whole story about that, just weaving in and out of them as they marched along. You have to think on your feet sometimes, that's the truth."

"You have to be quick on your feet, too," I said. "When there's a locomotive bearing down on you, for instance."

"Oh! You saw that one, did you? That was a closer shave than I meant it to be, I don't mind tellin' ya!"

There was a knock on his open door, and we saw pretty Mabel Normand wanting a word.

"Mabel, get in here," Sennett called out. "Come and meet the guy we saw in New York, remember, the one I said I'd hire if I ever got the chance."

"Chaffin?" Mabel said, walking straight over to Stan. "Pleased to meet you."

"No, that's Stan. This is Charlie Chaplin, this guy here."

Mabel had been working in the silent movies so intensively that her facial expressions were easy to read, and she was currently playing 'But I could have sworn...'

Charlie got to his feet, took her hand and kissed it, saying "Enchanté," in his rather oily simpering fashion.

Now Mabel's eloquent face was saying 'What the hell...?'

Sennett swung his feet onto the floor and leaned across the desk, using his big ham hands for emphasis.

"So listen. I've got three star dressing rooms over there in the big barn. Sterling, Arbuckle and Normand. How about a fourth, for Chaplin? Eh? Whadda ya say?"

"Aha!" Charlie said.

"When can you start?"

"Oh, well, the fact is, I am tied to Karno until December."

"That's all right, I can wait another month or two, it's been quite a while already, hasn't it? That's why I thought I'd get you over here, thrash this thing out man to man."

"Mmm," said Charlie, running through his repertoire of non-committal wriggling noises.

Sennett turned to me and Stan. "Tell you what. There's a job here for you two guys as well if you want it."

That floored us, and no mistake. "What? *Us?*" Stan said. "Work for you?"

"What are you making now? I'll double it."

"That sounds very tempting," I said. "Very tempting indeed."

"Well, think about it, boys, an' just let me know," Sennett said amiably.

Charlie got to his feet, abruptly cutting off that line of conversation. "Thank you for your hospitality, Mack," he said, thrusting out his hand. "I will certainly give you an answer very soon. But just now we really need to be getting back to the Empress for the matinée."

"Of course, of course," Sennett said, looking a little deflated. He put a brave face on it, though, and showed us down the stairs and out through the bungalow to the car he had waiting for us with the same energy and bonhomie he had exhibited throughout our visit.

Charlie was quiet during the drive to the theatre, and during the afternoon's show, and again in the evening, he seemed distracted.

423

At one point, during his now-celebrated dry cracker-eating bit, he seemed to have forgotten that it was a comic turn altogether, and just sat on the stage looking off into the distance, simply eating one cracker after another, while the audience wondered what the hell was supposed to be so great about *this*.

In the dressing room at the end of the night Stan and I were ready to go out and find ourselves a drink or two, but Charlie was still in his stage costume in front of the mirror, just sitting and staring, staring and thinking.

"Charlie? We'll be round the corner," Stan said, but Charlie didn't so much as flicker. He was in a world of his own.

Once we reached the bar and lined up a couple of beers, Stan and I were finally able to discuss the day at Keystone.

"The most difficult moment was when Mack offered us a job," Stan said. "I didn't know what to say. I mean, can you imagine working there? The racket!"

"I know, yeah," I said. "I think he probably thought that if he invited us along too it might help swing Charlie round to the idea."

"Do you think he will go for it? Charlie?"

"I can't tell. I just can't tell."

Just then, Charlie walked into the bar. He spotted us and walked slowly over to where we were sitting, the weight of the world on his shoulders.

"Stan? Arthur? I thought you might be interested to know," Charlie said, very seriously. "I have reached a decision."

I realised my heart was racing as he held the moment. "So?" I said. "Are we looking at the next star of the silver screen? The next titan of the tintypes?"

Charlie looked at us levelly, then delivered the verdict.

"No."

38
HE WORE A
WORRIED LOOK

YOU'D think Charlie would have been relaxed after making his momentous decision. After all, it had been hanging over him for months now, even if, as he claimed, he'd only been stringing Sennett along. But no, he was still worrying away at it, I could see that, from the way he was biting his nails and staring into the distance whenever he had a moment to contemplate his lot. I'd have given plenty to know exactly what he was thinking, but the chances of him confiding in me were somewhere between negligible and nil.

Stan was another case, though. The two of them were still pretty thick, even though they didn't share a room any more. So Stan might well be privy to the workings of the Chaplin mind. I knew he sympathised with Charlie, and believed his decision to stay with vaudeville was actually the right one – so did I, for that matter – and even if Charlie was still having doubts, and confided them in Stan, would Stan then pass that on to me? He might, he might not, that was my anxiously considered opinion.

So when I happened to pass by Charlie's door one morning a couple of days after our Keystone visit, and heard two voices engaged in earnest discussion, I paused. Then I sidled up close, taking care not to squeak the old floorboards, and pressed my ear to the panel.

"What if, though?" Charlie was saying. "What if pictures really are the future, and I've passed up a brilliant opportunity to get in on the ground floor?"

"Do you really think so?" Stan's voice replied.

"Oh, I don't *know*!" Charlie moaned, and I had the impression he might actually be wringing his hands.

"Listen, you've decided now, haven't you? Vaudeville, vaudeville is the thing. It's booming, anyone can see that, so ride the boom and aim for the top. You know, I heard that there are so many vaudeville theatres in the Greater New York area alone that you can work a whole year without unpacking a bag, let alone cramming yourself into that accursed boxcar. Then there's Broadway, and that *Ziegfeld Follies* or... what's the other one?"

"*George White's Scandals*,[17]" Charlie offered.

"Exactly," Stan said. "So why not just say 'What the hell!' and try to forget all about it?"

"Well, for one thing Mack was so very affable when I told him I wasn't interested, and he said: 'Any time you change your mind you just give me a yell, y'hear?' So the door is still open, and it almost feels like I haven't decided, not really, not definitively, not yet."

"Hmm."

"And then there's the money. Karno flat out refused to give me the raise I asked for, even though I made sure that Syd knew what I am being offered by Keystone, which is the same thing as telling the Guv'nor himself."

Outside the door I was nodding to myself – that was just as I'd thought.

"But he's given no ground at all, which means that all those months of dangling Sennett on the line have been for nothing. I'm going to resent working for so little, I can feel it."

"Well, you'll just have to keep your eye on the prize, my friend."

"I suppose so." There was a shuffling of feet, and a squeal of bedsprings, as though the two of them were standing up and making ready to leave. I was just about to dart away out of sight when I heard Charlie ask one last question.

"Tell me straight, Stan. Should I have gone with Keystone?"

Well, I could hardly tiptoe away before hearing the answer to that one, could I? "Come on Stan!" I thought. "Here's your chance. He got you the sack, remember, because you were just too damn'd funny."

"It would have been a bold move," Stan's voice said after a pause, and I sighed and sagged against the doorframe in impotent despair.

Suddenly I saw and heard the handle turning, and there was no time to take cover, so I quickly raised my fist as if I was just about to knock on the opening door.

"Aha!" I said as my presence was revealed, and Charlie took half a step back in surprise, throwing an arm up to ward off what he thought was going to be a sucker punch.

"I was just thinking I might head over to Sausalito on the ferry," I said, with a jollity that sounded forced, even to me. "Take a look at the giant redwoods over there. Apparently they're quite something. Any takers?"

"No, no, thank you," Charlie said, regaining his equilibrium. "I think I will just go for a stroll in the city. Stan?"

"I'll join you, I think," Stan said to his roommate, giving me a quizzical frown.

"Righto," I said, brightly. "Well, have a good day, you two. See you at the theatre later."

When I pitched up at Sid Grauman's Empress a few hours later it was to find Charlie sitting in the corner of the dressing room staring into space. He was pale and seemed to be trembling. Stan was sitting nearby, keeping a close eye on him, and when I walked in he shot me a wide-eyed look.

"Everything all right?" I said.

"How were the giant redwoods?" Stan asked.

"Oh, you know. Huge. Inspiring. Red."

Alf Reeves came in from the corridor behind me and peered anxiously at our near-catatonic number one.

"Whatever is up with him?" I said to Alf, who grimaced, nodded to Stan and then furtively beckoned me to follow him. He led me out of the dressing room and along to the theatre manager's office.

"I tell you," he said, sitting heavily in a leather covered desk chair that swivelled around under his weight. "It has been the damn'dest day."

"Why? What on earth has happened?" I said, sitting opposite the company manager as he opened a bottle of bourbon and poured himself a couple of fingers. I looked around for a second glass, but he soon put a stop to that thought.

"Not you," he said. "You are on stage in less than an hour."

"So? Tell me."

Alf took a long drink, exhaled through his teeth, sighed, and began. "This morning," he said. "I was just out stretching my legs when I bumped into Charlie and Stan, heading down Market Street, over on the sunny side. They weren't going anywhere in particular so I thought I might as well tag along, you know, bit o' company, kind of thing."

428

"Right," I said, not seeing anything too remarkable just yet.

"Well, we came to this small storefront, bead curtain across the door, smell of something oriental slow-burning away inside. There was a sign up advertising that there was a fortune teller inside, and Stan goes: 'Hey, look at this. You want to try?'

"I wasn't too fussed, but Charlie pipes up: 'I think I came here once before, when I was by myself and bored, and in the mood for a bit of mumbo-jumbo', and he's peering into the darkness like he's tempted, you know, so Stan and me, we say all right, and in we go, the three of us.

"Inside it's all dark, and it takes a moment for our eyes to adjust from the bright sunshine outside. Sitting in the corner is a Chinee with a long narrow drooping moustache. He has a small folding table with cards laid out in front of him, dealing more from his hand."

"This was the fortune teller?" I said.

"No, it turned out he was just playing patience," Alf said. "We asked him, we said 'Fortune?', and he gives us a flick of his pig-tails, like, to show that we should go further in, through another doorway into the back room.

"So then we are in the inner sanctum, and it's pretty murky in there. The only light is from a couple of scented candles, smelling of jasmine or some such. And we can just make out, hunched behind a small table in the centre of this chamber, there's the fortune teller herself, an ancient Chinese woman. Her head's bowed and covered with a hood, and she is just staring into a bowl on the table in front of her. This bowl has some kind of liquid in it, and it's giving off this vapour, maybe smoke, maybe steam, couldn't really say."

"Maybe she had a chest cold," I said.

"Yes, you wouldn't be so flippant about it if you'd been there, I'll tell you," Alf said, pouring himself a quick refill.

429

"Sorry Alf," I said. "Go on, what happened then?"

"The old Chinese woman beckons us forwards, see, and we take our places across the table from her. It's hard to see her clearly through the fug even though she's sitting just a couple of feet away. Charlie is squinting at her. 'You are not the same woman I saw here two years ago,' he says. 'She gone,' the woman goes, and her voice is harsh and kind of rasping.

"'The other one read the tarot cards,' Charlie says to me and Stan. 'She told me I had money-making hands, that I would be a big success.'

"'That is true,' this old Chinese woman says. 'You will be big success, *very* big success.'"

"Yeah, but I expect she says that to everybody, doesn't she?" I scoffed. "Doesn't mean it's true, does it?"

Alf shrugged. "Anyway," he said. "The old woman starts waving her hands around slowly in the smoke emanating from the bowl, and she seems to be trying to read patterns forming there. Charlie takes the hint and slides a dollar across the table. Now she's closing her eyes, and rocking back and forth, going: 'I see... I see... You have now big decision in your life, big. Maybe you change direction, maybe you stay the same.'

"Charlie gives us a wink, and says, 'Well that covers a multitude of eventualities, doesn't it?'

"Suddenly then the old woman gasps, like she has just had some truth revealed to her in the vapour, and she starts this awful wailing. 'You have made *wrong* choice, you make very *ba-a-ad* choice!'"

"Crumbs," I said. "Really?"

"Well, you know what's been going on with Charlie and these movie people, don't you? So this hits him like a thunderbolt. 'What?' he goes, and his bottom lip is all a-quiver. 'What do you mean, old woman?'"

Alf started wafting and waving his hands around, his eyes tight shut, mimicking the fortune teller's trance. "'You should not stay on old path,'" he said in the old woman's rasping voice. "'You must change direction. New start. New business. Break off with your past forever.'"

"She said that? 'New business'?"

"Yes, then there was more wafting and waving. 'Is difficult to see,' she says, and she's acting puzzled now, like she can't work it out. 'Not really new. Like old business, but... different. I cannot see clearly. All I see is you must make this big change. If you do, big success, *big* success. If you do not, very bad, very miserable, end badly.'"

Alf paused, shook his head, and took another drink. Clearly the encounter had affected him profoundly.

"End badly? What did she mean by that?"

"Well, that's exactly what Charlie asked her, and do you know what she did then?"

"No, what?" I whispered.

"She lifted her head slightly, and drew her finger across her throat. Well Charlie gasped, and his hands went to his neck, and it was dark in there but I swear he was white as a sheet."

"What was she saying?" I said, frowning. "That if Charlie stays with Karno... he will *die*? That's a bit much, isn't it? For a buck?"

"I know," Alf said, sitting back in his chair, shaking his head. "Well, after a minute or two Charlie recovers a little, starts laughing it off, you know? Saying it's all a bit vague, and that's how the trick is done. I mean, everyone thinks about changing direction, don't they?"

"I suppose they do," I said.

"So then Stan says why doesn't he ask her something she couldn't possibly fake."

431

"Good idea, yes."

"Like maybe his family, something like that. So Charlie says: 'All right, old woman. Tell me about my family,' and he's smiling now, feeling a bit more chipper..."

"And she couldn't do it?"

"Wait till you hear this," Alf said, mopping his brow with his handkerchief. "She wafts her hands about a bit more, swishing the smoke this way and that, and we start to reckon she's playing for time, you know, waiting for some more specific question she can get a hint from. 'I knew it,' Charlie says, and starts getting up from his seat. 'Let's go, come on.'"

"So you just left?"

Alf shook his head. "'Wait!' she barks. 'Father... *dead*!' 'Huh, lucky guess,' Charlie snorts, and makes for the door. The old Chinese woman is swaying now, from side to side, almost toppling off her chair, and she suddenly cries out: 'Mother... *mad*!'"

"Hey, that's right, isn't it? She is a bit cracked?"

"So I believe, so I believe. Charlie, poor lad, faints clean away."

"No!"

"Drops like a stone. Me and Stan wrestle him back into his chair, and we're slapping his face, and Stan goes looking for a drink of water. After maybe half a minute Charlie comes to, and I say 'Let's get you outside into the fresh air, son', you see, but the old woman ain't finished yet, not by a long chalk. 'You have brother, older than you!' she shrieks out. 'He is brother, but not brother!'"

"Syd, Syd's his half-brother," I said. "Same mother, different father."

"That's it," Alf said. "You've got it. 'Your brother walks the same path as you,' she says then, 'but you will be more successful than he. You will change your path, but he will stay on same road.'"

"Good Heavens!"

432

"And Charlie asks; 'You mean Syd stays with Karno and I do not? Is that what you see, old woman?'"

"What did she say to that?" I prompted.

"Oh, but now Stan has had enough, you see. 'Come away, Charlie,' he says, 'this is all just nonsense, don't pay it any mind.' Charlie's up on his feet again, and we're just about to walk out of there when she comes out with the topper."

"The topper?" I said.

"You ready for this?" Alf said, mopping his brow. "'You have a *son*,' she says."

"A son? Charlie has a son?"

"First I've heard of it. And I'm thinking you've blown it now, love! You've taken a pot shot and you've missed by miles, but strike me down if Charlie hasn't started shaking like a leaf. 'What do you mean I have a son?' he sneers, but the crone is absolutely certain of it. 'He is very small,' she says, 'and he has never seen his father. You stole the mother of your son from another, and then you sent her away.' Charlie whispers 'I had to do it,' or something like that."

"What the hell?"

"Search me," Alf shrugged. "And then all of a sudden she stands up, this crazy old fortune teller, and she's taller than we thought she was, actually, and she sweeps a great cloud of the smoke into Charlie's face, whoosh! And she starts shouting at him in this horrible croaking voice. 'You are bad, selfish man! Very bad, very selfish man!' Over and over, like that, and tears are streaming down Charlie's cheeks, and Stan's trying to get between the two of them, I've never seen anything like it in all my born days."

"Whew! And was that it? Was that the end of it?"

"Not quite," Alf said. "Stan starts giving the old woman a right telling-off. 'Listen here, that's enough,' he says. 'We came in here to be told our fortunes. You will meet a tall dark stranger, that sort of nonsense. Just a bit of harmless fun. We haven't come here to be told we are bad and selfish men. What about the big success he's going to have, eh? Tell him about that, and don't meddle in matters that are none of your concern.'"

"Good old Stan," I said.

Alf leaned over the table, glass clenched in his fist, and his story was clearly reaching its climax now. "'As you wish,' the old fortune teller says, with a nasty sort of leer. She reaches behind her for a bowl, like a fruit bowl, full of something that rattles and jingles as she swirls it around. She tips it out onto the table, and we see hooks, coins, buttons, cutlery, leaves, shells, corks, brooches, all kinds of odds and sods. And she closes her eyes and tips her head back, swooshing this junk around with her fingertips, until suddenly, as if guided by some mysterious power, she quickly snatches something, some items, one in each hand, and holds her closed fists out to Charlie.

"'What is in there?' Charlie asks, and his face is ashen with fear. 'I do not know,' the crone says. 'It is your future, not mine. If you would know your fate you must look and find out. Do you dare?'

"Charlie looks at us, and he licks his lips, and then he nods, and the old woman slowly opens her hands to show." Alf took a big swig from his glass, and then wiped his mouth with the back of his hand.

"Christ Almighty!" I said. "It's like an Arthur Conan Doyle or something. What were they, these objects?"

Alf looked at me as he reached again for his bottle, and it was the chilling look of a man who believed, sincerely believed, that he had been in contact with something outside of the natural world.

"One was a key," he said. "And the other... was a stone."

434

39
A FILM JOHNNIE

CHARLIE was like a wraith for the rest of that week at Grauman's. An automaton. He drifted through the performances, distracted, going through the motions, and Alf became quite concerned.

"We should never have gone into that bloody chinky shop," I heard him saying to Stan. "It's tapped his head."

On the Sunday the boxcar rolled down to San Diego, which meant passing through Los Angeles once again. Shortly after we set off, I noticed Charlie was deep in conversation with Alf across the folding table in his makeshift office, and our long-suffering company manager was looking far from happy.

I nudged Stan and pointed. "The game's afoot," I said.

"Do you think?"

When we pulled into Los Angeles station for a one-hour layover everyone spilled out onto the platform to stretch their legs, some wandering off to look for a sandwich or a coffee (or something altogether stronger). Alf bustled past me, his face drawn with anxiety.

"Arthur! Hold the fort, will you? And don't let the train leave without me."

"Why? What are you doing?"

"I have to send a wire to the Guv'nor," he muttered, and hurried off to the Western Union office.

Stan and I stood there watching him, and Stan suddenly grabbed my arm. "There, look!" he hissed. Further along the platform, stepping up into one of the Pullman carriages on our train, was a familiar figure – big face, big hands, dirty-straw hair, clumsy demeanour. It was Mack Sennett.

An hour later the stop in Los Angeles was almost up. Everyone bar myself and Stan was back in the boxcar, and there was still no sign of Alf. The guard was striding busily towards us, red and green flags in one hand, whistle in the other.

"Gentlemen, please, we are about to depart, please take your seats," he called.

"Erm... one of our party is on his way, he will be here any moment," I said.

"I can't help that," the guard said. "If he's not here on time we'll have to go without him."

"But..."

"Look!" Stan said, suddenly, pointing at the wheels. "Did you see that?"

"What was it, sir?" the guard said, whirling round.

"A child, I'm sure of it, crawling on the tracks right underneath the carriages... there! Again! Did you see?" He pointed urgently underneath a car a couple further forward from ours.

"Oh! Oh my!" the guard said, a look of panic on his busybody face. He crammed the whistle in his mouth, and blew a few sharp blasts, then he scuttled off, waving his red flag above his head, while crouching to try and catch sight of this imaginary child beneath the train.

"Nice," I said.

"Should buy Alf a few minutes," Stan smirked. "And look, here comes the man himself."

Our company manager was indeed barrelling along the platform towards us, clutching a beige telegram in one fist and a large spotted hand kerchief in the other.

"Everything all right, Alf?" I asked.

"No," he panted. "Everything is most definitely *not* all right. It's a bloody disaster! I just wired the Guv'nor and told him to offer the boy more money so he'd stay, but look!"

He thrust the telegram at us and mopped his sweaty brow as we clambered aboard.

"'NO MORE MONEY STOP CHAPLIN TRYING IT ON STOP'" I read, and Stan's eyebrows shot up.

"Where on earth did he get such an idea from?!" Alf gasped, exasperated.

Where indeed.

Back aboard the boxcar once again a further three hour slog to San Diego lay ahead. Ordinarily we might have tried to get involved in George Seaman's game of cards, or tried to borrow a copy of *Variety* to flick through, but on this occasion there was a rare old pantomime to keep us enthralled.

At the far end of the seating compartment, Charlie and Alf were once again in earnest conference. It was plain to see that Alf was pleading with Charlie, and he finally handed the telegram over to Charlie, although he plainly didn't want to. Charlie snorted derisively and got to his feet. He offered Alf his hand, and the company manager shook it. Then our number one turned on his heel and left the boxcar without so much as a glance at anyone else – not us, not the card game, not anyone – heading for the forward part of the train.

Alf sat back down, exasperated, and then slumped forward, laying his forehead on his forearms. Stan raised a quizzical eyebrow at me, but all we could do was wait, and speculate.

Charlie didn't re-join us in the boxcar for the rest of the journey, and when we spilled out onto the platform at San Diego he was nowhere to be seen. A couple of cars away, however, Mack Sennett was clambering clumsily down the steps, and we contrived to waylay him.

"Hello there, Mack," I said.

"Oh! Hello fellas!" he said with a big grin. "Nice to see ya again. Sorry I can't stay for the show, I gotta get back. Just had a bit of business to do with Charlie, you know?"

"Has he...? I mean, is he...?"

"He sure is. Got the contract right here." The big man patted his jacket pocket.

Stan and I looked at one another, trying to contain our astonishment at this news, and Sennett seemed to interpret this in his own way.

"Say, listen," he said, hanging his head sorrowfully. "I sure am sorry about this, and I know I did say I could take you boys on as well. Turns out that isn't going to be possible after all. I hope you understand."

"I think I do," I said. In fact I understood perfectly that Charlie would have made it a condition of signing his contract that Stan and I would be frozen out.

"Don't worry about it, Mack," Stan said.

"If I can put in a word for you with any of the other companies, like Biograph or Cosmos then I'll be happy to do it, just let me know, all right?"

"We will," I said.

"Well, I guess this is 'Cheer-oh!'" he said, in a lamentable attempt at an English accent. "I need to hop on the next train back to Los Angeles. Heck of a way to do business, eh?"

438

Charlie confirmed the news himself later that evening in the tiny dressing room we were sharing at the San Diego Empress.

"It's a hundred and fifty dollars a week, rising to one-seven-five in the second year," he said, smugly.

"Really? Whatever happened to that offer of five hundred you told the Marx boys about?"

"Oh that was just a mistake. I mis-spoke. No, it's one fifty, which is double what Karno's paying me, and actually more than he's paying Sydney, so it's a pretty good deal."

"Well," I said, putting on a worried frown. "I hope you've done the right thing."

"Eh? What do you mean?"

"Turning your back on all the groundwork you've put in. Dropping out of vaudeville before you've really reached the top."

"It certainly is a courageous move," Stan chipped in.

"But I reckon I could do this movie racket for a year and come back to vaudeville as a huge name," Charlie said.

"Like...? Who, exactly...?"

The fact was that nobody had yet attempted to convert film notoriety into a return to stage comedy. Probably because those vaudevillians who had gone over to the flickers were, as Charlie himself had pointed out when we visited Keystone, not exactly from the first rank. You might even say that none of them even had the name Charlie himself had acquired touring the Rocky Mountain Empresses for Sullivan and Considine. So making a success of moving pictures and then converting that into vaudeville bankability was not a path anyone had yet trodden.

"I can't think of anyone," Stan said, helpfully, as Charlie went quiet.

"Oh well," I said with a smile. "I'm sure you know what you're doing."

"I'm not," Stan murmured as Charlie wandered away, lost in thought. "I think he's off his blinking rocker!"

━━━━━

That seemed to be that, but it turned out that the world of vaudeville had one more card still to play. A couple of weeks later we were back in Colorado Springs, that small flat town nestling in the shadow of Pike's Peak on the Eastern edge of the Rockies. There were just two more weeks left of Charlie's Karno career, with the curtain due to come down just before Christmas in Kansas City (Missouri).

Arriving at the theatre one afternoon, lost in thought thanks to an astonishing snippet I had just read in the newspaper, I found two large fellows lurking by the stage door. There was something familiar about them, and as I came alongside I recognised the two man-mountains I had last seen dragging their knuckles along the floor in the wake of Big Tim Sullivan, co-owner of the Sullivan and Considine circuit. What on earth were they doing so far from home?

"Hey buddy," one of these creatures said as I approached, shoving himself away from the wall and spitting a toothpick onto the floor. "You Charlie Chaplin?"

In a second I had it. These guys had come to 'persuade' Charlie not to abandon Big Tim's vaudeville circuit. Presumably the New York gangster's paranoia hadn't abated any in the sanatorium where he had been incarcerated due to his tertiary syphilis. I couldn't let them work their knuckle-based magic on Chaplin – it was far too likely that they might succeed. It might mean taking a beating, but there was nothing else for it.

"Yes," I said with a heavy sigh. "I'm Chaplin. What can I do for you fellows?"

Without a word the two of them grabbed me, an elbow each,

440

and 'helped' me around the corner into an alleyway. I don't think my feet touched the ground.

"Now see here," one of them said, leaning on my windpipe with a massive forearm. "It has come to our attention that you no longer wish to work for Mr Sullivan. 'Zat right?"

I looked into the slow eyes of this chap, who I seemed to recall was named Brick, and tried to gulp past the blockage caused by his arm.

"True," I admitted.

"Well, Mr Sullivan would like you to know that he don't take kindly to that notion, and he would like you to reconsider."

"I see," I gurgled.

"And he has asked me and my colleague here to make the necessary arguments on his behalf."

"Unngh!" I replied.

"So. The first point he would like us to make is this..."

"Wait!"

Brick paused, his huge ham of a fist suspended in mid-air, poised to smash into my breadbasket. He looked at me inquiringly, and eased the pressure on my larynx a little so I could speak.

"Couple of things you should know," I said, gulping down some welcome fresh air – or as fresh as it came in an alleyway full of detritus, which I was very much afraid of joining unless I could talk fast. "First of all: I change my mind. I won't leave the vaudeville to go and make pictures. Why would I? It's a crazy notion. No, I will happily stay in Mr Sullivan's employ, although technically employed by Mr Fred Karno and only booked by Mr Sullivan and Mr Considine, I'm babbling, I apologise."

"You change your mind?"

"I do, with all my heart, you are such persuasive fellows, why would I ever go against your wishes?"

441

"Oh." Brick and his sidekick frowned at one another, a little perplexed by this development.

"The other thing that you should know? Is that - and I'm very sorry indeed to be the one to tell you this - Big Tim Sullivan is dead."

"What?" The two goons stared at me in disbelief.

"It's true, I was reading it in the paper just now. Here read it for yourself - no, tell you what, why don't I read it for you?"

I managed to free my arm and bring the newspaper round in front of my face. "Here it is, listen: 'US Congressman and leading light of Tammany Hall Timothy Sullivan, known to all as 'Big Tim', who has been suffering from ill-health, has been found dead on railway tracks in the Eastchester area of the Bronx, New York.'"

"Big Tim? Dead?"

"I'm afraid so."

"Dead? I can't believe it..." Brick turned to his pal. "Maybe we should still beat this feller up, though, what do you think?"

His mate nodded sombrely, taking off his hat. "It's what Big Tim would have wanted."

"No, no," I put in quickly. "What he *wanted* was for me to change my mind, wasn't it?"

"That's right."

"And I've done that, so your mission, your very last mission for your beloved boss, has been completed. I'm sure he's very pleased, wherever he is."

"Right..." Brick stepped back from me, allowing me to massage my squashed throat a little, and then he straightened my jacket lapels, and solicitously brushed some stray filth from my sleeve. "We'll be on our way, then."

"Back to New York City," the other man mountain added. "Pay our respects."

"Yes indeed," I said, bowing my head. "Sad day. Sad, sad day."

40
HIS PARTING SHOT

On Charlie's last night with the Karnos in Kansas City (Missouri) I was jubilant. I didn't want him to leave without knowing exactly how I felt, so I put together a little leaving present for him. I found an old tobacco tin left lying around, and filled it with some old ends of make-up. I made sure to tear the paper off, and tried to shape the brown bits and bobs as much as possible into pellets of... well, you know what it would have looked like.

I squinted down at my handiwork, and wasn't really satisfied, I have to say. It just looked like the gift of an oddball, rather than a righteous avenger reaping the visceral satisfaction of finally outwitting a deadly rival. There was nothing for it, I would have to harvest samples of the real thing.

Once that bit of business was taken care of, I mixed them in with the stubs of old make up. It wasn't so much the collecting that was unpleasant, it was the... shaping. But anyway, you don't want to know about that.

Then I wrapped the tin up in the fanciest foil paper I could find, finishing the whole thing off with a big pink ribbon. I found a card, and appended an appropriate inscription. Then I tucked the whole surprise behind a mirror and went to wash my hands again. And again.

The show, the last show, Charlie Chaplin's last ever show with the Fred Karno comedy company, was surprisingly emotional. Charlie was on the most tremendous form, even I had to admit that, and he would be a hard act to follow.

I have spoken many times about the Power, that mystical force that envelops you when you are onstage and everything is working perfectly. It is headier than the strongest drug, more intoxicating than the hardest spirit.

Well, Charlie certainly had the Power at his fingertips that last night, and the audience would have done anything for him. It suddenly struck me that this, this was what Charlie would be missing. Because you can't possibly achieve the same rapport with two thousand people through a camera, and a screen, and with maybe several weeks of time interposed between the performance and the response. They may laugh at your antics, on screen, they may howl with delirious abandon, but even if you are there in the room, watching with them, you are not exercising the Power, the control. There's a whole dimension missing to the experience, as far as the comic is concerned.

This, I saw now in a moment of piercing clarity, was why he clung to the Karno life with such tenacity, why he found it so hard to commit to Keystone. He told us it was bargaining, he may even have believed himself that he was playing Karno and Sennett off against one another, but deep down it was the Power he didn't want to relinquish.

And I'd backed him into a place where he had to give it up. Maybe my revenge was more complete than I knew.

That night in Kansas City, Charlie achieved something I had never seen before. I had seen the Power exerted by some masters in my time on the halls and in vaudeville. George Robey was the first, but then also Fred Kitchen, the great Karno number one, Little Tich at the Folies Bergère, Julius Marx positively oozed it from every pore, W.C. Fields wielded it as effortlessly as his banana-shaped pool cue. Stan Jefferson, too, that night in New York. I myself had felt it tingling at my fingertips like an electric charge.

But what Charlie did that last time was this. He brought the Power to bear, full beam, on that helpless audience, and then quite deliberately managed to spread it, to widen it, to exert it upon everyone onstage with him as well. Yes, we laughed along with everyone else. Guiltily at first, unprofessionally, but then quite shamelessly enjoying the little man and his boundless skills.

Of course, an audience loves it when actors lose it onstage, it just drives the mirth to a whole new level, and by the time Charlie was taking his many curtain calls, with those vivid violet eyes glistening with tears, two thousand people were literally holding their sides, not merely using the international language of pantomime to indicate their jollity, but genuinely fearing that they might laugh their insides out. I looked down into the aisles, and there were people there lying on their backs kicking their legs in the air, like stranded insects.

What a night that was.

———

Alf Reeves gathered us all in the green room at the end of the evening.

"As you know," he said, once he had clambered up onto a chair. "Charlie is leaving us."

"First I've heard of it," Charlie Griffiths said. "Where am I going?"

445

"Sss, sss, ssss!" tittered Bert Williams, which set everyone off.

Alf quelled the giggling with his two hands. "As you know, Charlie *Chaplin* is leaving us for pastures new. I should just like to say what a pleasure it has been to be his company manager for the last... good Heavens, is it really three years? And I'm sure you'd like to join me in wishing Charlie the very best of British luck in his new venture in Los Angeles."

"Hear, hear!" mumbled a few dutiful voices, and Albert Austin brushed away a tear, the sap.

"Now I thought we really should do this in style. Amy?" Alf turned to the doorway, where, right on cue, his wife came in with an ice bucket in each arm, and champagne bottles peeping out. "So while I open these up, I'll hand you over to the man himself, Mr Charles Spencer Chaplin, to say his farewells."

Alf jumped down from the chair, and slowly, thoughtfully, Charlie took his place.

"My friends," he began, and I must say I saw one or two quizzical expressions at that. "I just want to thank you all for your support, and your sterling work over the last many months. Without you I should never have been able to..."

POP! went the first bottle of champagne. "Woooh!" went the crowd, which began inching towards the sound reaching for glasses.

"Sorry, Charlie," Alf said. "Go on. Shush everybody."

"I was just saying, I wanted you all to know how much you all... mean to...!"

Then, to our utter astonishment, he was overcome. Cold, emotionless Charlie, aloof, distant Charlie, arrogant, unsentimental, unfriendly Charlie burst into tears, jumped down and fled.

"Aaahh!" the ladies sighed, but we were all frankly a little perplexed, since Charlie had spent most of our time together acting as though we were just ants he could squash beneath his heel at any moment. Partly that was just his manner, of course, that strange mixture of arrogance and shyness, but partly it was what he really thought of us, and people can always tell.

I looked around at them all, the company that would soon be mine. Stan would be a trusty number two, Charlie Griffiths another reliable pillar of support, Freddie Karno Junior was coming into his own, maybe he could take over my parts once I was number one, I thought. Edgar Hurley I was not quite so comfortable with. He was not an easy fellow to like, and his wife, the lovely Wren, was sitting alone, I noticed, with her hair down shading her face again. Surely the brute hadn't hit her again, had he? Maybe I'd ask Alf to move him on. A shame, in a way, because she was a definite asset.

I wondered whether any of them would really miss Charlie. Or did they feel, as I did, that a great burden was about to be lifted from our collective shoulders, and a new egalitarian era of team work and enjoyment was about to begin? Certainly, in the immediate short term, a new era of drinking champagne was getting under way, and the mood was decidedly celebratory.

After about half an hour, and with no one else particularly bothered about what had happened to him, I started to wonder where Charlie had got to. I didn't want him to slip away without giving him my present, not after all I'd... put into it... so I left the impromptu party behind and set off to look for him.

The theatre was dark and deserted, with all the other turns and the hands having left for the bar next door, and the audience long gone. I hadn't found him in any of the dressing rooms, or in the wings, and I was just about to give it up as a bad job when I heard a sob.

A sob, somewhere in the darkness. I screwed my eyes up and squinted, and there, out on the apron, I thought I could see a small shadowy figure barely illuminated by the spill from the safety light.

I stepped slowly onto the darkened stage towards the tiny form.

"Charlie?" I said.

The figure half-turned, and then I could make out that it was him, sitting on the front edge of the stage, dangling his legs into the orchestra pit.

"What are you doing?"

"Oh, Arthur, it's you. I'm sorry to leave the party. I just wanted a moment by myself."

I turned the tobacco tin in my fingers, feeling its unpleasant contents bumping gently against the sides as I did so.

"Well..." I began.

"I was just thinking of what I would miss, leaving all this. It has been such a big part of my life."

I thought then of all the things Charlie had done, done to me, during the time we had spent together. The rivalry that had come to define my life. The times he had done me down, sabotaged my chances, wrecked my romance with Tilly. I thought of Whimsical Walker, callously hounded to his end. Of Stan, for whom betrayal was the reward for friendship, because Charlie simply couldn't bear to live with someone every bit as funny as he was. Most of all I thought of Tilly, dismissed, paid off, pregnant, alone, all to save his wretched selfish self.

Yes. If anyone deserved what was in this tin it was him.

"Do you know what, Arthur?" Charlie said then, breaking the contemplative silence we were both momentarily lost in.

"What?" I said.

"I know we have had our differences over the years, but deep down I feel we are firm friends, don't you?"

That stopped me in my tracks.

448

I was all fired up to let it all out, tell him what I really thought of him, had been thinking about him for so many months and years. To crow about manipulating him down the ludicrous cul-de-sac of moving pictures, reducing his precious career to so much pointless trash, and then to crown it all with my cruel, disgusting, and yet perfectly appropriate leaving gift, but do you know what?

I couldn't do it.

He seemed so vulnerable just then, and so genuine, so lacking in his usual haughtiness, and smugness, and that awful superior sense of entitlement, that when he held out his hand to me I took it, and felt myself beginning to choke up as I said:

"Good luck, old man."

"Thank you, Arthur. And to you too."

We shook hands, holding on longer than we normally would have, knowing this was the last time, perhaps, that we would see one another. But, do you know, even though Charlie was in benign and misty-eyed mood, he couldn't resist unleashing one final little salvo at me.

"You could have been a number one, I suppose, Arthur," he said. "I dare say you will be now, now that I'm gone, but I don't think you have the range to be a big success. You are not a good enough character actor, is what I'm saying. You just play versions of yourself, that rage, that thwarted sense of injustice, it leaks out of all your characterisations. You can't lose yourself, you always give yourself away."

I ground my teeth and walked away, but as I reached the dark and dusty tabs I turned back and said,

"Maybe you're right about me, maybe I won't be as good a number one as you. On the other hand, maybe I will be..." – then I suddenly switched to the rasping voice of a wizened old Chinese lady fortune teller – "*big success, big success!*"

Charlie's eyebrows shot right to the top of his head. "What? What did you say?"

"Nothing. All the best, old chap."

I walked off the stage to the sound of my own footsteps – and I wish I could say it was the only time *that* happened. There was a broad smile on my face as I imagined Charlie's brain whirring and ticking furiously like an over-wound pocket watch.

My own thoughts turned then to Tilly and little Arthur. I'd sent a wire up to Mike's Place in Seattle, but a wire couldn't possibly convey all I was bursting to say – not with the amount of cash in my pockets, anyway – that would have to wait until the New Year. All I had sent was 'KARNOS RETURNING IN SPRING WITH NEW NUMBER ONE' – the rest I left for her to read between those lines for now.

Back downstairs in the dressing room Stan was waiting for me, but everyone else had called it a night.

"Well? Did you give him that nasty present, you revolting fellow?"

"I couldn't do it," I said. "He was being too nice to me."

I tossed the parcel into the bin, and threw the card down on the dressing room table. Stan picked it up and read it, an involuntary snort of laughter bursting from his mouth and nose.

"'*Some shits for a shit*'," he said. "Is that really what you wrote?"

I shrugged. "Well, you know..."

"You just don't know how to win gracefully, do you?" Stan grinned.

"In fairness I don't really have much experience," I muttered.

Stan poured out the last of the champagne into two glasses, held one out to me.

"Well, he's finally gone," Stan said.

"*Sic semper tyrannis*," I said.

"What does that mean?"

"Death to the simpering tyrant."

"Ha! Who'd have thought that old Chinese fortune teller would spook him so?" Stan chuckled.

"I know. Best twenty bucks I ever spent, borrowing her clothes and her room for an hour. I felt sure he was onto me at one point. And it was all I could do not to own up to poor old Alf, later on, he was so upset."

"The key and the stone was a bit on the nose, I thought."

"Maybe. But you trying to drag him away, that's what sold it. Thanks for your help."

"Well, I owed you a good turn, didn't I?" Stan said. He had been feeling guilty about keeping the news of Tilly's pregnancy from me, and I'm afraid I rather took advantage of that by awarding him a key role in my little deception. Mind you, one day I would have to tell him *my* secret, that Mack Sennett had been so impressed with him and not Charlie, and I didn't realise then quite what a big deal *that* would turn out to be – but that, as they say, is another story.

"It worked, that's the main thing," I said. "He's out of our lives for good."

"I wonder if we'll ever see him again."

"Oh, I expect we'll see the odd Keystone flicker over the next couple of years, you know, with Charlie stuck in the background complaining about the lack of a proper scenario and refusing to get involved in the chase. I might learn to lip read, just so I can enjoy that properly."

Stan chortled, and we clinked our glasses together. "Here's to 1914! Should be a good one!"

"Indeed," I said. "Onwards and upwards with the Karno company, heading for the very pinnacle of American vaudeville, eh?"

"That's the plan," Stan said. "And finally – *finally* – I get to be number one."

"Cheers to that!" I took a long draught of fizz, some of which crept down the wrong pipe. "Wait...! What?"

THE END

NOTES ON CHAPTER TITLES

PART ONE

1. OFF TO AMERICA
There were two music hall songs with this title, one performed by Fred Albert, the other by James Fawn.

2. CITY LIGHTS
The title of a classic 1931 full-length silent film, written by, directed by and starring Charlie Chaplin.

3. THE WOW WOWS
A sketch performed mostly in American vaudeville by the Fred Karno comedy company between 1910 and 1912.

4. BLITHERING, BLATHERING ENGLISHMEN
Taken from the *New York Clipper* review of *The Wow Wows* on its first appearance in New York in October 1910.

5. GENTLEMAN'S GENTLEMEN

"A gentleman's personal gentleman" is how Jeeves, P.G. Wodehouse's creation who first appeared in 1915, describes himself. He was not a butler, although Bertie Wooster observes that he "can buttle with the best of them".

6. MUMMING BIRDS
A classic Fred Karno sketch, his most successful, which toured the UK more or less constantly in the decade before the First World War, and toured America many times too, where it was usually known as *A Night in an English Music Hall*.

7. A NIGHT IN THE SHOW
The title of a 1915 silent film in which Charlie Chaplin shamelessly plagiarised Fred Karno's *Mumming Birds*, playing the roles of Mr Pest and Mr Rowdy himself.

8. AND THE NEW YEAR IN
A line from the chorus of *The Miner's Dream of Home*, co-written and performed by Leo Dryden. He had an affair with Hannah Chaplin and they had a son, George Dryden Wheeler, who was half-brother to Charlie and Syd, and ended up working in Hollywood with both of them and also with Stan Laurel.

9. CLAMBER CLOSER CLARA
A music hall song by Vesta Tilley, the popular male-impersonator, who set herself the tongue-twisting chorus: 'Clamber closer, Clara, can't you, clamber closer, do!'

10. OUT WHERE THE BLUE BEGINS
A popular music hall song by Kate Carney.

11. 'E'S TAKIN' A MEAN ADVANTAGE
A popular music hall song by Alec Hurley.

12. SHADOWS ON THE BLIND
Another popular music hall song, this one performed by Georgina Lennard.

13. A LITTLE IDEA OF MY OWN
A song by the Prime Minister of Mirth himself, Mr George Robey.

14. HOG WILD
A 1930 Laurel and Hardy film, where they start out trying to put a radio aerial on the roof, and end up sitting in a mangled car squashed between two trolley buses.

15. LET ME CALL YOU SWEETHEART
Popular song from 1910, featured in the 1938 Laurel and Hardy film *Swiss Miss*.

16. THE SIGH OF THE DOVE
A line from the Vesta Tilley song, *Sunshine and Shadows*.

17. CONTINENTAL DIVIDE
The line of the continental divide follows the Rocky Mountains down through America, close enough to be regarded as a tourist attraction at Butte, Montana, and Colorado Springs, amongst other places.

PART TWO

18. HIS LUGGAGE LABELLED 'ENGLAND'
Line from the 1914 music hall song *Belgium Put the Kibosh on the Kaiser* by Mark Sheridan. It was the Kaiser himself whose luggage was labelled 'England', but the plucky Belgians seemed then to have stopped him in his tracks.

19. THE RUM 'UNS FROM ROME
A music hall sketch performed by Stan Laurel, Arthur Dandoe and Ted Leo in England, 1911.

20. HARD BOILED EGGS AND NUTS
This was the gift brought by Stan Laurel to Oliver Hardy when paying him a visit in the 1932 film *County Hospital*. When Ollie asks why he hasn't brought candy, Stan explains that Ollie never paid him for the last box he brought him.

23. AND IS THERE HONEY STILL FOR TEA?
A line from the 1912 poem *The Old Vicarage, Grantchester* by Rupert Brooke.

24. CHANCE MEETING
A piece of music written by Charlie Chaplin for his 1925 film *The Gold Rush*.

PART THREE

25. THE STOWAWAY
Stowaway is the original title of the last film directed by Charlie Chaplin, the 1966 critical failure *The Countess of Hong Kong*,

which starred Marlon Brando and Sophia Loren.

26. A FELLOW OF INFINITE JEST
This is how Shakespeare's Hamlet remembers the dead clown Yorick in the famous graveyard scene.

27. K-K-K-KISS ME AGAIN
Another music hall favourite, this one performed by Florrie Forde.

28. A DISH BEST SERVED COLD
A proverbial saying about revenge that was current from the mid-19th century onwards, and has featured in many films, including *Kind Hearts and Coronets*, *The Godfather*, and *Star Trek II: The Wrath of Khan*.

29. A LITTLE OF WHAT YOU FANCY
The title of a music hall song by Marie Lloyd.

31. QUITE CHOP-FALLEN
This is how Hamlet describes Yorick to Horatio, now that all that remains is a skull.

32. MONKEY BUSINESS
The title of a 1931 Marx Brothers film.

PART FOUR

35. CAUGHT IN A CABARET
A 1914 short film, written and directed by Mabel Normand, in which she co-starred with Charlie Chaplin.

37. KEYSTONE KAPERS
Mack Sennett's Keystone Cops films inspired this, a 1983 video game for the Atari 2600.

38. HE WORE A WORRIED LOOK
A music hall song which was performed by Harry Randall.

39. A FILM JOHNNIE
A 1914 Keystone Picture, in which Charlie Chaplin disrupts the movie-making on the Keystone lot, and his co-stars include Roscoe Arbuckle, Mabel Normand and Ford Sterling.

HISTORICAL NOTES

Although many of the characters in *The Fun Factory* are based on real people, the incidents and relationships depicted contain a measure of speculative invention on my part.

Arthur Dandoe was a real person, a member of the Fred Karno company, and he toured the UK and America with Charlie Chaplin and Stan Jefferson (later Laurel), the three of them performing hundreds of shows together and living virtually in one another's pockets for several years.

Despite this there is only one reference to Arthur in Chaplin's massive 528 page house-brick of an autobiography – imaginatively entitled *My Autobiography* – and no mention at all of Stan, who was Charlie's understudy and roommate, and by all accounts (bar Charlie's own) a close friend.

The single reference to Arthur that you will find, should you be inclined to look, is to an incident on the night Charlie left the Karno company in Kansas City to take up a job offer with Keystone Pictures. He writes: "A member of our troupe, Arthur Dando (sic), who for some reason disliked me..."

Is it just me, or is there a wealth of contempt in that casual mis-spelling of Arthur's name? Anyway, Charlie goes on to describe a leaving present that Arthur prepared for him, the

459

very leaving present that he so nearly receives in the final chapter.

Some commentators believe that Stan Laurel was omitted from *My Autobiography* because he was the one genuine threat to Chaplin's supremacy over the world of comedy, the one performer who could actually hold a candle to the genius. For myself, I was fascinated by the kind of man who could have come up with that leaving present, and the relationship that is somehow defined by it.

When I started writing I was attracted to this period of Chaplin's career precisely because it was covered so imprecisely and unreliably in his own autobiography and the many various biographies, which naturally rely heavily on his own account. It seemed a dark, shady area that gave me a lot of elbow room. Then A.J. Marriot brought out his book *Chaplin: Stage by Stage*, which shone a great forensic searchlight beam onto the whole period. It not only details where Chaplin was and what he was up to day by day throughout his Karno career, it also pulls the great man up on a surprisingly large number of inaccuracies and deliberate obfuscations, taking him to task in a most entertaining way. I recommend it, it's a lot of fun.

Thanks to A.J. Marriot and others I have tried, as far as possible, to stick to known chronology as far as the actual careers of Charlie Chaplin, Stan Jefferson, and Arthur Dandoe are concerned.

The three of them did indeed set off to America together in the autumn of 1910 on a converted cattle boat. Things went badly for the company at first, but after a triumphant night in front of an audience of English servants they were booked to tour the Sullivan and Considine circuit. After one tour of the continent Arthur and Stan returned to the UK following a dispute over money, and they devised an act called *The Rum 'Uns From Rome*, which flowered briefly and then expired. Stan later said in an interview: "Like a couple of silly schoolgirls Dandoe and I had a difference of opinion, and our partnership fizzled out like a seidlitz powder."

Charlie meanwhile toured America a couple more times before returning home for what turned out to be a brief interlude. When he headed back across the Atlantic Stan Jefferson was a last minute addition to the company, while Arthur actually seems to have joined even later as a replacement for someone. All three of them toured the States twice more, for some of the time as a colleague of the great Drury Lane clown Whimsical Walker, whose participation was cut short by ill health. And they did become friendly with the Marx brothers along the way.

When Charlie left to join Keystone at the end of 1913 his Karno colleagues thought he was crazy, and they looked forward to continuing to conquer the burgeoning vaudeville circuits as before.

Most of the rest of what Arthur does in the book is fiction. As is what he will do next.

NOTES

1 *The Birth of a Nation* was released in 1915. Directed by D.W. Griffith, it was a silent epic set in the aftermath of the American Civil War, and it dramatised the foundation of the original Ku Klux Klan, which had all but died out. The success of the film arguably inspired the formation of the 'second era' Ku Klux Klan, and it was controversial even then for its portrayal of black characters (by white actors in blackface) as ignorant and sexually aggressive towards women.

2 Perhaps the Derren Brown of his day. As well as an electric chair Bodie also had a Röntgen X-Ray machine, and would use it to show the inner workings of volunteers in all their skeletal detail. He would perform acts of healing using hypnotism and electricity, without asking for payment, and at the 1909 law suit brought by the Medical Defence Union he presented no fewer than 900 testimonials from patients who claimed he had cured them where doctors had been unable to do so. The lingering fallout from the case during which many of his secrets were revealed meant that Bodie was refused membership of the newly-formed London Society of Magicians in 1913, despite the support of the president, his great friend Harry Houdini.

3 The Battle of Liège (5-16 August 1914) was to be the first battle of World War I. The city lies on the main rail routes from Germany to Brussels and Paris which the Germans intended to use in the invasion of France, and this master plan was delayed by several days by the need to lay siege to Liège and its twelve doggedly-defended forts.

4 ABC stood for Aerated Bread Company, and they ran a chain of self-service tea shops second only to that of J. Lyons.

5 In the years before the start of the First World War, one in ten waiters in London was German.

6 Mutt and Jeff are characters from a comic strip which first appeared in the *San Francisco Chronicle* in 1907. Mutt is a tall, greedy dimwit, and Jeff is short and bald as a billiard ball.

7 'Moral turpitude' was, as it happens, one of the reasons given when the US Attorney General rescinded Chaplin's re-entry permit in 1952.

8 Whimsical Walker was indeed the negotiator when Barnum and Bailey purchased Jumbo the celebrated elephant from London Zoo in 1882. The whole transaction, including transportation – which was cannily delayed by several weeks driving the press on both sides of the Atlantic into a frenzy – cost all of £3,000, but the great showmen recouped this massive sum in no time, taking $1,500 (£300) a day for the next eighteen months until their prize attraction was hit by a train and killed. Whimsical Walker also, as he mentions several times, trained a donkey to sing and performed with it in front of

Queen Victoria at Windsor Castle. These and other stories can be found in his memoir, *From Sawdust to Windsor Castle*.

9 Harry Langdon (1884-1944) headlined in vaudeville for many years until venturing into motion pictures in the 1920s. He became a major star with Mack Sennett's Keystone studio, and the success of his wide-eyed child-like innocent screen persona saw him ranked alongside the other comedy greats of the silent era – Chaplin, Buster Keaton and Harold Lloyd.

10 The IWW – the Industrial Workers of the World – is an international radical labour union formed in Chicago in 1905. They promoted the concept of 'One Big Union', asserting that workers should be united as a social class as well as being organised into smaller unions within the industry of their employment. They contend that workers and employers have nothing in common, and that a struggle must go on between these two classes until the workers of the world rise up and take control. The origin of the nickname "Wobblies" is uncertain.

11 Mount Baker, Washington. 'Kweq' Smánit' means 'white mountain'.

12 The Marx brothers – Julius, Arthur, Leonard and Milton – did not acquire the names by which they would become famous until a couple of years later, in 1915. The story goes that they were playing cards with a monologist called Art Fisher, killing time between shows on the Pantages time. As he dealt, Fisher began referring to them by the nicknames they might take if they were clowns, as that was the jokey conversation they

were having at the time. So Arthur became Harpo (because he played the harp), Leonard was dubbed Chicko (because he chased the chicks), Julius was given the name Groucho (perhaps because of his temperament, or because he carried his cash in a grouch-bag), and Milton was rechristened Gummo (he had a 'gumshoe' way of sneaking up quietly on you backstage). These names somehow stuck with them, although Chicko became Chico after a publicity misprint, and this seemed to suit his cod-Italian schtick better. The fifth brother, Herbert, took the stage name Zeppo when he joined them later, just to fit in.

As Harpo remarks in *Harpo Speaks!*: "You never could tell what you might be dealt in a poker game in those days."

13 At this time the Motion Picture Patents Corporation had established a monopoly on all aspects of film-making, controlling patents on cameras, projectors and film stock, and obliging film-makers to use, through an exclusive licensing system to its members, equipment patented by the Edison Manufacturing Company. They would use federal law enforcement officials to enforce their licensing agreements, and sometimes hired thugs and even used mob connections to disrupt unlicensed film production with violence. As a result, many independent companies established themselves in California, out of reach of Edison's New York-based enforcers.

14 *The Ziegfeld Follies* were a series of lavish productions on Broadway, which ran from 1907 to 1936. They were staged by Florenz Ziegfeld, and the shows featured many of the top names of twentieth century entertainment, including W.C. Fields, Bert Williams, Ed Wynn, Eddie Cantor, Fanny Brice, Ray Bolger, Louise Brooks, Josephine Baker, Bob Hope, Will

Rogers, Sophie Tucker, and British music hall duo Nervo and Knox. The champion boxer Gentleman Jim Corbett brought his vaudeville comedy act into the *Follies* after retiring from fisticuffs in the 1920s, and would even appear as a blackface minstrel.

15 Roscoe 'Fatty' Arbuckle (1887-1933) began his career in vaudeville as a singer, then became a comedy star at Keystone. He was, by 1921, one of the most popular and highest paid actors in Hollywood. His career was then ruined by a scandal when he was accused of raping and accidentally killing a young actress, Virginia Rappe. Arbuckle was tried three times and eventually acquitted, but worked only infrequently thereafter.

16 The famous racing driver was immortalised in the commonly-used put down of someone in an immoderate hurry: "Who do you think you are? Barney Oldfield?"

17 *George White's Scandals* were Broadway revues, modelled on the *Ziegfeld Follies*, that ran from 1919 to 1939, and featured such luminaries as Ethel Merman, the Three Stooges, Bert Lahr, Jimmy Durante and W.C. Fields (when he wasn't appearing in the rival *Follies*).

ACKNOWLEDGEMENTS

I would like to thank Ben Yarde-Buller of Old Street for taking a punt, and for his enthusiastic support and insightful input.

I would also like to thank Matt Baylis for some great editing and many good suggestions, and James Nunn for the splendid cover.

Thanks to those descendants of the real Arthur Dandoe who got in touch both before and after the first book came out, and furnished interesting titbits from their families' collective memories – June Russell, Sandra Stickler and Linda Barber.

Also thanks to Charles Walker, Jo Unwin, Rob Dinsdale, Jo Brand, David Baddiel, Mark Billingham and David Tyler.

And lastly my appreciation to Susan, Peter, John and Michael for being prepared to live on gruel, bread and water while I get all this out of my system.